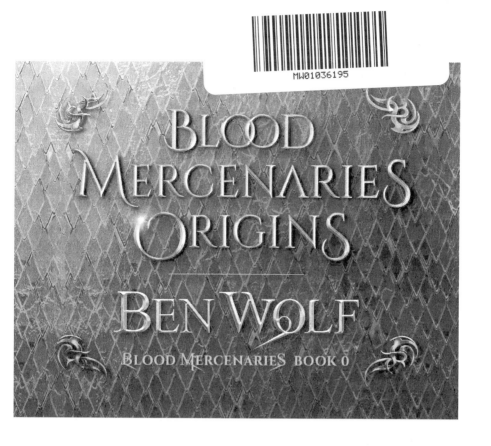

FOUR SWORD & SORCERY DARK FANTASY PREQUEL NOVELLAS

To The

BLOOD MERCENARIES SERIES

Published by

PUBLISHING GROUP

WWW.SPLICKETY.COM

Blood Mercenaries Origins

Published by
Splickety Publishing Group, Inc.
www.splickety.com

Ebook ISBN: 978-1-942462-33-0
Print ISBN: 978-1-942462-34-7
Copyright © 2019 by Ben Wolf, Inc. All rights reserved.
www.benwolf.com

Cover design by Kirk DouPonce of DogEared Design
www.dogeareddesign.com

Available in print and ebook format on amazon.com.

Contact Ben Wolf directly at ben@benwolf.com for signed copies
and to schedule author appearances and speaking events.

Printed in the United States of America.

This book is dedicated to Kirk DouPonce,
the world's greatest (and most patient) cover artist.

You are the real legend.

CONTENTS

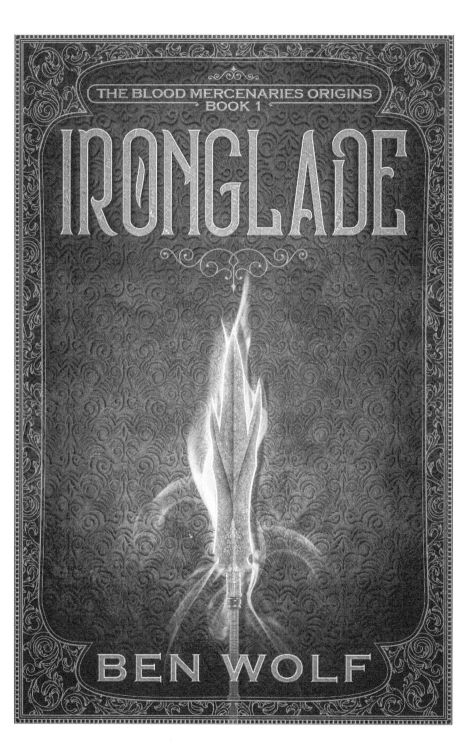

THE BLOOD MERCENARIES ORIGINS
BOOK 1

IRONGLADE

BEN WOLF

CHAPTER ONE

The heavy bronze doors slammed shut in Aeron Ironglade's face, ending his sixteen-year career with the Govalian Army and locking his best friend inside. He shifted his footing, and a small pouch of gold and silver coins stamped with the emperor's head jingled on his hip, half the amount it should've been.

"Goodbye, Wafer," he muttered and rubbed his aching back. "It's been real."

He started down the path toward Govaliston, the capital city of the realm of Govalia, but his bond with Wafer, the wyvern mount he'd raised from birth, thrummed in his chest. He stopped and turned back.

The high fortress walls loomed above him, mocking his failure and keeping him separated from his mount.

"I'll see you again, buddy. I promise I'll find a way to get you back."

As he walked away from the fortress, the bond dulled and dulled until he felt nothing but remorse and sadness. With each successive step, his anxiety burgeoned, and he wanted to turn back, but instead he kept walking.

Even if he had turned back, it wouldn't have mattered.

Aeron's journey back to Govaliston led him through rolling green hills marked with sporadic trees. He soon reached the town of Dreynoth, the nearest settlement to the fortress and a regular haunt for members of the Govalian Army due to its proximity.

Normally, Aeron could make the trip in three minutes or less thanks to Wafer's wings. But today, his boots had gotten him there in about fifteen minutes, and already his lower back pain had reignited.

He rubbed it as he walked into the town and past a stable for horses, a pub, and a brothel—all of which catered specifically to soldiers. The idea of a drink and a rubdown sounded great, but Aeron needed something stronger. Something he'd grown accustomed to over the last few months since he'd sustained his injury.

And the local apothecary shop undoubtedly had what he needed. They always did.

A handful of people bustled through the town's dusty streets, but at midday in the middle of the week, most were tending to their shops and businesses in preparation for the nightly influx of off-duty soldiers and the even larger weekend crowds.

Aeron sighed. He'd miss the camaraderie he'd shared with some of his unit. It bothered him to know he'd never be a part of that world again, but the lack of a connection to Wafer grated on him even more. He felt empty, powerless, and alone.

And he was.

"Come down from there!" a tiny voice chirped to his left.

Aeron turned and saw a little girl staring up at one of the few trees in the town square. Her hair color ranged somewhere between blonde and light brown, and she was probably seven or eight years old.

In the tree above her, among the branches of orange leaves preparing to drop for the winter, sat a fluffy, white cat.

"I said come down!" the girl repeated. She glanced around at some of the people walking by, but none of them moved to help her.

Aeron shook his head. *That cat is not gonna come down on its own.*

Then the girl's blue eyes locked onto his. "'scuse me, mister?"

Aeron cursed to himself. He never should've made eye contact.

"You're a soldier, right?" she asked.

Not anymore, kid. He waved at her. "Sorry. I'm—"

"Can you please help me get my cat out of the tree? He's not allowed to be up there." When Aeron didn't stop walking, the girl said, "Aren't soldiers supposed to help us?"

Aeron hesitated, and his steps stalled. He may not have been a soldier anymore, but that wasn't any real excuse not to help. Then the pain in his back flared and deepened as he stopped walking. That *was* a reason not to get involved.

He started rubbing the spot in his lower back again. "Look, kid… I'm—"

"Everlee. That's my name," the girl said as she started toward him.

"Everlee," Aeron corrected himself. He held up his hands. "I'm on my way to the apothecary to buy some—"

"It'll just take a second. I'm not tall enough to reach him." She took hold of one of his hands and started tugging on it. She repeated, "It'll just take a second."

Aeron exhaled a sharp breath. He knew where this kid was coming from—all too well. She clearly cared for the cat. She ached for it just like he ached from being away from Wafer.

As far as he knew, humans couldn't form the kind of bond with any other animal that he'd attained with Wafer, but it didn't mean Everlee loved the cat any less. This cat was probably her best friend, and this tree had unfairly separated them.

So how could he refuse? He may not be a soldier anymore, but he could still be a decent person.

"Alright," he said. "Fine."

The tree had no branches low enough for Everlee to reach so she could climb up after the cat, and even if she could have gotten up there, getting down with a big ball of fur in her small arms would be risky, if not outright dangerous. And fortunately for Aeron, the cat was on a branch low enough that Aeron could just reach up and grab him.

But as he raised his arms to take hold of the cat, the pain in his back spasmed, and he yelped.

The cat issued a low growl, and it darted along the branch and jumped onto an even higher branch.

Everlee gasped. "What happened? Why did you do that?"

"Sorry." Aeron rubbed his back with both hands. "My back. It's—"

"You scared him!"

"I didn't mean to," Aeron said.

Tears pooled in the corners of Everlee's eyes, and she whimpered. "Now how will I get him down?"

Where are this kid's parents? Aeron crouched in front of her and cupped her shoulders. "It's alright, kid—Everlee. I'll go up there and grab him. It's alright."

She nodded and sniffed. "Alright."

Aeron stood and faced the tree, which loomed even taller over him now that he had to consider the whole thing instead of just its lowest branch. He muttered, "What did I just agree to?"

If he'd had Wafer with him, he could've climbed onto Wafer's back and had Wafer lift him up. It might've scared the cat to death to see a gigantic, reptilian predator like Wafer peering up at him through the leaves, but at least Aeron wouldn't have had to climb.

But he didn't have Wafer now. He had to make do with his own strength and ability.

He quickly stretched out his back and his arms, trying to relieve some of the pain. Then he jumped, grabbed the lowest branch, and hauled himself into the tree.

Aeron immediately realized what a terrible mistake he'd made. His back pain dug into his nerves, scraping against them and agonizing his every movement. He never should've volunteered in the first place.

But now he was committed, and if he let go, he'd fall and hurt himself even worse. So he worked his way to a sitting position on the branch and took a few deep breaths to try to calm his rebelling muscles.

Gods... how many trees did I climb as a kid? And now I can barely get into this one? Getting old sucks.

The cat lay on a branch above him, staring down at him with blue eyes the color of Everlee's. Its paws hung over the branch as if it were a rag someone had tossed into the tree, and it mewed at him.

"I'm coming," Aeron grumbled to it. "Don't move. And don't you dare go any higher."

All he'd wanted to do was get something for his pain and get back to his parents' house in Govaliston. Tomorrow he'd start his new life doing... whatever. One thing was for sure—he had no intention of rescuing cats for a living.

He wove his thin body between the branches, resisting and ignoring the pain in his back until he finally managed to reach the cat. It mewed at him again and nipped at his hand.

"Hey!" Aeron snapped. "Cut that out. I'm trying to help you."

"No biting, Cracker!" Everlee called from below.

Cracker? The cat's name was Cracker? And he had a wyvern named Wafer? Aeron shook his head. Weird coincidence.

He managed to get Cracker by the scruff of his neck, and Aeron gently pulled him off the branch. Cracker loosed another low growl, and he squirmed a bit, flailing four paws tipped with sharp claws all around, but Aeron maintained control and slowly lowered him through the branches.

"You can drop him," Everlee said. "Cats land on their feet!"

"Yeah," Aeron grunted, "but I don't want to drop him from too high up."

He repositioned himself on the lowest branch, took hold of another branch with his free hand, and carefully lowered the cat low enough that Everlee could've caught him if she'd wanted to, but she wisely stayed back.

"Good?" Aeron wheezed.

"Yes!" Everlee bounced on her toes.

Aeron dropped Cracker, and he landed firmly on his feet. Then he promptly leaped into Everlee's outstretched arms and nuzzled her chin with his forehead.

Despite his aching back, Aeron smiled. He knew that feeling—the sensation of a long-awaited reunion with a close friend. He envied Everlee in that moment, and he resolved anew that he would get Wafer out of the fortress someday, even if it meant—

SNAP.

The branch Aeron had been holding broke, and he slipped from the tree and fell. At the last second, he reached out for the branch he'd been sitting on and grabbed hold of it, straightening out his fall, but racking his back in the process.

He somehow managed to land on his feet, but he immediately staggered back against the tree trunk and leaned on it for support. He exhaled labored breaths and clutched at his miserable back. His eyes clenched shut from the overwhelming pain.

Aeron finally opened his eyes to the sound of giggles. There before him, Everlee was spinning in a circle with her arms outstretched and with Cracker in her hands.

Now he understood why the cat had jumped into the tree.

Everlee's spins stopped, and she wobble-walked toward Aeron with Cracker clutched to her chest. Breathless, she said, "Thank you so much!"

"My pleasure," Aeron lied. He groped at his back and winced as he dug his knuckles into his own flesh.

"What's wrong with you?" Everlee asked.

"My back is… messed up."

"What happened to it?"

Aeron closed his eyes again. He really didn't want to have to recount the whole story to an eight-year-old kid whom he'd likely never see again. He summarized, "A friend of mine was in trouble. I saved her."

"Her?" Everlee asked. "What's her name?"

"Faylen." Now she *was* something Aeron didn't mind recalling. He smirked at the thought of her bright blonde hair and her slightly pointed ears, then his pain pulled him back into the present. "Anyway, I'm going to get something for the pain from the apothecary here in town. Glad your cat is safe."

"The apothecary? Why didn't you say so?" Everlee grinned at him. "He's my papa!"

In spite of his pain, Aeron smiled. *Finally some good news today.*

AERON LEFT DREYNOTH BEHIND, ALONG WITH A HAPPY EVERLEE, A GRATEFUL apothecary, and a cat named Cracker.

He'd managed to purchase a sack of magic mushrooms from the apothecary for only five coins, a significant discount over what he would've otherwise paid for them. It was the apothecary's way of thanking Aeron for saving Cracker from the tree.

One yellow-spotted shroom, glowing blue from the magic infused into it, had deadened most of his pain and enabled him to keep walking toward Govaliston, but he'd limited himself to just one for the time being. He didn't know when he'd be able to buy more, so he wanted to ration them.

An hour later, Aeron reached the outskirts of Govaliston. He made his way through the city, passing ramshackle homes and fine stone residences alike as he headed to the only home he'd ever known outside of the fortress.

Soon after, he stood before his parents' house. It looked the same as when he'd left, only sixteen years worse. Graying, worn-out pine boards made up its two-story exterior, secured with sturdy iron nails and brackets. A pair of windows hung open on the second floor, facing the street.

The front door looked newer, though—probably a recent addition from within the last five years. It didn't look as wretched as the rest of the house, and it still retained a hint of its original pine color.

Aeron exhaled a long breath. That house held a lot of memories for him, most of them sour. He looked down at his bag of shrooms and abandoned his rationing plans entirely. "There's no way I'm doing this sober."

He dug his hand into his bag.

"WHAT DO YOU MEAN, YOU WERE DISCHARGED?" PA FOLDED HIS ARMS.

Aeron shifted on the chair at their kitchen table, thankful the shrooms had started to relieve his back pain. They'd also cast his vision in an orange hue and made his body feel nearly weightless—a happy state to counter his father's grating interrogation.

Pa pressed his weathered palms flat on the oak table separating them and leaned closer. "I asked you a question, boy."

Aeron scoffed. *Boy? I'm not a boy anymore.*

A pinwheel of fiery colors ignited the gray wall behind his father, and Aeron cracked a smile. His anxiety had faded, virtually nonexistent thanks to the shrooms' effects.

"Something funny to you?"

Aeron's smile faded, and he shook his head. "I don't owe you any explanation."

"You do if you mean to live under my roof again."

Aeron glanced at his mother. The same range of colors spiraled slowly behind her. They made her look as radiant as she had the day he left. "It's mum's roof, too."

Pa's eyebrows arched down, and he stood upright again. "When she brings in the kind of coin I do on a daily basis, she'll have an equal say. Until then, *I'm* the rule of law in this house. Make no mistake about that."

Mum didn't look up from her embroidery, nor did she say anything.

Aeron frowned. *So much for the sympathy vote.*

The colors evolved, blending in touches of purple and pink—effects of the two shrooms he'd taken mixing together. He'd combined these types many times before, specifically for the effect now playing out in his vision, for the relief they gave his back, and for how well they quelled his anxiety.

Gods... I. Am. Lit. Aeron fought off a smile. *High as a spire.*

He could've climbed ten trees and saved at least forty cats, feeling the way he was feeling now. Maybe forty-five.

"What in the third hell is wrong with you?" Pa snapped his fingers in front of Aeron's face, and sparks of bright green light flickered in and out to accompany the sound. "You need to answer my question. Why did they discharge you? Your last letter said things were going well. Is it because of your injury?"

"No." Aeron sighed. That was sort of the reason, but not entirely. His injury didn't bother him when he took the shrooms. "Well, kind of."

Pa just stared at him.

"It doesn't help my case that I have chronic back pain…"

"But?"

"…but that's not the only reason I got discharged."

More staring. More silence.

"I had a difference of opinion with my commanding officer," Aeron continued. "He saw fit to use it as a reason to discharge me."

It was true, broadly speaking.

The colors morphed again, this time deepening from oranges into reds and browns. The effect was heightening. Normally he'd take another shroom right about now, but he doubted it would fly with his parents in the room.

"You only got half your severance pay," Pa said. "The army only does that when the discharge happens under sour terms."

Aeron glowered at him. "How would you know? You never served."

Pa's jaw tightened. "No, but I've shod their horses and hammered out their armor, swords, and shields for the better part of forty years." Pa pointed a calloused finger at Aeron. "So don't try to play high and mighty with me, *boy.*"

"Stop calling me that," Aeron grunted.

"Come again?"

"I said, *stop calling me that,*" Aeron repeated, louder. His voice sent the colors into a brief tizzy, then they resumed their calm flow. The effect calmed his emotions as well. "I'm thirty-one years old. Not a boy by any stretch of the imagination."

His mum looked up at him with a hint of sadness and longing in her tired eyes, then she returned to her embroidery.

Pa leaned close to him, squinting. A wreath of earthy colors encircled his head. That, combined with the scowl on his face, made him look like a pissy old lion.

"Are you..." he started. "...*high?*"

"What?" Aeron blinked and looked away. "No."

"You are! You're high." Pa huffed. "You come into my house, hoping for a handout—"

"I don't want a handout!"

"—and you're high as a cloud. What in the third hell are you thinking?"

"Pa, no." Aeron looked at him again. "I would never—"

"Don't lie to me, boy. I can see it in your eyes. All bloodshot and glazed."

Aeron blinked hard and stole a glance at his mum. His anxiety was building, but the shrooms kept pushing it back down. The push-and-pull made it hard to focus on what he wanted to say and how he wanted to say it.

Mum's eyes held even more sadness now. She softly shook her head and frowned at him.

Aeron couldn't keep looking at her. A pang of regret hit his stomach. He didn't want to see her cry. He didn't want to cry, either.

"Admit it," Pa growled. "You're on something."

He turned back to Pa. "I'm just tired, Pa. It was a long walk from the fortress, and I didn't get much sleep last night. I'm tired."

"Admit it, or I won't give you a thing. Not coin, not a job, not a place to stay."

Mum said to Pa, "Farico, that's—"

"Not another word from you, wife," Pa snapped. "It's you he takes after."

Mum's mouth clamped shut, and she resumed her embroidery with tears in her eyes.

"Don't talk to her that way." Aeron had wanted to yell it, but the shrooms were inhibiting his will to be aggressive.

"Don't change the subject." Pa's eyes narrowed. "You're high, and I know it. We all do. So stop pretending you aren't. Admit it, or you're out of here right now."

Aeron hesitated. He didn't want to let Pa win the argument, but he had to stay somewhere for the night. His family home was all he knew, all he could rely on.

"Last chance."

Aeron caved. "I—I took something for my back pain."

"I *knew* it. You blitzed little bastard." Pa shook his head. "This ends *today.*"

Aeron rolled his eyes. *Yeah, Pa. Your commands will just stop it altogether. They tried that in the army, and look how that ended up.*

"Here's the bottom line," Pa said. "If you mean to live here, you *will* pull your own weight. You'll work at my blacksmith shop *without complaining*, you'll pay room and board, and you'll do it all respectfully and without being high. Crystal?"

"Forget this." Aeron pushed himself up.

The room folded in on itself, then it reset. He'd seen it before when on shrooms, but it always tripped him out. The reds and browns had faded back to oranges, pinks, and purples again. The shrooms' effects were beginning to fade.

"You wanna leave?" Pa snapped. "Shut the door behind you on your way out."

"Go to hell, Pa."

"Curse me all you want. Walk out that door, and you're never walking back in."

Were it not for his mother, Aeron would've left right then and there. He could live without them both if he had to—he certainly had for the better part of the last sixteen years. But never being able to see Mum again was a steep price.

Something touched his hand—soft, like the fur of a cat. He looked down.

Mum held his hand in hers. Callouses and dry skin marked his fingers and hers, but she still felt soft and warm against him. Definitely the shrooms again.

She squeezed his hand, and the sensation calmed him.

"Stay tonight," she said. "Decide in the morning."

Aeron blinked, but the colors and the sensations remained.

"No," Pa said. "He decides now or he—"

"*Farico,*" Mum hissed at him. "Enough."

Now Pa went quiet.

Mum turned back to Aeron. "What'll it be, Aeron?"

CHAPTER TWO

Aeron woke up the next morning in his old bed, totally sober and totally in pain. A pair of blue eyes stared down at him from a familiar round face—but one sixteen years older than he'd remembered. He smiled, and so did his sister, Kallie.

"You're home," she said softly, then she wrapped her arms around him and squeezed.

His back pain heightened, and he yelped.

Kallie let him go and recoiled, her hands cupped together under her chin. "Oh... I'm so sorry. Mum told me, but I forgot."

"It's fine." Aeron labored to get himself upright on the bed, wincing all the way. The fingertips of his right hand tingled with numbness, and the muscles in his right forearm near his elbow ached, two of the more recent side-effects of his back pain.

He looked Kallie over. When he'd left, she was only five—a surprise baby, eleven years after he'd been born.

Now she was a full-grown woman of twenty-one, but with the same long, blonde hair, and absolutely stunning. She wore a blue dress that made her look like a princess.

"You're all grown up," he said.

"Yeah." She smiled again, her teeth white and bright but not straight, just like Aeron and the rest of the family. "You were gone a long time."

"Yeah. I was."

"Pa told me what happened. About you being discharged."

Aeron rubbed his eyes. "Don't believe everything you hear."

She sat next to him. "So it's not true?"

Aeron stopped and looked over at her. "It's complicated."

"What about Wafer?"

Memories of flying among the clouds on his wyvern's back surfaced in Aeron's mind. "They kept him. Wouldn't let me take him with, even though we're bonded. They're going to try to bond him to someone else, but it won't work. I've researched it. Best they can do is make him fly for an unbonded rider, and that won't go well."

Kallie nodded. "I don't know anything about it except what Mum read to me from your letters."

"I feel empty now that I can't be around him. Like a part of me is missing." Aeron rubbed his back. "I want nothing more than to get him back, but I have no idea how I'd even do that."

"I'm sorry. You're smart. You'll think of something." Kallie put her hand on his shoulder. "Anyway, Mum sent me up here to fetch you for breakfast."

"Alright. I'll be right down."

Kallie kissed his cheek then left the room and closed the door behind her.

Alone again, Aeron dug under his lumpy old mattress stuffed with ancient goose down, pulled out the sack of shrooms, and opened it.

Despite being somewhat squished and flattened from hiding under the mattress all night, they glowed up at him with familiar, faint blue light and a myriad of colored spots and stripes.

As Aeron reached into the bag, Pa's threats echoed in his memory, and he hesitated.

⁂

BY THE END OF THE DAY, AERON HAD RE-FAMILIARIZED HIMSELF WITH HIS FATHER'S blacksmith shop, despite his claims sixteen years prior that he would never return to it. Pa had done well in Aeron's absence; the shop had doubled in size thanks to the gradual growth of his business over time.

But that just meant Aeron had twice as much to despise.

His back was killing him. Blacksmithing made for hard labor, albeit with some craftsmanship involved, and his back couldn't tolerate it without the aid of painkillers. And he'd neglected to take any shrooms that morning out of a noble but foolish attempt at obedience to Pa's demands.

And worst of all, nothing he did here would bring him any closer to getting Wafer back. He was just wasting time, performing the same mind-numbing tasks he'd done before he left to join the army sixteen years earlier.

After his day at the shop concluded, he headed back to his parents' house, headed straight up to his room, dug out the bag, and scarfed down two shrooms—one with yellow spots and one with purple stripes, both irradiated with that familiar blue hue.

Their effects hit him immediately; the yellow one dulled his back pain, and the purple one cast his vision in the same orange hue he'd enjoyed last night. The purple one also relaxed his body and soothed his anxieties—the color show was just a bonus.

Aeron considered grabbing another shroom, one with green specks on its cap, to eat once the color show really got going, but he held off. He was already risking a lot by showing up to supper high again.

5555555555

"Aeron?" Mum called from downstairs.

Aeron jumped and stuffed the sack under his mattress again, careful to make sure it wasn't sticking out, then he draped his blanket over the edge just to be safe. "Yeah?"

"Supper's on the table."

The color show intensified, and his back pain numbed. "Be right down."

AERON SOMEHOW MANAGED TO SURVIVE SUPPER WITHOUT PA REALIZING HE'D TAKEN shrooms. Aeron retired early that evening, but right as he went to grab another shroom to help get him through the night, a knock sounded from his door.

"It's me," Kallie called. "Just wanted to say good night."

Aeron abandoned his search and beckoned her inside.

She shut the door behind her and sat on the bed next to him. "Pa was right, wasn't he?"

Aeron swallowed. "About what?"

"Your back. And how you deal with it."

Aeron sighed, then he nodded.

"Why do you take them?"

"Kallie," Aeron said, his voice low. "I wouldn't wish my back pain on you, or Mum, or even Pa. Ever since the accident, it's never been the same. I take the shrooms to *manage*. That's all I can hope for these days. I'll probably carry this ailment for the rest of my life, and I have to do something, otherwise I can't even function."

She nodded. "I wish there were another way."

"It's not illegal. It's not even immoral. Lots of people take them for far less noble reasons."

She nodded again, staring at the floor. "I know. I just wish I knew of a way to help you permanently."

The numbness in Aeron's fingertips prickled, and he closed his hand into a fist. "Me too. Believe me, I'd rather I was whole."

"So..." She paused. Then she looked up at him again. "What's it like?"

"Magic mushrooms?"

She tried to stifle a grin but failed.

"Or chronic back pain?"

She rolled her eyes. "The mushrooms, obviously."

"It depends," Aeron replied. "There are lots of different kinds. Probably an endless number of combinations between enchantments and types of mushrooms. Aside from magical creatures and sentient races, mushrooms are one of the only other things capable of retaining magic. I know a little bit about it, but I'm by no means an expert."

"Well, what happens to you?"

"The ones I take dull my back pain and relax my body," Aeron said. "Not usually to the point of putting me to sleep—though those types of shrooms are out there. They're crazy potent, though, so I stay away from those.

"These ones do enough to get the muscles in my back to stop fighting whatever it is that's causing the pain. That combination is my usual preference."

"Come on." Kallie nudged him. "They do more than that. What aren't you telling me?"

Now Aeron fought to quell a smile, and he failed as miserably at it as she had. "I see... vivid colors. And they change. Things kind of slow down, and I get sloppy and lazy, but in a good way."

"Like at dinner tonight?" She elbowed his ribs lightly.

Aeron grinned. "Do you think Pa noticed?"

"No. And if he did, I know Mum told him to lay off you for it anyway."

"And he listened?"

"I guess we'll find out." She shrugged. "I wouldn't recommend flaunting it in front of him, though. You never know what he'll do."

"Believe me, I won't."

"Well, I'm off to bed." Kallie kissed his cheek and stood.

"Hey, before you go, I've been meaning to ask you something."

"Yeah?"

"Are there any young men after you that I need to beat up?" Aeron asked. "I mean, I have all this combat training, and I can't let just anyone near my pretty little sister."

She smirked. "With your back the way it is, you wouldn't be able to beat any of them up anyway."

He tilted his head and eyed her. "Hey, that's not nice."

She giggled.

And then it hit him. "Wait—what do you mean by '*them?*'"

"Good night, Aeron." She winked at him and slipped out of his room.

She's too spunky for her own good.

Aeron fetched a yellow-spotted mushroom from his sack, devoured it, and stashed the sack again. Then he eased himself down onto the bed, careful not to agitate his back, and he fell asleep.

Morning came far too quickly, and fresh pain accompanied it. He took the yellow painkiller shroom alone. It didn't make him trip as hard, and he hoped it would be enough to keep him from hurting all day.

Thinking better of it, he stashed a second one in a pocket for later. It didn't matter if it crumpled or broke—the effect would still be the same.

The hours at the blacksmith dragged by, but at least Aeron managed to stay busy. The old skills he'd learned working alongside Pa for so many years came back quickly, with a few stern reminders on how Pa liked things done.

Aeron had just started hammering on an iron shield when the sound of approaching hoofbeats caught his attention. He leaned to the side and glanced out the nearest window.

A green flag crested the hill in the distance, heading toward the blacksmith shop. It bore a golden insignia that Aeron couldn't make out from such a distance, but he knew what it was anyway. He'd worn it and served under it for sixteen years.

It was the sigil of Govalia and her armies.

Human heads, then torsos bounced into view as their horses trotted up the hill. All of them wore forest green armor, including their helmets.

Aeron's heart pounded, and he worked to still it. He hadn't spent much time around the cavalry since his promotion to wyvern knight some twelve years before, so they likely wouldn't know or recognize him. He wouldn't have anything to be embarrassed about.

Then he heard the shriek of a wyvern high above, distinct against the repeating hoofbeats and the harsh sounds of the blacksmith shop. Wingbeats followed, growing ever closer, ever more ominous.

Aeron both reveled in the familiar sound and knew its terror.

His eyes widened, and he searched the skies. He saw nothing at first.

Then a massive gray reptile landed on the street no more than twenty feet from the window with a *thud*. Townspeople scattered, and the wyvern spread its wings and hissed.

He knew that wyvern. He'd seen it hundreds of times. Its name was Strife.

The wyvern lowered its wings and its body, bracing its front half on the street's surface with the knuckles atop its wings, now folded inward.

The knight atop the wyvern wore unique gray armor, specially crafted for him. Long, black hair draped over his shoulders from under his matching helmet. A small, silver wyvern wing was stamped on the left shoulder of his armor.

It was Commander Larcas Brove, the man who'd discharged Aeron from the Govalian Army.

CHAPTER THREE

Aeron swore a slew of profanity and ducked. The sharp motion sent pain shooting up his back, and he jerked upright again to counter it.

On his way up, he bumped the shield with his elbow. It toppled off the anvil and landed hard on his boot.

Fresh agony erupted in his toes, and he hopped around on one foot, cursing the shield, the shop, and everything else he could think of.

"What in the third hell's going on back there?" Pa called through the ruckus.

"Nothing," Aeron answered. "I'm fine. Everything's fine."

But everything was not fine. Not even close.

Aeron couldn't face Commander Brove now, not like this. Not as a damned blacksmith—or a blacksmith's apprentice, more accurately.

Brove had been Aeron's commander in the army. But Aeron had consistently beaten Brove in training combat, both on the ground and in the air. That success hadn't endeared Aeron to Brove in the least.

Brove had also personally ensured Aeron's discharge.

Aeron couldn't stay. He slipped off his heavy leather apron and padded gloves and draped them over the shield.

Voices sounded from the front—Pa's voice and the unmistakable timbre of Commander Brove's severe Urthian accent. They were heading toward Aeron, but the shop's layout obstructed their line of sight to him. He didn't have much time.

He left the apron and his hammer behind and hurried out the shop's back door.

✳

ONLY WHEN COMMANDER BROVE MOUNTED STRIFE AND FINALLY TOOK OFF DID AERON return to Pa's blacksmith shop. By then, the cavalry soldiers were trotting down the street and beyond the crest of the hill.

From Aeron's vantage across the street, he could see Pa pacing inside the shop with a red face and fists clenched. Aeron needed to get back there, and fast.

He hustled over, every step prickling up his back.

Pa noticed him coming and stopped in place. He jammed his fists into his hips and puffed his considerable chest out. Afternoon sunlight glinted off of his mostly bald head, dotted with sweat.

When Aeron closed within normal talking distance, Pa shouted, "Where in the third hell have you been?"

Aeron withstood it all. "I'm right here. You don't have to shout."

The skin on Pa's face tightened around his eyes and mouth. Very calmly, he said, "I beg your pardon, boy, but..." Then he shouted, "Yes I *damn well* do!"

Aeron grimaced and closed his eyes to quell his inner anxiety. He hadn't brought any of the purple-striped shrooms along. *What I wouldn't give for a fix right now.*

"Where did you go? Why were you gone so long?"

"I really had to piss."

"Pissing doesn't take a half-hour, and we've got a can in the back for that."

"It became more than a piss once I got there." Aeron rubbed his belly. "You know how sometimes you eat something that just churns and swirls and—"

"Enough. I don't care about your bowel movements." Pa waved his hand. "Next time you intend to run off, you tell me. Got it? We've got more work now than ever. I stand to make plenty of extra coin, even as useless as you are to me."

"Your confidence in me is ever-inspiring." Aeron sighed. "What kind of work?"

"You might've missed the soldiers who showed up when you were on your walkabout, but they delivered a huge order. A fresh batch of swords, shields, lance heads, and spearheads. Twelve pairs of shackles, both hands and feet, keys for the shackles, a bunch of sets of armor, and plenty more."

Aeron sighed again at the thought of what all of that would do to his back. After all he'd learned in the Govalian Army, did he really have to resign himself to a life of blacksmithing under his father's abrasive rule?

"Great," Aeron said flatly.

"So we're staying late tonight, and we're coming in early tomorrow, and we'll maintain that schedule until this job is finished." Pa added, "And I don't want to hear any of your griping about it."

Aeron mock-saluted him. "Yes, sir."

Pa glared at him. "Get back to work."

Aeron did, and all the while he wished he'd brought two more shrooms along that morning instead of just one.

More than that, he wished he could find a way to free Wafer and just leave this place once and for all.

A COUPLE OF WEEKS LATER, KALLIE VISITED AERON IN HIS ROOM AFTER DINNER. NOW A nightly tradition, they could talk and get caught up on each others' lives, a time to make up for all they'd missed over the last sixteen years.

"Aeron, you'll never believe what I found in Capital Square today." Kallie stood before him with her hands behind her back.

As much as Aeron loved her, he would've rather gone to sleep early. Exhaustion and pain racked his body, and he'd have to be up early again the next morning.

Plus, he needed a shroom and didn't want Kallie to find out where he kept his stash. Better if she didn't know, just in case. So the sooner she left, the better.

"What is it, Kallie?" he asked, monotone.

"Don't sound so excited, big brother."

"Sorry." He tried to stretch his back, but doing so sent a sharp spasm up his spine, down his right arm, and into his tingling fingertips. He quickly abandoned the motion. "Long days. I'm beat."

"Well, I won't keep you waiting, then." She produced a piece of parchment from behind her back and handed it to him.

"What's this?" he asked.

"Read it."

He did. It was an auction notice from the Govalian Army. Apparently, they'd put several old pieces of equipment up for sale.

Wagons, wheelbarrows, and various plundered goods from a recent campaign. Aeron had seen a hundred of these notices throughout his tenure with the army.

But this marked the first time they'd ever offered a wyvern for sale to the public.

CHAPTER FOUR

Aeron looked up at Kallie. "Wafer?"

She smiled. "I don't know who else it could be. Have any other wyvern knights been unceremoniously discharged recently?"

He frowned at her. "No, and thanks for phrasing it so delicately."

"Then it's got to be him."

"They're auctioning off a living weapon of war? That's unprecedented."

"Maybe they figure it's better to try to get something for him rather than just killing him or trying to force something that can't work because he's bonded to you."

"Maybe."

Kallie's smile widened. "Whatever the reason, you've got a real chance to get him back, free and clear. Well, not free, but you know what I mean."

It was a chance, but a small one. Miniscule. Aeron tempered his hopes.

"There's no way I'll be able to afford him. I've got six gold coins and three silver ones left from my army severance package. Even if I'd been paid my severance in full, he'd still be worth a dozen times that amount. Maybe more."

Kallie sat next to him on the bed. "I have some coin put away. I'd chip in to help. I know he means a lot to you."

"He means *everything* to me. He's my best friend, and we're bonded for life."

"So I'd help you."

"I can't let you spend your coin."

"I want to. I've been saving it up for a good reason, and I haven't found one that's good enough until now."

"Yeah, like a dowry for your wedding."

She snorted. "What wedding? I'm in no rush. Pa and Mum got married young, and now they pretty much hate each other. That's not something I ever want."

"What about the many prospects you told me about right after I came home?"

18

"Oh, I'm not serious about any of them. And they're not serious about me, either. It's fun to flirt with them, but none of them are husband material. So a dowry is something I won't need for a long time. I may never get married, actually. I like being independent, and that way, when Pa dies, I'll inherit the blacksmith shop."

Aeron blinked. "What?"

Kallie stared him down. "Well, you didn't seriously think he'd leave it to you, did you?"

She had a point.

"So let me help you, yeah? I don't even know that I'll have enough to make a difference, but we have to try." Kallie took his hand in hers and squeezed it.

Her hands were rough, like his. She'd put in more than her fair share of days at the blacksmith shop over the last sixteen years.

"So how do we come up with the rest?"

"We can ask Mum to help. She won't admit it outright, but she has a stash of her own."

Aeron's eyebrows rose. "I'm surprised no one has seen fit to rob this house yet."

Kallie chuckled. "Once we have a wyvern sleeping on the roof every night, we'll be safe forever."

"He might fit on the roof, but it would never support his weight."

"You know what I mean."

"You really think Mum will help?"

"I know she will. I already showed her this, and she said she would," Kallie replied. "I know you're tired when you get home, but you should really talk to her more. She misses her boy."

Hearing Kallie refer to him as a boy didn't grate on him nearly as much as when Pa said it. "I know. I'll try to get better at that. You probably don't remember because of how young you were, but Pa used to call me 'Mum's special boy.' At first it didn't bother me, but the older I got, the more I hated it."

Kallie nodded. "It's not hard to imagine why you left, seeing the way Pa's treated you since you got back."

"Yeah. I don't know what I did to make him hate me so much. I wish I had a father."

She curled her arm around his shoulders and gave him a faint squeeze, but not enough to tweak his back. It just felt good. Comforting.

"If we could convince Pa to chip in, too, you'd be all set," Kallie said.

Aeron scoffed. "Maybe we could sell him on the idea that I'd be out of his life again if he helped."

"He really likes his coin. I don't think he'd go for it, even with a reason as compelling as that." Kallie's lips curled into a grin. "But I'll ask him. He has a hard time saying no to his little girl."

"Mum's special boy and Pa's little girl. What a pair."

"What a pair indeed."

"The auction's in a week." Aeron's heart fluttered, and he smiled. "I'll save what I have, and whenever Pa decides to start paying me, I'll save that, too. Maybe with all of it combined, we'll have a chance."

Kallie squeezed him again, this time a little too hard, and his back protested.

He grunted, and she backed off.

"Sorry," she said. "I wish I could hug you like normal."

"Me too, kid. Me too."

She kissed his cheek, said goodnight, and then she left. Aeron pulled out his sack of shrooms and spread the opening wide.

Only a handful remained, and most of them were bonus shrooms—not ideal for helping his back. Instead they provided added "bonus" experiences to his trips.

He needed more shrooms to be able to function at work. But how would he save enough coin for the auction in a week and buy enough shrooms to survive?

Aeron sighed. It wasn't possible. He'd already resigned himself to it. Unless by some miracle Pa intervened, Kallie and Mum wouldn't have enough coin.

He popped one of his two remaining painkilling shrooms, stuffed the sack under his mattress, and looked into his coin pouch next. It was worse than what he'd told Kallie. He had three silver coins but only five gold, not six.

What did it matter anyway? One gold coin wouldn't make the difference when a military-trained wyvern would cost hundreds or even thousands.

He shut the pouch and tossed it to the floor. *It's hopeless. I'll never get him back.*

As the shroom's effects began to kick in, his attitude shifted along with it.

I have to try. I'd never forgive myself if I didn't. And now it could actually happen.

It meant going virtually without shrooms for the whole week—and back pain galore. But if he got Wafer back, none of it would matter. He could tolerate the back pain if he had Wafer.

He had to try, and he would.

The next week dragged by. Aeron helped Pa shoe over two dozen horses, and together they forged twenty new shields and eight swords. Pa also made most of the shackles, along with their complementary keys.

Aeron also caught a glimpse of a much larger skeleton key Pa had crafted. He'd tried to ask about it, but Pa shushed him and told him to mind his own business.

The back pain proved excruciating, but Aeron powered through it, just like he had for close to two months after the accident. After those two months, he'd finally given in and tried the shrooms one of his army comrades kept offering him.

By midweek at the shop, he'd completely run out of shrooms. He'd arranged for Pa to pay him something—anything—in time for the auction, and he'd saved the remnants of his measly severance payment instead of buying more shrooms.

Whether or not it would all be enough, he didn't know, but he'd made up his mind either way.

The night before the auction, Aeron couldn't sleep, despite the usual level of physical exhaustion he'd incurred from a long day of work.

The morning of the auction, he was ready to go an hour earlier than Mum and Kallie, so he sat at the kitchen table, waiting for them.

Pa came in, grunted, and sat at the opposite end.

Aeron watched him. Pa was uncharacteristically quiet, and he was avoiding eye contact with Aeron. Normally, Pa didn't shy away from anything even resembling conflict or personal interaction, but this morning was different. It was… strange.

Aeron had just worked up the nerve to ask about it when Pa spoke.

"Your mum told me what you're going to try to do today," Pa said, "and I have to say, I don't approve. You have a good thing going with me at the shop. Even if you don't like it, it's steady pay and steady work."

Aeron's heart sank. Pa meant to ban him from the auction right here and now. But it didn't matter. *I'm going whether he wants me to or not.*

"Pa, I'm—"

"I told your mum she was a fool for wanting to help." Pa still wasn't making eye contact with him. "Kallie is perhaps an even greater fool. She ought to be saving coin for her dowry, not throwing it away on some stinking beast."

Aeron bit his tongue. *That stinking beast means more to me than you ever did.*

"And even if you win the auction, which you won't, we've got nowhere to keep it. We live in the capital, for the gods' sakes, and we've no land to speak of aside from that which lies under our feet and the shop. It's beyond foolish—it's *reckless* to think we could properly board a pony, let alone a beast five times that size."

"Pa, I don't ca—"

"Let me *finish*, Aeron." Pa's eyes met Aeron's, then he looked down again. "Your whole life, you've done nothing but vex me," Pa continued. "I've tried to teach you how to live right, but you've only ever thrown it back in my face with disrespect and disdain. Then you fled my home while you were still a child and—"

"I was *sixteen*," Aeron cut in.

Pa glowered at him again until Aeron finally had to look away this time.

"And you joined the army instead of running the shop with me." Pa's voice wavered. "Worst betrayal I could've imagined. I deserved better from my own son."

Aeron scowled at Pa, livid. Leaving home wasn't a betrayal for Aeron—it was an act of survival. For Pa to suggest that Aeron had somehow done him wrong showed just how oblivious Pa was to his own demeanor and failures as a father.

It wasn't Pa who'd deserved better. It was Aeron who'd deserved better.

Aeron had never wanted to smash his Pa's head into a table so much. And he could've done it, too. He had the training. He had the strength. The only thing he didn't have was a fully functioning back.

"And then, on top of all that, you're wasting a perfectly good workday on your fool's errand. Trying to throw away hard-earned coin that, were it not for me giving you a job, you wouldn't have to begin with."

A job I never wanted. Aeron folded his arms.

"You're costing me work hours and production. You're costing yourself coin you might've used to move out of my house and get your own place. You're raiding your mum's savings and your sister's. And you're wasting my time, too."

Aeron's patience burst, and he slammed his palms on the table. "How am I wasting *your* time? I'm not asking you to come. I don't harbor any expectations of you, except that you'll be rude, demeaning, and cruel like you've always been.

"You've never wanted me. You wanted a son who would carry on your business, who would do whatever you said without question and without delay. You wanted to hammer me into your own image, but I'm not at all like you, and I never will be. I'll never be anything but a disappointment to you.

"So I don't care what happens today, Pa. Win or lose, I'm leaving your house, and you can go to hell. Go to *all* of the hells, for all I care. I said it the first day I came home, and I should've stuck with it. Well, I'm saying it now, again, and I mean it. One hundred times, I'd say it. Go. To. Hell. I'm done with you."

Pa's eyes had found Aeron again, and a fury the likes of which Aeron had never seen simmered within them. But lines of sadness deepened the wrinkles on his worn face as well. Aeron didn't know what to make of it.

Pa cleared his throat. "Are you done?"

Aeron stilled his breathing and wished he'd had one of the purple-striped shrooms. His anxiety level was threatening to go volcanic.

"Yes," he said.

"Because I wasn't finished."

Aeron sighed. *Of course you weren't.*

Pa looked down again. "I know I've not done well by you as your father."

Understatement of the ages.

"And I know I'm harder on you than I probably ought to be."

Aeron squinted at him. *Obviously.*

"And if I'm honest with myself, I know you haven't deserved that treatment."

Aeron blinked and leaned back. *What?*

"I—I should've done a lot of things differently. But I didn't. And I regret it."

What's happening? Am I dreaming? Am I high right now?

"And while I can't change the past—nor would I, if I could..."

Oh, never mind. That's the Pa I know. He's back.

"...I can still try to change the future." Pa paused, folded his weathered hands, and leaned with his forearms against the table. He met Aeron's eyes. "So I'm going to try to help you get your wyvern back."

CHAPTER FIVE

A eron's mouth hung open for a full minute of silence. Maybe longer.

Pa glanced around the kitchen. "Well? Aren't you going to say something?"

Aeron blinked back tears and shifted in his seat. "I, uh…"

Pa waited.

"I… I don't know what to s-say, really." Aeron sniveled, and a tear escaped and rolled down his cheek.

"A damned 'thank you' would be nice," Pa said, his voice flat.

Aeron chortled, then his lip started quivering. He didn't know if he could even get the words out. "Th-th-thank… thank you."

Pa nodded once, then he sat upright. "Don't get too excited. I do well at the shop, but I've got limits. I can't go past, say, 2,000 gold without having to sell off property or equipment."

Aeron's heart stuttered. "Gods, Pa. 2,000 is plenty. I think. I hope."

Pa chuffed. "Yeah, I hope so too. I hope it'll be a lot less than that. A *lot* less. I don't know if I conveyed this thoroughly or not, but I think this is a stupid idea, and I'd rather not spend any more on it than I have to."

Aeron chuckled and wiped the tears from his eyes. "Yes, you made that very clear."

"And maybe this way, your mum can keep her savings, and your sister can keep some shadow of hope that she may one day find a husband."

"Yeah." Aeron nodded. "Maybe."

They sat in numb silence for a moment, then Pa stood and said, "I've got to run by the shop to pick some things up before the auction. I'll meet you and the girls there."

Pa headed for the door.

"Alright." Aeron stood, too. "Pa?"

Pa stopped and turned back.

"Thank you again. Seriously."

And again, Pa just nodded once and didn't say anything, then he walked out the door.

✳

The auction took place in Capital Square, a sprawling opening in the center of the city used for commerce, large events like festivals and fairs, for citywide meetings, and as a rallying point for the army and civilians should the city ever be overrun.

Aeron had attended a handful of auctions before, always while on duty, but he'd never seen it this crowded—not for an auction, anyway. Throngs of people pressed each other within the square, talking, laughing, eating, and carousing.

The sight sent tingles ratcheting through Aeron's nerves, and his anxiety spiked. The thought of someone jostling him by accident and hurting his back made him physically queasy. He craved his shrooms—they could've helped him deal with it all.

"Hey." Kallie took him by his wrist. "It'll be good, yeah? We're here with you."

Aeron nodded, and he took Mum's extended hand also. She smiled up at him, one of the first genuine smiles she'd donned since his return.

"I can see the platform from here," Mum said, her voice barely audible over the commotion. "Let's make our way down there."

Kallie led the way.

When they got there, Kallie found them a spot near the front.

"Hopefully your Pa will find us quickly," Mum said. "I've never done anything like this before. I'm worried I'll mess something up."

"I've been to a few, Mum. We'll be alright," Aeron said. "What's our maximum spend amount?"

"Pa said 2,000 gold from him," Mum replied. "But I've got another 680 if we need it."

"And I've got just shy of 800," Kallie said.

Aeron and Mum gawked at her in unison.

"What?" she asked.

"Where did you come up with that much coin?" Mum asked.

"I have my ways." Kallie covered her mouth, her eyes wide. "No, Mum. I didn't mean it like that. I'm not... uh..."

"Selling yourself?" Mum finished.

"No! I would never."

"You're damned right you would never," Aeron said. "I'd strangle you."

"She's a good girl," Mum said. "Mostly, anyway. I believe her."

"*Thank you.*" Kallie shook her head and folded her arms. "I can't believe you'd even suggest such a thing."

"Well, I still want to know where all that coin came from," Mum said.

24

"I'll never tell. A girl needs her secrets." Kallie winked at her and Aeron. "You didn't tell us where *you* got *your* coin from, Mum."

"A few thousand embroidered clothes, shirts, cloaks, pillows, towels, handkerchiefs, and more over the years," Mum said. "Sold them to friends, took special orders. It adds up when you never have to spend any coin." She looked at Kallie. "Your turn."

Kallie's lips pursed shut, then she said, "Sorry. I'm keeping my secret."

"Oh, whatever." Mum waved her hand. "How much do you have Aeron?"

"Not much. About a hundred. Little more, I guess."

"So about 3,600, if we round up?" Mum said. "A fine sum. Well, if this falls through, I'm going to press your father to remodel the house."

"For that amount, we should build an entirely new one, Mum," Kallie said.

A loud clack-clack-clack sounded from the platform—the auctioneer smacking a wooden block against a lectern of some sort. The crowd hushed, and the auctioneer briefly explained the bidding process and then called for the first item to be brought out.

It was a black sail from a captured pirate ship near the port. It bore the traditional snake-eyes insignia of the Septerran, high seas pirates that terrorized the southern coastline. It stretched so wide that it took six soldiers and two ladders to properly spread it out for the crowd to see.

Aeron had seen sails like it a few times before while serving in the army and fighting enemies abroad and in Govalia's ports, including the Septerrans themselves. It was an appealing item, and were he wealthy, he would've wanted to bid on it, but it didn't measure up to getting Wafer back. Not even close. So he let it pass.

The auctioneer chased the bids, and Aeron noticed that those bidding held up small paddles. The sail sold to a bidder, and then the next item came out—a serpentine masthead from the same pirate ship as the sail. Bidding commenced yet again.

From behind, Aeron couldn't see what was on the front of the bidders' paddles, but when someone a few people back placed a bid on the masthead, he got a glance at it. The paddles displayed family crests and sigils.

Aeron's family had neither a crest nor a sigil, nor did they have a paddle to put it on nonetheless.

"What are we going to do?" Aeron asked. "We don't have a paddle to signal with."

"I guess we raise our hands? I've seen others doing that," Kallie said.

"I see Pa." Mum pointed at a bald head jerking through the crowd at about the same height as everyone else's heads. "Kallie, would you go fetch him, please?"

She headed off, weaving toward him. They returned a few minutes later, and Pa grumbled something about having missed breakfast, and why were there so many people here because it's just a stupid auction, and how long was he expected to stay?

"I wish I knew." Aeron rubbed his back. All this standing was beginning to take its toll on him. "They're bringing the auction items along that path behind the platform. I imagine they'll somehow bring him down there, but I don't know how long it will take until they get to him."

"Then I guess we'll wait." Pa grunted, then he handed Aeron a bronze paddle.

"You'll need this. I've only used it once before, at one other auction. Use it well today."

"This is fantastic." Aeron held it up to get a better look at it.

"400 to the blacksmith," the auctioneer called. "Do I hear 450?"

"What?" Aeron's eyes widened. He glanced between Pa, Mum, Kallie, and the auctioneer. "I didn't mean—"

Pa snatched the paddle from him and whacked his shoulder with it. A tinge of pain stung Aeron's shoulder and spread to his back, then it subsided.

"Are you an imbecile?" Pa growled. "You're going to bankrupt me on useless garbage."

Another bid surpassed Aeron's errant one, and then another overtook that one, and only then did Aeron begin to breathe easily.

An hour passed, then two. The hard ground continued to bother Aeron's back, and he took to contorting his body and stretching however he could. He earned himself several peculiar glances from others in the square, but he didn't care. If they hurt like he did, they'd be doing the same thing.

Kallie left for a few minutes and then returned with seared meat on sticks for everyone, and the smell of it set Aeron's stomach rumbling.

It subdued his appetite but didn't sate it, and he wished she'd brought him a second one. Fortunately, Mum let him finish the rest of hers.

After another hour and a half, Pa was ready to leave, and Aeron's back was rebelling almost as badly as if he'd been working. But all his discontent faded when the auctioneer announced the last item of the auction.

Twenty lance-wielding soldiers guided four large horses pulling a massive, burlap-covered cart toward the platform.

The soldiers pulled the burlap covering from the cart, revealing a gigantic cage with thick bars and an unmistakable blue-green wyvern locked inside.

Wafer immediately locked his golden eyes on Aeron.

CHAPTER SIX

A familiar rush of trust, comfort, and security filled Aeron's chest. A fleeting warmth spread throughout his body in waves, not as hot as if he were riding Wafer, but more of a presence than he'd felt in weeks.

Relief. That was the best word for how he felt. His anxiety melted away the longer he stared at Wafer. Even his back felt better, though he knew it was more of an influx of optimism than actual, physical healing.

One of the soldiers prodded Wafer with a lance, and Wafer screeched and thrashed against the bars to no avail.

Their bond faltered, and Aeron's anxiety returned. He couldn't relax yet, not when there was an auction yet to be won.

The auctioneer announced Wafer in the most generic of terms, stating that he was a common wyvern who'd been trained for battle and bonded to a rider whose tenure with the army had come to an end. As such, now he was of no additional use to the army since he refused to cooperate with anyone else.

"So buyer beware," the auctioneer concluded.

All in all, Aeron couldn't have hoped for a better explanation of Wafer's relative uselessness to anyone but him. He hoped it would be enough to dissuade anyone else from purchasing him.

The sight of much of the crowd recoiling at Wafer's unveiling, including some of them even leaving, filled Aeron with additional hope. Fewer people around the auction platform meant less buying competition. Probably.

The auctioneer started the bidding at 300 gold pieces, which was even lower than Aeron had expected. He moved to raise the brass paddle, but Pa blocked his arm.

Aeron half-glowered, half-gawked at him.

"Wait. Let's see how it shakes out," Pa said. "It may be a better strategic move to come in late and buy him with an over-the-top price."

Aeron squinted at Pa.

"Trust me. Like I said, I've done this once before."

"Once." Aeron scoffed.

"And how many times have you done it?" Pa fired back.

"I've been to at least five of these."

Pa's eyes narrowed at him. "Then we're both rookies, at best. I've got coin, and you've got experience. We can work together."

Aeron clenched his teeth but nodded. "Fine."

Someone matched the initial bid of 300, and the auctioneer called for 350. Another bidder called it, and the bid rose to 400. They played back and forth for a few hundred more, and the interplay seemed to level out around 750.

The auctioneer called for 800, but the other bidder didn't respond.

Pa nudged Aeron and nodded.

Aeron raised the bronze paddle, and Pa called, "One thousand."

The auctioneer started, then he smiled. "Very well. 1,000 to the blacksmith. Do I have 1,100?"

Aeron searched the crowd for the other bidders, but enough people had lingered that he couldn't spot anyone in particular.

"1,100, yes. Thank you," the auctioneer called. "The bid is called at 1,100. Do I hear 1,200?"

Pa nudged Aeron again, and he raised the paddle as Pa called, "1,500."

The auctioneer recognized it and called for more.

"1,700," came the response.

"Do I hear 1,800?" the auctioneer inquired.

"Maybe those big jumps weren't such a good idea after all," Pa muttered.

"Yeah. Maybe they weren't," Aeron muttered back. He raised the paddle to signal 1,800 gold pieces.

"1,900," came the immediate response.

Pa cursed, but he nudged Aeron a third time. "Go ahead and take it to the full 2,000."

Aeron did.

"2,100," called the other bidder.

Aeron's hands started shaking. What was going on?

"It's alright," Mum said. "We've got more. We'll put it to use if we have to."

Aeron nodded and raised the paddle for 2,200.

"3,000," came the counter.

Who the hell is bidding against me? Aeron scanned the crowd again, but he still couldn't get a look at the bidder.

"Kallie, Mum, try to keep watch on the crowd. See if you can spot the bidder."

They nodded.

Aeron called it for 3,100, and a call for 3,500 came back immediately.

"I see him!" Kallie pointed. "Well, I see where he is. I can't tell who it is."

Aeron craned his neck for a look, but he couldn't discern anyone from anyone else around where Kallie was pointing. He turned to Pa. "If I call 3,600, we're at our limit."

Pa groaned and rubbed the bridge of his nose. "Then you'd better do it."

Aeron swallowed and signaled it, and the auctioneer logged it.

"Do I hear 3,700? Sir?" the auctioneer extended his hand, palm up, in the same direction Kallie had been pointing.

He only got silence back.

"Sir, the bid is to you. Do I have 3,700?"

Please don't bid more, Aeron pleaded. *Please, please, please.*

He locked eyes with Wafer again and smiled.

We're close, buddy. So very close.

"4,000," came the bid.

Aeron's heart plummeted into his churning stomach. That was it. He'd been outbid. They didn't have enough. It was over. He stared at the ground in shock.

"4,500," Pa's voice tore through Aeron's malaise.

Aeron jerked upright and looked at Pa as the auctioneer logged the bid. "You said 2,000 was your limit. Even with my gold plus Kallie's and Mum's, we're still short."

"I'll find a way," Pa said. "I always have, and I always will."

"Pa, I can't let you—"

"Shut up before I realize what a moronic thing I just did."

"Sir, the bid is yours." Again, the auctioneer pointed toward the mystery bidder. "Do I hear 4,600? Or perhaps 5,000?"

Pa moaned. "Don't go there. Definitely don't go there."

"Very well. Going once," the auctioneer crooned. "Going twice..."

Aeron held his breath.

CHAPTER SEVEN

"Ten-thousand gold pieces," the mystery bidder called.

What?! Aeron's legs shook, and he almost toppled over. Who would want Wafer so badly that he'd pay 10,000 gold pieces for him?

No wyvern was worth 10,000 gold pieces. Even the best wyverns sold for no more than 4,000-5,000, and Wafer was already bonded. It just didn't make sense.

Aeron looked at Pa and hoped, but Pa shook his head.

"Sorry, but I'm not even worth that much," Pa said. "The house, the shop, the forge tools and our combined cash wouldn't even come close to covering that sum."

Aeron's last shred of hope fizzled to nothing.

The auctioneer called for other bids once, then twice, and then he pronounced the sale in favor of the other bidder without using his name.

Aeron didn't bother looking back this time. Instead, he found Wafer's sorrowful, golden eyes and begged for forgiveness.

"I NEVER DID SEE WHO BOUGHT HIM," KALLIE SAID AS THEY WALKED HOME. "COULDN'T pick him out. Just saw a hand go up every other bid, but no face."

Aeron processed her words and understood them, but right now, nothing could make him care. It was done. Over. He'd lost Wafer again, this time for good.

"We're almost home," Mum said. "Pa, Aeron will be staying home for the rest of today from work. There's no need to subject him to any more stress right now."

Something within Aeron spoke for him. "No, Mum. It's alright. I'm fine with working. It might take my mind off of things."

Mum hesitated at first, but then she nodded.

"Well," Pa said, "No good reason to stop by home. See you at the shop, Aeron."

"Yeah. Sure."

At home, Aeron changed into his grime-stained work clothes, pocketed some coins, and then headed back downstairs.

Kallie tried to say something to him as he walked out, but he heard Mum say, "Leave him be. He needs time."

No, Mum. Time isn't what I need.

Aeron didn't head toward the shop. Instead, he headed toward the apothecary.

I need magic mushrooms.

✦

THREE SHROOMS LATER, AERON'S PAIN HAD SUBSIDED, AND HE'D MADE HIS WAY TO PA'S shop with the remainder of his shroom purchase in a new sack.

He didn't say a word to Pa; he just headed straight for his apron and his gloves, through the vivid displays of colors transforming around him, and got to work.

The haze didn't keep Aeron from working, but nor did it dull his sorrow. Thanks to the shrooms, he felt no anxiety, but he hadn't found a shroom to combat sadness or to fill the emptiness in his chest where his bond with Wafer should have been.

He hammered through his work. The shrooms' swirling, colorful effects had just started to wear off when the familiar sound of hoofbeats clopped outside.

At that point, he didn't care. He'd already lost everything he'd wanted, so what did it matter if the soldiers recognized him and called him out in front of Pa?

The telltale wingbeats of a wyvern approached next. The sound broke Aeron's heart anew, but he shook it off and ignored his feelings as best as he could.

Before long, Commander Brove's Urthian-accented voice came from the far end of the shop. Where Aeron had wanted to hurt him before, now he just wanted to be left alone. He hoped Pa would get Brove out of there quickly.

"Aeron?" Pa called.

Aeron lowered his hammer and looked up.

Commander Brove stood next to Pa, wearing his telltale gray armor with the silver wyvern wing stamped on his shoulder and a smirk. That smirk sparked rage anew in Aeron's belly, but the remaining shroom effects subdued it.

"The commander wants to speak with you," Pa continued.

Well, I don't want to speak with him. Aeron said, "I'm busy."

"What's wrong, Leatherwing Ironglade?" Brove taunted. "Oops. Forgive me. It's just 'Aeron' now, isn't it? You don't have a rank since we stripped it from you."

The spark reignited in Aeron's gut, and this time he had to fight to stanch it instead of the shrooms doing it for him. "I have nothing to say to you."

"I suppose you didn't explain the real reason why you were discharged, did you?" Brove brushed something off of his armored shoulder and smirked again.

"He told me enough," Pa said.

"He told you that he took magic mushrooms, endangered his fellow knights on a critical mission, and summarily got discharged?" Brove tilted his head and eyed Pa.

Aeron stayed silent.

Pa glanced between them and nodded. "Not in so many words, but I've gathered as much over the last few weeks, yes."

"Hmm. Except that's not what happened." Brove chuckled. "Would you like to know the real reason?"

"Commander, please..." Aeron said.

Now Pa remained silent.

"Did he tell you that he committed..." Brove lowered his voice. "...*treason?*"

Aeron fought the lingering shroom effects and said, "That's not strictly true."

Brove shrugged. "It is according to the oath you swore. The part about serving the Govalian Army for life wasn't a suggestion."

"Daydreaming about leaving doesn't constitute *treason*," Aeron countered, more to Pa than to Brove. He'd already pled his case to Brove and failed, but Pa needed to hear the truth. "I would've stayed with the army forever, but with the accident, my back made it hard to do much of anything without... help."

"And that's where the magic mushrooms came in. They hindered your judgment in this area, certainly." Brove turned to Pa. "Do you know that he wrote you a letter outlining his plans to steal army property and abandon his post?"

Aeron's rage bubbled over. "That's not true! You're twisting my words!"

"Whether I am or not doesn't matter. We intercepted the letter, of course, and General Cadimus saw fit to expel you all the same."

"And he also refused to execute me, despite your multiple requests," Aeron said.

"The punishment for treason is death. Though General Cadimus showed you mercy, the law is the law. But since he passed judgment, I cannot contravene his ruling." Brove bared his teeth in a wicked smile. "And that includes his decision to auction off your precious wyvern."

Aeron clenched his fists, but Brove's admission came as little surprise to him. As a general, Cadimus oversaw much of the Govalian Army, including the ranks of wyvern knights. He typically allowed Brove to control the riders' assets and operations, but wyverns without riders weren't a simple matter.

Apparently, Cadimus had decided that a wyvern bonded to a rider who was no longer employed in the army was more of a liability than an asset. It still needed to be fed and stabled, and it would require additional attention and training to get it ready for another rider—if it ever would be.

"If I'd had things my way, I would've just killed your mount and fed its carcass to the other wyverns at the roost," Brove continued. "It would've made for a better use of our time and resources. But General Cadimus forbade it. He insisted we sell the wyvern to recoup some of our losses.

"So I auctioned him, as ordered," Brove smiled again, "and bought him myself."

CHAPTER EIGHT

Aeron's jaw hung open, and he sobered up immediately. "Why?"
"Because your discharge was a miscarriage of justice. You should have died for your treason," Brove said. "But since I can't bring justice to you, I'm going to bring it to your mount instead.

"He will return to the roost," Brove continued. "He will be killed, and he will be fed to the other wyverns. And you will live the rest of your meager existence knowing every detail of his fate."

"Get out of my shop," Pa uttered slowly, menacingly.

Brove turned toward him. "Excuse me?"

"I'll forge your weapons and shoe your horses, but I won't tolerate harassment." Pa pointed toward the front door. "So get out of here."

Brove stepped closer to him and leaned his face near Pa's. "Keep talking to me like that, and you won't make so much as a door knocker for us ever again. I'll have you put out of business faster than you could whistle the Govalian Anthem."

Pa didn't flinch. "I know the law. A proprietor may refuse service to anyone whom he chooses for any reason. I'm exercising that privilege right now, and I'm refusing to service you and your men by allowing you to enter my place of business."

"You really don't know who you're dealing with, do you?" Brove asked.

"That makes two of us, then," Pa said, stone cold.

Brove stepped back. "You'd be on the floor, begging for your life right now if you didn't do such impeccable work."

"If I didn't do such impeccable work, you'd be training naked every day."

Silence.

Aeron blinked.

More silence.

Brove nodded. "I suppose I can't argue with you there."

"I'll send word when your order is finished," Pa said.

"And I'll send word when the wyvern is dead." Brove sneered at Aeron. "He's already been transported back to the roost. Pretty soon, he'll be dinner for all of his pals."

"You're jealous because I'm better than you," Aeron fired at him. "That's all this ever was. I beat you, and your ego can't take it."

"Maybe that was true, once, but certainly not anymore."

"You're sick," Aeron continued. "You spent *10,000 gold* just to get back at me?"

"It was nothing," Brove said. "My family, back in Urthia, is quite wealthy. It's how I earned my officer's commission in the army, in fact. And if paying 10,000 gold means that some measure of true justice is served, and if it sets the right example for other treason-minded soldiers, then it is a worthy price to pay."

"I hate you," Aeron said.

"I know." Brove grinned, turned, and headed out of the shop with his soldiers following.

Pa watched the soldiers mount up through the window. "You must have really pissed that bastard off."

Aeron didn't answer. He just stood there staring past the window, past the soldiers and Commander Brove and Strife, past the city itself. He saw nothing.

The first mighty beat of Strife's wings broke Aeron's absent focus, and he blinked. "I have to do something."

"What is there to do?" Pa asked. "It's done. He's won. The best you can hope for is to live well in spite of him."

"That's not enough. They're going to kill Wafer."

"I know he's important to you, but sometimes this is how life goes."

"No, Pa. You have no idea what you're talking about. To you, he's just a pet or a horse that flies. But to me, he is literally my best friend. We're linked. Bonded. If they kill him, a huge part of me dies as well."

Pa shrugged. "I don't know what to tell you. But we have work to do. Real work that will earn us real coin."

Aeron sighed. Pa would never understand.

"But…" Pa started. "But first I need to run an errand."

"Whatever."

"And you can either mope around all day or you can accomplish something." Pa headed over to his favorite workstation and pulled something small and metal off of a nearby rack. He held it up—a large skeleton key. "Before I go, I wanted to make sure you knew to take special care of this key."

Aeron blinked. "You want me to… take care of a key?"

"This key is very important," Pa said. "It's a key commissioned in secret by our very own Commander Brove. It can open most of the fortress's external doors, and only ranking officers are allowed to carry keys like this."

Aeron tilted his head. *Interesting.*

"I'm not really supposed to tell anyone about keys like these. But I'm telling you so you can take care of it while I'm gone. On my errand. Which will take quite some time to accomplish."

What is he doing? It didn't make sense. If Pa had wanted the key safe, he could've taken it with him, or he could've just left it hanging there as another anonymous, innocuous part of the shop.

"Do you understand?" Pa asked. "I want you to *take care of it* while I'm running my errand."

Aeron's eyes widened. He nodded. "Yes. I understand. Thank you, Pa."

Pa gave him a single nod in return. "You've ruined a lot of things in your life recently. Don't mess this up, too."

And with that, Pa turned and left.

Aeron rushed over and grabbed the key.

IN ORDER FOR AERON'S HASTY PLAN TO WORK, HE'D NEED TO STOP BY THE APOTHECARY again. He hurried inside and pointed to what he needed.

"How long until these take effect?" Aeron asked.

The old apothecary rubbed the two long, silver hairs sprouting from her chin. "Both should be instantaneous. I wouldn't touch the blue one with any part of your skin until you're ready to use it. It's rather potent."

"Good to know." Aeron nodded. "How long do their effects last?"

"Oh, normally about a day, each. But they're older mushrooms than what I normally sell, so I wouldn't count on more than six hours," she added. "I just don't get a lot of folks asking for these."

Plenty of time. "Will these mix well with the purple-striped and the yellow-spotted ones?"

"I seem to recall that mixing either of these with anything else is a recipe for disaster, but as I said, I don't sell many of them these days." She gave a soft chuckle. "My memory's not what it used to be."

Aeron cursed under his breath. "I'll make it work. How much?"

She told him, and he paid the steep price. But what did a few dozen gold coins matter if they helped him ransom Wafer from his fate?

The apothecary donned leather gloves, wrapped the blue magic mushroom in a cloth, and handed it to him along with another orange-and-black mushroom, not wrapped.

"Don't squeeze the blue one. It releases spores that are just as effective."

"I know. That's why I wanted it." Aeron thanked her, ran out, and headed back toward Pa's shop.

When he got there, he found Kallie waiting for him.

"Aeron." Sadness etched her words. "I'm so sorry about the auction. We tried."

"I know we did. But I'm fine now. Really, I am." He passed her by and scurried around the shop, piecing together what he needed.

"What are you in such a rush about?"

"No time to explain." Aeron pointed at a shield he'd finished the day before, hanging from a hook on a wooden post. "Hand me that, would you?"

She paused, then she complied. "Alright."

He set it to the side where he could find it again and began to look around the shop for something he hadn't made since he'd started working at the shop again. "Gauntlets, gauntlets... I need gauntlets."

Kallie pointed across the shop. "Pa usually keeps them over there."

Aeron found them and slipped them on over the sleeves of his work clothes.

"You look like you're going into battle. What's going on?"

"Nothing. Can't talk about it." Aeron fiddled with the straps and buckles on the gauntlets but couldn't quite get them tight enough. "Help me tighten these?"

Kallie planted her feet. "Not unless you tell me what's going on."

"It's better if you don't know anything. That way, if someone questions you—"

"For the gods' sakes, Aeron. You're my brother. I want to help." She lowered her arms to her sides. "You're clearly up to no good, so let me help you with it. I'm good at being up to no good."

Aeron grunted, but he *would* move faster if she helped him. He held out his arms toward her. "Fine. I'm going to break into the fortress and set Wafer free."

"What? How?" Kallie tightened one greave, then the other.

"Pa made a special key that ranking officers use to get inside. I'm... borrowing it." Aeron grabbed a forest green breastplate next. "Help me with this?"

"The back isn't painted yet. It's just raw iron."

Aeron swore. "Didn't see another one near my size. It'll have to do. Strap me in."

She did. "Now that you've told me, I'm not so sure I want you to do this. You're going to get yourself caught or killed. Maybe both."

"I'll be fine. I'll be wearing a disguise."

"A pretty mediocre one."

"It'll work. Once I reach Wafer, we'll fly out. The roost is open air—no ceiling."

Kallie's protests continued, but she kept helping him don the armor. When they finished, he looked mostly like a soldier again—at least from what Aeron could tell.

"Something's missing." She held up her forefinger. "Wait."

Kallie grabbed a lance from a rack and handed it to him.

Aeron looked it over. "This lance isn't up to army code."

Kallie rolled her eyes. "Neither is the unfinished back of your breastplate. But as you said, it'll have to do. Are you sure you want to do this?"

He nodded. "I *have* to do it. If I die, at least I'll die with my best friend."

"Gods, Aeron. Don't say things like that." Kallie shook her head and looked away. "We just got you back."

"I'm sorry." He approached her, leaned the spear to the side, and took her hands in his. "I don't want to die. I'd much rather get away with it. But if I do..."

She looked up at him.

"Well, I was going to offer to let you have all of my belongings, but I'm poor as dirt. So you'll just have to remember me on your own."

Kallie smacked his breastplate and smiled. Even so, tears ran down her cheeks. She grabbed him and curled her arms around him. "Love you, brother."

"I love you too, sis." He patted her back and pulled away. "Gotta run."

"If you make it, when will you be back?"

He picked up the shield again and yanked the lance free from the floor. Then he patted his pockets to make sure he had the key, and he tucked the shrooms into a small pouch and secured it to his waist.

Aeron also grabbed a key for shackles, just in case he did get caught, and he tucked it inside the wrist of his left greave.

"Tonight. But I don't know how long I'll be able to stay."

She nodded. "Don't tell me goodbye now. Tell me when you get back."

Aeron smiled. "Alright."

"Well, go already," she said.

Aeron bolted out of the shop and made for the path that led to the fortress.

Each successive step racked Aeron's back as he trudged up the path.

His anxiety about what he meant to do assaulted his senses and shortened his breath, but he forced it down and moved ahead with the rationalization that *not* doing this would be far worse.

He completed the two-mile hike to the fortress in about forty-five minutes and stopped before the very same bronze doors he'd faced several weeks earlier.

Aeron sucked in a long breath to still his nerves. "Told you I'd come back."

A keyhole in the center of the right-side door gaped open at him. He tucked his lance under his armpit, dug out the unwrapped orange-and-black shroom, and ate it. It tasted a bit like honey—if it had been mixed into a bowl of dirt.

He waited a moment and felt nothing. After five minutes, he still felt nothing, but it had to be working. Its effects weren't necessarily supposed to be noticeable.

Aeron pulled out the skeleton key, looked it over, and gulped. "Here we go."

He inserted the skeleton key into the lock and turned it with two hands. The effort tweaked his back. Nothing else happened.

He tried again, twisted it the other way, and this time it turned. A heavy clank sounded, and Aeron pushed the huge bronze door open and stepped inside.

He only made it three steps into the courtyard.

CHAPTER NINE

"You there! Halt!" a voice shouted from above Aeron.

He cursed under his breath and slowly looked up. Three steps and he'd already been caught.

A soldier on watch duty atop the fortress walls pointed down at him. "What do you think you're doing?"

Aeron gulped back his fear but couldn't muster the courage to respond. If the wrong words spilled from his mouth...

"Close the door! You'll let in bugs."

Relief swept over Aeron, and he pivoted, headed back, and pulled the door shut.

Bugs? It was a courtyard. It didn't have a ceiling. Bugs would get in anyway. *Maybe it's just an expression the wall watchmen use.*

He looked up, but the soldier had already gone back to watching the horizon.

So far, so good. He kept his head and eyes down and tried to look like a soldier. He'd been one for so long, it should've been more natural, but nothing felt right.

Was he walking too fast? Too slow? Would someone notice the back of his armor and say something? Was he carrying his shield right?

Stop overthinking it, and just move.

Most of the soldiers milled about, talking and chatting. Some sparred with each other. Wooden practice swords and spears clacked and banged against iron shields. Other soldiers grappled, both upright and on the ground. A handful climbed ropes and ladders, racing each other to the top and back down again.

Aeron scanned for anyone who might recognize him, especially Commander Brove or any of his former wyvern knight comrades, but so far, he hadn't seen any.

He hoped they wouldn't all be at the roost, either, but with Govalia at peace with her neighbors, the wyvern knights had nowhere else to be. It didn't bode well for Aeron's chances of going unnoticed.

The courtyard ended with a set of doors leading into the fortress. Brown-gray stones formed the corridor walls, and iron-wrought torches mounted at regular intervals cast flickering light along his path. He wondered if perhaps his father had forged the torches and their mounting brackets.

A fresh pang in his back severed his flippant thoughts. The sooner he got to the roost, the sooner he could free Wafer and get to the rest of his shroom stash.

He reached a familiar spiral staircase made from the same brown-gray stones, gripped the wrought-iron railing mounted to the wall, and proceeded upward. Despite his attempts to take softer steps, the weight of the armor clanked when he moved, jerking and pinching his back.

"Just a few more steps," he whispered. "Just a few more."

The last time he'd taken these stairs was the day he'd been escorted out of the fortress. One of the benefits of being a wyvern knight included not having to worry about those stairs. He could just fly Wafer directly in and out of the roost, and the mess hall was just down the corridor from the roost.

Five minutes later, he crested the final stair and took a right turn into the corridor, which opened into the roost itself.

From outside, a commoner might see the fortress's massive size and wonder what could possibly take up so much space. Even considering the fortress housed and fed the bulk of Govalia's soldiers, the fortress was huge.

But in fact, the roost claimed the largest chunk of space within the fortress, including the throne room. Rightfully so—wyverns required a lot of maintenance.

As Aeron ventured into the roost, he sucked in a sharp breath to fend off his burgeoning anxiety. It didn't help much.

Under the open ceiling, the roost looked and smelled the same as it had when he'd left several weeks earlier. Wyvern stalls, each wide enough to accommodate a wyvern's twenty-foot wingspan and corresponding length, lined the walls around a large central platform known as the launch pad.

Antechambers for the knights' bunks and personal effects lay to Aeron's right, along with an antechamber for latrines and a bath. Long before his promotion to the wyvern knight ranks, as a Featherwing—a new recruit—he'd hauled buckets of water up the very staircase he'd just summited to replenish the latrines and the bath.

He didn't want to imagine what that kind of strain would do to his back now.

Beyond the launch pad and the stalls lay the hatchery. Female wyverns laid eggs only once a year, almost always one single egg per wyvern, and only at certain ages.

Certain male wyverns were permitted to fertilize the eggs soon after, and then the attendants brought the eggs into the hatchery.

Aeron had watched, side-by-side with a dozen other rider prospects, as Wafer's tooth pricked through the eggshell.

He'd watched as a shimmering blue-green creature covered in scales clawed its way into the world and scanned the hatchery for its lifelong partner—its rider.

And then Wafer's golden eyes made contact with Aeron's. The bond forged in an electric instant. A tingle started on the tip of Aeron's nose and shot down his neck, into his chest and arms and legs and fingers and toes. Wafer had leaped at him, tackled him to the floor, and wrapped his newborn wings around Aeron's torso.

Aeron loved thinking of that moment now, but it had repulsed him at the time. Bloody, slimy afterbirth had still covered Wafer from his time inside the egg, and when he'd plowed into Aeron, the stuff got all over Aeron's chest, face, and arms.

But that's also how Wafer had gotten his name: a piece of the egg had stuck to the top of Wafer's head, like a little hat. It was no bigger than a wafer.

Aeron snapped out of it. He could reminisce later. Time was of the essence.

He walked toward the launch pad and veered to the left. A trio of soldiers had led one of the wyverns out of its stall, saddled it up, and positioned it on the launch pad. It crouched low and exhaled a serpentine breath, and its rider mounted it.

Aeron recognized the mount immediately. The roost only housed one orange wyvern with purple striping—Nilla.

And its rider's unmistakable white-blonde hair gave her away just as clearly. Faylen Uridi, one of only three female wyvern knights commissioned by the army. She was the friend he'd saved, and in doing so, he'd injured his back.

Faylen was stunning both in appearance and prowess, and Aeron had always harbored an attraction for her, so he was glad when Nilla reared back, spread her wings, and launched into the blue expanse above the roost.

It meant she wouldn't be a part of what happened next, whether good or bad.

Once the other two soldiers cleared out, Aeron made for Wafer's stall. As he approached, his connection to Wafer strengthened, and Wafer's head popped up over the wall, searching with those unforgettable golden eyes. Aeron wished Wafer hadn't been so obvious about it, but maybe it wouldn't matter in a few minutes.

He made it to Wafer's stall unhindered. Wafer made a few reptilian chirping noises, and Aeron shushed him gently. Aeron checked over his shoulders to make sure no one had taken notice. It seemed as though they were still safe.

"I'm happy to see you too," he whispered. "I'm here to get you out."

Wafer's head bobbed, and he chomped his mouth open and closed lightly.

"We'll get you something to eat later."

Wafer huffed, loud and short.

Aeron winced. It shouldn't have mattered; the wyverns made all kinds of noises on a regular basis. But it sent his anxiety spinning all the same.

"Easy, boy. One thing at a time. I have to get you out of here first."

Aeron checked the shackle on Wafer's right ankle. The same as always—connected to a thick, black chain so Wafer couldn't just fly away but made to unclasp easily and without a key in case of an emergency or an attack.

"Straighten up. I'm going to unshackle you." Aeron reached down.

Then a gruff, Urthian-accented voice behind him said, "Welcome back, Aeron."

CHAPTER TEN

C ommander Brove had Aeron subdued and then shackled.
Aeron had tried to fight back, but too many knights came at him, and the first tweak of his back sent spasms of sharp pain ratcheting throughout his body. He gave up far quicker than he would've preferred.

They set up a feeding post near the edge of the launch pad. Normally, they'd hang animal carcasses from it so the wyverns could feed without assistance, but this time the knights hooked the chain of his shackles to the long hook embedded near the top. It stretched his arms high and ensured that his back pain persisted nonstop.

Then Commander Brove summoned the entire unit to the edge of the launch pad.

"A wayward son has returned," Brove announced to them. "Leatherwing Ironglade has come back to us, despite our best efforts to keep him out."

The knights and the hatchery attendants surrounding them chuckled.

"As you all know, he was discharged for treason, but General Cadimus saw fit to spare his life." Brove shook his head. "But now he has committed treason once again by violating the terms of his discharge and through his attempt to steal a weapon of war. And the punishment for such treason is, unquestionably, death."

No one said anything.

Brove drew a dagger from his belt.

A few of the wyverns stirred in their stalls.

Aeron flinched, partly from the sight of the dagger, but mostly because of his back. The fingers on his right hand had gone partially numb, and the effect had also started in his forearm, too, only it hurt more than it tingled.

"But," he continued, "it would be imprudent to kill him without a proper interrogation, first. We ought to have some fun with this, don't you think?"

The crowd's reaction was mixed. They'd all been Aeron's comrades only a few weeks prior, and some of them had stood by Aeron when Brove had first accused him.

Others, though, saw fit to side with Brove immediately. That divide separated those in enthusiastic agreement now from those who saw the injustice of it all.

"Unanimous enough for me." Brove pressed the flat of the dagger against Aeron's cheek. "An honest answer keeps you from getting cut. Any questions?"

Aeron very carefully replied, "No."

"Good. How did you get in here?"

Aeron didn't want to betray his father's trust, so he'd come up with an alternative story just in case something like this happened. "I stole a key on my way out of here, and I used it to walk right in the front doors."

Brove's eyes narrowed, and he turned the dagger so its edge pressed against Aeron's right cheek.

"It's the truth," Aeron uttered from the opposite side of his mouth. "The key's tucked under my breastplate."

The dagger's edge pressed harder against Aeron's cheek, then it relented. Brove lowered it and then motioned with it toward two of his men. "You two, remove his breastplate."

They complied, but not gently. Their tugs and pulls on the breastplate's straps delivered new agony to Aeron's back, and he winced and gritted his teeth.

Sure enough, the key his father had made fell out and thudded on the launch pad. As the two wyvern knights tossed Aeron's breastplate aside, Brove picked up the key and examined it.

Aeron fought to still his thundering heartbeat. It should be innocuous enough. After all, Pa had supposedly made dozens of such keys over the years.

But the fear of being caught in the lie racked Aeron's nerves. For all he knew, Brove might've somehow been able to identify it as a new key.

Brove turned toward the same two men and tossed them the key. "Hold this. We're not finished yet."

One of them caught it and held it down by his side.

Brove placed the flat of his dagger on Aeron's left cheek next, harder than he had before. The slightest twitch and it would cut him. "Second question, and this should be an easy one. Why did you come back?"

Aeron's jaw tightened. Brove was fishing for a full confession. But what other choice did Aeron have? "I came back to free my wyvern."

Brove twitched.

Fire raced down the side of Aeron's face, and warmth oozed out after it. Brove had cut him.

Wafer roared from behind Brove and pulled against his chain, but he'd never break free from it.

"I told the truth!" Aeron snapped.

"No, you didn't." Brove lowered the dagger and sneered at him. "That wyvern is not *yours*. He never was, and he never will be. He's strictly the property of the Govalian Army."

Aeron rolled his eyes. "You *knew* what I meant."

"And you *knew* the rules." Brove pressed the dagger's edge against the thin, tight skin on Aeron's forehead. "Next question."

Aeron groaned and moaned, but he did so without moving his head. No sense in getting cut again if he didn't have to.

"I haven't even done anything yet," Brove said.

"It's my back. It's still wrecked from the accident."

"And you came unprepared? What happened to all your magic mushrooms?" Brove taunted. He retracted the dagger.

Aeron tried to shift, but the pain didn't subside. "They're wearing off. I need another one."

Brove tilted his head and smiled. He pressed the dagger against Aeron's forehead again, and Aeron stilled.

"Did you bring any with you?"

Aeron swallowed. "Yes. In the pouch on my belt."

Brove cut the pouch from Aeron's belt and tucked his dagger under his armpit. He unfastened the pouch, pulled out the cloth, and unwrapped it, revealing the blue mushroom.

By that point, Aeron's right arm had gone almost completely numb, and he tried to adjust his position to give his right arm some relief. It didn't do much. The shackles just didn't allow him much range of motion.

With one hand, Brove held the blue mushroom between his bare fingers and thumb and studied it. He still held the dagger in his other hand.

"If I let you have this, will it help your back feel better?" he asked. He'd neglected to put the dagger against Aeron's body, but Aeron didn't mind.

Aeron nodded. "Tremendously."

Brove smiled his wicked smile again. Then he held the mushroom out toward Aeron.

Aeron leaned forward and opened his mouth. This was all about to end, one way or another.

Then Brove dropped the mushroom to the launch pad and stomped on it. Dust-like particles puffed out from it in plumes, and they wafted toward the edge of the launch pad—toward the rest of the soldiers in the roost who had gathered around.

Brove twisted his heel, grinding the mushroom into crumbles, and more spores shot out. He looked up at Aeron. "How does your back feel now?"

Aeron stifled a smirk and turned it into a scowl. His backup plan had worked even better than he'd expected. "Have I ever mentioned how much I hate you?"

"You have. I suppose I can't cut you for that, though." Brove laughed. "I know it's the truth."

Aeron remained silent.

"Last question." Brove extended his free hand, and a soldier stepped onto the launch pad and put the blunt end of a spear into his palm. Brove shifted his grip on it and sheathed his dagger. "How would you feel if I killed *the army's* wyvern right in front of you?"

Aeron stayed silent again. It had to work. He'd touched the mushroom with his bare skin. It just *had* to work.

Brove stalked across the launch pad toward Wafer, the spear clenched tightly in his hands.

A rush of concern flooded Aeron's body, but not of his own conjuring. The emotion originated from Wafer and transferred to Aeron through their bond.

Aeron tried to convey hope back to Wafer, as well as the courage to defend himself against Brove, but his anxiety got the better of him, and he lost focus.

Come on! Aeron's body tensed. *I need this to work!*

Then Brove stopped halfway to Wafer's stall. He shook his head, rubbed his eyes with his free hand, and then continued forward.

Three steps later he stumbled, but he caught himself on the launch pad with the spear like it was a walking stick. His legs wobbled, and he swayed noticeably.

Gods, it's working. Aeron smiled. He looked at the rest of the soldiers.

Several of them traded yawns around the group, and he caught a few leaning on their comrades or on the edge of the launch pad with their eyes closed. One guy had even sat down against the launch pad, and all Aeron could see was the back and the top of his head.

Brove glanced back at him, blinked four or five times, and then tried to stagger toward Wafer again, but he slumped down and lay near the far end of the launch pad near Wafer's stall. His spear clattered over the edge and to a stop on the roost floor.

Aeron beamed, and Wafer looked at Brove with ripe curiosity.

The rest of the soldiers started dropping as well. Some of them had gotten wise to what had happened and started coming Aeron's way, but slowly, like slugs crossing a vacant street.

It was time. Aeron maneuvered his arms and reached into the wrist of his left gauntlet. He could barely feel anything with his fingers being so numb, but he pushed through the sensation.

It was a hard action to pull off, what with contorting his back and having to work around the shackles, but he managed to fish the shackle key out all the same, and he passed it to his left hand. Now he just had to hope that his father had made that set of shackles.

He worked the key into the lock and wiggled it around until it bit. Then he twisted it hard.

The shackle opened, and his wrist slipped out.

Aeron freed his other wrist next, much easier than the first one, and he left the shackles hanging on the post. He rolled his shoulders and tried to stretch out his back, and slowly the feeling returned to his right arm.

Then he started walking toward Brove.

One of the soldiers, a man he recognized as Porgus Darleton, reached for his leg, but in slow motion. Aeron hopped over it with ease.

Porgus looked up at him with eyes full of grogginess and confusion. Then he sprawled out on the launch pad, eyes closed, and started snoring.

44

Aeron reached Brove and looked down at him. Brove wasn't asleep yet, but he wouldn't last much longer, either.

"Whaa... how'd you..." Brove's words slurred out of his mouth.

"You probably won't remember what I'm about to tell you," Aeron began, "but that blue mushroom was grown and imbued to put even the realm's most dedicated insomniacs asleep. When you stomped on it, you sent thousands of tiny spores shooting out at the other soldiers, and now they're falling asleep, too."

"But... why n... not... you?" Brove managed.

"Before I let myself in the front door, I took a mushroom that was grown and imbued to keep even the most hopeless narcoleptics awake." Aeron smiled. "It totally negated the effects of the blue mushroom."

Brove blinked long and hard, and drool oozed from the corner of his mouth onto the platform.

Aeron had to hand it to him—he was really fighting to stay awake, and he'd outlasted most of his soldiers despite directly touching the blue shroom.

"You gunn... na kill... m... me?" Brove asked.

Aeron shook his head. "No."

"Wh... y?"

"Because I'm not a heartless piece of trash like you."

Brove couldn't keep his eyes open anymore, and he fully succumbed to the shroom's effects.

Aeron went back and grabbed his breastplate, found his helmet and shield, and recovered the key to the bronze doors next.

Then he picked up Brove's spear. It was on the heavy side, but it was a wicked weapon with a three-pointed steel spearhead. It would do some serious damage in battle.

Aeron wondered if his father had made it. Whether he had or not, Aeron was taking it.

Then he turned to Wafer, who perked up immediately. Either Wafer was far enough away that the shroom spores didn't reach him, or they just plain didn't work on wyverns.

"I think I deserve a souvenir, don't you?"

Wafer snorted. It was a yes.

Besides, he couldn't find the lance he'd brought in with him. This was more than a fair trade for his trouble thus far. Aeron opened the shackle on Wafer's ankle, and Wafer nuzzled his scaly snout against Aeron's chest and face.

Aeron thought back to Cracker, who'd nuzzled Everlee in much the same way after Aeron had freed him from the tree in Dreynoth. Now he'd had his glorious reunion, too.

"Alright, boy. I know. I missed you, too." Aeron coaxed Wafer out of his stall and onto the launch pad. "Don't step on the commander."

Wafer growled at Brove's sleeping form, but he stepped over him, as ordered.

"I hope you're ready to fly. We've got time for one stop at home, and then we're off to who knows where, and for gods know how long."

Wafer's head bobbed up and down, and he made the same chomping noises as before.

"Yes, buddy. We'll get you fed, too."

With his tail, Wafer flung the post aside as if it weighed nothing. It skidded off the edge of the launch pad toward the empty stall left by Nilla and Faylen.

Then Wafer lowered himself so Aeron could saddle him up. Aeron hooked the breastplate and shield to the saddle, then he mounted Wafer. It hurt his back to do so, but otherwise, he'd never felt better.

"You ready for a new adventure?" Aeron asked.

Wafer didn't have to reply. Aeron could *feel* that he was.

They both were.

Aeron sent Wafer a command through their bond, and Wafer sprung off the launch pad and shot through the opening in the ceiling, carrying Aeron to the clouds high above.

THEY LANDED A FEW MINUTES LATER IN FRONT OF PA'S SHOP.

Several people on the street eyed Wafer as he set down, careful to back away to give him plenty of space. They stared but didn't do anything else. Thanks to Commander Brove's repeated landings at that spot, the folks around the shop had grown accustomed to seeing wyverns around the area.

Aeron hopped off of Wafer and ran inside. The sun had started to set, and Pa wasn't there anymore, so Aeron deposited the borrowed armor and the key where he'd found them—more or less. He kept the shackle key, though, just in case he might need it again.

Satisfied, he hurried back out, locked the shop door behind him, and then he and Wafer flew toward his parents' house.

Wafer set down in the street in front of the house, and Aeron beckoned him to roar with three taps on the nape of his neck. Wafer complied, and Aeron watched as the folks in his parents' neighborhood scattered.

At least they weren't being nosy about it. The last thing Aeron needed was neighbors alerting the authorities to his whereabouts.

His parents and sister scrambled out of the house and stopped when they saw Aeron and Wafer. Kallie squealed.

"He's beautiful!" She bounced up and down on her toes and inched closer. "Can I ride him?"

Mum grabbed her by both arms and hauled her back. "It's bad enough that one of my children flies around, cheating death on a regular basis. You'll stay here with your feet stuck firmly to the ground."

Aeron laughed. "Come on, Mum. It's perfectly safe, even for two. Wafer knows what he's doing."

Mum held her ground. "Some other time, perhaps. I can't abide it today."

Aeron looked at Kallie. "It's up to you."

She sighed and nodded. "Yeah. Some other time."

As Aeron dismounted, Pa shook his head.

"What?" Aeron asked.

"I can't believe you actually pulled this off."

"Yeah. Maybe I'm not worthless and stupid after all." Aeron meant it as a joke. Mostly.

"You're not worthless or stupid," Pa said.

Aeron grinned at him.

Pa continued, "You just pursue worthless ideas and make a lot of stupid decisions."

Aeron's grin dissipated, and his voice flattened. "Thanks."

"May I..." Mum raised her hand toward Wafer, tentatively. "...touch him?"

"Of course." Aeron smiled. "He only bites when I tell him to."

Mum shot Aeron a glare, then she reached forward and stroked the side of Wafer's scaly neck. Kallie joined her. Wafer leaned into the affection and made the same contented chirps that he'd made when Aeron showed up at his stall in the roost.

"Pa, you can pet him too, if you like," Aeron said.

Pa held his ground. "No, thank you."

"Suit yourself." Aeron turned to Mum and Kallie. "Watch him for a moment while I go fetch some things from my room?"

They nodded, and Aeron headed inside the house. In his room, he collected his sack of shrooms and stuffed the remainder of his clothes and personal effects into a pack. He slung it all over his shoulder and headed back outside.

"You're leaving?" Mum's eyes bore the same sadness as they had the day he'd arrived.

"I'm sorry, Mum, but it'll be better for all of us if I go. I'm a fugitive from the Govalian Army now, so I can't stay." He took her hands in his. "But I'll write often, and I'll stop by whenever I'm in the area. And if Pa ever lets you leave the city, maybe you could come and visit me sometime with Kallie."

"Where will you go?" Pa asked.

Aeron knew the type of answer Pa wanted, and he knew Pa had asked more for Mum's benefit than anyone else's. "I'll go wherever Wafer and I can find work. But I have to leave Govalia, at least for now."

Pa nodded, his face sullen.

Mum's eyes teared up. "It was lovely having you back at home, even if only for a few weeks."

Aeron wrapped her in a long hug and kissed her cheek. "I love you, Mum."

Kallie hugged him next, before he could say anything. She let him go after a moment and said, "Don't get yourself caught or killed out there, yeah? If I do have a wedding someday, I want you to be there, intact. And I want Wafer there, too."

Wafer snorted and bobbed his head, then he chomped his jaws open and shut.

Aeron chuckled. "He said that if there's food, he'll be there."

Kallie laughed and hugged Aeron again.

Pa extended his hand, and Aeron shook it.

"I know we rarely see eye to eye, but I'm proud of the man you've become," Pa said.

Aeron waited.

Pa added, "Mostly, anyway."

There it is. "Thanks, Pa."

"Take care of yourself, boy."

Aeron smirked. "I will, old man."

Pa's neutral expression soured, and he released Aeron's hand. "Call me old again, and I'll kick your ass."

Aeron rolled his eyes. "I'd better go. No telling how or when they'll figure out what's happened."

He mounted Wafer again, waved goodbye one last time, and then they vaulted into the air.

As they flew, Aeron called out, "Wafer, how would you feel about becoming a mercenary?"

Wafer bobbed his head and chomped with his mouth.

As long as I get to eat.

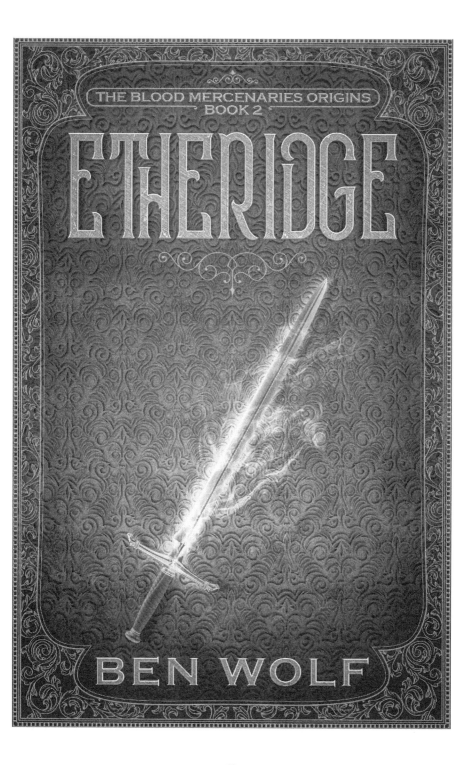

CHAPTER ONE

E lectric energy tingled in the tips of Kent Etheridge's fingers. He clenched his fists to subdue the sensation.

"Father is waiting," Kent said from his brother Fane's side. "I do not know why you insist on delaying."

"It is not my intention to keep him waiting, nor do I wish to vex you, brother," Fane countered. "And I would prefer if you didn't hover over my shoulder. I am perfectly capable of dressing myself."

Kent scoffed. *With the aid of no fewer than three of our servants.* "Fine. I am heading downstairs. At least one of us should be punctual."

"Then just wait one more minute, and I will be ready." Fane shifted his stance so the servants could secure his long, green cape to the triangle- shaped fasteners attached to his jacket.

Kent frowned. His younger brother's vanity had irked him for decades, but over the last several weeks, Fane had developed an even more demanding demeanor. It frustrated Kent beyond what words could describe.

The tingling in Kent's hands persisted, and he kept his fists clenched. He needed to get out of there and regain control of himself before Fane noticed.

"No, Fane," Kent said. "I am leaving now. The succession ceremony is not dependent on your attendance."

As Kent turned and headed out the door, Fane spoke again. "Kent, your selfishness is the one thing about you I do not covet."

Kent didn't turn around but said, "And thanks to your recklessness, your carelessness, and your flippancy, there is nothing about you worth coveting."

That ought to be enough to silence him. Where his brother was concerned, stern and decisive words proved most effective in reminding him of his place.

Hearing no reply, Kent continued out of Fane's chambers.

Breathe, Kent. Thinking about his brother's insolence intensified the tingling in his fingertips again, even though his fists remained clenched.

As he headed for the grand staircase that swooped down to the manse's lower floors, he noticed his fists giving off a faint blue glow.

Kent cursed and tucked them under his armpits. He abandoned his trek down the stairs a floor early and receded into the shadows behind a marble support pillar near a wall paneled with dark wood.

But the blue glow from his fists was even more noticeable there.

Breathe, Kent. Control yourself.

But how do I control that which I cannot control? Others have learned to control it.

And they are our sworn enemies. Cursed and damned. Like you. Just breathe. That is all you can do.

Kent breathed. His pounding heartbeat slowed, and his stress dwindled again. He checked his hands.

The blue glow had vanished, and the electric sensation no longer teased his fingertips.

Why the gods had seen fit to curse him, of all people, with the scourge of magic, he didn't know, but he marveled at the irony yet again.

He straightened his red waistcoat and checked his own cape, also red, and then he headed out of the shadows and toward the staircase.

Fane met him there. "For all your posturing, you are now as tardy as I am."

Kent's jaw tightened, but he refused to let Fane damage his calm. "I elected to wait for you out of my deep sense of magnanimity. You may thank me whenever you are ready."

They proceeded down the remainder of the grand staircase together.

Fane said, "In that case, I will thank you when I have succeeded Father in your place as the lord of house Etheridge."

In other words, Fane would never thank him, unless Kent was dead and had failed to remarry and produce an heir. Fane's words didn't quite amount to a blatant wish for Kent's death, but they came treacherously close.

Now on the first floor, they headed into a large gathering hall adorned with dark wood paneling and bronze candelabras affixed to the walls. A hearth at the far end glowed with vivid orange flames.

A painting of the late Lady Etheridge, Kent and Fane's mother, hung from the stones overhead. In recent years, Kent's dark hair had begun to gray, matching the silver locks depicted in his mother's portrait, though Fane's had not yet started to lose its color. They both shared their mother's bright blue eyes.

Morning sunlight poured into the room through towering, arched windows paned with glass. It glinted off of gold-colored flecks in the room's white-and-black marble floors.

Their father, Lord Oswin Etheridge, sat in an overstuffed leather chair, facing them as they entered the room together. He looked frailer than he had just the night before.

He was wise to plan the succession early. Kent, now at forty-eight years old, had handled their family's affairs for the last three years almost exclusively, so it made sense for Father to name him Lord Etheridge once and for all.

They approached their father at a casual pace, and he grinned and motioned to the two servants standing next to his chair, one on each side. They hooked their arms under his armpits and gently pulled him upright until he could stand, albeit slightly hunched over.

One of the servants handed him his cane, a twisted, wooden stick polished to a high shine and topped with a bronze gryphon—the very symbol of House Etheridge. He leaned on it for stability while he addressed his sons. "Kent. Fane. Good morning."

Kent nodded to Father, and he and Fane echoed Father's greeting in unison.

Father's gaze fixed on Kent. "Are you ready, my son?" Kent nodded.

"Father, before we proceed…" Fane stepped forward. "…I would like the opportunity to speak."

Wonderful. What could it be now?

"Fane," Kent began, his voice stern, "you always have something to say. There will be ample time to speak after the ceremony concludes."

"Your cunning tongue strikes again, dear brother," Fane quipped. "But what I have to say must be said before the ceremony proceeds."

Kent stood his ground. "Whatever it is, it can wait."

"It cannot. I must be indulged."

"I have *indulged* you your entire life."

"Nonsense. You have merely tolerated me."

"As one does when dealing with a nuisance," Kent cut back.

Fane shook his head. "Such a loving response from my dear brother."

"And soon to be your lord," Kent countered. "Know your place."

"I know my place, and it is here, in this room, between you and Father."

The familiar tingle returned to Kent's fingertips.

No… not now. Fight it. Be in control. Kent clenched his hands into fists again.

"Father?" Fane looked at him, and Kent did as well.

Father turned to his two servants, the only other people in the room. "Leave us."

They obeyed immediately and shut the room's heavy wooden doors behind them, joining the manse's other servants and guards in awaiting further orders.

Father exhaled a long breath through his nose, and then he straightened up as much as he could manage. "Fane, it is most irregular that you would ask to speak before a ceremony so important to me, to your brother, and to our family."

"Father, please," Fane nearly pleaded.

"Let him speak, Fane," Kent growled.

Father held up a withered hand then quickly returned it to his two-handed grip on the cane to stabilize himself. "If Kent will grant you the opportunity to speak then I, too, will allow it. But know that whatever you might say will not affect my decision to pass on my title preemptively."

Kent eyed Fane. *Whatever he has to say, it won't be anything good.*

Fane scowled at Father, then he turned to Kent, still scowling, but expectant.

The decision was easy. Kent stared daggers at him. "I do not grant you the right to speak prior to the ceremony."

"This is outrageous," Fane muttered.

"As I said, *know your place*, little brother," Kent snapped.

Fane shook his head. "No. I refuse to remain silent."

Father held up his hand again. "Fane, you must yield to—"

"Father, please forgive my interruption. This must be said. Your oldest son is a traitor to our family name."

Kent gawked at Fane, and Father glanced between the two of them.

"That is utterly absurd." The tingling in Kent's fingers intensified. He had to rein it all in. "I have been nothing but totally loyal, diligent, and *relentless* in protecting and expanding our family's name and holdings since the day I came of age. Father, you *know* this to be true."

"This is a serious allegation," Father said. "I know your dedication is beyond reproach, yet I must know why your own brother would make this accusation."

"Because he is an envious, treacherous leech who has always wanted that which he cannot have: the right of the firstborn," Kent said.

"I will gladly expound, Father," Fane said.

"*No*," Kent nearly shouted. "There is nothing to expound upon. Father, I have never given you any reason to doubt my commitment and loyalty. You personally trained me and guided me and taught me how to care for our holdings and reputation over the last thirty-five years. This family means everything to me. I would never do anything to jeopardize us."

Fane started again. "Father, if I may—"

"No, you may *not*." Kent pointed at him, then he quickly pulled his hand back to his side. The tingling had spread to his entire hand.

This cannot be happening. I must regain control.

But how? Kent could storm out, perhaps. But while that would serve to conceal his secret, it would show a measure of weakness and instability.

His father was ready to pass his title on to Kent, and now that Fane had sown a measure of doubt into the process, Kent didn't want to foster its growth any further.

No, Kent needed to stay and fight for what was rightfully his. He worked to still his breathing and to quell the flux of magic in his fingers.

"Fane," Father said, "the accusation you are bringing against your brother is of the utmost seriousness. Without evidence, it appears as though you merely desire to usurp him and claim his place as Lord Etheridge. Your aspirations to my title are well-known to many, not least of all your brother and me."

"Father, I would not make such a claim without absolute certainty." Fane stepped closer to father, and it irked Kent all the more. "I am not trying to usurp his claim. I am trying to protect this family—"

"That is a *blatant lie*."

"—from the influence of our enemies—"

"Our enemies hold *no* sway over me whatsoever." Kent moved his hands behind his back, hidden carefully by his cape. He couldn't be certain, but at the level of tingling they'd reached, they would likely begin to glow soon, if they weren't already.

"—and those who would seek to do us harm."

"He is conjuring false rumors without any proof," Kent said. "He is and always has been a jealous little boy. He has always opposed me, and now, on the most important day of my life, he opposes me yet again."

Father shook his head. "I know all of this, but I cannot allow an accusation of this magnitude to go untested and unanswered. The truth must be known before we proceed, one way or another."

"I have told you the truth," Kent replied. "I have never done anything to adversely affect our family. He has yet to share any evidence to the contrary."

"You want proof?" Fane gave Kent a wicked grin and looked at Kent's waist—or perhaps at his hands, hidden under his cape. "It is in this very room."

Kent swallowed. *Impossible. I've hidden the curse so well—from everyone. No one knows. How could he possibly...*

"Show us your hands, dear brother." Fane's eyebrows arched down, but his wicked grin remained.

He knew. Kent didn't know how, but somehow Fane knew. He'd found out about Kent's magical affliction and now meant to use it against him.

"What do his hands have to do with anything?" Father asked.

"Even the smallest child in Muroth knows that our fair country has been at war with the wicked Inoth for a hundred years," Fane said. "And House Etheridge has long since defended Muroth's southern border against Inothian incursions.

"Their use of magic is an abomination, a curse from the gods, which is why such practices are forbidden here. Anyone caught practicing magic of any kind in Muroth is subject to judgment and, ultimately, execution."

Kent swallowed again. Fane had the advantage now, without question.

Father leaned forward. "What do Kent's hands have to do with any of this?"

"If he would only show them to us, I will explain." Fane turned toward Kent.

Kent looked at Father. "This is preposterous."

"Please, Kent," Father said more than asked. "Show us your hands."

Kent steeled himself, clenched his fists hard, and inhaled a long, shaky breath. He now regretted not having stormed out when he'd had the chance.

But he complied, slowly pulling his tingling hands from behind his back and holding them, palms up, toward his father and Fane.

They weren't glowing.

Kent exhaled a silent sigh. "What have you to say now, brother?"

Fane grinned that same wicked grin again. "I do not need to say anything else. Instead, I will show you."

Fane pulled a green crystal from within his coat and placed it in Kent's open palms.

Then Kent's hands ignited with blue flames.

CHAPTER TWO

K ent dropped the crystal to the floor and recoiled. But painless blue fire still enveloped his hands.

How had he not seen that coming?

The crystal was scorallite, a type of mineral Murothians used to identify Inothian mages. His own men, soldiers who guarded the border and interrogated those trying to pass into Murothian lands, used scorallite crystals to identify those cursed with magic.

And Fane had set one in Kent's hand. Such a simple tactic, yet profoundly effective.

"Your eldest son is cursed, Father," Fane said.

Kent closed his eyes and willed the flames to depart and the tingling to subside. His concentration paid off, as both diminished to nothing.

Father gasped. "By the gods..."

"Father, allow me to explain," Kent said.

"There is no explaining this," Fane countered. He squared himself with Kent and stared at him with cold blue eyes. "You are anathema to our people, cursed, and eternally damned. As such, you may not succeed our father as Lord Etheridge, and you are condemned to die."

"Wait, Fane," Father said.

Fane turned back. "Father, you know the law. You've been enforcing it for three quarters of a century."

"Fane, stand down," Father ordered. "I will speak with my son, and you will remain silent."

Fane stepped aside in silence, but his triumphant expression did not change.

Kent started to speak. "Father, I—"

"Be silent, Kent." Father didn't say it loudly, but he said it firmly. "I will speak, and you will listen. There will be no explanations, no excuses. You will only speak if I grant you permission to do so. Do you understand?"

Kent's insides shuddered, but he stood tall and nodded.

"You are my eldest son. You are the successor to my title, my lands, and my responsibilities."

"Father?" Fane stared at him in disbelief.

"*Quiet*, Fane," Father snapped. "I will not warn you again."

A sliver of hope parted the dismay in Kent's gut.

"Kent, you are what you are, and I cannot change that. No one can, unless the gods see fit to emerge from their realms to remove this curse from you."

Tears welled in Kent's eyes. He believed in the gods as much as the next Murothian, but he knew they'd never care enough for the affairs of men to intervene in such a way.

"Regrettably, your brother is right. The law is the law, and I must enforce it in my role as a Lord of the Realm of Muroth." Father's old, blue eyes met Kent's once more. "As such, I strip from you all of the rights and privileges associated with your name, as I strip the name Etheridge itself from you."

"Father, no!" Kent begged.

"And I hereby banish you from all of Muroth under penalty of death."

Kent gasped. Everything he'd done over the last thirty-five years—every preparation he'd applied, every scrap of education and training he'd received, every sacrifice he'd made, every risk he'd taken—none of it mattered anymore. None of it could ransom him from his fate.

"*Banishment?*" Fane spat. "You are merely *banishing* him?"

Kent and Father looked toward Fane.

"The Murothian penalty for being a magic-user is death, and death alone. He must be executed. You have seen the proof with your own eyes."

Kent's fingers began to tingle again. He clenched his fists to stave it off.

Things were already bad enough.

"And as Lord of House Etheridge and protector of our southern borders, I am granting him the only mercy I can," Father fired back. "Your brother may no longer call himself an Etheridge, nor may he reside in this realm. But I refuse to execute him."

"Then you refuse to see that Murothian justice is served!" Fane shouted.

"Control yourself, Fane." Father pointed a gnarled finger at him. "I *am* Murothian justice in this province, or have you forgotten your studies?"

Fane hissed, "You are nothing but an old man who lacks the resolve to do what must be done."

"How dare you!" Father growled. "Your impudence is reprehensible. Your talk is bordering on treason. Be silent, for I do not wish to lose two sons today."

Fane shook his head and glowered at Father. "You already have."

The silver glint of a dagger flashed into Fane's hand, and then it disappeared again, driven through Father's chest.

Kent recoiled in horror. "No!"

Father gasped, staggered back a half-step, and clutched at his chest. Fane released his grip on the dagger, and Father slumped into the leather chair near the hearth, wheezing with wide, sunken eyes and covered in blood.

"Father, no!" Kent shoved past Fane and rushed to Father's side. For magic being a curse, he'd seen and heard of its extraordinary properties, not the least of which was its ability to mend broken bones, torn flesh, and even brutal wounds.

But Kent had no knowledge of such uses. His entire life, he'd been taught to hate magic and to oppress, kill, or report anyone found using it. So he'd never learned anything about how to use it. He had only fought to repress it within himself, to hide it.

That didn't mean he couldn't try.

Kent pressed his hands on either side of the dagger as his father stared up at him in shock and disbelief. Kent's hands ignited with blue light again, and he willed the magic flowing through him to somehow heal his father.

"Guards!" Fane shouted from behind him.

At that moment, Kent looked down at the dagger lodged in his father's chest. He recognized it.

Father had given it to him two years prior as a gift for a victory Kent achieved in battle against an incursion of Inothian warriors, powerful magic-users who'd threatened the Etheridge fortress in the southeastern quadrant of the province.

The doors burst open, and two guards clad in bronze armor and wielding swords barreled inside.

"He murdered Lord Etheridge!" Fane shouted.

Fane had stabbed Father with Kent's own blade, and Kent was trying to use magic to save him. And now the guards' first impressions were of Kent standing over his dying father with glowing blue hands.

It was a setup. A perfect setup.

And suddenly, Fane's remark about thanking Kent only when he could instead succeed Father as Lord Etheridge made perfect sense.

The guards rushed toward Kent.

He was unarmed, but he'd faced two armed men many times before, and oftentimes more. It was never easy, but he knew how to prevail. He'd trained relentlessly for most of his life to overcome situations like this and far worse.

The first guard swung his sword laterally, and Kent stepped into his swing with his arms up. He blocked the guard's arm from moving forward and got a grip on it. Then stepped across the guard's body, bent at his knees, and flipped the guard over his shoulder.

The back piece of the guard's breastplate smacked hard on the marble floor, and Kent easily pulled the sword from his hand. He spun back and met the second guard's blade with his own.

Kent's hands still glowed with blue light, but blue flames no longer emanated from them. As he exchanged blows with the second guard, the glow continued to fade to nothing.

The guard proved a proficient fighter, probably one of the more capable soldiers in the province. It made sense; highly skilled soldiers were assigned to protect that which mattered most—the Etheridges themselves.

But Kent was better. He parried a swing, stepped in, and drove his elbow into the soldier's face instead of simply running him through. He was, after all, just being a loyal soldier, and he didn't deserve to die for Fane's sins.

The guard staggered back, but he didn't go down, so Kent stepped in again and planted his left foot behind the guard's right foot, and he shoved hard with his arms and pulled with his leg.

The guard dropped back, and his helmet slammed against the marble floor. He wasn't moving.

Kent whirled back toward the first guard, who'd recovered but no longer held a weapon. Kent started toward him, full of confidence and rage while Fane looked on.

"Guards!" Fane called again. "More guards!"

The guard dove for Kent's knees, and Kent sprawled out to stop his advance. He used his body weight to smash the guard's helmet, face-first, against the floor. Then he sprung to his feet and started toward Fane.

But Fane was ready for him with a pair of long knives, one from each of his boots. The morning sunlight from the huge windows behind him lit up his green cape and his matching waistcoat and trousers.

"You murdering bastard," Kent growled. "I will kill you for this."

"Not if we kill you first, you cursed scum." Fane's gaze flitted past Kent toward the doors, and the telltale clanking of metal and shuffling of leather- soled boots announced the approach of several more guards.

Kent kept a safe distance between himself and Fane's knives and assessed his predicament. The room had one set of doors, seemingly the only exit.

But any of the massive windows behind Fane would afford Kent a reasonable escape. Those options aside, only the chimney leading up from the fireplace remained, but with the fire burning in the hearth, Kent doubted his chances.

And escape was the only option now. He wouldn't have time to kill Fane and the two unconscious guards he'd left on the floor before the rest of the guards arrived.

They'd still accuse Kent of murdering Father, and they'd kill him for being cursed once the other guards woke up and spoke of what they'd seen.

Kent tried to reposition himself so as to get a better angle on approaching the windows, but Fane matched his movements, cutting him off from the easier escape.

Like Kent, Fane had trained in the art of combat since childhood. Getting past him would come at a cost, either to one of them or perhaps to both of them.

The guards appeared in the doorway and began filtering into the room toward Fane and Kent.

"He murdered Lord Etheridge and used magic to dispatch those guards," Fane called to them. "His dagger is in Lord Etheridge's chest."

The guards wouldn't normally have trusted Fane's word over Kent's, but given the look of the room and the fact that Kent was holding one of the guards' swords, they didn't argue. Instead, they moved to encircle him.

If Kent didn't go now, he'd be pushing past not just Fane but also whatever guards would reach the windows in the next few precious seconds.

So he went for it.

He charged Fane, his eyes keen on the blade in Fane's right hand but aware of the one in his left as well.

Fane braced himself and tensed, ready.

Kent swung his sword, and Fane shifted under it, over to Kent's right side. Fane lashed his knife blade toward Kent's torso, but he no longer stood between Kent and the windows.

Kent didn't stop his momentum. He swung the sword back the other way as he leaped at the window.

Fire lit up Kent's hip. His sword hit something on its backswing, and the glass shattered against his body as he plowed through it and onto the manse's lawn.

Somewhere behind him, Fane screamed.

Kent hit the ground, rolled, and sprung up to his feet. Pain seared his hip, and he glanced down as he ran. He'd been cut, probably when Fane had sliced at him. The blade had carved through Kent's wool clothing, but he couldn't tell how deep the wound was.

It hurt to run—but not enough to stop. His breath puffed out as mist in the cold winter air.

Stately walls formed an sturdy perimeter around the Etheridge manse, and more elite soldiers clad in bronze armor stood guard in watchtowers placed at strategic points.

Getting through the gate would prove challenging, but not by any means impossible; none of these soldiers knew what had happened, or even that anything *was* happening.

He ran across the lawn, jumped over flowerbeds, and dodged ornamental stones and trees until he reached the front gate.

The soldiers manning the gate stared at him in confusion, but he didn't care. Near the gate, one soldier was tending to a white horse with small, sporadic black spots. It was already saddled.

At least something is going right today.

"Open the gate!" Kent shouted as he ran.

The soldiers looked at each other, but no one moved. "Open the gate!" Kent yelled again.

Still no action. One of them shouted back, "We're under orders from your brother to keep it shut."

"I am overruling him!" Kent winced as he ran. Every step spiked his hip, but he'd gained a substantial lead ahead of the guards who now inevitably pursued him. Even so, he didn't look back.

"My lord..." Another soldier looked him up and down. "Are you bleeding?"

"I am fine," Kent snapped. "Open the damned gate, or I'll have you all executed."

The soldiers rushed to comply, and the gate inched open.

"You, there." Kent pointed toward the soldier tending the horse and tucked his sword in his belt without a sheath. It would have to do for now. "I am taking that horse."

"Yes, my lord." The soldier bowed and then stood by to steady the horse while Kent mounted it. Then he handed Kent the reins.

Unintelligible shouts sounded from behind them, and Kent finally looked back. Halfway to the manse, the bronze armor of about a dozen soldiers glinted under the sunlight.

The soldiers looked up at him.

"My father has been murdered," Kent told them, "and I am personally riding north to Lord Frostsong's estate to petition him for aid. My brother Fane is the culprit."

"My lord!" said the soldier who'd helped him onto the horse. "Please allow me to gather a proper escort for your journey."

Kent couldn't allow any of them to come with. Based on the tingling in his hands, it was only a matter of time before his magical curse manifested again, and then he'd have to fight off more of his own soldiers. All he could do was flee.

"There is no time. I will be fine on my own." Kent checked the gate— almost wide enough to fit the horse through. "See that my brother is arrested for the murder of my father, and have him executed before I return."

I can never return, even if that should happen. But they didn't need to know that.

"Yes, my lord," one of the soldiers said.

The gate was close to being open wide enough. Kent urged the horse toward it.

The shouts from behind him crystalized in his ears.

"Don't let him out! He killed Lord Etheridge!" someone yelled. Kent glanced back at the soldiers around the gate.

They stared up at him, as confused as they'd been when he'd come running.

The pursuing guards shouted the same directive again, and the soldiers at the gate turned toward Kent. They were putting it all together, making sense of the scenario, Kent's injured hip, the sword in his belt.

"My lord," one of them said. "You need to come down off that horse."

Kent kicked the horse's sides and cracked the reins, and the horse bolted toward the gate.

"Close the gate!" someone behind him shouted.

The gate stopped opening and started closing, but Kent was already close enough. The horse squirted between the gate doors and carried him into the expanse of hills and trees beyond.

He disappeared into the forest to the north of the manse, then he curled east, and finally, he turned south.

KENT DIDN'T STOP RIDING UNTIL THE WALLS OF RANHOLD FORTRESS, MUROTH'S southeastern border fortress, loomed on the horizon, just before the setting sun. He looked back. So far, no one was following him that he could see.

He'd calculated his options during the ride away from his estate—well, what *was* his estate—and decided that he had to keep heading south. He would go to Inoth, the one place where they could not follow him. Not without risking a full-fledged war.

Kent urged his horse forward.

He'd told the soldiers at the gate he was heading north, to Lord Frostsong's estate. But even though the Etheridges and the Frostsongs had maintained comfortable relations for decades, Lord Frostsong would undoubtedly have Kent killed upon learning of his curse.

That was Muroth's law, and it was inescapable as long as he remained in the country. No one in Muroth would help him.

Ranhold Fortress was about two miles away now, and Kent took solace in knowing that his arrival would far precede any news regarding his cursed condition or of his father's demise.

As such, Kent would still command some measure of power, respect, and even privilege upon his arrival, and he intended to parlay all of that into a good meal and possibly some rest.

Fane... that bastard.

Kent exhaled a shaky breath. He'd hardly taken time to breathe, much less to process what had happened. Sorrow racked his chest, and tears stung the corners of his eyes.

I swear... by the gods, I swear I will have my revenge.

Kent blinked away his emotions and refocused on his plans.

He'd entertained the idea of fleeing to Urthia or Govalia, two countries that bordered Muroth to the northeast and due east, respectively, or of heading due north toward Xenthan, the continent's largest country, part of which bordered Muroth in the north along with the neighboring country of Etrijan.

But he'd dismissed those ideas just as quickly. Any of them would mean spending far too much time traversing now-hostile territory.

Aside from Inoth, his only other option was finding a ship on Muroth's western coast and boarding it.

But where would it take him? Plus, that path would lead him through even more of his home country along the way, and any soldier with a scorallite crystal could quickly identify him as being cursed.

As much as he hated to admit it, Inoth was his only viable option—and in some ways, his best option.

Since Muroth and Inoth refused to trade or negotiate in any manner, he'd had no contact with anyone of significance within the country. No one there would know him, and in anonymity, he could begin a new life.

What's more, as a fellow cursed magic-user, he would no longer have to hide his abilities, meager as they were. At least the tingling in his fingers might finally normalize once and for all.

Kent muttered curses anew upon Fane. Were it not for Fane's lifelong jealousy and deceit culminating the way it had, Kent would be ruling the province instead of trying to flee it.

Father hadn't needed to die, particularly the way that he'd been killed. Murdered by his own son.

Rage boiled in Kent's chest, but he had no way to release any of it. He wished Fane were there with him. Then Kent could wrap his glowing blue hands around Fane's neck and squeeze the life from his body.

Someday. Someday, Fane will pay for his crimes.

Within minutes, he'd closed to within a half-mile of the fortress, and in the waning sunlight, he could make out the shapes of soldiers patrolling atop both the border wall and the fortress.

The sight filled him with nostalgia and sorrow simultaneously. And then the sorrow took over.

Kent pushed it all aside. He could deal with his emotions once he was truly safe.

A few minutes later, his horse approached the fortress's northern gate. He identified himself to the soldiers on duty and requested that they send General Calarook to the wall to confirm his identity.

Shortly afterward, a stocky man about Kent's age with black-and-gray hair and wearing dark bronze armor emerged from the now-open portcullis at the gate— General Calarook. Four soldiers clad in white-iron armor flanked him, two on each side.

Kent urged his horse forward but didn't dismount. If they somehow knew what had happened, he wanted to be ready to bolt away without any delays.

Furthermore, forcing General Calarook and his men to look up at him projected a useful air of superiority that he could leverage.

"My lord," General Calarook rasped. He bowed. "We weren't expecting you."

When Calarook straightened up, Kent noticed the thick scar that traced from his left cheek down his jaw and down the left side of his throat. Long ago, something or someone had carved a remembrance into Calarook and damaged his voice in the process, but Kent had never heard the entire story.

"Of course not," Kent said. "Otherwise you would have been prepared with a proper welcome. But that is the nature of surprise inspections, General. They are meant to be surprising."

Calarook grinned and nodded. "I've been known to execute surprise inspections myself from time to time. You can expect to find everything in good order here. I run a tight ship."

Kent matched his grin. "I know you do, General. Will you escort me inside?"

"It will be my pleasure."

The portcullis soon closed behind them, sealing them inside the fortress.

KENT PASSED OFF HIS INJURY AS A MINOR WOUNDS HE'D SUSTAINED WHILE RIDING TO the fortress. He claimed he'd scraped against a low-hanging tree branch that gouged his hip.

General Calarook had given him a curious eye upon hearing it. He had certainly seen his fair share of wounds throughout the years and likely doubted the veracity of Kent's tale, but he didn't question it openly, and he made sure Kent received proper care for it.

The "inspection" went well. The soldiers demonstrated attention to detail and thoroughness. Their dedication to developing and maintaining the fortress's rich history of defending against Inothian attacks made Kent proud, albeit a proudness laced with sadness.

They prepared a hasty feast in Kent's honor, and all the while General Calarook asked him gentle questions that pinpointed the holes in Kent's story.

What happened to your escort? Where are your personal effects?

Did you not think to bring warm clothes for your journey?

What inspired your choice to carry a common soldier's sword instead of your own?

What led you to dress so well for a simple inspection?

Kent tactfully answered them all, but he sensed that Calarook understood that something was off. After all, he hadn't risen to the rank of general by being stupid.

After the meal concluded, Kent excused himself and allowed Calarook to escort him to the private chambers they'd prepared for him for the evening. They stopped at his door, and Calarook paused with the skeleton key in the lock.

He turned toward Kent and rasped, "My lord, forgive me for my forwardness, but I know there is more you are not telling me. I only ask you now out of concern that I may need more information in order to best prepare for any potential threats. Is there anything else I need to know?"

Kent smirked. "General, your skills of perception are as sharp as ever. There is more to this story, but as my father and I are still developing a plan, we cannot share much more than what I am about to tell you."

Calarook turned the key and opened the chamber doors. "Perhaps it's best we speak inside."

Kent hesitated. Of all the people in Muroth he didn't want to be alone in a room with, particularly under the current circumstances, Calarook ranked near the top of the list. His fighting prowess and tactical mind surpassed that of the majority of the Murothian Army's top commanders.

What's more, he had insisted on overseeing Ranhold Fortress personally, despite Kent and his father's attempts to move him somewhere more comfortable. Calarook had refused to leave the protection of the southeastern border to anyone else.

But Kent obliged him, entered the room first to get a sense of its size and the resources available should he need to make use of them. He saw a bed with simple wooden posts, a wardrobe in the corner, a simple writing desk with a chair, and little else.

Calarook shut the door and locked it behind him. "Have a seat if you wish, my lord."

Kent tried to read Calarook, but he couldn't discern what he was thinking. Calarook's face remained hard but emotionless, like usual, and his damaged voice didn't betray any audible cues one way or another.

So Kent pulled the desk chair out and sat down.

Calarook sat on the corner of the bed, tucked the key into his left gauntlet, and stared at Kent.

"Thank you again for your hospitality, General," Kent said.

Calarook just nodded, interwove his armored fingers on his lap, and kept staring.

"What I am about to tell you, you must promise not to share with anyone."

"I am bound by the blood covenant I swore to Muroth and her emperor to respect and obey your lordship." Calarook gave a slight bow. "Your wish is my command."

"I understand. Thank you."

Kent took a breath and then launched into a fabrication about how his father suspected Inoth had sent spies into Muroth to discern their defense capabilities and to assess for weaknesses. Therefore, Kent had personally come to visit the most crucial intersection between the two countries.

He'd developed the tale hours earlier while riding from his family estate toward the fortress, and it rolled off his tongue as smoothly as any lie he'd ever told, though he usually shied away from lying at all.

"And my task tomorrow will be to infiltrate the kingdom of Inoth so we may glean what information we can about their plans concerning our great nation."

"Alone?" Calarook asked.

Kent nodded. "Alone. I have been preparing for this day for months. Bringing anyone with me would risk damaging my chances for anonymity."

Calarook nodded.

They sat there in silence for a long moment.

Finally, Calarook sucked in a sharp breath and said, "You know, I had hoped it wasn't true."

Kent's heart started beating faster. "I beg your pardon?"

"Of all the lords I've dealt with in this country, you were by far my favorite." Calarook's hands separated and rested on his knees. "You always treated me with fairness and respect. Your father was a good man, but I always knew you were better."

Kent squinted at him. Calarook had distinctly spoken of Kent's father in the past tense. It wasn't an accident. "Thank you."

"That's why I found it so disconcerting when I received word by raven this afternoon of what happened at your family's estate this morning."

The familiar tingle returned to Kent's fingertips. He clenched his fists.

"I was aggrieved to hear of your father's untimely demise, and I was even sadder to hear of your brother's succession as Lord Etheridge." Calarook shook his head. "Between you and me, I've always thought he was a wretched, spoiled brat."

Kent nodded. "So have I."

"But unfortunately, if the story I read was true, what I think of him doesn't change what I must do now."

Calarook reached for something at his belt, but he hadn't brought in any weapons—at least none that Kent had seen. He still wore his full armor, minus his helmet. Kent doubted he'd been able to conceal any weapons within his bulky armor.

Even so, Kent remained on his guard; he'd given up his sword prior to dinner, so he was unarmed, too.

Calarook extended his arm toward Kent with his hand closed, palm up.

Then he opened it.

A piece of vivid green scorallite lay in his palm.

"I need you to take hold of this, my lord." Calarook kept his eyes fixed on Kent, and Kent returned his stare. "Then we will know the truth."

Kent swallowed. He uttered, "I did not kill my father."

"That, I believe," Calarook said. "But I need to know for sure about the rest."

Kent stared at the scorallite for a moment, then he refocused on Calarook's hard brown eyes. "Please do not make me do this, General. Just let me leave."

Calarook shook his head. "You lords wrote the laws. I just enforce them."

The tingling in Kent's fingers heightened and spread to the entirety of his hands. "Very well, General. Please forgive me for having failed you."

Kent leaned forward, reached for the scorallite with his left hand, and balanced himself on the edge of his seat by grabbing the top of the chair with his right hand.

Then he stood upright and whipped the chair at General Calarook's head.

CHAPTER THREE

General Calarook raised his left arm, and the chair shattered against his shoulder and side rather than his head. The scorallite and broken pieces of wood scattered across the floor and the bed.

Unfazed, Calarook sprung to his feet and charged Kent, who sidestepped a little too late. Calarook's right arm caught Kent's waist, and they both hit the floor in a mass of well-dressed and well-armored fury.

Amid the scramble, Kent smashed his elbow into Calarook's cheek, and it earned him a brutal head-butt to his chest. The air pushed out of Kent's lungs, and he struggled to breathe as he found his footing and tried to back away.

Calarook pursued him and lunged forward again. Kent tried to sprawl, but the force of Calarook's attack kept him upright. Kent's back smacked into the wall next to the wardrobe, and he grunted and moaned and sucked for air.

They fought for positioning, and Kent managed to grab Calarook's head with his hands and anchor it between his forearms.

Kent pushed forward with his torso and forced Calarook upright for the first time in the scuffle, then Kent pulled him back and drove his right knee into the armor covering his belly.

A dull *clunk* sounded, and Calarook expelled a sharp breath.

Kent seized his chance. He yanked Calarook's head to the right and kicked at his ankles with his right leg.

The head motion set Calarook off-balance, and the kick swept his feet out from under him. Kent let him go, and Calarook hit the floor on his side with an armored *clank*.

The wardrobe. Calarook was lying right in front of it.

Kent grabbed the top of it and hauled it down. It slammed on top of Calarook with a loud crash, and Kent had to wonder if more soldiers might come to Calarook's aid because of the noise.

One thing Kent had learned in all his decades of fighting training was to press an advantage whenever he had one, so he did. Kicking Calarook's armored ribs wouldn't afford Kent anything except broken toes, so Kent aimed elsewhere.

As Calarook hefted the wardrobe off of him, Kent delivered a hard kick to his exposed head. The blow struck hard, and it stunned Calarook for an instant—long enough for Kent to drop down and pin him to the floor.

Pain smashed into Kent's forehead, and he rolled off of Calarook to recover. Calarook had bashed him with one of the wardrobe's doors.

Kent hurried to his feet and dabbed at his head. His fingers came back red and wet, but he realized the tingling had subsided, just as it had during his fights with the guards and his brother back at the manse.

Calarook got to his feet as well and flung the door at Kent, who dove to the side to avoid getting hit. When he reset, Calarook had reached him and wrapped his arms around Kent's waist. The pressure pinched the bandaged cut on his hip, and he winced.

Kent tried to squat down to counter, but Calarook proved too strong. He hefted Kent off his feet, twisted and arched his back, and drove Kent into the floor.

The blow racked the bones in Kent's arms and shoulders, and Calarook's body weight kept Kent struggling to breathe.

Calarook pinned Kent on his back, mounted him, and bared his bloody teeth. He raised his right arm to throw a punch.

Kent shifted hard to his right and pumped his knees into Calarook's back. The force sent Calarook's punch careening wide, and Kent wrapped his arm around Calarook's head, anchoring it close to his shoulder.

It gave him a moment to breathe, but it didn't last long. Calarook twisted and reared back up.

Kent's red cape lay half under his own body and half to his right side. He could use it if he could get enough of it in his hands.

Calarook readied himself for another punch, Kent performed the same evasion as before, only this time he didn't try to hold Calarook's head down with his arm.

Instead, he wrapped a length of the cape around Calarook's head and fed it to his other hand. Then he wrapped it around again.

When Calarook straightened up, the cape slipped down from around his face to under his chin—around his neck.

Kent pulled it and adjusted his grip until it tightened around Calarook's thick neck.

Purple-faced, Calarook pulled on the cape at first, then he changed tactics and dropped his elbow on Kent's nose.

The blow hurt, but it failed to loosen Kent's grip. Instead, Kent pulled tighter, adjusted his grip again, and kept his elbows and forearms near his head to better protect himself.

Calarook dropped a few more elbows, all of which Kent deflected, and then he resorted back to pulling at the cape. He should've just done that all along.

Kent had no room to his right, so he planted his left foot just on the outside of Calarook's right foot, braced his forearms against Calarook's bronze chest, and shoved hard, up and to the left, with his torso and his hips.

Calarook's stocky body toppled over, and Kent tightened the cape further, now from on top. Kent pressed his advantage.

He cleared Calarook's legs, got on his side, and used his shoulder and one temporarily free hand to roll Calarook onto his side. Then Kent got behind him, hooked his legs around Calarook's ample waist, and yanked with all his might.

Calarook's hands fought the cape, and he snorted and gurgled, but before long, his hands slipped down to his sides. By now, his whole head had turned purple, like one massive bruise.

If Kent wanted to kill him, all he had to do was keep the pressure consistent for about another minute. Not much effort at all.

But doing so would leave the fortress in far worse shape and less prepared to defend itself against incursions from Inoth.

Then again, Inoth was about to become Kent's new home. Perhaps Muroth, the country that had both borne him and branded him for execution, deserved whatever it got.

But General Calarook didn't deserve to die.

Kent sighed, and he released his grip on Calarook's neck. He unwrapped his cape, and a labored breath sucked into Calarook's mouth and nostrils.

Kent pushed him to the side and stood. The choke had put Calarook to sleep, but he would eventually wake up disoriented, and he'd miss the time that had passed since he went out.

Kent needed to leave before that happened. He fished the room key out of Calarook's left gauntlet and headed toward the door.

He caught sight of a mirror on his way out, and he used his red cape to wipe some of the blood from his face. It didn't help much, but it would have to do.

Kent left the room and locked Calarook inside. If anyone in the fortress had the strength to break out by sheer will, it was Calarook, but it would take even him some time to manage the feat, especially while weakened and confused once he woke up.

With the key in hand, Kent headed down the corridor toward the exit. He made his way into the fortress's courtyard, reoriented himself to his surroundings, and headed for the south gate. Once he passed through it, he'd be in Inoth, and he'd be safe.

Relatively.

What do I tell the soldiers?

Cold air chilled his face and hands, and once again his breath exhaled as vapor. As he approached the gate, he realized he didn't have the horse he'd stolen from his own estate.

There's no time. You're already in too much danger.

It was true. He would have to make his way on foot.

He reached the portcullis, and the ranking soldier on duty gawked at him.

"Lord Etheridge? What happened?"

Kent opted for honesty. "General Calarook attacked me. I overcame him and locked him in my chambers."

"By the gods... I'm glad you're unharmed!" The soldier looked him over. "Mostly."

"Send men to tend to General Calarook, then raise the portcullis." The soldier's back straightened. "My lord?"

"Raise the portcullis *now*, soldier."

"My lord, it's clear you're unwell. You're poorly dressed for the elements, and we never open the portcullis after dark, for safety reasons. Why—if I may ask—do you want us to do such a thing?"

"Because I am going out. I am on a secret mission from my father, and I am not to be hindered in any way." Kent said slowly, menacingly, "Open. The. Gate."

The soldier gulped, then he relayed the order.

Kent checked behind him as the portcullis rose, but no one came for him, including General Calarook. When the portcullis reached halfway up, Kent handed the soldier the key.

"If your men cannot otherwise get inside those chambers, here is the key."

The soldier took it and stared at Kent with confusion etched on his face.

"Wish me good fortune, soldier?" Kent asked.

"I wish you all the good fortune this world has to offer, my lord." He gave a slight bow.

Kent ducked under the portcullis and headed into the darkness beyond the fortress. All the while he wondered if that soldier's wishes were the last kind words he would ever hear from one of his countrymen.

WHEN KENT AWOKE THE NEXT MORNING, THE BLOOD FROM HIS HEAD HAD DRIED AND crusted on the side of his face, and the blood from his nose had crusted over the left half of his chapped lips.

He worked his finger along his top row of teeth and separated his lips carefully, and then he smacked his lips together a few times to get them working again.

He'd fallen asleep under a tree some three miles from Ranhold Fortress, now hidden from his view thanks to a series of hills and the small forest that surrounded him. His cape had done just enough to keep him warm the night before, but now, in the morning light, he could see how stained and soiled it and the rest of his clothes were.

He took his time getting to his feet, in part because he wasn't in any rush to begin his new life, but mostly because his body ached all over from the last day's travails.

At his age, his body took far longer to recover than it used to. Kent intended to give it as much time as it needed to accomplish that feat.

Sometime later, he pushed himself up to his feet, and his body ached anew. His

head swam and pounded for a moment, then it equalized and gave him a respite from its harassment.

He leaned against the tree for a few minutes while he collected himself, cursing Fane all the while. But with each new strife Kent endured, his resolve to kill Fane further ingrained itself in his will, in his very being.

His brooding done, Kent stretched his sore limbs and started walking south.

Father had many times mused aloud at the possibility of invading northern Inoth with a large, organized force, but he'd never acted on the impulse. Neither had Emperor Bouwen, Muroth's ruler.

As such, Kent had only been to Inoth a handful of times, and always with a small army accompanying him. So he didn't really have any sense of where he was going.

He decided to just head south until he happened upon something manmade—a farm, a road, a town—and figure it out from there. As long as he avoided Inoth's northern fortresses, he would be fine.

Half a day later, he saw a farmhouse in the distance. He headed toward it.

Rather than stopping in and petitioning for aid, he visited the water trough set out for the livestock and used the frigid water to clean off his face and hands. The animals likely wouldn't be pleased, but he didn't revel in having to use their water to clean himself either.

He left the farm shortly after and found a road—more like a path with a couple of ruts—and he followed it for another two hours. The midday sun went from warming him to baking him and then back to warming him again as he walked.

Another hour later, he happened upon a good-sized town, and he ventured into it.

He got no shortage of strange looks from the townspeople. Probably his two-day-old clothes and their bedraggled condition. Or perhaps their initial quality and decadence, especially compared to what everyone else was wearing, set him apart.

A little boy, perhaps six years old, with short brown hair wandered up to him. "What happened to your face?"

Or... that. Kent crouched down and looked the lad in his dark green eyes. "I got into a fight."

The boy's eyes widened. "Did you win?"

Kent grinned. "Just barely."

The boy smiled, then he turned and ran off.

Kent hadn't eaten since the night before, and now it was early afternoon. A few shops, street vendors, and a local inn seemed to offer food, but Kent had no coin. He hadn't had time to grab anything from his personal coffers at the manse, and he'd brought nothing from the fortress aside from the clothes on his back.

Ultimately, Kent managed to trade his cape, ruined as it was, for a good meal and a sack of fruit that he could carry as he walked. As the vendor stuffed the sack with apples and oranges, Kent wondered whether or not she was cursed as well.

After all, he was in Inoth. Yet, strangely, he hadn't seen anyone using magic in any capacity since he'd arrived.

Hundreds of years earlier, Muroth and Inoth had been one nation that became embroiled in a civil war. The southerners had aligned to form a nation of magic-users, and the northerners, who relied on traditional weapons of war, tried to prevent their secession.

In the end, the southerners prevailed. Inoth formed in spite of its parent country, Muroth, and all Murothian magic-users fled to the south under penalty of death. Little had changed since then, except that Muroth had developed a much stronger military as a result.

The small town had little to offer him, and it was still far too close to the Murothian border for his liking. Perhaps if he headed farther south to Goldmoor, Inoth's capital city, he'd find some sense of purpose.

What's more, a bigger city meant he'd disappear more easily. Now, above all else, anonymity was his friend.

So Kent asked the vendor for directions to the capital, and he got the information he needed. Then he set out toward Goldmoor, hoping his meager sack of fruit would last the full three-day walk.

IN THREE DAYS TIME, KENT ARRIVED AT THE WESTERN GATES OF GOLDMOOR WITH NO more fruit and no more sack. He'd washed himself and his clothes in an icy stream along the way, but he still felt... poor. There was no other way to describe it.

Then again, he *was* poor now, in every sense of the word. Yet as much as he longed for the comforts of his home in Muroth, he would've given it all away to have found a way to save his father—and to kill his brother.

From what Kent had observed, the soldiers at the city's western gate allowed people to walk in and out generally without bothering them, but on occasion, they would stop travelers and ask them questions. Kent expected he'd be stopped, and he had prepared a story in advance, should it happen.

He'd opted to walk the extra half-day to reach the city's western gate precisely to help avoid suspicion. Entering the city's northern gates would cast his story into doubt due to the gate's relative proximity to Muroth, so the extra travel time made sense, tactically, to mitigate the risk.

Sure enough, as Kent approached, a pair of low-ranking soldiers clad in brown leather breastplates and matching greaves stopped him.

"You look tired, traveler," the first soldier said.

Kent studied them both from top to bottom. He could see no weapons on either of them. But then again, he was in Inoth now.

The Inothian Army relied on the use of magic to fight, so Kent assumed these soldiers could handle themselves without the aid of weapons.

He did, however, notice little pouches hanging along their belts.

Kent had seen comparable pouches up close only a handful of times before, on captured Inothian soldiers near Muroth's southern border, but he still didn't know what purpose they served.

Whenever his men had captured an Inothian and searched him, they only found nature's castoffs in those pouches—grass, leaves, sticks, pebbles, and the like.

"I'm talking to you, guy," the first soldier said.

Kent smiled. "Forgive me, sir. I have had a long journey, and I am indeed tired."

"You've got a strange accent." The second soldier stepped closer, his hands on his hips. "Where are you from?"

"Northern Urthia." Kent had chosen the country based on its distance from Inoth. He figured few common folk would ever have had occasion to travel so far from home, so it seemed like a safe bet. And since Inoth and Urthia had maintained peaceful terms for decades, these soldiers likely wouldn't have been sent there for any reason either.

"Certainly explains your ridiculous clothing," the first soldier said.

"Long way from home, aren't you?" the second soldier asked. "Alone and without so much as a pack?"

"I ran into bandits on my way here," Kent lied. "They were magnanimous enough to let me keep my clothes, but nothing else."

"What did they look like?" The second soldier's eyes narrowed.

"Like bandits." Kent sensed that wouldn't be enough, so he added, "It was dark. I couldn't see them well. My vision isn't what it used to be."

The soldiers had to be at least fifteen years younger than Kent, so playing up his "old man" status seemed wise.

The first soldier nodded. "Not much to be done about it, but you could report the incident to the constable, if you like."

"I just reported it to you."

"We just work the gate, sir," the first soldier said. "We don't deal with anything beyond these walls, as per our assigned posting."

"The constable won't do anything either, to be honest." The second soldier had loosened up a bit, and now his hands hung at his sides instead of resting on his hips, near those pouches. "No sense getting your hopes up. Your property's long gone by now. Best to accept it and move on."

"You got any friends in the city who can help you out?" the first soldier asked.

Kent shook his head. He could tell the truth for this one. "Not a soul."

"And I assume they took your coin as well?"

Kent nodded.

"Here." The first soldier dug into one of his pouches and produced a few small copper coins. He extended them toward Kent. "It's not much, but it should buy you a warm meal, at least. Maybe even a room for the night."

Kent accepted the coins and marveled at them. This soldier, this man who'd been the embodiment of his sworn enemy less than a week earlier, had just given his own coin to help ensure Kent's wellbeing.

Yet Kent's own father had disowned him, his brother had tried to have him arrested and executed, and General Calarook had tried to kill him. The vast difference between the two sets of experiences left him stunned.

"Thank you," Kent managed to say.

"And be sure to stop by the Temple of Laeri. They can help you more."

"Laeri? The Goddess of the Light?"

"The same." The first soldier grinned. "You worship her up in Northern Urthia as well?"

Not a question Kent had wholly prepared for, but... "I worship her wherever I am."

"You'll be right at home, then." The first soldier gave him a nod. "Now, sir, if you don't mind, we ought to inquire of some other travelers. Go on into the city, if you still wish."

Kent nodded to them both, and he repeated, "Thank you." Then he went inside.

He'd heard that Inoth's capital city got its name from the vivid sunrises seen from its harbors. Given that it was afternoon now, Kent resigned himself that he would view it eventually. He'd be living here indefinitely, so he had plenty of time to explore later.

The city rose before him to the north, gradually elevating on a steady slope, but it lowered to sea level in the east and south. High above, a series of white-stoned spires loomed over the rest of the city.

He guessed it was Hunera Palace, where Inoth's queen resided. Goldmoor bustled with people of all shapes and sizes, not unlike Muroth's capital city, Drion. But in many ways, Kent liked it better than Drion. He especially liked being near the sea. The warm, salty air filled him with hope.

As instructed, he asked around and made his way to the Temple of Laeri, a massive, pillared structure made of sleek black stone. Kent marveled at it as he approached, and he wondered why a temple of light would be made of black stones.

But inside the temple, an all-white sanctuary greeted him. White walls, white floors, a white altar. White tapestries hung from the walls, and white light streamed through the crystalline ceiling.

A white statue of Laeri towered over the altar with her hands extended out to her sides, palms up, majestic and beautiful. But a dark circle hollowed out the center of her chest, just under her covered breasts.

The statue vaguely resembled the icons of Laeri he'd seen in comparable temples in Muroth. Behind her, a massive marble triangle framed the altar, with its lower point down, and the upper points spread wide beyond Laeri's head.

He wondered at the possible symbolism of the design aesthetic. Was it a metaphor for the outside world as compared to that of a life of dedication to the goddess Laeri? Or had black stones simply been more economical to purchase, given that Hunera Palace was made of white stones?

Whatever the case, Kent gathered with a group of others inside the temple and repeated the liturgy and incantations spoken by the priestess in pure white robes embroidered with star and triangle shapes. It almost matched the ceremonies in Murothian temples to Laeri, except for a few minor deviations.

Then again, he hadn't attended any type of ceremony in years. He couldn't claim even remote expertise in this area.

But as the ceremony concluded, the priestess raised her hands over her head and looked toward the crystalline ceiling. She put her left hand into the stream of light, now angled toward the temple's eastern wall thanks to the setting sun, and she closed her eyes.

When she pulled her hand away from the stream, the light still clung to her hand, and an arc of light traced from the stream of sunlight down to where she'd lowered her hand and hung in the air. Then she molded the light into a small orb, twice as bright as the streams of sunlight.

Kent watched the sight in awe. He'd seen plenty of forms of magic in his days of fighting Inothians, but he'd never seen anyone manipulate light itself before.

The priestess turned back toward the image of Laeri and raised her hands again, this time with the orb glowing between them. She released it, and it hovered in the air over her head. Then it slowly rose up to Laeri's chest and lodged in the hollow, dark circle under her breasts.

As it did, the statue itself began to glow, but not on its own. The orb was casting light throughout the statue, and millions of microscopic cracks glowed with the warm afternoon sunlight the priestess had captured.

Incredible. And an incredible tribute to the Goddess of Light.

Kent wondered how the priestess had managed such a feat, but more so, he wondered what practical value the magic had outside of illuminating a statue.

He didn't get a chance to ask the priestess. She walked behind the statue of Laeri and disappeared, possibly into a back room.

Kent caught a temple worker afterward and tried to get a meeting with the priestess, but the temple worker refused to accommodate him. So Kent explained what the soldier had told him, and the temple worker escorted him through the temple to a separate chamber.

Kent found himself standing among dozens of foul-smelling, disheveled people, waiting in some sort of line. He surveyed the room and realized he'd stumbled into some sort of communal sleeping room.

Unlike the pristine whiteness of the sanctuary, this chamber housed simple wooden beds stacked three high and spaced no more than a few feet apart. The line curled around the beds to a wooden table set up at the far side of the room.

Another temple worker, distinct because of his white robes, sat at the table and scribbled on a piece of parchment for each person who approached. Then the person at the front of the line would leave and meander through the forest of beds. After what looked like intentional searching, the person would claim one.

Kent realized the beds were numbered.

He'd slept outdoors for nearly a week, and while he would've preferred not to share sleeping quarters with dozens of filthy street people, it beat actually *becoming* one of those filthy street people by sleeping on the street that night.

And with winter drawing to a close, the nights were still cold, even so much farther south than Muroth. So Kent sighed and resigned himself to his fate.

The line took a little less than an hour to get through, and Kent claimed a bed— number 268, a bottom spot.

Shortly after he did, the doors to the chamber closed, and no one else was let in, despite much shouting and complaining coming from just outside. The temple's shelter service must've capped around 300 beds.

Temple workers ushered the human mass into another larger chamber, sat them at worn wooden tables like the one where Kent had received his bed number, and fed them a hot, albeit bland, meal.

Better than an empty stomach.

Back in the chamber of beds, Kent made his way back to number 268.

When he got there, a large, bare-chested man was laying in it.

The man was chatting at a young woman in the next bed over who appeared as if she wanted nothing to do with either him or the conversation they were having.

"Excuse me, sir," Kent said to him. "But I believe you have the wrong bed."

The man looked up at him with brown eyes so dark, they were almost black. "Piss off." Then he resumed his talking.

Kent squared himself with the bed. "I said, you have the wrong bed, *sir.*"

The man looked up at him again. "An' I said, *piss off.*"

"I apologize, but I will not be doing that. Now, will you comply nicely, or must you be made to cooperate?"

The man scoffed, then he rolled out of bed and stood to his full height— a good six inches taller than Kent.

His skin carried a grayish, ashen pallor, albeit faint, and black, bristly hair sprouted from his chest, arms, neck, face, and shoulders. Kent imagined it must've carried over to his back as well, but he decided he'd rather not know for sure.

His scarred face seemed swine-like in shape, and when he spoke, his teeth looked abnormally large for his mouth. He looked strong, but in an unrefined way. His thick arms lacked tone, and under his sagging chest muscles, his gut lolled over his belt.

Still, he had to weigh a solid seventy pounds more than Kent, and in a fight, that would make a considerable difference. Avoiding a scuffle, if possible, was Kent's prerogative, but if one were to start, he would end it quickly.

"Who in the third hell d'you think you're talkin' to?" he growled.

Kent wrinkled his nose. The man's breath stank like day-old, half-digested mead and rancid meat.

"Perhaps I was not clear," Kent said calmly. "I do not care who you are. I only care that you remove yourself from the bed allotted to me for this evening."

The man's mouth opened, and he blinked. Then he carried on as if Kent hadn't said anything. "I'm Trag Gadzag. Ya mus' be new in town if ya don' know who I am."

Is he slow in the head? "I simply require my allotted bed. Please step aside."

"No one tells me what t'do. I'm the best fighter th'dockmasters ever seen."

Definitely slow. But if he was telling the truth about his status among fighters down by the docks, then Kent had cause for concern.

Kent had engaged in only a few street fights in his day, nearly all of them as a youth. But he'd learned one thing through his extensive combat training over the years: street fighters usually didn't know much actual technique.

However, many had more tenacity than even dedicated soldiers. And that made them dangerous.

But Kent had handled far worse in his day. "Trag? As in, Trag-ic? Tragic? Is that your full name?"

Trag squinted at him. "No. Just Trag. Trag Gadzag."

Kent shook his head. "No, I am certain it is short for 'Tragic.' With a face like yours, that name is perfect."

The young woman Trag had been talking to stifled a giggle, but she slid off her bed and watched from behind it.

Trag's fists tightened, and his pitiful chest puffed. "You're gonna pay f'r that."

By now, a loose crowd had encircled them. Their presence had all but necessitated that Trag choose to fight, especially since Kent had publicly damaged his ego.

Kent was ready for it. As the smaller man, he had the advantage of speed and added mobility in a smaller space.

"Last chance, friend," Kent said calmly. "Walk away, and I will have my bed, and you may return to yours."

Trag smacked his chest with his right hand three times, loosed a piglike roar, and swung a big overhand right at Kent's head.

CHAPTER FOUR

K ent slipped under the punch with ease, got on Trag's right side, and used his momentum to smash Trag's head into the wooden bed rail where he'd just been standing. Quick, hard, and decisive.

Trag went down hard.

Fight over.

The crowd gasped, and Kent casually sat on his allotted bed. But then Trag stirred and began to push himself up.

Kent scrambled to his feet. *Fight not over.*

"He's half-orc," someone hissed from behind Kent. "Thick skull."

That explains a lot. And it wasn't just his skull—all of Trag's bones would be thicker due to his half-orc heritage. No wonder Trag was the best fighter the dock-masters had ever seen.

Kent readied himself.

Trag turned around slowly. Rage abounded in his dark eyes, and dark blood streamed from his nose and bubbled from between his large teeth. He beat his chest three more times.

Tenacity. Street fighters have tenacity.

Kent had to make the fight not worth continuing, and breaking Trag's half-orc bones would prove too difficult.

Joints, though—no species that Kent knew of had impossibly strong joints. Movability meant vulnerability.

So when Trag swung again, Kent didn't bother with counter-punching or throwing a kick or an elbow. Instead, he avoided the punch, repositioned himself, and latched onto Trag's left arm with both hands.

He raised his left shin up to Trag's hip, then he jumped off of his right leg, swung it over Trag's head, and planted his heel in Trag's face.

Kicking Trag's face was just a bonus. The real effect was that Kent's weight pulled Trag to the floor.

They hit the ground, but Trag's resistance ensured Kent a soft landing. Kent shifted and squeezed his knees together, and he straightened Trag's arm along his torso.

Trag grunted and struggled, but Kent raised his hips hard.

SNAP.

Trag bellowed, and Kent released him and rolled up to his feet. Trag remained on the ground, clutching his broken elbow joint and wailing.

Now the fight was over.

A bright light burst into view between Kent and Trag, blinding Kent with pain. He tried to shield his eyes, but it was too late. He couldn't see anything.

Something swept him off of his feet, and he hit the floor on his side.

"Stay down, both of you!" a sharp male voice commanded.

Kent still couldn't see. The light continued to blaze, and he didn't want to open his eyes to face it. Something curled around his body, and it lifted him off the floor with ease.

What is happening?

He scrambled and strained, but he couldn't break free. The form kept him restrained, all while it seemed to carry him along—though he couldn't be sure. He still couldn't open his eyes against the bright light.

A moment later, he hit the ground again, and the light vanished. He opened his eyes and sat up. The Temple of Laeri loomed over him, a black void against the starry night sky.

What...?

He looked around. He was in some sort of alleyway paved with crumbling stones and framed by the temple's black exterior wall on one side and a handful of other stone buildings on the other.

The stench of rotting fruit and urine hit Kent's nostrils, and then he heard a wheezing, moaning sound nearby.

Kent turned to his left and saw Trag lying on the ground next to him, writhing and clutching his injured arm.

Did they... throw us out?

He stood and hurried back to the temple walls, but he couldn't find a door anywhere. It didn't make any sense—how had they removed Trag and him without carrying them through a door? Was the door just hidden within the wall?

Or was it magic, perhaps? Light magic. It explained the brightness that kept him from seeing anything while it was happening. And with Laeri being the Goddess of Light, it made sense.

Kent wished he better understood how it all worked.

"Ya bastard!" Trag shouted from behind him.

Kent whirled around, ready, but Trag still lay on the alley floor with his elbow broken.

"Ya broke my damn'd arm!"

Kent relaxed. "I gave you ample warning, and you chose the wrong path."

"An' you got us kicked out f'r the night!"

"Again, that was your doing. I did not start the altercation." Kent smirked. "I simply finished it."

A river of profanity spilled from Trag's mouth, some of it in Orcish, presumably.

But Trag was right about one thing—they'd been expelled from the temple. That meant finding other accommodations for the night. And with no coin or other resources to speak of, it likely meant sleeping on the street.

Kent scanned the alley again, consumed by indecision.

For all Kent's knowledge, he knew nothing about such lifestyles. He didn't know the city, so he didn't know his way around.

He didn't know which areas tended to harbor more criminal activity and which areas tended to harbor less. He didn't know whether other institutions offered shelter, and he didn't know if they'd let him in at such a late hour anyway.

Trag struggled to his feet, wincing.

Kent faced him again, wary and ready. "I do not need to warn you again, do I?"

Trag glowered at him and pointed with his good arm. "I never wanna see ya again."

With that, Trag turned and headed out of the alley, his left arm hanging limp and awkward from his shoulder.

Kent watched him leave. If there were anyone Kent might observe to see how such a life was to be lived, Trag exemplified the lifestyle. So Kent followed him out of the alley at a distance.

Trag's hulking form staggered through the streets amid dozens of others out and about at night—a fraction of as many as Kent had seen during the day. Trag maneuvered through them all, heading east, toward the coast and the harbor.

It made sense; if Trag genuinely was the best fighter the dockmasters had ever seen, then he would know the area. He'd likely even worked on the docks at some point.

Sure enough, Trag led Kent to the harbor, and he took up residence on a wooden bench against a massive warehouse of some sort. Or perhaps it was a building where they constructed ships.

As with homelessness, Kent knew little of the practice of shipbuilding, thanks to living in a landlocked province of Muroth all his life.

Kent watched Trag from afar, and he ultimately elected to steer clear of him for the rest of the evening. It would be far better if Trag didn't happen upon him while he was sleeping.

Revenge is far easier if your target is asleep.

Kent thought of Fane. He definitely wanted Fane awake and comprehending every detail when Kent finally claimed his vengeance.

Instead of further pursuing Trag, Kent headed down one of the docks toward one of the smaller ships. He'd picked it out because it appeared unoccupied.

And what could be better than a covered lodging that offered the added benefit of rocking him to sleep with the push and pull of the waves?

He boarded the vessel with ease, found his way below decks, and lay across a pile of some sort of fabric. Not as comfortable as the bed he'd inadvertently vacated at the temple, but it beat sleeping on the street or on a wooden bench.

Within minutes, the waves coaxed Kent into fitful dreams of his father and brother.

"WHAT IN THE THIRD HELL ARE YE DOIN' ON ME SHIP?"

The voice snapped Kent awake, and he recoiled from the direction of the sound.

A man in a fine coat and trousers pointed a curved sword down at him. "I asked ye a question, mate."

"Forgive me, sir." Kent raised his hand as if to submit, but he also used it to gauge his distance from the man's sword.

There, on the floor and on his back, Kent could only hope for mercy or a mistake.

"I have only just arrived in town and needed a place to sleep," Kent continued. "Your fine vessel looked inviting, so I took it upon myself to—"

"I want ye off me ship in ten seconds, or I'll flay yeer skin into strips and use it as bait."

The man wasn't as big as Trag, but from the way he carried himself, Kent could tell he knew how to handle that sword.

"Yes, sir. Right away." Kent stood slowly so as not to surprise the man or give him a reason to attack.

"Ye've got seven seconds," the man said. "I suggest ye hurry."

Kent nodded and maneuvered around him, then he charged up the steps to the main deck and back onto the dock, leaving the ship behind.

In the distance, massive merchant ships and Inothian Navy frigates floated under the golden sunrise, poised to set out on whatever new adventures lay beyond the bay.

Goldmoor, indeed.

"And don't ever come back, ye hear?" the man called from the ship. Kent wouldn't come back. That was for certain.

He headed west, and the city swallowed him whole. He passed several beggars in the streets and wondered if he'd soon end up sharing their lot in life.

No, Kent reasoned. He had a lifetime of applicable skills in economics, combat, and business to rely upon. Certainly he could find some way to put that knowledge to practical use.

But where? And how? He walked the streets for hours, searching for answers.

As he wandered the north side of the city, a loud commotion arose from one street over. It intensified as he proceeded onward, and he heard a flurry of screams next.

Kent cut through an alley toward the street. If someone was in danger, he wanted to be on hand to help, if he could.

When he got to the scene, he found two men facing off in the middle of the street, surrounded by an ever-growing circle of scattering people.

One of them, a short man wearing a dark robe with red accents, was drawing black symbols in the air with his fingertips. Shafts of eerie red light swirled around him like vipers pursuing prey.

The other man wore a hooded brown-and-gray cloak. A dozen fist- sized rocks floated around his body on their own. He held a brown stone in his left hand, and he extended his right hand toward the man in the dark robe.

The rocks orbiting him shot toward the man in the dark robe, but as they drew near, the red light swirling around the man in the dark robe accelerated, spiraling faster and faster.

The rocks hit the red light, and it crushed them into dust. Then the red lights slowed into their snakelike shafts once again.

"You're weak, bounty hunter!" the man in the dark robe shouted. "And no match for my dark runes."

Bounty hunter? Kent marveled. What, exactly, was transpiring here?

"I'm not done yet, Eusephus," the bounty hunter shouted back. He raised his hands, one still holding the rock, and one open.

Various stones arose from the street and began to encircle the bounty hunter again.

The man in the dark robe, Eusephus, thrust his arms forward, and the red lights shot toward the bounty hunter like spears.

The bounty hunter smacked his hands together, pressing the rock between them, and the stones formed into a wall. Then the bounty hunter dove to his right.

The red lights shattered the wall of rock and streaked through the air where the bounty hunter's body had just been.

The bounty hunter rolled up to his feet, closer to Kent's position, and dropped his rock to the ground. His hood slipped off of his head, revealing short blonde hair. Tan skin showed on his arms, legs, and face where the cloak didn't cover them.

His green eyes flashed toward Kent, then he refocused on Eusephus and rushed forward.

The bounty hunter's rock remained where he'd dropped it, now just a fraction of its original size, and smooth and shiny. Kent wondered what had happened to it.

As Eusephus hurled more streams of red light, the bounty hunter extracted a white crystal from a pouch on his belt. He extended the crystal toward Eusephus, and the red lights collided with a previously invisible crystalline wall and dissipated harmlessly in a prism of red hues.

Eusephus cursed, and the bounty hunter continued to press forward.

From behind Eusephus, a group of leather-clad Inothian soldiers approached. The one in the lead wore a captain's diamond-shaped rank on the shoulders of his armor. He shouted an order that Kent couldn't make out.

Eusephus stole a glance back and cursed again, then he traced a new set of symbols in the air before him, one for each hand. His right hand pointed toward the approaching bounty hunter, and his left pointed toward the soldiers.

He finished completing the symbols, and his hands ignited with pale green fire. The flames erupted from his palms and traced lines between the two sets of encroaching opponents and himself. Green fire blazed from each line, creating an impassable barrier that stopped them all short.

Kent stared at the green conflagration, amazed. He had produced blue fire from his fingertips before, but he had never achieved anything close to the magical prowess that either the bounty hunter or Eusephus had displayed thus far.

The bounty hunter's skills reminded Kent of battles he'd had with other Inothians near the border. They'd hurled rocks at his men along with fire, water, metal, and more, but in all his years of repelling the Inothians, he'd never seen anything like the magic Eusephus was wielding.

While Eusephus began drawing his next symbols, the bounty hunter removed a feather from another of his pouches. He held it in his right hand, then he spread his arms wide like bird wings and swung them toward the flames.

A gust of wind ripped through the center of the flames, and the bounty hunter walked through the opening. The feather was no longer in his hand.

On the other side, the soldiers manufactured a stone bridge of sorts, also using magic. It blocked enough of the fire so they could pass beyond it.

But Eusephus was ready for them. Two new symbols, different in shape, yielded two violet weapons covered with glowing runes, one in each hand.

In his left hand, Eusephus held a glowing blade, sharp on one edge and lined with long saw teeth on the other. In his right hand, an irradiated flail, covered in spikes, hung from a purple chain.

Kent marveled at the sight. Eusephus had just conjured those weapons out of nothing—out of magic, to be precise.

Eusephus swung the sword across his body at the bounty hunter, but the bounty hunter recoiled back.

Then Eusephus spun and whipped the flail at the encroaching soldiers. It hit one of them square in his chest and sent him careening into one of the buildings lining the street, but the others managed to avoid it.

Eusephus's eyes flared with vivid red light, and he cackled.

Another soldier rushed over to help his downed comrade and called, "His weapons drain essence! They'll kill you in one blow!"

"They'll fuel his magic, too," the captain called. "Be cautious!"

Kent didn't understand what the soldiers were saying, but the soldier Eusephus had hit was clearly dead. What kind of magic was Eusephus using?

Something evil, without question.

Eusephus had just killed one of the soldiers. He'd kill more if he had the chance—that much was clear.

As the skirmish raged on, Kent scanned the street for something he could use to help. A tent had collapsed nearby him, and along with it, its tentpoles.

He slipped one out of the tent and held it up. At about ten feet, it was far too long to make a useful quarterstaff. Kent glanced back at the fight.

The bounty hunter hurled a blue blast of magic—Kent didn't know what kind—at

Eusephus, but Eusephus batted the magic away with a well-timed blow from his flail. The blast exploded in a spatter of blue light, then it dissipated altogether.

A soldier approached Eusephus with a shield of metal hovering in front of him. He also held a metal rod of some sort in his hand.

Eusephus cackled again and batted the shield to the side with his flail. On his follow-up swing, he drove the spiked edge of his sword into the soldier's chest.

The soldier screamed at first, but his voice faded to nothing as his face shriveled to black, decayed skin. His hands crumpled into curled, arthritic hooks. Then the soldier dropped onto his back, his white teeth bared from his black skull.

Eusephus's eyes blazed with red light anew.

Kent watched it all, horrified. It had to be dark magic. He'd never encountered it firsthand, but he'd heard tales of such things. Having seen light magic in action at the Temple of Laeri, it made sense that its antithesis should also exist.

As the bounty hunter stormed in for another attempt, Kent leaned the tent post against a nearby building's stone wall and braced it against the cobblestone street. Then he kick-stomped on it about three feet up from the ground. The pole snapped, leaving a sharp, splintered end where it had broken.

Now about seven feet in length, the tentpole would work well as a long quarter-staff. More than sufficient for what Kent had in mind.

He'd personally felled dozens of magic-wielding Inothians over the years, and they all shared a few common weaknesses. If Kent could exploit those weaknesses again today, he could help put an end to Eusephus's terror.

He turned back toward the battle.

As Eusephus swung at the bounty hunter, his back turned toward Kent.

Perfect. Kent rushed forward, clutching the tent rod as if it were a spear, with the jagged end facing toward Eusephus.

The bounty hunter rolled away from Eusephus's attacks, and as Kent expected, Eusephus rotated to take on whomever else might be coming for him. He had good battlefield awareness, which was part of why he'd proven so dangerous thus far.

Eusephus's irradiated eyes fixed on Kent, and he swung his flail.

CHAPTER FIVE

Kent's tentpole would've never held up against a blow from either of Eusephus's weapons. But if he maneuvered correctly, it wouldn't matter.

As Eusephus's flail careened toward Kent's head, Kent lowered his level and slid feet-first toward Eusephus. The flail howled over Kent's head.

Eusephus brought his sword around next, but he was too late.

Kent's feet collided hard with Eusephus's shins, and Eusephus dropped to the street face-first, just on the other side of Kent's legs. Then Kent sprung to his feet and brought the tentpole down hard on Eusephus's head.

Crack.

Eusephus went limp. His eyes, still open, stopped glowing red, and the violet weapons in his hands evaporated into a purple mist that drifted away on the wind.

Kent looked up. The bounty hunter stared at him with an expression caught somewhere between surprise and anger.

Meanwhile, the soldiers encircled Kent and Eusephus, all with their hands up and holding various natural objects.

"Back away from him," one of them, a soldier with brown hair, said to Kent. "And put the stick down."

Kent tossed it to the side, raised his hands in surrender, and backed away.

"Did you kill him?" the same soldier asked.

"No," Kent replied. "But you should check all the same."

"Stay back, alright?" the soldier said.

Kent nodded and obliged, but the bounty hunter continued forward, closer.

"And you." The soldier pointed at the bounty hunter. "You're under arrest."

"No, I'm not," the bounty hunter replied. "I'm Ronin Shroud, a bounty hunter. This man is wanted for murder in three countries, and I've pursued him here to catch him and claim the bounty. I have documents to confirm my intentions and his identity."

"Then let's see them."

Ronin Shroud produced the documents, and the soldier looked them over while his men checked Eusephus.

"He's breathing, Captain," one of the other soldiers said. "Restrain him," the captain ordered.

Though Eusephus was still unconscious, the soldiers knelt on his back to keep him pinned while they clamped his wrists together with a pair of metal shackles colored a vivid blue. Kent had never seen anything like them before.

"You didn't do much of a job catching him," the captain muttered.

Ronin scowled at him. "It got done in the end."

"Seems more like that man deserves the bounty than you," the captain remarked.

"He's not a bounty hunter," Ronin said.

"You do not know that," Kent interjected.

They both looked at him, and Ronin said, "Then let's see *your* papers."

Kent smirked, but he didn't say anything.

"That's what I thought." Ronin sneered at him. "Besides, you haven't been tracking him from Urthia for the last three months, have you?"

Kent kept quiet. If Ronin was telling the truth, he likely knew Urthia better than Kent did. If they asked who Kent was, he'd have to change his story.

Maybe this time Kent would claim to be from Etrijan, instead. He'd visited its capital city of Sefera a handful of times on diplomatic visits.

"Again, that's what I thought." Ronin turned toward the soldier. "He's mine, and so is the bounty."

"I won't argue with you," the captain said. "But I intend to make it known how poorly you handled this. He killed two of my men, caused extensive property damage, halted commerce on this street, and scared off the citizenry because you chose to engage him here."

"I—" Ronin hesitated. "I regret that his actions caused such turmoil, of course, but this carnage can hardly be attributed to me."

"He will doubtless pay for his crimes, but I will recommend to the royal treasury that a portion of your bounty should go toward helping the families of my men in the light of their demises."

"Their recompense should come from the satisfaction of knowing their loved ones' murderer will be executed for his crimes, not from *my* pockets," Ronin snapped. "I did not kill those men." He pointed at Eusephus. "*He* did."

"But you chose to engage him in public rather than—"

"I don't have to explain myself to you, Captain." Ronin held up his hand. "File your grievances, but give me the signature I rightfully deserve to submit my claim on his bounty."

The captain didn't move.

"It's mandated by law, now that you've seen the required documentation,

Captain." Ronin extended the parchment forward. "Unless you intend to relinquish him into my care so that I may turn him in personally."

The captain frowned, but he extended his forefinger toward the parchment. It began to glow blue, like Kent's hands had done so many times before, and he ran it across the parchment in a series of up-and-down motions.

When he finished, he scowled at Ronin. "Get off my street, bounty hunter."

Ronin gave him a slight bow. "Much obliged, Captain."

He shot a sideways glance at Kent as he rolled up the parchment and tucked it inside his cloak again, and then he headed down a side street.

Kent waited a moment, then he followed Ronin at a distance.

It didn't take long for Ronin to realize Kent was following him.

Within five minutes of leaving the street where Kent had downed Eusephus, Ronin cut into an alley. When Kent followed, Ronin wasn't there. Kent turned back to find Ronin standing right behind him, in the street again.

Clever trick.

Ronin shoved Kent into the alley and pinned him against a brick wall covered in thin, green vines. "Why are you following me?"

Kent batted Ronin's hands away and shoved him back hard.

"Tough guy, are you?" Ronin glared at him and removed something from one of the pouches on his belt, but Kent didn't see what it was. Then Ronin extended his right hand toward Kent's feet.

Something grabbed Kent's legs, and he tried to scamper out of its grip, but it held him tightly. He nearly fell, but something else grabbed around his waist and anchored him in place.

He looked down. The vines that had been on the wall had grown and stretched to entangle his legs and waist. They snaked up his back and snagged his arms all the way up to his wrists, pinning him against the wall.

Kent strained against them. They gave slightly, but they held strong.

Ronin advanced toward him. "Why are you following me?"

"Half of that bounty should be mine," Kent said.

Ronin scoffed. "No, it shouldn't."

"Do you want to know what you did wrong?" Kent asked.

Ronin's eyes narrowed, and he raised his right hand again.

Vines scraped their way around Kent's throat, and he tightened his jaw.

Ronin said, "I could kill you."

"You are a bounty hunter," Kent said. "Not a murderer. You catch criminals, but you are not one of them."

"Then I'll just leave you here."

"No, you will not." Kent glanced at the thin vines restraining his right arm. "For two reasons."

Ronin folded his arms. "Enlighten me."

86

"First of all, it will bother you not knowing what you did wrong, especially now that I have said something. And second…"

Kent jerked his right arm forward, and the vines restraining him tore free of the wall. He mimicked the motion on his left side, then he quickly stripped the vines from his throat and leaned forward. He ignored the ones around his waist and legs for now.

"…And second, you magic-users always overestimate your powers. These vines are too frail to hold someone with any physical strength whatsoever."

Ronin recoiled a step, but he didn't re-engage the vines. "'Magic-users?' We're called 'mages.' Where are you from that you don't know that term?"

"That is none of your concern." Kent bent down and tore the vines from his left leg, then his right.

As he did so, Kent noticed that the lower part of his right trouser leg had ripped, probably when he'd slid into Eusephus. Then he wrenched free of the vines around his waist and stepped forward again.

Kent caught a glimpse of something green as Ronin stuffed the object in his left hand back into a pouch.

"I'm not giving you any of my bounty," Ronin said. "I earned that coin. All you did was show up."

"Yes. I showed up and ended the confrontation in five seconds," Kent said. "Something you have failed to achieve for the last three months, by your own admission."

"It's *not* that simple." Ronin glowered at him.

"But part of you agrees that I am entitled to some of those earnings." Kent folded his arms. "You know splitting the bounty is the right thing to do, especially since you were in over your head."

"I was not."

"How old are you, kid?" Kent asked. "Seventeen? Maybe nineteen?"

"I'm *twenty-six*," Ronin snapped. "And I've been a bounty hunter for the better part of five years now. Seven, if you count my apprenticeship."

"You were still definitely out of your league."

"I would've handled it."

"I think I deserve at least forty-five percent." Kent grinned. "You keep the larger share since you were after him for so long."

"You won't get a single coin. He's my bounty, and I've got the parchment to prove it," Ronin said. "You've got nothing."

"Then why are you still talking to me?"

"I don't—" Ronin's eyes narrowed, and he turned down the alley. "I'm leaving now."

"Do you want to know what you did wrong?" Kent called after him.

Ronin didn't stop. "No."

"I mean, aside from underestimating him and engaging him in a public place?"

Now Ronin stopped. He turned back. "Are you looking for a fight, old man?"

Kent smirked. "Please. You would not last three minutes with me."

"I'm not so sure about that." Ronin reached into another of his pouches.

"Your mistake was the same mistake I capitalized upon to end the confrontation as quickly as I did."

Ronin froze. He swallowed. "Fine. Tell me what it was so I can get out of here."

Kent shook his head. "There is still the issue of how we will split the bounty."

Ronin's face scrunched, then it relaxed. "I'll give you fifteen percent. Not a coin more."

Kent extended his hand.

Ronin hesitated at first, but then he shook it.

Kent smiled and released his grip. "I would have accepted a hot meal and a change of clothes."

Ronin glared at him. "So what did I do wrong?"

"I will tell you," Kent said, "over that hot meal. And I would like to ask you some questions in return."

"I don't have time for this, old man."

"Kent. You may call me Kent."

Ronin eyed him. "Just 'Kent?'"

"For now, yes."

"Fine. One meal, after I collect the bounty."

"You mean, after *we* collect the bounty."

"Yes. After *we* collect the bounty."

Kent motioned down the alley. "Lead the way."

WITH A POUCH OF ONE HUNDRED FIFTY GOLD COINS TIED TO HIS HIP, KENT SAT ACROSS the inn's wooden table from Ronin.

They'd visited a local magistrate's office, submitted the bounty warrant, complete with the captain's signature, and collected the sum owed—a thousand pieces of gold. A considerable amount, even given the trouble Ronin had endured to subdue Eusephus.

Kent would've stopped to purchase new clothes if Ronin had let him, but Ronin insisted on sitting down to conclude their conversation first. They'd placed their orders with the innkeeper, and now they sat facing each other, each with a frothy mug of ale before them.

"Get on with it, then," Ronin said. "What did I do wrong?"

"First, I want you to agree to answer my questions."

Ronin sighed. "How many?"

"Very many."

"I don't have time for this," Ronin grumbled. "I need to start chasing my next bounty."

"It will be well worth your time." Kent grinned at him. "I promise."

Ronin rubbed his forehead. "Fine. I'll answer your questions."

"Good." Kent leaned back in his chair. "Your mistake was the same as every other magic-user—*mage* I've encountered. You rely too much on your magic and not enough on what your physical body can do."

Ronin squinted at him. "Go on."

"Eusephus was so wrapped up in trying to kill us with his magic weapons and dealing with magic attacks that he failed to properly address my non-magic attack."

"He was physically swinging his magic weapons, though."

"That did not mean he knew what he was doing." Kent sipped his ale. It had a pleasant hint of sweetness to it. "I will credit him this: he handled them better than I would have expected, but he was by no means as capable as any trained fighter I have ever encountered. Had he been otherwise, I doubt he would have fallen so easily."

"I'm strong and physical. I dodged every one of his attacks."

"Yet you could not breach his defenses."

Ronin looked down at his ale, then he refocused on Kent. "No. I couldn't."

The innkeeper returned with beef stew and bread for each of them.

Due to a lack of funds, Kent hadn't eaten since breakfast that morning, when he'd spent the last few coins given to him by the soldier at the city's gate. The warm aromas set Kent's stomach rumbling, and he tore off a piece of the bread, dipped it in the stew, and ate it.

He finished chewing and swallowed the bite, then he said, "But I could. And I did."

"Normally my skills are enough to subdue my marks. Even other mages." Ronin took a bite of his own.

A few moments passed as they ate, and then Kent resumed the conversation.

"This may seem like a silly question," Kent began, "but how does magic work?"

Ronin looked up at him again. "You're a mage, and you don't know?"

Kent narrowed his gaze. "How could you possibly know that I am a mage?"

Ronin shrugged. "I can just tell. It's sort of a latent ability I got when my powers awakened. I can sense it, somehow."

Kent wondered if he had any sort of latent ability tied to his magic, but he couldn't pinpoint anything specific. "So when a mage's powers appear, that manifestation is called an 'awakening?'"

Ronin eyed him. "You really don't know anything about this?"

"Pretend I am a small child, and you are explaining it to me for the first time."

Ronin eyed him for a long moment. "Awakening is one term that is used. 'Age of discovery' is another. 'Manifestation,' like what you said, isn't common, but I've heard it before. It just depends on what region you're from."

Kent drank from his ale again.

"Speaking of which, you never did tell me where you're from." Ronin ate another bite of stew.

"I would rather not say."

"Your accent sounds Murothian."

Kent's heart started beating faster, but he made sure not to convey any stress.

"I hail from elsewhere, though I spent quite some time in northern Muroth," Kent said. "That was, of course, until my magic 'awakened.' I immediately left the country when I discovered it. As you know, Muroth does not take kindly to mages or the use of magic."

Ronin eyed him again. "Where did you go when you left?"

"Northern Urthia."

"For how long?"

Careful, Kent.

"I am asking the questions," Kent said. "Not you."

Ronin scooped another spoonful of stew into his mouth and motioned toward Kent with his free hand.

"Again, I would like you to explain to me how magic works."

Ronin wiped his mouth with the sleeve of his coat. "That's like asking how the world works."

"Simplify it for me."

"Alright…" Ronin pressed his elbows into the table on either side of his bowl of stew and put his hands on his forehead. "Basically, you concentrate on what you want to happen, and then the magic within you makes it happen."

"How?"

Ronin glanced around, leaned back, and spread his arms wide. "It's *magic*, Kent. Ever heard the expression that something works 'like magic?' People say that because they can't explain how magic works. It just *does*. And that's what makes it *magic*. If I could explain it, I'd be a god instead of a bounty hunter."

"You kept reaching into the pouches you wear on your belt and grasping various objects. I am observant enough to comprehend that your magic revolves around whatever you are holding at that time." Kent nodded at him. "Explain how that works."

"Alright, sure." Ronin dug into one of his pouches and pulled out a bright green leaf.

It might've been the same one he'd used to entangle Kent in the vines, but Kent couldn't be sure. Ronin might've had a lot of them in there for all he knew.

Ronin held it up in his left hand. "See this leaf? Watch this."

Ronin pressed his forefinger against the top of the table. Blue light emanated from under his finger, then it turned green. As he slowly lifted his finger from the table, a green stem sprouted from the dead, gray wood of the table's surface.

It grew another two inches, and leaves formed along its shaft. At five inches in height, a bud appeared, and then a vivid yellow flower bloomed.

Kent watched, enraptured. Until that moment, he'd never considered what beautiful, creative properties magic could have.

Perhaps Muroth had gotten it wrong—perhaps magic wasn't a curse after all.

"If you can imagine it, you can probably make it happen." Ronin removed his hand, and it stopped growing, but it stayed there, a beacon of hope amid the otherwise dark atmosphere of the inn. "But you need fodder to make it happen. And there's a cost."

He held up the leaf again. Instead of being bright green and full of life, it had shriveled and turned brown.

Kent took it from his hand. "What happened to it?"

"I channeled its properties into my magic, and it drained the leaf's essence," Ronin explained. "That's how anima magic works. We use the essence of natural objects to direct the flow of our own magic."

Essence. The soldiers had mentioned that word after Eusephus started wielding his violet weapons. He basically understood what Ronin meant by the word, but he didn't know what "anima" meant. "What is anima?"

Ronin's eyebrows rose. "You know about the three types of magic, don't you?"

Kent stayed quiet.

Ronin face-palmed. "Alright. This is basic stuff. Anima describes natural, or nature-based, magic. Light magic is derived from holy sources and involves light and goodness and happiness and religion and all sorts of other pleasant things. Dark magic comes from the exact opposite sources."

"Evil sources?"

Ronin nodded. "Demons, dark gods, evil magical creatures—whatever you want to believe."

"I see."

"Anima magic is low-cost and easy to learn. The cost of light magic is lots of time and dedication. It's arguably the most powerful magic, but it requires absolute sacrifice of one's self to use it, let alone master it. By contrast, dark magic requires the sacrifice of others."

"As in, murder?"

"More or less. Or the killing of animals or legendary creatures."

"Animals wouldn't fall under anima?" Kent asked.

Ronin shook his head. "It's a fine line. Plants, trees, rocks, water, air, fire, and other elements all fall under anima. Animals, while natural, are living, breathing beings with some capacity for intelligent thought.

"So extracting their essence will kill them, and that blurs the lines between anima and dark magic. The more sentient a being, the graver the sin of stealing their essence becomes."

Kent nodded. "So taking the essence of a bear is worse than taking the essence of a fish."

"Sure." Ronin nodded. "I wouldn't feel good about taking either, but if I were shipwrecked and might drown, I'd grab a fish and try to use its essence to help me breathe underwater or swim better, or both.

"Intent matters, here," Ronin continued. "It would die, but I'd live. And we eat fish all the time, and that's not wrong. But good luck trying to take a bear's essence anyway. It's a damned bear. It would kill you before you succeeded."

"Point taken." Kent sloshed the remainder of his ale around in his mug.

"But dark magic has other manifestations as well," Ronin added. "You don't have to use an essence to become like that thing. You can just use the essence to power other spells. Dark spells."

"And that's what Eusephus was doing?" Ronin nodded.

"You said 'essence,'" Kent said, "but you mentioned things like rocks and water and fire as options for anima users. How can a thing have essence if it is not alive?"

"This was confusing for me at first, too," Ronin replied. "Try not to think of 'essence' and 'life' or being 'alive' as all the same. They're different. A thing's essence *is* tied to its life if the thing is alive, but 'essence' more closely means 'existence.' If it exists, you can probably use its essence for magic."

"You were using a stone earlier, against Eusephus. Explain that."

"Maybe you didn't see it when I grabbed it out of my pouch, but it was a normal-looking, bumpy, decent-sized rock at first. By the time I was done, it had shrunk to a small, smooth stone."

Kent recalled noticing the stone's smoothness when Ronin had dropped it. "Because you used some of its essence."

"I used most of its essence for that one, yeah." Ronin smiled. "I like using rocks because they're durable and laying around everywhere. Leaves are plentiful, too, and they're light. They're not anywhere near as durable, but they have their uses, so I carry a bunch of those as well."

"Does the type of leaf or type of rock matter as far as what you can do with it?"

Ronin shook his head. "The gods were kind to us. If I have a limestone, I can still manipulate basalt. If I've got an oak leaf, I can make the grass do my bidding."

"Or you can make vines on a wall obey your commands."

"Exactly." Ronin scoffed. "I can't believe you don't know any of this. Didn't anyone use magic where you're from?"

"I only recently had my own awakening," Kent confessed.

"How long ago?"

Kent debated whether or not he should admit it to Ronin. He relented. "About eight years ago."

Ronin leaned forward, his eyebrows raised. "You've been sitting on your magic for *eight* years? What in the third hell is wrong with you?"

"I did not know what was happening. Therefore, I did not know whom to turn to."

Ronin nudged his bread around his plate with his knuckles. "That makes sense, I suppose. Your awakening happened really late in life. What are you, fifty-five?"

Kent grunted and shot him a glare. "I am forty-eight, thank you very much."

"Still, an awakening at forty years old is later than anyone I've ever heard of." Ronin smirked at him. "What happened? Did you catch a unicorn or something?"

"Hardly." Kent sighed, remembering that day. "I woke up one morning with blue light coming from my fingers."

"Sounds about right." Ronin held up his hand, and it began to glow with blue light. "You know raw magic is this blue color, right?"

"I do now."

"Watch." Ronin reached for the flower he'd grown on the table and touched one of the flower petals with his glowing forefinger.

The flower petal blackened, but only where he touched it. Then Ronin pulled his hand away.

"Magic is corrosive on a low level, so you can throw a burst of raw magic and do damage," Ronin said.

"But it's more effective if paired with the essence of something else."

"Yep."

Kent nodded. "I think I am beginning to understand."

Ronin smacked the table next to the flower. "Good. It's time I get going, then. These bounties won't turn themselves in."

As Ronin began to stand, Kent said, "I just have one more question."

Ronin sat back down. "Last one."

"More of a request, really."

"What?"

Kent grinned. "I want you to take me with you."

Ronin stared at him. "What?"

"You heard me."

"Is this some sort of sex thing? Because I'm not into men." Ronin looked him over again. "Least of all older men."

"That is very crass." Kent blinked. "No, nothing like that. I want to learn how to use my magic, and I need to earn an income in the process. I have extensive combat and military training with a variety of non-magical weaponry, and as I have proven to you more than once, I know how to take care of myself. I would be an asset to you."

Ronin squinted at him. "So... you want to be a bounty hunter?"

"I more so want to develop my magical skills, but I need to make a living as well. Being a bounty hunter seems like an ideal avenue to achieve both simultaneously."

Kent mused, *And it will better prepare me to one day find my brother and right the wrongs he has done to me.*

"I don't need a partner."

"You mentioned that you had done an apprenticeship prior to striking out on your own. Consider me an apprentice instead."

Ronin shook his head. "Don't need an apprentice, either."

"With two minds, we will capture bounties twice as quickly." Kent smiled. "And I will only require a forty-five percent split, as I am the trainee and you are the experienced one."

"Apprentices get ten percent. That's less than what I gave you for Eusephus."

"I am no mere apprentice. Given my background, I would require far more than ten percent."

"I'm just telling you what apprentices usually get."

Kent grinned. "So you *are* willing to take me on?"

"I—" Ronin's voice stalled. "I didn't say that."

"Sixty-forty split, in your favor." Kent extended his hand. "Do we have an accord?"

"I said I don't need a partner."

"But you cannot deny how much more effective we would be should we work together." Kent kept his hand extended. "And I will teach you physical combat so you can become a more well-rounded bounty hunter."

Ronin hesitated again.

"Come, now. Let us make a deal."

"I want seventy percent," Ronin blurted.

"Nonsense. Sixty percent is more than fair."

Ronin scowled at him. "Fine. We'll try it for one bounty, and we'll see how well it works. If it doesn't, then we'll go our separate ways, no questions asked. Agreed?"

Kent smiled. "Agreed."

They shook hands.

CHAPTER SIX

Six Months Later

"I have to admit, I never could've imagined we'd bring in fourteen bounties in only six months' time." Ronin passed Kent his cut of the most recent bounty, a cool four hundred seventy-five gold coins. "And dangerous ones, at that."

It marked their biggest score since they'd started working together, and it had been one of their easiest hauls yet, thanks to Kent's strategic planning and their combined execution.

"Who is our next target?" Kent stuffed the coins into his satchel.

"Whoa, easy there." Ronin held up his hands. "Why don't we take some time off instead? I've got a cousin who owns an estate on the island of Caclos. It's going to get cold here within the next few months, but Caclos is supposed to be incredible this time of year."

"It is supposed to be incredible *every* time of the year."

"All the more reason to go." Ronin leaned nearer to him. "And the women there are said to be the most exotic beauties on the continent."

Kent smiled. "I have heard that as well."

"Then let's go. We have more than enough coin, and the only bounties currently available are from Muroth. As mages, we can't go there."

"No." Kent shook his head. "Certainly not."

Though he wanted to go back and avenge himself upon Fane, Kent still wasn't ready to do so. He'd grown in his abilities to use his magic over the last six months, but he had much more to learn. The parchment in Kent's pocket was a prime example of how much he still did not know.

"So how about it? Why don't we take a holiday?"

Kent rubbed his chin. He hadn't had anything resembling a holiday since before he'd taken over most of his father's affairs nearly four years prior. "I suppose it would not hurt to spend some of our coin. We have accumulated quite the sum over the last six months."

"Yes, we have." Ronin grinned. "I'll go book us passage."

Kent raised his eyebrows. "Right now?"

"We're only a few hundred yards from the docks. I'm sure we can charter a vessel to leave within a few days. Maybe even tomorrow."

Kent smiled again. "If you say so."

As Ronin hurried off, Kent picked a stone up from the street. He held it in his left hand and summoned his magic.

It pulsed through his body like a flow of cool water and pooled in his fingertips. Several other stones from the street rose into the air and began to orbit him, just as Ronin had shown him.

But what Ronin hadn't shown him interested him far more. He'd invested in some rare texts and tomes about magical techniques since he'd started earning coin, and he'd realized that he knew only a fraction of what could be known about anima magic.

Kent carefully pulled the old parchment from his trouser pocket, unfolded it, and began to read it. It instructed him to focus on the technique of making the element in question—in this case, rocks— form a barrier around his hand.

He concentrated hard on the technique, and the stones stopped orbiting. Instead, they formed into a shell that covered his right fist and part of his wrist, just as the parchment had described.

Incredible. It was working.

Six months ago, he'd lacked any semblance of control over his magical abilities. He could barely manage to keep them hidden, let alone use them to achieve his own ends. Despite all he'd lost, Kent regretted not having studied magic sooner, even though such practices were strictly forbidden in his world.

He read the parchment some more. The language was ancient Aletian, named for the long-extinct culture that had discovered and colonized the continent of Aletia. He'd only begun to learn the language over the last several months, but he'd managed to fill in the gaps with critical thought and cross-referencing with other tomes and texts.

The writing was faded, too, and the parchment was worn, but he'd pretty well determined what he needed to do next—he needed to test the magic.

Tacitly maintaining his concentration on the technique, Kent glanced around for a target to test the effect on. Across the street stood a stone building in disrepair. A signpost extended from the front of the building above the door, but no sign hung from it. Its windows were dark, vacant, and devoid of glass.

Perfect. Kent headed over to the alley adjacent to it. He positioned himself in front of one of its side walls, also made of stone, glanced up and down the alley, and checked the parchment again.

He hesitated. If it didn't work, he'd break his hand.

But there is only one way to know for sure if it works. Kent folded and tucked the parchment back into one of his trouser pockets.

He concentrated his magic into his knuckles, pulled his rock-covered hand back for a punch, and then slammed it into the wall.

Kent's fist broke through the stone with a burst of blue light and punctured into the building itself. His shoulder caught in the hole, stopping his momentum.

Kent couldn't believe it. He had literally just punched through a stone wall.

He pulled his arm out of the hole. The rocks covering his hand and wrist were mostly gone, and what few remained fell off to the alley floor. The rock he'd been holding dropped from his open hand, now a small, smooth pebble.

Unbelievable. Yet he'd just seen it with his own eyes. The technique had worked.

Was there anything magic *couldn't* do? With enough study and practice, perhaps it had no limits.

No wonder the Murothians feared Inoth's power. If it was possible to break through stone walls with the aid of magic, what good were the walls and fortresses Muroth had constructed over the years?

Kent imagined what he might be able to do to Fane with power like this.

The possibilities were endless.

He brushed the dust off of his sleeve and turned back toward the street.

Ronin stood there, glancing around, looking for him.

Kent started to wave and opened his mouth to call out, but another man approached Ronin instead. Kent stopped, wary.

The man wore a dark blue cloak, accented with diamond-shaped patches of gold fabric on the back. The cloak's hood was down. He handed Ronin a piece of parchment and then left.

As Ronin studied the parchment, his face scrunched into a scowl. Then he lowered the parchment to his side and shook his head.

Kent exited the alley and approached him.

"There you are," Ronin said.

"Bad news?" Kent nodded toward the parchment.

"I'm afraid so." Ronin sighed and rubbed his forehead. "I've been summoned to appear before the head of the Inothian Army, General Deoward, over the incident with Eusephus. Apparently the captain who signed for the bounty all those months ago really did lodge that complaint."

"And they are just now broaching the subject?" Kent squinted at him.

Ronin nodded. "They want to question me regarding what happened."

"When?"

"Now, it seems. I am to report to the palace immediately."

"Hunera Palace? They mean to question you in the queen's palace itself?"

"Yes. The barracks are adjacent to the palace." Ronin crumpled the parchment and threw it into the gutter that ran along the street. Soiled, stinking water soaked into it, and it began to unfold again as the water saturated it. "So our trip to Caclos is on hold for the time being."

"I should accompany you," Kent offered. "I was there, after all. I can provide testimony to your benefit."

"You told me I had indeed endangered everyone there because of how I handled the situation." Ronin eyed him. "And now you want to help me?"

"You have upheld your side of our bargain honorably. The least I can do is stand by your side at such an inquiry and try to cast you in a favorable light," Kent said.

Ronin grinned. "I'd wanted to ask you, but I didn't want to assume anything."

Kent waved his hand. "Please. We are partners. Of course I will stand by you."

"Thank you." Ronin's grin widened, and they started walking north, leaving the parchment behind them in the gutter. "Never been to Hunera Palace, have you?"

Kent smirked. "I have never had occasion to visit."

"Well, let me tell you—you're in for quite the experience." Ronin patted Kent's shoulder. "Maybe we'll even catch a glimpse of the queen. She's supposed to be very pretty, though I've never seen her up close."

Forty-five minutes later, they reached the palace gates. Despite his growth in using magic, Kent had made a habit of carrying a sword with him, and he had to turn it in to the guards waiting at the palace gates. They catalogued it and stored it for him in a small shed nearby.

Then Ronin led them past the dozens of guards and through the robust, gold-plated doors that led to the palace's courtyard.

Kent could hardly believe any of it. He'd just walked onto the palace grounds of Muroth's sworn adversary, and he'd done so uninhibited, without an army, without a single weapon, all because someone he knew had been summoned.

If only Father could have seen me now. The memory of his father stanched his excitement, but he pushed it aside.

Flowers, trees, and bushes, all expertly groomed, embellished the white- and light-gray marble that made up the courtyard's pathways, planting beds, and the palace's exterior. Crystalline water flowed from a fountain topped with a statue that resembled the goddess Laeri that stood in her temple.

Kent took in the palace's beauty and recalled his many trips to Lowmir Keep, the emperor's home, in Muroth. The keep had conveyed a rugged, darker feel, especially compared to the brightness of the Inothian queen's palace. The countries really did contrast sharply with each other.

Another contingent of guards protected the grand entrance to the palace itself, and they directed Ronin to a building on the far right side of the courtyard.

It, too, was constructed of comparable white-and-light-gray marble, but at three stories tall, it stood only about a fifth as high as the towering palace. Windows only marked the top two stories.

A matching building sat across it from the courtyard, and together they formed two of the courtyard's three perimeter walls, with the palace itself being the third. Kent guessed they were military barracks used for housing soldiers, and when they entered the building, his suspicions were confirmed.

As he took in the nuances of the barracks, Kent couldn't help but marvel at what value this experience would have held for him less than a year prior. To be able to enter the heart of his worst enemies' military operations and report back could have totally altered Muroth's approach to dealing with Inoth.

A man with the double-diamonds' rank of major on the shoulders of his tan uniform met them just inside the door. He led them through the barracks, past soldiers' dormitories, past a large library full of worn tomes and papers, and past a modest armory with several racks of weapons crammed inside.

Kent smirked. Perhaps the *library* was their armory instead.

The major brought them into a huge, high-ceilinged room paneled with maple wood. Modest windows adorned the upper half of the room's back wall, spaced several feet apart. Their height, and the iron bars that reinforced them, made for effective security measures, should the palace ever be attacked.

A long table stretched before Kent and Ronin, and five silver-haired men sat in a row on the other side of it. Each of them wore tan military coats and scribbled on sheets of parchment spread out on the table before them.

Three diamonds accented the shoulders of the two on each side, but the one in the middle wore four diamonds. Kent had seen high-ranking Inothian officers' uniforms only twice before, both times on the battlefield near the Murothian wall.

The major bowed and introduced Ronin and Kent to the five men, but he addressed the bearded man in the center as General Deoward.

"Thank you, Major," General Deoward said. "Proceed with your other duties."

"Yes, General." The major bowed again, then he turned and left the room.

Kent glanced back. Aside from the five men in the room with Ronin and him, only two guards stood near the doors, and they followed the major out and shut the grand doors behind them.

"Which of you is Ronin Shroud, the bounty hunter?" General Deoward asked.

Ronin stepped forward, but twenty feet still separated him from the edge of the table. "I am, General."

Deoward turned toward the man seated directly to his left and muttered instructions to him. The man began writing anew on his parchment.

Deoward faced Ronin again. "You're aware of why you've been summoned?"

"I am, sir." Ronin swallowed. "I hope my immediate response to your summons will be credited to me in light of this matter."

"Noted." Deoward studied him for a long moment, and then turned to Kent.

At first, Kent thought nothing of it. But when Deoward's bulldog face shifted with a subtle smile, a ripple of concern hit Kent's gut.

General Deoward stood and said, "Welcome to Inoth, Lord Etheridge."

CHAPTER SEVEN

Kent froze at first, then he glanced at Ronin.

Ronin refused to make eye contact with him and continued staring straight ahead.

Kent quickly scanned the room for potential exits. With the windows high up and covered in bars, the doors through which he'd entered appeared to be the only way out—short of trying to summon enough magic to blow through one of the walls. He'd already done it once today, but he couldn't pull enough rocks from anywhere nearby to do it.

As Kent considered his options, the doors behind him swung open. He looked back.

The major had returned with a half-dozen other soldiers, and the two guards who'd been posted at the doors entered as well.

Kent wished he hadn't given up his sword. He reached into one of the pouches on his belt for a match to ignite some fire magic.

"Halt!" the major shouted. "Or we will strike you down where you stand."

Kent released the match in his fingers and slowly pulled his hand out of the pouch. He'd never get it lit in time.

Despite how quickly his skills had developed and the size of the room affording plenty of space to maneuver, he stood no chance against fifteen skilled mages, possibly including Ronin.

"I'm sorry, Kent," Ronin said.

Kent turned toward him with his hands at his sides and glowered at him.

"Had you told me the truth when we met, I never would've had to do this," Ronin continued. "But I had no choice. Once I learned who you were, I had to comply."

The parchment. Ronin had crumpled it up and thrown it into the gutter—not because he'd been upset about what it said, but because he'd wanted to hide it from Kent without seeming obvious about it.

Worse still, he'd managed to get Kent to walk right into his own demise without even a hint of hesitation.

Kent smirked. Ronin had been clever ever since the day Kent had met him. It was part of why they were so effective in bringing in bounties together.

"Lord Etheridge," Deoward said. "I hereby place you under arrest as a foreign combatant, agent of espionage, and enemy of the state."

Kent shook his head and chuckled. "If only you knew how grossly inaccurate all three of those claims were, General."

Two of the soldiers grabbed Kent by his arms while another stripped the pouches from his belt. Then the major clamped a pair of vivid blue shackles around his wrists, just like the ones the soldiers had put on Eusephus six months earlier.

Kent had since learned that the enchanted blue metal would block him or any other mage from doing any magic.

Deoward motioned with his head, and two of the guards ushered Kent toward the doors. But the rest remained in the room.

As Kent watched, the major produced another set of shackles and started toward Ronin.

"What?" Ronin recoiled several steps deeper into the room, away from the soldiers. "General, I complied with your summons! I turned in a known enemy of Inoth. I should be rewarded, not arrested!"

"You aided him in his efforts to spy on our lands and country," Deoward said. "Therefore, you are guilty of those crimes as well."

"Unknowingly!" Ronin yelled. "I didn't know who he was!"

"Major, arrest him and get him out of here. I don't have time for this," Deoward grunted.

"Yes, General." The major moved toward Ronin with his shackles held high.

Ronin kept his distance from the soldiers and reached into one of his pouches, and then the soldiers hauled Kent out of the room.

KENT HAD SEEN WORSE CELLS THAN THE ONE THE SOLDIERS THREW HIM IN, BUT HE'D never actually ventured *inside* any of them.

Long ago, Inothians had carved and dug into the ground beneath where the barracks now sat and shaped out several long rows of dozens of six-by- eight-foot cells in the caverns beneath. Sporadic torches provided the only lighting down there, and it stank of feces, urine, and rotting flesh—typical dungeon smells.

They'd taken the blue shackles off of Kent's wrists, probably because bars made of the same vivid blue metal framed his cell on three sides. Over the last six months, he'd often mused how much easier the fight against Inoth would've been if Muroth had learned about that metal long ago.

A jagged, uneven rock wall formed the back of the cell. They'd locked him inside, leaving him to little more than his own thoughts and a bucket in the corner.

Kent's nose wrinkled. Come what may, he didn't want to be in that cell for any longer than necessary.

He assessed the cell and considered what it would take to make a way out. Manipulating the bars wasn't an option. The enchanted metal would repel any magic-based attempts to create an escape.

The rock wall at the back of the cell didn't appear much better. Even if he replicated his rock-punching feat from earlier that day, he'd be punching into a wall of solid rock that never ended. Likewise, he couldn't hope to escape through the straw-covered floor, either.

Perhaps if he did it enough times on the ceiling, he'd eventually break through to the upper level, but what then? He'd be back in the barracks, surrounded by Inothian soldiers and guards, and they'd either kill him or just put him in another cell.

Kent was stuck there, at least until they decided what to do with him. No question.

Part of the back wall curved down and protruded out, shaped almost like a long seating area. With no bed in the cell, he'd either need to sleep on the floor, or he could try to make do with the rock protrusion.

Perhaps some thoughtful mage had reshaped the wall specifically for that purpose.

Kent headed over to it and sat, then he lay down. The flattest part of its surface was too short for him, even if he curled his legs close to his chest.

But he was a tall guy—a solid three inches north of six feet. Maybe he could make it work if he let his legs dangle over the end.

As he sat upright again, something crinkled in his trouser pocket.

He cursed and bolted to his feet, then he gingerly pulled out the archaic parchment he'd stuffed into his trousers earlier that day. It had ripped, and some of its edges had flaked off, but it hadn't crumbled.

Kent cursed under his breath all the same. He'd been careless, and he'd damaged it. Now, on top of translating ancient Aletian, he'd have to take extra care to preserve what remained of the parchment.

Fortunately, he'd absorbed the technique of the first side of the parchment. He'd reserved the back side for learning some other time, though, because of its increased complexity.

No time like the present. If Kent had anything, he had time. He sat down again, flipped the parchment over, and started mentally translating where he could.

Five minutes later, he'd only scratched the surface of the translation when the familiar sound of the cellblock door opened down the corridor.

Kent stood, carefully folded the parchment, and tucked it back into his pocket. He'd be more careful with it from now on.

He approached the bars and tried to look down the dim corridor.

Before long, a pair of guards dragged a limp form past Kent's cell and opened the door to the vacant cell next to his.

BLOOD MERCENARIES ORIGINS

Kent recognized Ronin's brown-and-grey cloak first, but he didn't recognize Ronin's face at all.

It was covered in blood.

The guards tossed Ronin into the adjacent cell, and he collapsed into an unmoving heap on the floor with a wet *smack*. He lay on his side with his right arm pinned under his torso and with his back facing away from Kent.

Part of Kent felt sorry for him, but the other part—a much, much larger part—didn't care. Ronin had gotten what he'd deserved for turning Kent in. And had Ronin not tried to fight back, he wouldn't be in the condition he was in now.

The guards locked the door, cast cold looks at Kent, and then headed back out of the corridor.

Kent waited for a few minutes after he heard the door shut before he removed the parchment from his pocket again. Then he took a seat on the rock protrusion and resumed his studying.

He started by rehashing the handful of words he'd translated prior to Ronin's arrival. Nearly an hour later, he'd ascertained the purpose of that page of parchment —if he was correct in his translating.

Evidently, mages of incredible power could marshal enough concentration to go beyond simply manipulating the properties of elemental magic; they could actually take on the physical properties of the element they wished to wield.

So a mage could *become* liquid, like water, or hard, like metal, or transparent, like air.

He thought back to how he'd punched through the wall with his hand wreathed in stones from the street. If his translation was accurate, and if he could master the technique the page described, he might not have to wreathe his hands in rock to achieve such feats anymore.

It was an ancient, wondrous power, known only to a few elite mages and arch-mages. And now that Kent knew it was possible, it put him closer to that select group. And that's where he wanted to be.

It's where he *needed* to be, if he meant to fulfill his quest for revenge on Fane.

Could a mage then learn to fly, if he were to take the essence of a bird? Kent wondered. *Or would he become a bird instead?*

The latter possibility seemed less appealing.

As Kent returned to his studying, a moan sounded from Ronin's cell.

Kent lowered the parchment and looked at him.

Ronin rolled onto his stomach and pushed up to his hands and knees. He gingerly dabbed at his red face with his fingertips, and then he crawled over to the bars separating his cell from Kent's and pulled himself up to his feet. He faced Kent.

Both of Ronin's eyes remained closed—his left eye was swollen shut, and dried blood had caked over his right eye. So far, Ronin hadn't realized that Kent occupied the cell next door.

Ronin winced, leaned his left shoulder against the bars, and started picking at the dried blood near his non-swollen eye. He bared his teeth and sucked air through his mouth as he gradually peeled the red-brown layer of film from his face.

He exhaled a sharp breath and dropped the flecks of blood to the cell floor. He blinked his now-liberated right eye a few times, rubbed it, blinked again, and muttered curses. Then he turned toward the bars and saw Kent watching him. He cursed again and turned away.

Kent just kept staring at him, silently. He carefully folded the parchment and tucked it in his pocket again.

Ronin staggered over to his own rock protrusion, one much larger and longer than Kent's. They should've put Kent in Ronin's cell, and vice versa. Then Kent might've been able to stretch out a bit more.

Ronin, five inches shorter, would've better fit the protrusion in Kent's cell. He sat on the rocks and leaned against the wall, his single good eye fixed on Kent.

Dried blood from his nose clung to his upper lip and chin, and more had caked on his forehead from a gash near his hairline. The blond hair on the right side of his head was now red-brown, and bruises colored his cheeks with purples and yellows.

"Kent…" Ronin started. "Look, I'm sorry."

Kent didn't move.

"I—I got scared. Inothians *hate* Murothians." Ronin shifted on the rocks. "If I didn't turn you in, and they found me out, I would've been committing treason."

Kent continued staring at Ronin.

"C'mon, man," Ronin continued. "The notice said you were Murothian *nobility.* Switch it around. If a Murothian man didn't turn in an Inothian when he had the chance, what would you, as a noble, have done to the Murothian?"

He would have died a traitor's death—far worse than what the Inothian would have gotten. Ronin had a point, but it didn't excuse his choices.

"Aren't you going to say anything to me?" Ronin asked.

Kent exhaled a calm breath through his nostrils.

Ronin huffed and blinked slowly. "What would you have done?"

"Were our positions reversed, I would have told you about the notice first," Kent said. "Then I would have given you a choice: comply or run. And then I would have given you a head start while I went to report you as missing."

"You think that would've worked out for you, given how I look right now?"

"I would have asked you to punch me to make it look more convincing."

"That only works in fables and fairytales."

"My point is," Kent continued, "I would have valued our friendship over my own life."

"Garbage," Ronin uttered.

Kent leaned forward, surprised. "I beg your pardon?"

"You heard me. That's garbage." Ronin's singular eye stared daggers at Kent. "If you had really valued our friendship, you would've told me who you really were when we first met."

Kent scoffed. "So you could have turned me in right then and there?"

"You don't know that I would have done."

"Yes, I do. If you were willing to turn me in after six months of building friendship and trust, you absolutely would have turned me in before."

"Then you should've told me at some point before this happened."

"I did not *know* this was going to happen."

"Don't play dumb with me," Ronin said. "You know what I meant. If you really meant to build trust with me, you would've told me the truth about who you were."

Kent remained silent.

"I should've known better anyway. Everything about you felt… off, especially when we got to talking. Your late magic awakening. Your Murothian accent. Your nice clothes. Not knowing the term 'mage' or anything about how magic worked." Ronin leaned back farther and rubbed his forehead. "Now it all makes sense."

Silence hung in the wretched air between them for a long moment.

"I am sorry I withheld the truth from you," Kent said.

Ronin looked at him again. "Well, like I said, I'm sorry I turned you in. I didn't know what else to do."

"I cannot fault you for turning me in," Kent admitted. "I understand the predicament you were in, and I forgive you for making the choice that you made."

Ronin nodded. "Thank you. I suppose I forgive you, too."

Kent cleared his throat. "I suppose I do not need to explain what a miscalculation it was on your part to try to fight that many Inothian soldiers."

"No." Ronin moaned. "The last thing I need is another tactical lecture from you. Consider this one a lesson learned the hard way."

"Then I suppose it is best that we focus on finding a way out of this mess."

"I'm open to suggestions."

"I am not very familiar with Inothian law. What will be done to us?"

Ronin sighed. "Execution, most likely."

Kent frowned. Execution meant he'd never be able to take his revenge upon Fane. There had to be another way.

Ronin added, "We'll get a trial before some sort of magistrate, but hardly any trials in exoneration. Usually the accusation is enough to bring forth some measure of justice. Or… punishment. That's probably a better word.

"And in our case, the evidence is clear. We're both more or less guilty. You definitely are, obviously. I'll be convicted of treason for being associated with you, because, well, I *was* associated with you. For six months."

"Will it help if I testify to your ignorance of my identity?" Kent asked.

Ronin shook his swollen head. "I doubt it. But if you want to try, I won't stop you. I need all the help I can get."

"How long until we can expect the trial?"

"Could be an hour. Could be days." Ronin shrugged. "I really don't know."

"Then I have more studying to do." Kent fished the parchment out of his pocket again. He couldn't afford to keep doing that, as the parchment wore out exponentially faster every time he did so, even with the great care he took to preserve it.

Ronin leaned forward. "You're always studying something."

"I have a lifetime of catching up to do in learning to master my magic. Studying is the quickest way to better myself."

"I'd say you've caught on pretty quickly over the past six months. You have a knack for it. That's for sure." Ronin leaned back again, and then he shifted so he could lie down on the protrusion.

Kent translated in silence, wishing he'd had the opportunity to write down his findings. Instead, he committed to memory what he could.

Hours later, after translating, checking, re-translating, and committing the text to memory, he felt ready to try the technique. He inhaled a long breath, then he exhaled it slowly and pressed his hand against the brown rock that made up the back wall of the cell. He closed his eyes and began to concentrate.

"Finally figured something out?" Ronin asked from his left side. Kent's eyes opened, and he lowered his hand and turned toward him.

"Possibly. I was just about to try it."

Ronin raised his hands. "Sorry. Go ahead."

Kent faced the rock wall again and pressed his hand against the wall again, on a spot about level with his head.

He resumed his concentration, closed his eyes again, and focused on the cool rock under his palm. He imagined his hand becoming one with the rock, melding to it, taking on its properties, and then he let his magic flow into the wall.

With his eyes still closed, Kent stood there, motionless. He pumped more magic into the rock, cycling it through the wall and pulling it back into himself, slowly. Tediously. He opened his eyes for a look.

"What in the third hell?" Ronin's voice snapped Kent's concentration.

Kent jerked his hand away. Blue light flickered in his fingertips, then it faded to nothing. He growled at Ronin, "What is the matter? I was making progress!"

Ronin nodded toward him, his gaze fixed on Kent's hand. "Look."

Kent looked down at his hand.

It had turned brown and bumpy, and the soft glow of torchlight glowed on its surface. It had turned to rock.

Kent held his hand up, and the effect crept away from his wrist, along his palm, and up his fingers until it disappeared entirely, restoring his hand to normal.

"Tell me you saw that?" Ronin grabbed the bars separating their cells.

Kent gave him a smile. "I saw it. I just cannot believe it worked."

"Look at the wall." Ronin pointed.

Kent turned to look where he'd touched it. What had once been a rough wall of rock now bore a faint indentation roughly the shape of Kent's hand. Very subtle—easily missed and certainly not clear to anyone but Kent in such low light.

Then again, maybe it had been like that before, and he just hadn't realized it?

No. He'd seen his hand take on the properties of the rock. So had Ronin.

It was unmistakable.

He hadn't been able to test what such a technique might do, but he'd achieved the technique itself. The parchment had been right.

Kent pressed his hand against the rock again. Perhaps if he tried again, he might be able to maintain the technique for longer and—

Clank. The familiar sound of the cellblock door opening halted the flow of Kent's magic, and he pulled his hand down. He quickly folded the parchment and slipped it back into his pocket.

Several sets of armored footsteps and jingling keys traipsed down the cellblock toward them. Kent met Ronin's eyes, and neither of them said a word.

Seven soldiers in Inoth's standard-issue leather armor lined up outside of Kent's cell and Ronin's cell—three at each door.

Kent recognized the extra soldier—notably by his perpetually grave expression— as one of the dungeon's guards. He'd been the one to open the door both for Kent and when the soldiers had thrown Ronin into his cell.

Now he unlocked Kent's cell.

The first soldier held a fiery torch. He reached into the torch with his right hand, and it ignited with flames that alternated orange and telltale magic-blue.

The second soldier held a fistful of straw, and the straw on the floor around Kent's feet trembled and wobbled as if ready to leap at him at any moment.

Kent smirked. It was a sound, simple strategy—if Kent resisted, one soldier would rally the kindling around him, and the other would ignite it with the magic flames enveloping his hand. In such a small space, Kent couldn't hope to fight back.

The third soldier produced a familiar pair of blue shackles. He clasped them to Kent's wrists as the grumpy dungeon guard opened Ronin's cell next, and those three soldiers matched the approach of the ones in Kent's cell.

"What's happening?" Ronin asked.

The guards didn't respond.

Ronin stepped toward the one with the shackles. "I said, what's—"

"Get back!" the soldier with the shackles snapped.

In Ronin's cell, the fire around the soldier's fist flared bright, and the straw on his floor lifted into the sky and began circling Ronin. The soldier with the flames drew his hand back, ready to hurl fire at Ronin.

CHAPTER EIGHT

R onin slowly raised his hands, and the soldier with the shackles drew in close and shoved him back hard.

Ronin landed on his rear-end on the rock protrusion. He braced his hands against the protrusion to steady himself, then he pressed his palms against his hips.

Kent caught a glint of blue metal sliding into Ronin's left sleeve, then he slowly raised his hands.

"Sorry," Ronin said. "Sorry."

As Ronin allowed the soldier to clamp the blue shackles on his wrists, Kent tried to make eye contact with him through the bars, but Ronin wouldn't meet his eyes.

Had Ronin managed to get a key? If so, what did he plan to do with it?

Whatever Ronin had in mind, Kent admired him for it. Snagging the key on its own was a bold move, and if it somehow led to their escape, Kent certainly wouldn't complain.

The six soldiers escorted Kent and Ronin out of the cellblock and back up to the barracks' ground floor. Afternoon sunlight poured in through the barracks windows near the ceiling, reminding Kent that he hadn't eaten anything all day.

Apparently, rumors about Kent's presence must've spread because every Inothian soldier along his path scowled at him as he passed by.

Eight months ago, he would've sneered back at them, his sworn enemies, but now he'd virtually become one of them—a magic-using citizen living and working in Inoth.

Kent couldn't fault them for their disdain, though. He'd overseen the killings of countless numbers of their countrymen over the years, mostly by way of battles along the Murothian border.

But he'd also led his fair share of raids into Inoth and presided over numerous executions of captured Inothian soldiers. At the time, it had all made sense to him. It didn't anymore.

It was far too late to make recompense now, though. The soldiers were undoubtedly taking Ronin and Kent to trial, and soon after, he would pay for his old transgressions.

As they walked, Kent's attitude soured. If Inoth executed him, he wouldn't get his vengeance on Fane. Perhaps even worse, he would die as a nobody, and then Fane would have truly won. The idea grated on him, and he resolved to fight for his life. He had too much to live for to give up now.

At the end of the barracks, the soldiers escorted Kent and Ronin through a guard station separating the barracks from the palace proper instead of taking them back outside.

Kent frowned. He would've liked to see the courtyard again, at least, before his inevitable execution.

They traipsed through halls that grew more and more ornate the farther and higher into the palace they climbed.

The raw utility of the barracks yielded to the regality of the palace corridors, rich with tapestries, art, and fine white marble walls. Doors made of dark wood, adorned with silver handles and keyholes punctuated the halls.

This will certainly be a nice place to die. Kent sighed. Then he shook the thought away. He'd determined to fight, and fight he would. He couldn't prematurely give in to defeat.

The soldiers ushered them around a corner and toward a pair of comparably decadent doors, spread wide open to reveal a cavernous room inside.

Its grandeur surpassed anything Kent had ever seen, yet it reminded him of the Temple of Laeri in many ways, namely how the room's black interior walls closely matched the temple's exterior.

But as they headed inside, walking on a floor constructed of white-and-black marble in a tessellation of hexagonal tiles, the ceiling captured Kent's attention.

At its height, the ceiling had to reach several hundred feet above them. From Kent's perspective, it likely fed into the palace's central spire, visible from virtually anywhere in the city.

Shafts of waning sunlight shined through the slim windows that stretched up at regular intervals as the ceiling ascended, and crystals lining the ceiling's ascending walls shimmered gold like a sunset on the Tahn Sea.

As Kent marveled, the soldiers shoved him farther into the grand room.

Ahead of them, a wide platform, black like the marble walls and raised two feet above the floor, lay on the far end of the room. Two rows of white, marble pillars framed a central walkway across the floor tiles. Golden lamps alight with fire stood near the pillars.

Dozens of sets of Inothian eyes watched Kent as he walked down the center aisle.

He passed a rainbow of nobles dressed in fine robes and cloaks, officials and heads of state clad in tailored Inothian garments, and merchants wearing exotic fabrics from all over the continent.

Among them, Kent saw commoners as well, albeit only a few.

Elite Inothian soldiers clad in white leather armor, gauntlets, and greaves stood at each pillar, their keen eyes searching everyone in the room except for Kent and Ronin. A line of five elite soldiers also stood between the edge of the platform and the court.

Behind the elite soldiers and atop the platform loomed an imposing white chair, tall, regal, and stark against the platform and the walls. As Kent drew nearer, he realized it had been carved out of translucent white crystals—or perhaps just one very large crystal.

Crystal jutted out from the top and the sides of the chair, giving it a raw feel, especially poignant against the otherwise immaculate room. The chair's arms were smooth on the top, and a plush, red cushion adorned the seat.

Kent's mind sparked with understanding at the sight. They weren't being brought before a magistrate. They were being brought before Inothian royalty, perhaps even the queen herself.

And that chair was the country's seat of power—the Inothian throne.

Two smaller chairs sat one on each side of the crystal throne, both white but not made of crystal. They looked to be made of marble instead, but Kent couldn't be sure.

The soldiers ushered Kent and Ronin forward, and the pattern on the floor changed. A straight line of five individual red hexagonal tiles, spaced equally, punctuated the sea of black and white tiles.

The soldiers positioned Kent and Ronin on two of the red tiles, one on each side of the centermost red tile.

Something hit the back of Kent's left knee, and it buckled. He dropped to one knee, ready to whirl around and bash the soldier in his face. Instead, he quelled his instincts, regained his calm, and only shot a glare back at the soldier.

Kent faced forward in time to see the black wall behind the throne open, revealing a passageway beyond.

Several figures emerged from the passageway, led by a dark-skinned bald man of impressive size. He looked to be near in age to Kent, and he wore black metal armor, polished to a high shine. It was some of the finest armor Kent had ever seen.

The man glowered at Kent as he stepped around the throne and stood next to it, between it and the chair next to the throne.

He looked formidable, and his perpetual scowl and the hulking sword hanging from his hip helped with the effect. Probably from Caclos, by the look of him.

Kent found himself hoping to stay alive if only for the chance to test his mettle against the man.

Four other soldiers, also clad in comparable black armor, came out next, and they stood on the outsides of the smaller chairs, two on each side. Likely the queen's royal guards.

Then a pale young man, probably in his early twenties, stepped forth.

He had blond hair and wore a fine white coat, embroidered with a white-on-white pattern that Kent couldn't discern from that distance, and white trousers. No sword hung from his side, but he wore a small, crystal crown atop his head.

Kent stifled a grin. It looked like the kid was wearing a tiara.

The kid sat down in the chair to the left of the throne, his posture upright and rigid.

But Kent's musings jolted to a stop at the sight of the next person to emerge, and the throne room descended into silent reverence.

She wore a white gown adorned with sparkling crystals—or perhaps diamonds—complementing her fair skin and blonde hair. Her full, red lips invited suggestion almost as much as the look in her light blue eyes. Her high cheekbones, the touches of age around her eyes and mouth, the neutral expression on her face—it all enraptured Kent.

He'd never seen anyone like her, not anywhere in his travels, and certainly not anywhere in Muroth. She exuded a maturity and an unparalleled grace to any woman he'd ever met, yet she looked younger than him, perhaps by five or ten years.

A crystalline crown sat atop her head, larger than the pale kid's tiara, but only slightly. It, too, sparkled, and it suited her perfectly. She wore both the crown and the heavy, invisible robes of power well.

She rounded the crystal throne and sat on it, and two female servants scurried to the front to straighten and adjust the drape of her dress. Then they scurried away just as quickly and took up posts near the passageway which remained open.

It made sense now why the soldiers had made Ronin and Kent kneel— though they could've just asked instead.

The queen reclined in the crystal throne and studied Kent and Ronin.

Because they were kneeling, and because of the height of the platform and the throne, she loomed over them, even from such a distance and from behind the line of elite soldiers separating her from everyone else.

The large Caclosian man bellowed, "All hail Queen Aveyna of House Armanix."

"All hail," came the crowd's unison reply.

Queen Aveyna's stern gaze fixed on Kent in the subsequent silence.

"You are Lord Kent Etheridge, of the noble Murothian house by the same name?" Her alto voice cut through the quietness.

Kent stared back at her. "I am."

No one said a word. Then the big bald guy nodded slightly.

Thwack. Sharp, quick pain hit the back of Kent's head, but it faded as quickly as it came. He glanced back to see one of the soldiers retreating into position.

"You will address Queen Aveyna as 'Your Highness' or 'Your Majesty,'" the bald guy grunted, his words heavily accented.

Kent cleared his throat and added, "I am, *Your Highness.*"

Queen Aveyna glanced at the bald guy. "Perhaps we ought to conclude the trial there. He has already admitted to being an enemy of the state."

The bald guy turned and bowed slightly, his gaze set on her. "If it so pleases Your Majesty, I will make it so."

She lifted her hand and waved it, a small dismissive action reinforced by a nation's-worth of power. "No, Grak. Not yet."

Grak, gave a slight nod and then faced forward again. "Rise, Lord Etheridge," Queen Aveyna said.

Kent rose to his feet.

"You are doubtless aware of our ongoing conflict with your country. So why are you, of all people, in Inoth?" Queen Aveyna asked.

"It is a long story, Your Highness," Kent replied.

"Abbreviate it."

Kent nodded. "My magic awakened nearly nine years ago, far later than is normal, as I have learned. Given my pedigree and standing within my country, I could not reveal this element about myself to anyone."

"But it came to light nonetheless," Kent continued, "and I was forced to flee my homeland. So I came here, the one place where I knew Muroth could not follow me."

Queen Aveyna studied him again, silent like the rest of the room. Kent quickly added, "Your Highness."

She blinked and then said, "I see the wisdom in your rationale. Your presumption that your anonymity in our nation would remain intact is what failed you in the end."

"Yes, Your Highness."

"That is, if your story is true."

Kent glanced at Ronin. "I am happy to demonstrate my abilities, if you will allow me to do so, Your Highness. Or my partner can vouch for them, if he is willing."

Queen Aveyna looked to Ronin, then she looked back at Kent. "That will not be necessary. You have already confessed to your identity, so whether or not your story about awakening to your magic is true, it is irrelevant given that you hail from the most scorned house in all of Muroth—by Inothian standards."

"I did not choose my birthright, nor did I choose to have my awakening."

"Yet here we are nonetheless. The fact remains that House Etheridge is notorious for having slain thousands of Inothians over the last century."

Kent bristled. "Many of whom attempted to violate Muroth's borders to inflict harm upon our citizenry. Do you not also wish to protect Inoth's borders, Your Highness?"

"And what of the countless raids Murothians have committed upon our northern lands? How might those be excused in light of your arguments against our incursions?"

"Sometimes it is necessary to—" Kent stopped.

He could continue arguing, or he could refocus the conversation in such a way that he might stand a chance of saving his life. His only hope now was talking his way out of this.

"Your Highness," he began again, "I have been stripped of my titles, lands, wealth, and privileges, and I have been banished from my homeland. I am no threat to you or your people."

Grak scoffed and shook his head.

"Except, perhaps, for him." Kent nodded toward Grak. "I would relish the chance to test my might against his."

Grak's expression soured, and he started forward.

"Grakios Petrakis," Queen Aveyna snapped. "Remember your place." Grak stopped, turned back, and bowed to her. "Yes, Your Majesty.

Forgive me."

Then he returned to his place at her side.

But Kent had learned something about him—he was a touch reckless and perhaps a touch overconfident.

He'd seen it before with other men in similar positions of authority, in Muroth and elsewhere. Complacency bred by a wealth of power could warp a man's impressions of himself.

As such, he'd feel an even stronger need to prove himself worthy of his position—often to his detriment if his skills had atrophied as a result of that same complacency.

Kent had never allowed that to happen. He'd always prioritized his training to forestall atrophy and complacency.

"Even if I were to believe your claims of losing your... everything," Queen Aveyna began, "it would not erase your past transgressions."

Kent's jaw tightened. "If you seek an apology, I cannot proffer one. Nor would I expect one from any of your soldiers who violated Murothian borders. All I can say in my defense is that I am not that person any longer.

"I am no longer a citizen of Muroth, and I no longer subscribe to their beliefs regarding Inoth, Inothians, or magic. Most importantly, I mean you no harm." He added, "Your Highness."

"In that case, I believe I have no more questions for you, Lord—excuse me. *Mister* Etheridge." Queen Aveyna set her focus on Ronin. "What is your name?"

Kent exhaled a silent, frustrated sigh and turned toward Ronin. Ronin, still kneeling, replied, "Ronin Shroud, Your Highness."

"And your vocation?"

Ronin stammered, "I'm a—a bounty hunter, Your Highness."

"And what is wrong with your face?" she asked.

"I—I beg your pard—" Ronin stopped. "Oh. The soldiers—they—"

"If I may, my queen," a voice from behind them said.

Kent recognized the voice and glanced back. General Deoward stood in the center of the walkway between the pillars, still clad in his tan uniform.

"He resisted arrest and sustained his injuries in that action. Three of our soldiers are infirmed with comparable injuries," General Deoward said.

"Thank you, General," Queen Aveyna said.

"My queen." He bowed and then receded into the crowd of people gathered in the throne room.

Queen Aveyna looked at Ronin but said nothing.

"Am I allowed to explain? Your Highness?" Ronin looked around, glancing between the soldiers behind him, Grak, the prince, and the queen. "Please?"

Queen Aveyna nodded. "Speak."

Ronin explained how he had received the parchment regarding who Kent was, how he immediately complied with the order to bring Kent in, and how General Deoward had decided to arrest him anyway.

"It's completely unfair. Unjust, Your Highness," Ronin said. "I am a native Inothian. I've never even *thought* of committing treason or betraying my country, much less committed any significant crimes. I just want to scrape out a living, pay my taxes, and be left alone."

Queen Aveyna tilted her head at him. "How old are you, Mr. Shroud?"

"I turned twenty-seven last month, Your Highness."

"You're very near in age to my son." Queen Aveyna turned to her right, and Grak stepped back in response as the prince leaned forward. "Prince Kymil, you are twenty-five, correct?"

Prince Kymil nodded. "Yes, Mother."

"And in your twenty-five years of life, have you learned much about Inothian law?"

He nodded again. "I have, yes."

"So you are aware that every Inothian is entitled to a hearing or a trial, regardless of the offense or accusation?"

Kent could see where this was going. He looked at Ronin again, but Ronin kept his attention on the queen and her son.

"Of course, Mother," Prince Kymil replied.

"Is it fair to suggest that an Inothian two years older than you, one whose vocation requires a better-than-average knowledge of our laws, ought to know that aspect of our law?"

Prince Kymil fixed his harsh stare on Ronin. "Unquestionably."

Ronin started, "Your Highness—"

"Mr. Shroud, you may speak when I have addressed you, but not before," Queen Aveyna said.

Ronin's mouth clamped shut.

"In my estimation, it is clear that you immediately complied with the order you received," Queen Aveyna said. "Yet you failed to take into account the very laws with which you intersect on a daily basis, given your vocation. What I must now determine is whether or not you knew of Mr. Etheridge's true identity before you received the order."

Ronin didn't say anything. "You may speak, Mr. Shroud."

"Thank you, Your Highness." Ronin pointed at Kent. "I met him six months ago, and he did *not* tell me what he just admitted to you."

"What did he tell you?"

"That he was from Northern Urthia but that he had spent some time in Muroth before his awakening." Ronin added, "By the way, I believe his story about his awakening to be true, Your Highness. When we first met, he didn't know anything about how to use his magic. He asked me the types of questions a small child would ask about magic."

BLOOD MERCENARIES ORIGINS

"Our focus is on you, now, Mr. Shroud. Let us keep it there." Queen Aveyna leaned forward. "So you claim he lied to you about his identity?"

"Yes. Completely."

"For what it is worth, Your Highness," Kent interjected, "Ronin is telling the truth. He knew nothing about me, and I told him a mixture of truth and lies to try to preserve my anonymity. It would be unjust of me to remain silent or say anything to the contrary because it is the truth."

"Ah, *truth* from the enemy of the state," Queen Aveyna mused. "What a marvel to behold. Miraculous, in fact. So much so that I hesitate to believe you."

"I have been nothing but thoroughly honest in my responses, Your Highness."

"But since not even a fragment of trust exists between us, I cannot take you at your word," Queen Aveyna countered. "You *are* an enemy of the state, after all."

Kent said nothing else. At that point, he couldn't be sure of helping Ronin's case, and he might very well harm it if he continued.

"Mother, may I speak?" Prince Kymil asked.

Queen Aveyna gave him a calm smile. "Of course, darling."

Prince Kymil's cheeks reddened, the first sign of color Kent had seen anywhere on his pale skin.

"The nature of our laws is such that a violation stands regardless of intent," Prince Kymil said. "While he claims innocence regarding the identity of this Murothian bastard, Mr. Shroud has nonetheless aided him over the last six months.

"Furthermore," Prince Kymil continued, "he resisted General Deoward's attempt to arrest him, and in doing so, he injured three Inothian soldiers— his own country-men. Therefore, I believe the law is clear: he is guilty multiple times over."

Kent looked at Ronin, and Ronin gawked at Prince Kymil in silence.

Queen Aveyna watched her son with rapt attention, a slight smile on her face. Then she turned to Ronin. "Do you have anything to say in response?"

Ronin stuttered, "Y-Your Highness, As I made clear, I had no idea he was Murothian, let alone a lord. How can I be held accountable for that? I did everything within my power to comply! I turned him in right away!"

Ronin's words stung Kent, but he realized why Ronin had to say them.

"And what of your attack on our soldiers?" Queen Aveyna asked.

"I only did that because I felt I was being positioned to suffer for crimes I didn't knowingly commit," Ronin said. "Wouldn't you have fought back if someone was unjustly trying to do you harm, Your Highness?"

"I am not the subject of this debate, Mr. Shroud."

"But isn't it a fair question?"

"I would have followed the laws of our land."

Of course the queen would err on the side of the law. She wasn't being scruti-nized. The argument carried no weight, but Ronin's lack of education was showing.

Ronin got down to his knees. "Please, Your Highness. I am a patriot. I am loyal to Inoth. I don't want to die for this."

Kent hated to see him begging, but Ronin had to stay alive somehow, and the trial wasn't looking good.

Queen Aveyna watched him for a long moment. She finally said, "As with Mr. Etheridge's claims of truth, which I cannot trust, I find myself wondering if I ought to trust your sincerity or not. You have broken the law, regardless of such, but I believe there is room for grace in our application of it."

Prince Kymil scowled at her, then he turned his scowl toward Kent and Ronin.

"The question is," she continued, "are you worthy of that grace?"

"I am, Your Highness," Ronin said. "I promise I am. My job is to collect wanted criminals and help bring them to justice. I only have Inoth's best interests in mind."

Queen Aveyna cast a lingering glance at Kent, then she refocused on Ronin. "Then I want you to prove it to me."

"Anything, Your Highness. I'll do anything."

Kent's shoulders stiffened. He could see where this was going, and Ronin had just committed to it unknowingly.

Queen Aveyna leaned forward. "I want you to execute Mr. Etheridge."

Kent looked at Ronin again, and he saw the expression he expected to see.

Ronin rose to his feet, his mouth hanging open, silently staring at the queen. He finally managed, "Your Highness, I—"

"Mr. Etheridge is an admitted interloper and sworn enemy of Inoth," Queen Aveyna said. "He is unquestionably guilty, and I now formally find him as such. I am sentencing him to death. You have sworn allegiance to me and to Inoth. Now you must prove your loyalty by fulfilling my sentence on Mr. Etheridge."

"By..." Ronin swallowed. "By executing him."

"Yes," she replied.

Prince Kymil sneered at Kent and rubbed his hands together.

Little prick. Kent scowled in return. *I could snap your neck in three seconds, if given the opportunity.*

Queen Aveyna asked, "Will you prove your patriotism to us all, here and now?"

Ronin cast a long look at Kent. Then he turned toward the queen and extended his shackled wrists. "If someone will unlock me, Your Highness, I will comply."

Something inside Kent shriveled. He understood Ronin's predicament, but Ronin's acceptance of his charge dug deep into Kent's core. Ronin had been his only true friend since he'd fled Muroth.

It felt like getting betrayed by Fane all over again.

Queen Aveyna nodded to Grak, and he ordered, "Unlock him."

The soldiers behind came around Ronin and unlocked his shackles. They clanked to the marble floor at his feet, and he stepped over them.

"How do you want it done?" Ronin asked.

Grak stepped forward. "Give him fire."

Ronin's eyes widened. "You want me to burn him alive?"

"He is an enemy of the state. No punishment is too severe," Grak said.

Ronin paused, then he nodded.

One of the soldiers in brown leather headed to one of the golden lamps standing nearby and picked it up. He carried it over, and Ronin reached into the flames.

His right hand ignited with swirls of blue and orange fire just like the soldiers' hands had in the dungeon.

The soldier then approached the five elite guards posted in front of the platform and offered the fire to each of them. They each let the fire wash over their hands in waves of blue and orange, and then the soldier returned the lamp to its spot.

Ronin furrowed his brow and looked at Grak.

Grak smirked. "Consider it insurance."

Ronin glanced at Kent again. "I'm sorry."

"Apologies mean nothing at this point." Kent straightened his posture.

Ronin closed his eyes hard for a moment, then he opened them and stared at Kent again. "I have to do it."

"I know." Kent stood firm, fully aware that he would die thoroughly unsatisfied.

Fane still lived, and if Kent perished, his treacherous brother will have won once and for all. The thought enraged him more than anything else.

Ronin extended his fiery right hand toward Kent. Then he put his left hand on his right shoulder and nodded at Kent.

It meant something. Kent didn't know what, but it meant something.

Ronin had no good reason to touch his right shoulder while throwing fire at Kent. It made no sense.

Kent's eyes narrowed, and he watched.

"What are you waiting for?" Grak rumbled. "Get on with it."

Ronin nodded again. Then he whipped his left hand toward Kent.

A glint of blue metal slipped out of Ronin's sleeve and careened toward Kent.

The key to the shackles.

CHAPTER NINE

K ent caught the key in his hands and immediately began to unlock the shackles.

Stupid, Ronin. Reckless and stupid. But Kent appreciated it nonetheless.

Meanwhile, Ronin let the fire in his right hand extinguish, and he dropped to his knees again with his hands up.

Grak must not have caught on right away, because he just stood there glancing between them, his face painted with confusion.

But when Kent's shackles clanked to the floor, Grak screamed, "Kill him!"

Ronin stayed still, but the five elite soldiers started toward Kent, their hands flaring with huge, vibrant flames.

Kent had nothing to fight back with. They'd taken his pouches long ago, and he was in the middle of a grand throne room with plenty of empty space around him.

He had only one choice. And if he failed, he would die.

Kent kicked the shackles away, dropped to his knees, pressed his hands flat against the red marble tile, and concentrated on the technique from the parchment. He flooded the red marble with magic and cycled it back into himself, just like he'd done to his cell wall.

Flames roared toward Kent from the elite soldiers. He bowed his head and closed his eyes, totally focused on the red marble tile beneath him.

Fire seared the top of his head and washed over his shoulders and back, then it cascaded down his neck and under his chin. It washed over his chest and stomach, and it consumed his legs and feet.

Brilliant heat enveloped every inch of his body, and he felt his clothes burning away.

He stopped moving, stopped hearing, stopped breathing. The world went quiet, and the heat subsided.

Kent raised his head and opened his eyes.

The elite soldiers stood there, their hands devoid of fire, their faces filled with shock.

Behind them, Queen Aveyna and Prince Kymil stood behind Grak and the four guards also in black armor, and they all stared at Kent.

He stood, slowly, scanning the throne room around him for other threats, ready to take them on.

The soldiers in brown leather who'd escorted Ronin and Kent from the dungeon marveled at him from across the throne room. Ronin still knelt on the floor, but he'd lowered his hands to his sides.

The crowd of people among the pillars watched him in stunned silence with fear written on their faces. No one approached him. No one threatened him. No one moved at all.

As Kent faced the queen again, he realized he was naked. He looked down at himself and saw shining red marble instead of skin. The technique had worked perfectly.

He wondered how long the effect would last. Since he'd bent down, he'd been continually activating his magic.

He wanted to keep circulating it, to test how long he could keep it up, but he was still in the Inothian throne room, surrounded by enemies on every side. He couldn't waste time.

Then the red marble receded from his skin, leaving him pink and cream-colored, like usual. A measure of fatigue hit him. He'd experienced it before when pumping out a lot of magic all at once, but he resisted its effects and maintained his focus. He had to—he still wasn't safe here.

A ring of ashes—his clothes and boots—encircled him. At his feet, two deep impressions in the shape of his hands dug into what remained of the red marble tile beneath him.

The entire tile now sat lower than the other tiles around it, as if he'd sucked half of its essence away. Then again, he *had* sucked half of its essence away.

Kent looked up at the queen and thought he should cover himself, but he decided against it. She had allowed this to happen, and she would now reap the consequences.

"Incredible," a voice said to Kent's left. Ronin's voice.

Kent glanced at him, then he faced Queen Aveyna again.

Grak drew his sword and started toward the end of the platform. The four royal guards accompanied him.

"Wait, Grakios." Queen Aveyna's gaze lingered on Kent.

Grak stopped. "Your Majesty, I mean to fulfill your mandate and execute this brigand."

"No. You will stay your hand." Queen Aveyna threaded her way between Grak and the other royal guards.

"Your Majesty, please! It isn't safe." Grak tried to hold her back, but she moved him aside with a stern look and nothing more.

Grak sighed and motioned to the other royal guards. Two of them accompanied him, following close behind her as she walked toward the edge of the platform.

The other two remained with Prince Kymil, doubtless protecting the future of Inoth's royalty if their comrades failed to protect the queen.

Queen Aveyna advanced to a set of steps before the throne and descended toward Kent. Grak and the two royal guards followed only two steps behind, ready to spring into action if Kent so much as moved.

"Mother?" Prince Kymil called from behind her.

"Be silent, Kymil," she said as she continued to approach Kent.

As Queen Aveyna drew nearer, Kent smelled a sweet, floral aroma. Some sort of perfume.

It smelled lovely, but he refused to let it faze him. She had just ordered his execution by the hand of his only friend, and her soldiers had nearly reduced him to charred bones.

Queen Aveyna stopped ten feet away from him and ordered, "Someone get Mr. Etheridge some clothes."

Kent squinted at her, still tense and ready for anything. He would drop to his knees and turn to stone again if anyone made any threatening moves.

But no one did. Instead, a rotund man from the crowd came forward at once and removed the elegant purple robe he was wearing. He approached Kent from the side and extended the robe toward him, and Kent accepted it with a nod.

The man gave Kent and the queen a slight bow and then receded back into the crowd.

Kent donned the robe, his wary eyes fixed on Queen Aveyna the whole time. The robe didn't have a drawstring or a belt, so Kent held it shut with his left hand, leaving his right hand free for action if necessary.

"Mr. Etheridge," Queen Aveyna began, "I believe I owe you an apology."

Kent said nothing.

"I am sorry for ordering your execution. Your skill with magic is remarkable."

Kent glanced at Ronin, who shrugged at him.

"Yet I find myself unsure what I ought to do with you."

So I am still your prisoner. Kent's eyes narrowed. "Let me go."

Queen Aveyna shook her head. "I'm afraid I cannot do that."

"Why not?"

"The sight of the sort of magic you just demonstrated is a rarity, even in Inoth. Many archmages I've met lack skill to achieve such a feat. Thus, you are simply too valuable of an asset to release." Queen Aveyna took a few steps closer to him, closing the distance between them to less than five feet. "And one does not simply throw away an asset."

Her reasoning made sense—to a point. Kent said, "I thought you found me untrustworthy."

Queen Aveyna smiled, and Kent admired her. She was even more radiant when she smiled.

"I stand by my claim," she said. "You *are* untrustworthy. You *are* an enemy of the state." She paused. "But I want to believe what you said earlier."

"I said a lot of things earlier."

"Specifically, you said you mean neither Inoth nor me harm." Queen Aveyna tilted her head. "Did you mean that?"

Kent inhaled a slow breath and glanced at Grak, whose snarl hadn't changed since he'd stepped off the stairs. Kent refocused on Queen Aveyna.

"Your Highness," Kent said, "if I had wanted to, I could have used the power I just demonstrated and attacked you or your men. I could have used it to walk out of here. I could have used it to bring down this palace on top of everyone in this throne room."

Perhaps that last bit was an exaggeration, but Kent didn't care.

"But I refrained from doing any of those things," he continued. "If that does not demonstrate the truth of my words, then I do not know what will."

Queen Aveyna nodded. "In that case, I am willing to learn to trust you, if you are willing to learn to trust me. I would like to invite you to remain in the palace as my guest so that we might begin to get acquainted."

"Mother!" Prince Kymil snapped from behind her. "He is *Murothian!* A Murothian *lord!* He will slit our throats while we sleep!"

Queen Aveyna whirled around. "Be *silent*, Kymil. I have made my decision, and you *will* abide by it."

Prince Kymil's mouth shut, but rage burned in his blue eyes.

Queen Aveyna turned back to Kent. "Will you accept my invitation, Lord Etheridge?"

Kent shook his head. "I am no longer the lord of anything, Your Highness."

"From now on, I refuse to acknowledge you as anything else. You are clearly highborn, and as the Sovereign in Inoth, I choose to recognize you for what you are."

"Your Highness…" Kent started, but he couldn't say anything else.

That she of all people, the queen of his homeland's sworn enemies, would in some small way restore his title to him, baffled him.

But it also filled him with boundless joy and pride, as if the last six months hadn't been a waste. As if he'd regained a minuscule, yet essential piece of himself that he thought he'd lost.

What's more, she was offering him yet another chance to pursue his revenge on Fane, and, perhaps, the beginnings of some essential connections that could help him succeed. How could he say no?

Kent cleared his throat and regained his composure. "Your Highness, I would be honored—under one condition."

"And that is?" she asked.

"That Ronin Shroud be allowed to go free and with your blessing," he replied. "I assure you, again, that he had no idea of my true identity. He is perhaps the most loyal Inothian in your kingdom. He deserves to be rewarded, not punished. As a compromise, I ask that you grant him absolution from all of his crimes and set him free."

Queen Aveyna looked past Kent at Ronin. "Mr. Shroud, come forward."

Ronin complied, and he stood next to Kent. They exchanged a glance of disbelief and then refocused on the queen again.

"Kneel," Queen Aveyna said.

Ronin knelt.

Queen Aveyna closed the remainder of the distance between them, and her guards came with. She placed her right hand on Ronin's head. Blue light shined from under her palm, and then it turned white.

"With my blessing, I release you." She pressed her glowing forefinger on Ronin's forehead. "And with this mark, I absolve you of all crimes, and I anoint you as a true Inothian patriot. Never again will your loyalty to Inoth be questioned, and anyone who dares to question it will be subject to my judgment."

Ronin blinked, and his lips spread into a wide, almost idiotic smile.

Queen Aveyna removed her finger from his forehead. "Rise."

As Ronin complied, Kent noticed a hexagonal mark glowing on his forehead. He glanced back at Queen Aveyna. Was she a practitioner of light magic?

"I hereby order that any and all confiscated property be returned to Mr. Shroud, and I order that he be paid a sum of ten thousand gold pieces as a reward and recompense for his troubles." Queen Aveyna looked directly at Ronin. "Mr. Shroud, you are free to go."

Ronin's jaw unhinged, and he stammered, "Th-thank you, Your Highness! I... I don't know what to say." He bowed to her and then faced Kent. "So... what happens next?"

"I will send word once I know more." Kent grinned. "Go. Enjoy your freedom."

"Will you be alright?" Ronin asked, his voice low.

"I believe so." Kent extended his hand. "Thank you for all you have done for me thus far. I am certain we will meet again."

Ronin took Kent's hand, shook it, and pulled him into an embrace. "I know it. We still have to go to Caclos together."

"We do. And we will." Kent released him. "Thank you. You are the brother I never had."

"And you as well." Ronin grinned. "Alright. I'll see you around, I guess."

Ronin bowed to the queen once more, and then he turned back and headed toward the throne room's doors with a fresh bounce in his step.

Kent watched him go, partially because he'd miss Ronin, but mostly because he needed to be sure Ronin got out of the throne room alive. No one followed him out, and no one brandished any weapons or used any magic from what Kent could see.

He hoped Queen Aveyna would remain true to her word. At this point, he couldn't do anything else but trust her.

Kent turned back toward her and waited in silence.

"I imagine you must be hungry," she said.

"I am." Kent hadn't eaten since breakfast that morning, prior to when Ronin received the notice. He'd spent the entire day in the dungeon, and they had neglected to feed him.

"My servants will attend to you and provide you with more suitable dining attire," Queen Aveyna said. "Then you shall join my son and me for dinner once you are refreshed. My servants will show you the way. Dinner will commence within the hour."

Kent gave her a slight bow. "Yes, Your Highness."

With that, Queen Aveyna turned and walked between her royal guards toward the platform stairs. They followed her, but Grak shot a long glare back at Kent as he walked.

Kent didn't return the animosity this time. He didn't know how long he might manage to stay in the queen's good graces, so further antagonizing the head of her personal guard would only prove harmful.

As Kent watched the queen and her entourage disappear into the passageway behind the throne, he noted that Prince Kymil didn't so much as make eye contact with him—yet another person Kent didn't want to aggravate if possible.

The wall closed over the passageway behind the throne, and the throne room again bustled with conversation—probably mostly about him, if he had to guess.

Then a trio of female servants approached Kent and ushered him out of the throne room. They escorted him through the palace to a private, ornate chamber where they measured his proportions for clothing and drew him a hot bath.

When he emerged from the bath and entered the bedchamber, he found multiple articles of clothing, most of them laid out in coordinated sets.

The female servants had gone, so he dressed himself in one of the sets of clothing. They fit him fairly well, though additional tailoring would have improved the overall look.

He slipped into the least stiff pair of boots they'd provided for him. If something adverse should happen, he wanted to be limber and ready for action. The looser clothes and the more malleable leather of the boots he'd selected would better allow for movement if he should need to do so.

Still, he wished his other clothes and boots hadn't burned up in the throne room. Those boots, especially, had fit just right. He'd finally broken them in not even two months earlier.

What he wouldn't have given to have his sword handy as well. To his knowledge, it was still under lock and key, held fast by the guards at the palace gates. It would do him no good there.

Kent positioned himself in front of the vanity positioned near the chamber door, and he examined his image in the mirror. The clothes were distinctly Inothian and not quite his taste, but the fabrics were fine quality.

All in all, he'd suffered far worse at the hands of both Muroth and Inoth thus far, so he reconciled himself to mostly ignoring his appearance. Satisfied, he headed to the door, opened it, and stepped into the corridor.

Two guards in black armor awaited him, along with Grak himself. Kent stopped just outside the door, so close to Grak that he could smell garlic and beef on his hot breath. At that range, Kent finally got the chance to size him up properly.

Grak outweighed Kent by thirty pounds or so, not including his armor, which looked heavier than it probably was. Well-made armor typically weighed less, not more, and someone in Grak's position could afford the best-quality armor available.

He had Kent beat in height by a little more than an inch, and he had a thicker, bulkier neck. Overall, Grak was broader and possibly stronger than Kent. Perhaps Kent's assumptions about Grak's complacency were unfounded.

Then again, size didn't necessarily translate to prowess.

Kent stood there, unflinching, inhaling Grak's tainted breath in silence, unwilling to speak first. He always refused to cede any ground in such confrontations. He'd stand there in silence all night if he had to, and Grak would pay for it since he'd been charged with bringing Kent to dinner.

Finally, Grak looked Kent up and down and said, "You look pretty."

Somehow, Grak had pinpointed one of Kent's few insecurities about what was to come, but Kent didn't show it. Stoic, Kent said, "You are not my type."

Grak smirked. A deep reservoir of intelligence lingered behind his cunning green eyes. "I don't suppose you have any weapons on your person, but I'm going to check anyway."

"I would prefer that you refrain from touching me."

Grak leaned in close, only inches from Kent's face. "I don't give two twigs what you would prefer."

Kent's nose wrinkled at the intensity of Grak's breath, but he remained otherwise unfazed. "Let me put this another way: you are not going to touch me."

"Is that so?"

"The queen gave you orders. If I arrive unmolested, you will have fulfilled your mandate. If I arrive in any lesser condition, you will answer to her wrath."

"I can say you resisted. Maybe you even tried to attack me."

"But you will not."

"And why is that?"

"Because I am an asset and an invited guest. I have no reason to resist. I have no reason to attack you, a nobody. If I meant to do someone harm, I would have already done it in the throne room."

"She trusts what I tell her," Grak said. "I'm the captain of her personal guard."

"The queen is intelligent and discerning. She would see through your lies. And I will be late if you persist in talking when we should be walking."

"I *need* to search you," Grak asserted.

"I am unarmed. You may either take my word for it, or you will fail your mandate one way or another."

Grak studied Kent's eyes for a long moment. Then he raised his finger and pointed at Kent's chest. "If you so much as *sneeze* the wrong way at dinner, I'll kill you quicker than you can say 'magic.' Crystal?"

Kent didn't respond.

Grak's brow furrowed, and he started down the corridor without Kent.

Kent glanced at the two other guards, and one of them motioned him forward. So Kent followed Grak, and the guards followed him.

As they walked, Kent noticed that Grak didn't have any pouches connected to his belt. Perhaps Grak wasn't a mage. Kent would have to investigate further later on.

The walk terminated in a grand hall about a quarter of the size of the throne room, adorned with white marble and dark wood paneling reminiscent of the room where he'd met with General Deoward earlier that day.

A long banquet table filled a good portion of the room but only had four chairs around it, and three tall windows divided the hall's western wall.

At the far end of the room sat Queen Aveyna. The space between them measured about the same as when she'd been sitting on her throne while Kent stood on the red tile in the throne room.

As Kent entered the room, Queen Aveyna stood. Prince Kymil, who sat to her left and on the corresponding side of the table, also stood, but considerably slower.

"Welcome." Her voice carried across the large room to Kent, and she motioned toward the chair on the side of the table to her right, Kent's left, across from Prince Kymil. "Please, have a seat."

"Thank you." Kent obliged her.

He waited for her to sit, then he sat down in unison with Prince Kymil.

When he looked at Prince Kymil, he received an artificial smile in return.

Kent had seen a few thousand forced smiles in his lifetime—perhaps tens of thousands. He'd had servants and soldiers under him, after all, and many of his fellow lords and ladies had mastered the art as well.

Kent returned it with a nod, but he didn't smile back.

Two royal guards already stood behind Queen Aveyna, and Grak joined them. The other two guards who'd accompanied Kent to the dining hall split apart. One stood against the wall behind Kent, and the other rounded the table and took a position on a wall behind Prince Kymil.

Good positioning, Kent mused.

If he were to attack either the queen or the prince, he'd have a hard time pulling it off because of the royal guards' potential to intervene. Grak clearly knew what he was doing.

A set of double doors opened behind Queen Aveyna, and a line of servants entered with extravagant platters of food. They arrayed the platters on the table and filled crystalline goblets with red wine and water.

Queen Aveyna thanked the goddess Laeri for her provision and blessed the food. Meanwhile, Kent offered a silent prayer of thanks that he'd survived today's trial, just in case Laeri had had anything to do with it, and then they set to eating.

"If it pleases you, Lord Etheridge," Queen Aveyna served herself a helping of roasted lamb, "I would like to hear the detailed story of how you found your way to our capital."

Kent took a sip of his water to buy himself time. It wasn't a topic he wanted to discuss, especially with any great detail, but he couldn't very well refuse her, either. And furthermore, she had referred to him by his birthright title again.

In the end, he reminded himself that he could never return to Muroth or his ancestral home, so he obliged her. "Certainly, Your Highness."

Kent started by sharing how nearly nine years prior, he'd experienced his awakening to magic. Then he shared about his father's ailing health, the succession ceremony, and all that transpired there. He detailed his journey to the border and his escape from his own border fortress, including his fight with General Calarook.

"Eventually, I found my way here," he continued. Kent explained how he ran across Ronin and the criminal Eusephus in the street, how he'd helped take Eusephus out, and how he'd teamed up with Ronin from that point on. "And now I am dining with the queen and the prince of Inoth."

Queen Aveyna smiled at him. "The gods have a peculiar way of throwing our lives into disarray, don't they?"

"To say the least, yes."

They continued conversing throughout the entirety of the meal and dessert, but Prince Kymil hardly said a word. Kent noticed, but he didn't press the issue. He just noted it and left Prince Kymil alone.

He also noted the changes in Queen Aveyna's demeanor throughout the course of the meal. She began the dinner as the pinnacle of proper conduct, but as the conversation extended, her mannerisms and speech relaxed.

Kent couldn't be certain, but at times between shared laughter, the queen might've been sizing him up—physically. And with the exception of Kent sharing the dark parts of his expulsion from Muroth, Queen Aveyna's smile remained fixed to her face.

Kent wondered whether his charm or the wine had played a more significant role in the conversation's evolution. Either way, he found himself relaxing as well, with a full belly and a never-empty goblet of wine.

"Mother, would you excuse me?" Prince Kymil asked. "I would like to retire."

"But it's so early, my love," Queen Aveyna said. "Are you sure you're well?"

He nodded. "I'm fine, Mother. Just exhausted from the day's excitement."

Kent looked him over. They sat about six feet across from each other, as close as they'd ever been.

Prince Kymil was built more like his mother than a man. For his age, his shoulders and arms should've begun to fill out by now. Furthermore, his sickly pallor didn't help with his overall appearance.

It wouldn't be a stretch for Kent to believe that Prince Kymil truly was exhausted from the day's excitement, given his relative frailty.

But more likely, from the occasional sullen glances Prince Kymil had cast at Kent throughout the evening and the way he'd barely touched his food, Kent discerned that Prince Kymil just didn't want to be there with him.

Kent didn't blame him. At Prince Kymil's age, Kent couldn't have tolerated eating across from an Inothian lord of any shape, size, or color either.

Ongoing wars had that effect on countries—people developed a deep- rooted disdain for their adversaries. Were it not for the whirlwind of experiences severing Kent from his old life, he would still harbor the same contempt.

"Of course, darling." Queen Aveyna smiled at him. "Good night."

Prince Kymil blushed like he had back in the throne room. His voice flattened. "Don't stay up too late, Mother. You know how you get."

Queen Aveyna chuckled and waved him away. "It's early, my love. I'll be fine."

Prince Kymil opened his mouth to say something else, but instead he bowed to her and then left the room with two of the royal guards following close behind.

With Prince Kymil gone, Queen Aveyna said, "He's such a wonderful boy."

"What happened to his father?" Kent asked.

Queen Aveyna's smile faded, and she reclined in her chair. "He died a year ago."

"I am sorry to hear that." Kent leaned forward. "May I ask what happened?"

Queen Aveyna broke eye contact and stared at her plate instead. "I don't think I've had quite enough wine to discuss that with you, Mr. Etheridge."

Back to "Mr. Etheridge" again? A slip of her tongue, perhaps? Or was it intentional, a way to remind him of his place?

"Forgive me if I came across as too bold," Kent said.

She waved her hand, dismissing his apology. "It takes far more than that to offend me. But all the same, I believe I ought to draw our time together to a close."

As she stood, Kent stood as well. She nodded to him, and he bowed to her.

"I will call upon you tomorrow," she said.

"Whatever Your Highness wishes."

Her wonderful smile returned. "Good night, Lord Etheridge."

Kent smiled back at her. "Good night."

Without looking back, Queen Aveyna reached out with her right arm. Grak moved hooked his arm around hers and started escorting her to the door. The two royal guards behind him followed, but they stopped short of the door.

Queen Aveyna didn't so much as make eye contact with Kent when she walked past him, even though he watched her every move.

Grak, however, glowered at him with each step until he led Queen Aveyna out of the dining hall.

The two remaining royal guards took Kent back to his chambers and left him there, unguarded, for the night. Perhaps it was the queen's first real attempt at establishing a measure of trust between them.

⚜

INSIDE HIS CHAMBERS, AS HE PREPARED TO RETIRE FOR THE NIGHT, KENT NOTICED A soft orange glow outside his chamber window. Curious, he peered through the glass. Down below, two figures stood before a stone mausoleum.

One was clearly Grak, based on his size and armor, and the other was just as obviously Kymil, small, frail, and pale. Grak held a burning torch while Kymil faced the mausoleum. After a long moment, Kymil turned away from the structure and headed back toward the castle with Grak close behind him.

Perhaps Kymil's father was buried in the mausoleum, and he was paying his respects. In a way, he Kent envied Kymil for it; Kent would likely never have the privilege to pay his respects at his own father's gravesite.

He turned away from the window, stripped down to his new undergarments, and retired. The bed welcomed him, easing his aching body and his tired mind.

But just as he began to fall asleep, a faint knock sounded from his door.

Bare-chested and barefoot, Kent rose to open it, wary. If Grak had come back for him, or if someone else within the palace has decided to attack the former Murothian noble now living as the queen's honored guest, he wanted to be ready.

In the moonlight streaming into his room, Kent searched for something he could use as a weapon, and he found a thick, iron candlestick. He removed the candle and set it on the vanity, then he advanced toward the door.

The knock sounded again, a bit louder this time.

Kent eased his way over to the door and reached for the knob, but he heard the jingle of keys on the other side, and he stopped short.

Metal clinked, then scraped as the key slid into the lock from the other side.

Whoever it was, they were coming in whether Kent wanted them to or not.

Kent stepped to the side, behind where the door would open, and readied his candlestick. He calmed his breathing, but his heart kept hammering in his chest.

The lock clicked, and the door latch clicked, and the door slowly swung open with a low groan. Faint footsteps padded on the floor, and Kent stiffened.

As the door closed behind the intruder, Kent raised his candlestick to strike.

CHAPTER TEN

K ent didn't swing.

It was a woman. A blonde-haired woman, very beautiful, and clad in only a thin, silky nightgown tied together at the top with silken string.

Queen Aveyna.

She shut the door, locked it, and looked at him in the moonlight. She glanced at the bludgeon in his hand and whispered, "That's not a very hospitable way to treat a late-night visitor."

Kent lowered the candlestick. His heartbeat accelerated, and he whispered back, "What are you doing here?" He added, "Your Highness?"

"You know why I'm here. And you don't have to call me that right now," she said. "Call me Aveyna."

Kent swallowed. By the gods, she was beautiful, and he wanted her. "Your High— Aveyna, this is not wise."

She let the keys drop to the floor, and she closed the distance between them and put her hands on his bare chest. The top of her head came up to just below his neck.

Aveyna inhaled a deep breath. "Whether it's wise or not, it's happening."

She rose up on her toes and kissed his chin. Her arms curled around his neck, and she pulled him down to her. Her lips met his in a long, passionate kiss, and he dropped the candlestick. It hit the ground with a dull thud.

Kent drank in her touch, reveled in the feel of her warm body against his. She still smelled like flowery perfume. And he hadn't been with a woman in such a long time.

Not since Miranda.

He gently pushed her back and held her at bay. "Forgive me, but I do not believe this is a good idea."

Aveyna stepped back and untied the strings at the top of her nightgown. "Kent, it's no use resisting. You want this as much as I do."

She slipped the nightgown down over her shoulders and let it drop to the floor. Kent swallowed again. *Incredible.*

Aveyna started toward him.

As she reached for him again, he slipped away from her—toward the bed. He regretted the decision immediately, as she took it as encouragement and headed straight over to it herself.

She crawled onto it and beckoned him over, every curve of her impeccable body outlined by moonlight.

"Aveyna," he began, "forgive me again, but I barely know you, and I am not in the habit of engaging women, no matter how beautiful or regal, in this manner so soon after meeting them."

"I knew I had to have you the moment you emerged from the flames," she said. "Your body is nearly as magnificent as your skill with magic."

Kent wiped sweat from his forehead. He felt it collecting under his armpits and on his back as well. "I appreciate the honor you are showing me, but mere hours ago you considered me an enemy of the state of Inoth."

"Perhaps I've decided to extend more trust to you." She eased one leg off the bed and then the other, and she took hold of his wrists and began to pull him back.

He stopped his forward motion with one step, but she kept pulling—not hard, but enough to continue her suggestion.

"You are the Queen of Inoth. I am no one. This is not right."

"I am the Queen of Inoth. Therefore, I *say* what is right," she countered.

Aveyna tugged him harder, and he took another step toward the bed.

"I—I—" he stammered.

"If you're afraid of what this will cost you, don't be. I'm not like other women."

There is no denying that, at least. Kent took another step forward.

"Almost there." She showed him that smile—that enrapturing smile that had captivated him all throughout dinner.

He stopped and gently rolled his wrists, breaking her grip. "Forgive me, Queen Aveyna, but I must ask you to leave."

She stood there, her smile halfway gone. "You really won't oblige me?"

Kent exhaled a quiet breath through his nose. "Please understand—it is not because I am disinterested. I find you very attractive, but I am not given to rash decisions."

Aveyna remained quiet.

"I believe that to engage in such an act with you now would risk the possibility of something far greater between us in the future."

"What makes you think I want something greater?"

Kent hesitated. "Do you not?"

Now Aveyna hesitated.

"There is no need to answer now," Kent said. "I understand what you are enduring with regard to the recent death of your husband."

Her composure faltered, and her face twisted with anger and hurt. "You know *nothing* about it."

"Actually, I do," Kent said calmly. "My own wife, Miranda, died many years ago, in childbirth. Our son, who would have been my heir, perished as well. Though, if given the choice, I would have preferred her to live a full life with me even if it meant never having an heir."

Aveyna's face softened some, and she sat on the bed, her arms wrapped around herself. "I—I'm sorry."

Kent nodded, and he walked over to her nightgown, still a pool of silk on the floor. He picked it up, brought it back to her, and handed it to her.

"Thank you." Tears streamed down her face. "Gods, I feel like such a fool."

Kent sat next to her on the bed. He wanted nothing more than to reach out and wrap his arms around her, but he refrained. He'd just stymied her advances, and though his carnal nature wanted more, he dared not do anything to reignite her ambition again.

"Is there anything else I can do for you?" he asked.

"No. You have shown me respect. That is precisely what I needed, even if it wasn't what I wanted." She slipped her nightgown onto her head and pulled it down her body. Then she looked up at Kent. "Thank you."

He chanced taking her hand in his. "Perhaps we can do this some other time."

Her perfect smile, albeit a teary-eyed version, returned. "I hope so."

"Very good. Then I will see you in the morning. Perhaps for breakfast?" Kent offered.

"Yes. I would like that very much."

Kent stood, helped Aveyna to her feet, and walked her to the door. He picked up the keys and handed them to her, then he picked up the candlestick and set it on the vanity again.

She opened the door, he bowed to her, and then she left.

With the door shut and locked, Kent returned to his bed and lay down in it.

The aroma of her flowery perfume still lingered on the sheets. He would have difficulty sleeping that night.

THROUGHOUT THE NEXT SEVERAL WEEKS, AVEYNA AND KENT GOT BETTER ACQUAINTED, and he gained more and more of her trust. He found it beneficial in a variety of ways, not the least of which was a gradual reduction in his paranoia that everyone in the realm wanted him dead.

Within two months, Kent had earned free rein throughout the palace, meaning neither Grak nor any of his royal guards had to escort Kent whenever he wanted to leave his room. He welcomed the freedom, and he used it to send word to Ronin of his wellbeing.

Even so, he still was not permitted to wear his sword around the palace. However, the soldiers at the palace gates kept it locked up for him to use whenever he wished to practice—under watchful eyes, of course.

As such, Kent routinely trained with some of the soldiers in the palace courtyard and even took up teaching them fighting techniques. He'd always found Inothian soldiers to be poor hand-to-hand and armed fighters, and they continued to prove him right, time after time.

But the more time he spent with them, the more they grew under his tutelage. In exchange, some of the ranking officers began to show him additional magic techniques useful for fighting. Kent drank it all in and committed the techniques to memory.

A week later, Queen Aveyna invited Kent to a meeting of her most trusted advisors. Kent agreed to attend.

When Kent entered the throne room that evening, two elite soldiers walked out and shut the doors behind them, sealing him and everyone else in attendance inside.

"Welcome, Lord Etheridge," Queen Aveyna's voice carried from the throne as Kent approached. "Come forward."

A round of welcomes, nods, and well-wishes from the other attendees greeted him, and most of them seemed genuine.

Ahead, Prince Kymil sat next to his mother, and General Deoward and several other high-ranking military officials stood near the edge of the platform.

As usual, Grak stood between Queen Aveyna and Prince Kymil.

As Kent approached, the group of military officials parted, leaving only General Deoward standing between Kent and the platform. He gave Kent a curt nod, and then he too stepped aside.

Kent knelt on the centermost red tile and bowed toward the Queen. He stole a glance to his right, at the red tile he'd occupied when he'd nearly been executed. Someone had removed the old tile and replaced it with a new one that didn't quite match the other four in color.

Kent smirked.

"Rise and come forward," Queen Aveyna beckoned him.

Kent rose, and he began to ascend the platform steps toward her.

She stood up and started toward him. When she stopped, he stopped.

Grak glared at him, but Kent ignored it. He did, however, note Grak's death grip on the hilt of his sword.

"Lord Kent Etheridge, formerly of the nation of Muroth, I have summoned you this evening to ask you a very simple question," Queen Aveyna began. "I would like to offer you the opportunity to become a full citizen of Inoth."

Kent granted himself a grin. *My, how far I have come.*

Queen Aveyna smiled and studied his face. "Do you accept?"

Kent nodded. He had nothing to lose by accepting, and he stood to gain much more. "I would be honored, Your Highness."

Queen Aveyna performed the same short ceremony on Kent as she had on Ronin the day of his trial, and she anointed Kent as an official Inothian. "Rise, Lord Kent Etheridge, loyal citizen of Inoth."

Kent rose. "Thank you, Your Highness."

"I have another request of you," she said.

"Name it, Your Highness."

"I would like you to serve as one of my chief military advisors, specifically with regard to our ongoing conflict with Muroth." Queen Aveyna's chin rose slightly. "But before I can allow you to serve in such a role, tradition dictates that I subject you to an inquisition by those with whom you will serve."

An inquisition? Interesting.

She motioned toward the throne room doors, and Kent looked back.

General Deoward stood on the centermost red tile. General Ruba, a man whom Kent had met only once thus far, stood on the off-colored tile where Kent had turned to stone.

A third man with tan skin and clad in an Inothian naval uniform, colored blue with vibrant orange accents, stood on the tile to the right of General Deoward. Kent had never met him.

Behind them, the rest of the military officials stood by, watching.

"You know General Deoward and General Ruba," Queen Aveyna said. "The third gentleman is Admiral Tagril, the leader of the Inothian Navy."

Admiral Tagril gave Kent a slight bow, and Kent returned it. Then Kent turned and refocused on Queen Aveyna.

"Would you like to serve your queen in this way?" she asked.

Kent grinned. They'd grown far closer over the last several months, and he'd begun to develop strong feelings for her. Her words conjured up memories of her visit to his chambers that first night, and he considered a variety of ways he would've liked to serve her.

"If my queen so wishes," he said, "I shall gladly oblige her."

Kent turned to face his inquisition.

General Deoward posed the first question. "How do we know we can trust you to provide good information regarding Muroth's intentions going forward?"

A loaded question.

"Would you please clarify further, General?" Kent asked. "Are you asking if I am trustworthy as a native Murothian who once held lands and power along the border, or are you asking if any information I might provide is still relevant despite several months having passed since my arrival in Inoth?

"Both," General Deoward replied.

"I am totally loyal to Her Majesty, Queen Aveyna," Kent began. "When my family learned of my magical abilities, they expelled me from my home, stripped me of my land and titles, and forced me to flee the country under penalty of death.

"Now Queen Aveyna has granted me Inothian citizenship. Under these combined circumstances, for me to return to Muroth would mean execution. Inoth is my home now, and it always will be.

"Regarding my knowledge of Muroth's defenses and preparations for battling Inoth, I can assure you that change comes very slowly to Muroth. Murothian strategies and tactics largely have not changed since nearly the beginning of this war, primarily because said tactics have proven useful repeatedly throughout the years.

"Furthermore, our fortresses and walls are fixed structures. They do not move, and I have firsthand knowledge of their intricacies. I coordinated their defenses for decades, particularly those under my family's purview, and I know precisely what to expect should we encounter one of them.

"Finally, regarding offensive approaches, I directed and led the Murothian Army's southern forces on numerous occasions and in numerous battles with Inothian forces. I am capable of accurately predicting their movements and tactics, and thus I can serve as an integral part of formulating an effective Inothian strategy to face said army."

General Deoward nodded. "A very thorough answer. Thank you."

Kent gave him a slight bow.

General Ruba spoke next. He asked a pair of questions dealing with specific situations in which Muroth had managed to overcome Inoth in past battles.

Kent answered that most mages and Inothians lacked any significant degree of physical training. He'd made the exact same observation about Ronin—mages relied too heavily on their magical abilities and forsook their physical potential.

"In order for Inoth to triumph over Muroth in any given battle, Inoth must learn to better utilize the physical attributes of its soldiers. Muroth's army has grown large and fierce, but Inoth could easily reclaim an advantage by implementing more physical combat training," Kent concluded.

General Ruba nodded, and Admiral Tagril asked Kent about whether he saw any practical use for the Inothian navy in future conflicts with Muroth.

"Where I come from," Kent replied, "we have small rivers and streams. Southeastern Muroth has no coastline but instead shares borders with Inoth and Govalia. The Inothian navy would likely prove cumbersome at best if it tried to navigate any of its ships through those rivers and streams.

"Perhaps a better approach would be to utilize the navy to attack southwestern Muroth in a coordinated effort involving a ground attack on Muroth's southern border. A powerful enough barrage could sufficiently divide the Murothian army to weaken the forces in the southeast, and it could make an invasion of lower Muroth easier for Inothian land forces."

Admiral Tagril bowed low to him.

"I must confess, Admiral," Kent added, "that I am no expert in naval combat tactics. I would yield such decisions to your wisdom."

For another two hours, the officials asked Kent their questions, and he answered them in earnest. He rather enjoyed the discussion, even when they disagreed on certain points. He hadn't engaged in such conversation since before he'd fled Muroth, and the Inothian perspectives fascinated him.

Queen Aveyna scanned the throne room. "I will now hear any dissenting opinions on this matter. Rest assured, your voice will be heard and your cautions considered, so no one should be afraid to speak up for fear of retribution."

She extended her hands toward the other military officials, but as Kent expected, no criticism came from anyone. He chalked it up more to good discipline throughout the Inothian army and navy rather than anything he'd personally said or done to convince them.

Had a soldier spoken out in such a scenario in Muroth, he'd be heard, but he'd

BLOOD MERCENARIES ORIGINS

also receive a stern lecture later on. Loyalty was prized above all in Muroth, and from what he'd witnessed thus far, it held true in Inoth as well.

Queen Aveyna waited for a long moment, and then she lowered her arms. "In that case, my esteemed generals and admiral, I call upon you to cast your votes on whether or not Lord Etheridge should be permitted to serve as one of my advisors and as one of your peers.

"Remember that a vote of 'yes' will establish his authority as equal to any of yours, and remember also that the final decision lies with me regardless of your votes. Understood?"

All three of them nodded.

Queen Aveyna looked at General Deoward. "General, yay or nay?"

General Deoward nodded. "Yay."

"General Ruba?"

"Yay."

"Admiral Tagril?"

"Yay."

"Then I believe I have made my decision. Lord Etheridge, please turn and face me."

Kent complied.

Queen Aveyna opened her mouth to speak, but the next words spoken weren't hers.

"I object," a voice from Kent's right said.

Kent, Queen Aveyna, and everyone else in the throne room turned to look.

Prince Kymil stood before his chair, his hands balled into fists.

CHAPTER ELEVEN

"I object," Kymil repeated. "May I speak, Mother?"

Queen Aveyna blinked at him, then she glanced between him and Kent. "My dearest, you are welcome to voice your concerns, of course."

Prince Kymil walked to the edge of the platform and addressed the crowd of officials rather than either Queen Aveyna or Kent.

"My fellow Inothians," he began, "this man is of foreign birth and is a former lord of our greatest enemy, Muroth. His intentions are not pure in the least. I believe he is a spy, sent to us by Muroth to weaken us, even at the cost of his own life, if necessary.

"He once led the very armies that plague our northern borders, and now we welcome him with open arms as a chief advisor? Are we mad?"

Prince Kymil pointed at Kent with absolute sincerity and concern in his eyes.

"This man cannot be trusted, especially not so soon. He is the equivalent of an enemy combatant. Whatever information he might offer us, we could extract from him as our prisoner, not as an *advisor*." Prince Kymil shook his head and lowered his hand. "What if he turns on us? What if he leads us into a trap on the battlefield?"

He paused and looked back at Queen Aveyna.

"What if he betrays and kills my mother?"

"Prince Kymil," Queen Aveyna said, "that is preposterous. If Lord Etheridge had intended to do me harm, he would have done it by now."

"You don't *know* that, Mother," Prince Kymil said. "Perhaps he is just biding his time, waiting for an opportunity to assassinate both of us, thereby throwing the kingdom into utter disarray."

Queen Aveyna looked at Kent, who didn't move except to calmly shake his head. Then she refocused on Prince Kymil. "Kymil, you're overreacting. Kent has proven to be nothing but loyal and kind over the last several months."

"We barely know him, Mother."

"No, *you* barely know him, Kymil," Queen Aveyna countered.

Prince Kymil folded his arms.

Queen Aveyna's pale cheeks reddened slightly. "I have taken the time to get to know his character, and I believe he is a man of honor and respect. He is not only worthy of this role; he is also equipped to provide immense value to our efforts against Muroth."

"He's a conniving, surreptitious spy," Prince Kymil nearly yelled. "He is a native, highborn Murothian at his core, and he always will be."

"*Enough*," Queen Aveyna snapped. "I have heard your concerns. Do you have evidence to support these claims beyond what you have already said and presented?"

Prince Kymil opened his mouth to say something, then he hesitated.

Queen Aveyna put her hands on her hips. "Well?"

Prince Kymil spoke quickly. "I believe more evidence will be uncovered in time, but it is simply far too early to—"

"Darling," she stopped him. She moved closer to him and, quietly enough for only him and those nearest to them to hear, said, "If you don't have any evidence, don't continue to speak. It makes you look foolish in front of the people you mean to rule when I am gone."

Prince Kymil blushed, but this time it spread to the entirety of his face, and his jaw tightened.

"Do you understand?" she asked quietly.

"Yes, Mother," he replied in a voice barely above a whisper.

Queen Aveyna turned back toward Kent and the officials. "I have heard the prince's concerns, and they are valid. I thank him for expressing them. However, I have deemed that it is in the kingdom's best interests to proceed with the promotion of Lord Etheridge to the role of chief advisor."

Prince Kymil sat in his chair again, folded his arms, and scowled at Kent.

Kent wished he had taken more time to get to know Prince Kymil over the last few months instead of solely developing his relationship with Queen Aveyna. He certainly didn't regret the inroads he'd made with her, but, admittedly, he hadn't shown enough interest in interacting with Prince Kymil.

Then again, he wondered if Prince Kymil even *could* view him favorably. Given Kent's background, Prince Kymil might never find him trustworthy.

"Lord Etheridge," Queen Aveyna said, "please kneel."

Kent knelt and looked up at her.

Afternoon sunlight shined through the ceiling windows, framing Queen Aveyna in a golden aura. She was more beautiful than anyone Kent had ever seen—even more so than his beloved Miranda had been, if he were being honest.

Queen Aveyna raised her hands above her head, and they shined with blue light, then white. She pressed her fingers together and slowly pulled her glowing palms apart, tracing a line of white light between them.

Her fingers separated from their corresponding twins on each hand, but the light between them lingered, brilliant and straight. When she lowered her hands, the light, now at least two-and-a-half feet long, hovered in the air over her head.

She reached up for it with her right hand and took hold of one end. As she pulled the light down, it took the shape of a crystalline sword that glowed with vibrant white light.

For all Kent had learned about anima magic, the practice of light magic still eluded him. Queen Aveyna had shown him several basic techniques, but he'd mastered only two or three of them. They always left him tired and weary, unlike most forms of anima magic, which he could do all day.

Queen Aveyna pressed the flat of the blade against the top of Kent's head. "May your mind stay sharp in the course of your service to Inoth."

She carefully touched the tip of the sword to his lips, and it felt cold, almost like ice.

"May your mouth speak only truth in the course of your service to Inoth." She nodded to him and said, "Your hands."

He held them out for her.

She touched the tip of the sword to each of his hands. "And may your hands only do good work in the course of your service to Inoth."

Again, the blade cooled his palms.

"And remember," she said with a smile, her voice low enough so only he could hear her, "I can use this sword to cut off your head whenever I want. So for your sake, my son had better be wrong about you."

Kent grinned. "I am loyal, I assure you."

"Good." She winked at him and released her grip on the sword. It dissipated into nothing before Kent's eyes. "Rise and present yourself, Lord Etheridge, Advisor to the Queen."

Kent stood and faced the officials, all of whom knelt to him and bowed, including General Deoward, General Ruba, and Admiral Tagril. If Kent were trying to infiltrate and cripple Inoth from within, he would've been well on his way to doing so.

Fortunately for Inoth, he had genuinely forsaken his old life in Muroth. And unfortunately for Muroth, Kent would now work against them for the rest of his days.

And Fane would pay the greatest price of all.

He stole a glance back at Prince Kymil. Aside from Grak and the rest of the royal guards, Prince Kymil was the only person not honoring him.

Instead, he continued to sit in his chair with his arms crossed, still scowling. It matched the expression on Grak's face perfectly.

No matter. Kent lived to serve Queen Aveyna's interests, not theirs.

"You may rise," Queen Aveyna said to the officials, and they did. "Now, let us celebrate."

KENT OCCUPIED THE SEAT OF HONOR THAT NIGHT. UNFORTUNATELY, RATHER THAN being seated next to Queen Aveyna, he sat directly across from her at the far end of the grand banquet table in the dining hall.

It was an Inothian custom, apparently, that the person being honored sat across from the royalty present so as to suggest a measure of equality in honor.

Kent would have much rather sat next to Queen Aveyna.

Several dozen chairs sat around the table, all filled with the ranking military officials who'd been present for the ceremony.

General Deoward sat to Kent's left, but on the adjacent side of the table, and General Ruba sat to Kent's right, across from General Deoward. Admiral Tagril sat to General Ruba's right, and the various officials sat where they pleased from that point on.

Though Kent could hardly make out Queen Aveyna's expressions from so far across the room, Prince Kymil's persistent glares cut across the table with perfect clarity. He sat to his mother's left, on the adjacent side of the table.

Grak, also scowling, stood behind them.

Kent wondered if Grak ever ate anything. He had to, given his size, but Kent had never seen it happen. Grak never ate when the queen or the prince ate. But it also made sense not to eat while protecting them—one fewer distraction.

Kent ate and conversed primarily with the two generals and the admiral. General Ruba and Admiral Tagril got thoroughly drunk and resorted to telling the foulest, dirtiest jokes and stories they'd ever heard, but General Deoward and Kent remained sober as they exchanged stories of various battles over the years.

They had much in common, including having stood on the opposite sides of several of the same battles. General Deoward didn't seem to be holding it against Kent, despite Kent's side having won the majority of them. Similarly, Kent no longer faulted General Deoward for having initially arrested him.

The night lingered on, and the wine continued to flow, but gradually the officials retired for the evening and walked or staggered out of the dining hall. Kent kept his eyes on Queen Aveyna as much as he could amid the loud joking to his right and the incessant war-storytelling to his left.

As he did, he noticed Prince Kymil summon Grak to his side while Queen Aveyna addressed one of the officers to her right. Prince Kymil uttered something indecipherable to Grak, who nodded, staring at Kent the entire time.

Kent watched them intently, but their conversation ended as abruptly as it began.

"Well, Lord Etheridge," General Deoward said as he rose to his feet, "if you'll excuse me, I should escort our two fellow advisors back to their chambers. I doubt they have the wherewithal to complete such a mission on their own."

Kent stood as well. "Thank you for your hospitality, General—our first encounter notwithstanding, of course."

"Yes." General Deoward's countenance hardened slightly. "I'm sure you understand I was merely doing my duty."

"Completely." Kent extended his hand. "I look forward to serving Inoth with you."

"Likewise." General Deoward shook Kent's hand. "Good evening."

With that, General Deoward rounded Kent's seat and grabbed hold of the other

BEN WOLF

two advisors and helped them up. They both leaned on him as the trio stumbled toward the dining hall doors, with Admiral Tagril and General Ruba still cracking jokes.

Kent no longer wondered why he had so consistently routed Inothian armies and incursions over the years.

He cast another glance at Queen Aveyna, but she was locked in a tense conversation with her son and didn't notice him.

Grak did, though, and he glared at Kent from across the room.

Only a handful of guests still sat at the table, so with a measure of disappointment he'd failed to capture Queen Aveyna's attention, Kent elected to retire as well. He left the room with Grak's harsh gaze still heavy upon him and returned to his chambers.

⚔

THAT NIGHT, FROM HIS ROOM, KENT SAW KYMIL STANDING AT HIS FATHER'S mausoleum with Grak again.

With his newfound freedom, Kent had taken to surveying the castle grounds, and he'd made sure to stop at the mausoleum for a look. Sure enough, it housed not only Kymil's father but several more of his ancestors as well.

And Kymil was once again paying his respects, perhaps to all of his ancestors, while Grak stood watch with his torch in hand. Why Kymil felt the need to have Grak accompany him for protection, Kent didn't know.

But perhaps if Kent were as scrawny and weak as Kymil, he would want a guard around all the time as well.

Kent crawled into his bed and began reading an ancient tome he'd borrowed from the palace library.

A wizened archmage by the name of Sobikal had written it several hundred years ago. It focused on the theory that a person could somehow master all three types of magic if only they could live long enough to achieve the feat.

Even without considering the additional lifetimes a mage would need to live in order to achieve mastery of all three, Kent didn't see how such a feat was possible.

From what he understood, the foundational principles of light magic and dark magic diametrically opposed each other. Light magic required a degree of self-sacrifice, and dark magic required energy and essence from other living things in order to wield power.

But Sobikal claimed he had found a path toward achieving that goal, the end result of which would be godlike power. Sobikal's biggest regret, as he'd written it in the book, was that he'd come to the realization of this possibility so late in life that he had little time to fully explore the path.

As Kent read, he heard the hiss of something against stone to his left. He shined his candle toward the sound and saw a thin, flat piece of parchment on the floor in front of his door.

Someone had slipped a note under his door?

He pulled the sheets aside and slid out of bed to examine the parchment. He picked it up and held it near the candlelight. It read:

Come to my chambers.
- A

Kent shivered. He wore only his undergarments, and though the nights had turned cold as winter approached, it wasn't the weather that had chilled him.

If he obliged the queen, he knew what it would mean.

She hadn't attempted to engage him in this manner since his first night in the palace, but they had certainly flirted and teased their way into closeness with each other since then. He'd been thoroughly smitten with her, and she clearly felt the same way.

Their relationship reminded him very much of his time with Miranda in that it felt natural and fluid. Were it not for the breadth of difference between Aveyna being queen and Kent being a makeshift lord and now an advisor, he could have called Aveyna a friend as well as a love interest.

Kent stared at the parchment. Her words read more like a command, but he knew she meant it as an invitation. But it was an invitation that he dared not turn down nonetheless.

With a sigh, Kent placed the parchment on his bed and closed his eyes.

Then he headed over to his vanity and lit two more candles so he could choose what clothes he intended to wear.

⚔

QUEEN AVEYNA OPENED HER DOOR. HER BLONDE HAIR HUNG DOWN BY HER SHOULDERS, and she invited Kent inside. He'd been to her chambers a few times before, but he'd always stayed outside.

This time, he went inside.

Aveyna closed and locked the door behind him.

Candles glowed with soft light around her considerable bedchamber, easily twice the size of Kent's. A burgundy canopy hung over her large bed, and thick furs covered the bed's surface.

A hearth burned with low flames across the room, and silver moonlight shined onto the stone floor through three tall windows. Kent counted at least another three sub-chambers attached to the bedchamber, but he didn't get a look at them because of Aveyna.

She walked up to him, barefoot and clad in a comparable nightgown to what she'd worn on her visit during his first night at the palace. She wrapped her arms around his torso. "I'm cold. Warm me up?"

She smelled like flowery perfume, as usual. It was wonderful.

Kent wrapped his arms around her and squeezed her close to him. The feeling of her body pressed against his sent his senses tingling. "Your fire is low. Would you like me to add to it?"

"Yes, please."

He released her and headed over to the hearth. He fed three thick logs into the dwindling flames and then stepped back. "There. That will help."

When he turned back, he found Aveyna sitting on her bed, wrapped in one of the furs, and he smiled.

"What are you smiling about?" she asked. "It's still cold."

"Give it time."

"Come sit with me?" She patted the bed next to her.

Kent sat next to her.

"Thank you for coming."

"Your note didn't leave me with much of a choice."

"You always have a choice. Especially now, *Advisor* Etheridge." She winked at him.

"Thank you again for placing your trust in me," he said. "I am honored, especially considering all that has happened."

"There is no one more deserving of the role," she said. "Do you know why I've summoned you tonight?"

He looked into her light blue eyes. "I have an idea."

"And you came willingly?"

"Yes," Kent replied quietly.

"Forgive me if I was too forward."

Kent chuckled. "Compared to last time, a note is not at all too forward."

Aveyna smiled and tried to hide her face under the furs. "Now I'm blushing."

Kent burrowed for her hand and found it. "You have no reason for concern. You simply wanted to rush to an inevitable conclusion."

Aveyna lowered the furs. "I don't want this to be the conclusion of anything. Unless it's the conclusion of our time apart from each other."

Kent nodded. "I can agree with that."

She smiled again. "Good."

Kent sat there, gazing into her eyes. He wanted her more than he had that first night in the palace—far more. His body flooded with emotion and energy, and he reached for her face with his hand and cupped her jaw.

She leaned toward him, and he pressed his lips against hers.

Within moments, she was tearing at his clothes, peeling them off layer by layer.

"Why are you wearing all of this?" she asked as she worked on his trouser buttons.

"I wanted to show up prepared for anything," he replied as he pulled his shirt off his shoulders. "You might have been summoning me to a private military meeting, for all I knew."

Aveyna giggled, and he loved the sound of it. She said, "I appreciate your thoughtful modesty."

The fire crackled behind them, brightening the room with golden light. They kissed again, with him shirtless and her still working on his trouser buttons.

"Here. Let me." He stood and finished working the buttons. Then he kicked off his boots, pulled his trousers down, stepped out of them, and rejoined her on the bed.

They made their way under the furs on the bed, and he made his way under her nightgown.

The fire in the hearth roared to life, and they spent the next hour locked in a passion the likes of which Kent had never known.

⁂

KENT LAY ON HIS BACK IN THE BED, AND AVEYNA LAY ON HIS CHEST, CLINGING TO HIM.

Across the room, the fire had receded again. Kent considered getting up to tend to it, but he decided to stay put instead. Aveyna was comfortable, and so was he. Beyond comfortable.

"Tell me about your wife," Aveyna said softly. "What was her name again?"

"Miranda."

"Yes. Tell me about Miranda."

Kent exhaled a long breath. He hadn't spoken of her in years, mostly because it stirred up old pains in his heart any time he did.

"She was the daughter of another Murothian lord from several provinces north. It was an arranged marriage, which I was not initially pleased about, but the instant I saw her, every single reservation I had extinguished," he began. "She had long, black hair and bright green eyes. Fair-skinned. A bit taller than you, and absolutely stunning."

"Mmm," Aveyna said. "She sounds lovely."

"She was." Kent smiled, and sadness trickled into his heart. "When we married, I was nineteen. She was only sixteen. Our love was slow to develop. I had my own ideas about what I expected, and they differed from hers. She was strong-willed and stubborn. But so was I.

"At first, her stubbornness bothered me, but it was one of the qualities I came to love the most about her. My mother had died some ten years prior, so the only consistent exposure I had had to women came in the form of servants. Whenever I tried to treat her like one of them, it did not go well for me."

Aveyna giggled. "I can imagine. Treating the daughter of a lord like a servant? What did you expect would happen?"

"I had been taught that women were subservient to men, but Miranda's mother had taught her otherwise. Needless to say, I had more than a few rude awakenings along the way, but it all worked out until…" Kent hesitated. It was a painful memory.

Finally, Aveyna said, "I don't want to make you talk about it."

"I am willing to do so. For you."

Aveyna sighed softly. "You told me she died in childbirth."

"She did."

"Is there much else to tell?"

"A little."

"I'd like to hear it."

Kent curled his arm around Aveyna and ran his fingers through her hair. "We were married for nearly three years before she became pregnant. She had endured two miscarriages during that time. I have long wondered if those failed pregnancies were her body's way of saying she was not built for childbearing.

"But we succeeded when she was nearly twenty years old. When she went into labor, I was happy and terrified and hopeful all at once, but those feelings slowly surrendered to fear and desperation when the midwives and our physicians told us she was dying."

Kent swallowed back his emotions and cleared his throat.

"It's alright," Aveyna said to him. "You don't have to say anymore."

"No. I need to." Kent forced himself to maintain his composure, and he continued. "They told us the pregnancy— my son—was killing her."

"Oh, Kent," Aveyna clung tighter to him.

"They gave me a choice. An impossible choice," he said. "I could either save my child and probably lose my wife, or I would certainly lose them both."

Aveyna squeezed him again.

"Miranda made me choose our son. She made the physician perform the surgery." Kent clenched his fists. "I have seen horrific acts exacted on the battlefield. I have *done* horrific things to my enemies. But nothing I have ever witnessed compared to what the physicians did to my wife."

Kent paused and closed his eyes, and he felt Aveyna kissing his shoulder and rubbing his bare chest.

"They cut her open and pulled the child, my son, from her womb," Kent opened his eyes to try to stanch the memories of Miranda's blood, of the carnage of new life. "And he was already dead."

Aveyna gasped.

Kent continued, "They tried to sew her back up, but she had lost too much blood. The idea of losing them was hard enough, but knowing I had forced my wife to endure such a bloody, pointless death made it all the worse.

"The physicians later explained to me that her hips were not wide enough to bear a child naturally. The gods had not made her that way, they said. So my guilt at ordering the surgery shifted to guilt at ever having lain with her in the first place. If I had not insisted on continuing my family name, she might still be alive today."

"You couldn't have known, Kent." Aveyna sat up and looked him straight in his eyes. "You couldn't have known. It wasn't your fault."

Kent nodded. "I know that now, of course. And yet, after coming to Inoth and witnessing miracles in action, seeing magic do things I could have never imagined, I cannot help but wonder if some form of magic may have saved her."

Aveyna shook her head. "It was an impossible situation. You cannot hold yourself accountable for any part of it."

Kent nodded again and cleared his throat to stave off the remainder of his emotion. "Forgive me for my demeanor. It is a difficult story to tell."

Aveyna cupped his cheeks with her hands. "You have no reason to apologize."

With a sigh, Kent leaned back and closed his eyes. "It has been nearly thirty years. I did not expect to miss her so severely after this long, but apparently I do."

"It's understandable. She was your first true love. That is a hard thing to grapple with, no matter how much time passes."

Kent opened his eyes and looked at her beautiful face. "It is. And I can only imagine how you must be struggling with the death of your late husband."

Aveyna's soft countenance changed, and she looked down at the bed.

Damn. You should have kept your mouth shut, Kent. He bit his lower lip.

"I understand the wound is still fresh. I should not have said anything."

Aveyna shook her head. "It's not that."

Kent squinted at her. "I apologize nonetheless. I have clearly upset you."

Aveyna said nothing.

Kent gently took hold of her arms. "If you will tell me how I transgressed, I can begin to make things right."

She shook her head. "It's nothing you did. It cannot be helped."

"What cannot be helped?"

"The way I feel."

Kent sat there in silence for several moments, waiting for Aveyna to say more, but she didn't. Finally, he started to speak again, but she cut him off.

"I poisoned my husband."

CHAPTER TWELVE

K ent sat up and looked at her. "What?"
"My husband," Aveyna repeated. "I killed him. I poisoned him, and he died."

Kent blinked. "Why?"

"He was cruel to me."

"As in, he—"

"He hurt me, physically. He was the king, and there was no one I could turn to for help." Aveyna pulled the furs over her bare chest and clung to them. "I feared he might kill me."

Kent considered her words. Killing a king was a high crime, but she hadn't done so out of greed or a desire to reign in his place. She'd done it to protect herself.

"He came close several times, but I recovered. No one else knew except for our royal physician, and he has since passed away."

Kent eyed her. "Did you..."

"*No*," Aveyna said. "Gods, no. Our physician, Archmage Ivelsted, was the only one who cared for me during those times. I could have never done such a thing to him."

"So the prince does not know?"

"He certainly doesn't know how his father died. Whether he knows about his father's behavior toward me, I do not know." Aveyna sighed. "Either way, it is done now."

"If your husband was the king, then why is Prince Kymil not king now?"

"He married into the royal family. My parents were the king and queen until they died, and then my husband, Theldus, and I took power. The line passes through me, not through him. I am and have been the rightful ruler since my parents died," she explained. "Though I think the discrepancy of power between us was the source of our contention."

BLOOD MERCENARIES ORIGINS

It made more sense that Aveyna would kill her husband under those circumstances. As the rightful ruler, she was removing a hindrance to her reign in the most expedient way she knew how.

Kent wasn't sure he liked the idea of it, but he had to admire her pragmatism. He'd heard of royal scandals throughout history, including murders for power-grabs and usurpations. Aveyna had acted in kind, but it was only to secure what was already hers.

Though there could possibly have been another way.

Kent asked, "If you were the rightful ruler, why did you not expose Theldus for what he was?"

"I was not always as strong as you perceive me to be now. For a man to lay his hands on a woman one moment and then grovel and apologize and swear his undying love the next moment—it is confusing and difficult." Aveyna clutched the furs tighter. "Then one day, something within me just snapped. The next morning, he was dead, in bed next to me.

"Archmage Ivelsted knew what I had done immediately, but he said nothing. Instead, he declared Theldus's death a tragedy, and we burned his body that night." Aveyna stared at the embers glowing from the hearth. "And that marked the end of my marriage."

Were Aveyna's husband to be exposed for what he was, Kent assumed he would have been executed anyway. And with Aveyna being the supreme law of Inoth, she would be the one passing the sentence.

Had Aveyna executed him publicly, her subjects would have known every part of this aspect of her personal life. So perhaps she had done it privately to avoid unnecessary public stigma and scrutiny of her actions from that point on.

It was, upon Kent's reflection, both a shrewd and necessary decision.

Though he had to admit it gave him pause all the same. Part of him had to wonder how quickly Aveyna might end his life if he were to cross her in some way, even just inadvertently.

But on the whole, Kent both felt sympathy for her for what she'd had to endure as well as admiration that she'd taken control of the situation to put a stop to it. "I am quite certain I will never understand what you went through, but I am glad you are safe now."

Aveyna's concentration broke, and she looked at Kent again. "So am I."

She shifted and lay back down, pulling him down with her. Then she intertwined her leg with his, pressed herself against him, and lay on his chest again.

"Will we get to do this again?" she asked.

"I would much prefer it to stopping," Kent replied.

"Good. I was worried I might scare you away." She rested her chin on her hands, which she laid on his chest with her elbows out to her sides, and she stared at him. "You're so handsome. It would be a pity to miss out on seeing you this close up on a regular basis."

Kent grinned and tousled a lock of her blonde hair. "I completely agree."

"I am worried about Kymil, though."

The mere mention of Kymil soured Kent's attitude. He tried not to let it enter his voice. "How so?"

"I suspect he would not approve of this."

Kent huffed. "You are the queen. It is not his place to approve or disapprove."

"I know, but it still bothers me to know he may be unhappy."

At that moment, half-underneath the most beautiful woman in all of Aletia, Kent couldn't have cared less about her pale, insolent son's happiness. But he cared about her, and if Kymil's unhappiness hindered her happiness, then perhaps there was something he could do about it.

"Would you like me to speak with him?"

She rose up and looked at him with those incredible light-blue eyes. "You would do that?"

Kent hesitated. What had he just committed himself to? "I will if you think it may help."

"I think it's worth a try," she said. "He really is a kindhearted young man.

And you're wonderful. Once you two forge a stronger relationship and understanding, I imagine his views on you will soften."

"If you say so."

"I do." She smiled at him. "He is going hunting tomorrow with Grak and General Deoward. I will ask him to include you on the excursion."

"Grak actually leaves your side?" Kent scoffed. "I didn't know he was capable of being away from you for more than a few minutes at a time."

Aveyna laughed. "He is very dedicated. And I believe he harbors a deep infatuation with me. So far, it has only manifested as protective feelings, but I would have you remain watchful all the same. He can be a bit vindictive at times."

"So I have noticed."

"To answer your question, yes. He is taking leave tomorrow to hunt with and protect Kymil. He accompanies Kymil on all excursions away from the palace because I do not trust anyone else to properly protect him." She kissed Kent's chest. "Except, perhaps, for you. I believe you could protect him, if need be. And that's all the more reason why you should go along tomorrow."

"If that is your wish, then I shall obey."

Aveyna beamed at him. "Thank you."

She pulled herself up to his face and kissed him again, deep and passionate, with her bare body pressed against his. The fire ignited again, even as the embers in the hearth continued to cool.

MORNING SUNLIGHT AND A CHILL IN THE ROOM WOKE KENT. HE CRAWLED OUT OF BED, still tired from the late night and its festivities, both during and after the banquet, and made his way into the bath chamber. He relieved himself and then returned to the bedchamber where Aveyna awaited him.

He positioned some logs in the hearth along with some straw and used two striking stones to spark a fire. Within minutes, he got it going, and he rejoined Aveyna in bed. She thanked him profusely for rekindling the fire, both with her words and with her body.

When they finished, she rose from the bed and donned a silk robe. "You should probably return to your chambers soon. We ought not push our good fortune."

"I agree," he said.

Aveyna sat at her vanity and began brushing her hair. "But before you leave, I wanted to explain to you my plans regarding Muroth going forward."

Kent tilted his head. "Certainly. But do you not also want to share these plans with your other advisors?

"I will," she replied. "But I want to make sure you and I are in agreement prior to any such meetings."

A sense of uneasiness filled Kent's stomach. *First, she reveals that she poisoned her husband to death. Now she wants to discuss policy regarding my former country solely with me, without the other advisors present?*

"I will admit, you have aroused my interest," Kent said.

Aveyna shook her head and looked at him through the mirror. "There's no cause for concern. I merely want to explain to you the steps I've taken to finally bring an end to the ongoing conflict with Muroth."

She kept referring to it as an "ongoing conflict." In Muroth, they'd always just called it what it was: war.

"And what would that be?" he asked.

"A temporary cessation of hostilities to provide space for a parlay. I have drawn up a treaty. If we can convince Muroth to sign it, we will no longer have to fight. Perhaps someday we may even become allies."

A parlay? A treaty? Allies? Kent couldn't believe his ears.

He sat up in the bed. "Aveyna, that is fine and noble thinking, but I fear it amounts to little more than a dream. A fantasy. Muroth is entrenched in its beliefs regarding magic and Inoth, and it is still bitter over having lost Inoth in the first place. I do not foresee much changing on that front."

"Perhaps you need a more positive outlook on the situation."

"Perhaps you need a more realistic outlook instead." Kent regretted it as soon as he'd said it, but it was too late.

Aveyna stopped brushing her hair and stared at him through the mirror.

"Forgive my impertinence, my queen," he said. "It is just that I have little faith that Muroth will go along with such ideas."

She stood and walked over to the bed, and Kent admired the way the robe clung to her in all the right places.

Aveyna sat on the bed next to him, put her finger under his chin, and kissed his lips lightly. "I already sent the letter."

Kent's eyes widened. "Aveyna..."

"I know what you're going to tell me. You're going to say that it's a sign of weakness and that Muroth is sure to exploit it."

Kent blinked at her. "That is almost word-for-word what I had in mind."

"Then there is only one way to find out, my love." She kissed him again, just a peck on his lips, and then she stood again and headed back toward her vanity.

That view was just as good as when she'd walked over to him.

Kent shook himself back to cognition. "Unless you can reach your messenger before he makes it to Muroth. Depending on when you sent him, and if you have a rider fast enough to catch up, we may be able to rescind the message in time."

Aveyna sat at the vanity and continued to brush her hair. "I'm afraid no rider in Inoth will be fast enough to catch this messenger."

"And why not?"

"Because I hired a freelance mercenary to deliver the message for me." She smiled at him. "A wyvern rider, formerly employed by the Govalian Army. He'll have arrived by now."

Kent cursed under his breath. She was right. And she'd purposely hired a wyvern rider knowing that once she sent the message, it could not be undone. "I do not know what else to say."

"Then I will speak," she said. "I promoted you to the role of advisor so you might advise me on how to forge peace between our two nations, not so you could help me overpower or subdue Muroth. I covet your knowledge of Muroth's internal politics because that knowledge means a quicker path to peace, not further extending this conflict."

Kent rubbed his eyes. "I am not trained in the art of peacemaking. I am trained in the art of war."

"But you are trained in the art of negotiation, are you not? And you know our negotiating partners better than anyone else in Inoth ever could," she countered. "Surely Muroth must've had plans for Inoth had you found a way to overcome us."

"Yes, but they all involved the subjugation and absorption of Inoth and its people into Muroth again. It would have included the enslavement or execution of any person using magic, regardless of their age.

"It would have meant the absolute end of life as you now know it," Kent blurted. "None of it is good for Inoth. No plans Muroth has for your country—for *our* country—are good."

"Then we must convince them otherwise." Aveyna set her hairbrush down and turned toward him. "I will be relying on you to help me achieve that end."

Kent shook his head. "I will do what I can, but the hatred and fear of magic are so deeply ingrained within Murothians that I doubt they will agree to any terms you propose."

"For now, we need only convince my other advisors and Kymil."

"You know I will obey you, of course," Kent said. "I will never oppose you openly, but I would like to request that you keep one consideration in mind."

"And that is?"

"If your call for peace fails," Kent said, "then we must prepare to fight."

"I am not opposed to violence and killing as a means to achieve peace." Aveyna walked over to him again. "But we have repeatedly tried those methods since this conflict began, and nothing has changed. I would prefer that my legacy be an attempt to resolve our differences with Muroth through diplomacy rather than on the battlefield."

Her actions would also likely make it harder for Kent to exact vengeance on Fane. If he were aiding Inoth in waging war on Muroth, then Fane and House Etheridge would naturally come within his circle of focus at some point. And killing Fane on a battlefield was just as good as anywhere else.

Kent nodded at her nonetheless. "That is admirable. As I said, I will support you, but in truth, I hold little hope for success."

"We will see, my love." She planted a lingering kiss on his lips, and then she pulled away. "Now I suggest you get dressed, get back to your chambers, and prepare to go hunting. You don't want to be late."

WITH A BOWSTRING ACROSS HIS CHEST AND A FULL QUIVER OF ARROWS HANGING FROM his hip, Kent rode north out of the palace stables next to General Deoward, following behind Grak and Prince Kymil.

They exited through a guarded, heavily reinforced gate on the north side of the city, but not the city's main northern gate. Deoward mentioned it was a sort of open secret.

The gate was not used for any other reason than to allow the royal family and those in the queen's court private access to everything that lay beyond the city's walls —or a private way into the city. When not in use, the gate remained shut, locked, and guarded by a small contingent of Inothian soldiers.

Beyond the northern city walls lay the vast forest. When Kent had arrived in Goldmoor, he had entered via the city's western gates, and thus he had only seen the forest from a great distance. Now they were headed straight for it to hunt deer, boar, and other wild game.

As they rode, Deoward explained the forest's history, particularly how it had long since supplied Goldmoor with timber for homes, firewood, shipbuilding, and more. Beyond that, he said, the animals in the forest made for good sport and even better eating.

Along the way, they passed through sprawling plains of farmland that alternated between growing crops and kept grazing cattle and sheep fed and occupied.

"Most of these lands belong to the royal family," Deoward said. "The lands that don't are owned by nobles who pay taxes. You know how it goes, having been a lord. I imagine lordship in Muroth is similar to here in many ways."

"It is," Kent replied. "Do you own any lands? ...are generals in Inoth permitted to own lands?"

Deoward scratched at his grey beard. "We are. I have a few dozen acres south of the city, along the coast. But I'm thinking of selling off ten acres or so. I don't get down there much these days, and at my age, I won't be able to properly care for it for much longer."

"You have servants and workers who handle that for you, do you not?" Kent asked.

"Of course. But I like to oversee their progress. I believe any group of people can become more cohesive and productive if a strong leader is willing to guide them." Deoward looked at Kent. "Another concept I'm sure you're familiar with."

"That I am, General. That I am."

As much as Kent was enjoying his conversations with General Deoward, the whole reason he'd come on this hunting trip was to grow better acquainted with Prince Kymil. So he excused himself and urged his horse forward.

Kent threaded between Prince Kymil's and Grak's horses and announced himself.

"Would you excuse me, Grak?" Kent said. "I would very much like to speak with the prince alone."

Grak eyed him, and then he leaned forward and looked at Prince Kymil.

"It's fine, Grak," Prince Kymil said with a nod. "We're almost to the tree line."

Grak shot Kent another glare, then he tugged his reins and fell back next to Deoward.

"Thank you, Your Highness," Kent said.

"You may dispense with the pleasantries, Lord Etheridge," Prince Kymil said. "You may call me Kymil, and I will call you Kent."

"If that is your wish, Kymil," Kent replied.

"It is." Kymil didn't look at him as he spoke. "What would you like to discuss?"

"Nothing in particular, I suppose. I inquired of the queen how I might best gain favor in your eyes, and she recommended that I accompany you on this trip." Kent kept trying to make eye contact, but Kymil kept looking forward. "And so I wanted to state that if you have any questions of me, I am happy to answer them."

"I have nothing to ask you, Kent," Kymil said.

Kent's jaw tensed. Kind of difficult to get to know someone better if they weren't willing to participate.

Or perhaps Kent needed to try harder.

He scanned Kymil, his horse, and the saddlebags hanging from the horse and saw no weapons of any sort. So how did Kymil intend to hunt?

Back in Muroth, he'd heard of young lords allowing servants to accompany them on hunts in order to do the shooting, tracking, skinning, and field-dressing of their kills. Then the young lords would claim credit for the kills. It had always felt dishonest to Kent, and so he'd never partaken in the practice.

If Kymil meant to do something along those lines, and he meant to have Grak do all the hunting for him, it would aggravate and annoy Kent for the whole excursion. The Murothian lords who'd done it ranged from age six to age ten or perhaps eleven. Kymil was more than twice that age.

"Would you permit me to ask a question of you?" Kent asked.

"You just did."

"Then permit me to speak freely?"

Kymil sighed. "You may."

Kent wanted to knock him off his horse for his attitude, but he resisted the urge. "I noticed you do not have any weapons with you. How do you intend to hunt?"

The question brought a smirk to Kymil's face, and for the first time since Kent had ridden up, he looked at Kent. He said, "You'll see."

They arrived at the forest's southern edge only minutes later, and they slowed their horses to an easy gait as they entered into the trees.

"Deep within this forest lurk dark and terrible creatures," Deoward said from behind Kent. "But as long as we don't venture too far into the woods, and as long as we don't stray too far from the trail, we should be fine."

Dark and terrible creatures? Kent had heard stories of mysterious creatures roaming forests in Muroth as well, but he'd never met anyone who'd encountered any, let alone seen any himself.

Still, he had believed magic was a curse less than a year prior. Anything was possible, he supposed.

They stopped a few hundred yards into the forest, and then Kymil dismounted. Kent followed suit, and he watched as Kymil opened one of the saddlebags on his horse and pulled out a pouch.

As Kymil tied it to his belt, Kent thought he saw the pouch itself move, but Kymil started walking, and Kent couldn't be sure of what he'd seen.

Grak stayed behind with the horses while Deoward accompanied Kymil and Kent deeper into the forest. Kent carried his bow in his hands now, and Deoward carried a trio of lightweight javelins.

But Kymil still carried no weapon from what Kent could see. He just carried a straight walking stick with several holes bored through it at regular intervals from the top to the bottom.

Perhaps he intended to use magic to hunt? It seemed like an unfair advantage, as magic had so many possible uses, especially compared to a simple bow and arrow.

The trees loomed overhead, blocking out most of the sunlight. To Kent's right and left—east and west—he could sort of see through the trees, but they seemed to go on forever. To the north, however, the sunlight faded far faster, cloaking the forest in deep shadows and darkness.

Kent didn't fear much in life, but nothing within him had any inclination to head farther north into this forest. It just didn't feel right.

"*Shh*," Kymil hissed. He stopped short, lowered his stick to the ground, and reached into his pouch.

Kent didn't have the right angle to see what Kymil had grabbed, and he didn't want to move for fear of scaring off whatever Kymil had seen.

Kymil's right hand began to glow red, and he lashed his hand forward from his hip as if throwing a skipping stone across a pond. A shock of red light zipped through the air, and a dull *thud* sounded in the distance.

"Yes!" Kymil pumped his fist and tossed the contents of his left hand into the underbrush. Kent would never find it there.

Kymil picked up his stick and walked toward where he'd thrown his magic, and Kent and Deoward followed. They found a brown rabbit pinned to a tree by a glowing red arrow, its back legs still kicking. The arrow had pierced under its neck, near its left foreleg, but the arrow hadn't killed it.

"Well done, Prince Kymil," Deoward said.

Kymil shook his head. "I'm out of practice. Usually my aim is fatal."

"Or perhaps it tried to flee," Deoward said.

Kymil set the stick down, took hold of the rabbit's head and its back, and twisted hard. A series of *cracks* announced its demise.

Kent raised an eyebrow. At least Kymil hadn't let it suffer.

The arrow evaporated into red smoke and disappeared, and the rabbit slumped to the ground.

"What kind of magic did you just use?" Kent asked.

Kymil picked up the rabbit and secured its legs to one of the holes in the walking stick with a leather string. "It's blood magic. A type of dark magic."

Now both of Kent's eyebrows rose. *Dark magic?*

From what Ronin had told him so many months earlier, and from he had read in his studies, dark magic was the most dangerous magic to try to master, both to the wielder and those around him. It had certainly proven dangerous for those around Eusephus back in the streets of Goldmoor.

"How does it work?" Kent asked.

Kymil grinned as he tightened the knot, then he held the stick and the rabbit out toward Kent. "If you will hold our lunch, I will show you."

Kent took it from him.

Kymil reached into his pouch again and this time held out his hand for Kent to see. A grey mouse with a fuzzy white belly and a pink nose squirmed in his left fist.

"Watch." Kymil held up his other hand, and it began to glow red.

The mouse in Kymil's hand writhed violently and squealed, and then Kymil hurled another red arrow into the woods. It embedded in a tree several yards away.

Kent looked back at the mouse which now lay in Kymil's empty palm. It had shriveled into little more than a skeleton covered in coarse, grey-brown fur.

"Blood arrow. The magic used its lifeblood, its essence, to create the arrow," Kymil explained. "It's a simple spell. It took me longer to learn to throw the arrows with any degree of accuracy than it did to learn to create them in the first place."

"So one mouse yields one arrow?" Kent asked.

"Essentially, yes. Bigger animals have bigger essences, and they yield more powerful arrows or other types of weapons with this particular spell."

Other types of weapons. Kent thought back to Eusephus's violet blade and flail. He hadn't seen Eusephus holding any mice or anything else while wielding them.

Kymil tossed the mouse's corpse into the brush, and Kent handed him the rabbit stick. "Shall we continue?"

"Yes, lets," Deoward said. "Perhaps the next kill will be mine."

Kent walked next to Kymil. "Nearly a year ago, I saw a practitioner of dark magic using a pair of violet weapons that he conjured out of thin air. He had drawn shapes with his hands first, and they just appeared in his hands."

"Runic magic," Kymil said. "Another type of dark magic. The mage creates ancient

154

BLOOD MERCENARIES ORIGINS

runes with his hands, and they create a variety of effects. It's high-level dark magic, and it comes at an incredible cost."

"The mage was not using any animals that I could see, though whenever his weapons hit his opponents, the weapons stole their essences."

Kymil nodded and stepped over an exposed root. "For runic magic to work, he would have had to harvest essences in advance. The weapons could perpetuate the spell, but he couldn't have created them without already being steeped in essence."

"He was an accused murderer."

"That likely explains it, then. He probably stole essences from other sentient beings and used them to fuel his dark magic." Kymil shook his head. "A tragic truth of the black arts. Dark magic, if left unchecked, can create urges within mages to seek greater power through more nefarious means."

And killing mice to create blood arrows isn't nefarious?

"Or perhaps some people are better used as sacrifices to secure greater power."

Kent's back straightened. "I beg your pardon?"

Kymil smiled. "Criminals. Murderers, pirates, bandits, brigands. The infirm, invalids. Rather than allow them to drain the resources and energy of those around them, perhaps it is better that they contribute to a greater cause, one far more significant than their harmful or dwindling lives."

While he understood Kymil's point of view, Kent didn't agree with it. There was a big difference between the execution of a criminal to achieve justice and the stealing of his essence to aid the executioner in gaining more power.

As for the infirm, how would Kymil have reacted if he'd been given power over Kent's father's fate? Kent didn't want to consider the outcome.

Kent certainly didn't begrudge Kymil the usefulness of the magic. On this small of a scale, it worked well and was practical; the death of one mouse yielding a good meal through the death of a rabbit didn't bother him.

But he'd seen what the magic had done to that mouse. The idea that a creature's life—or a *person's* life—could be stolen to feed a mage's appetite for power, that it would simply be reduced to a means to an end, left Kent with a sick feeling in his stomach. It was unnatural and cruel.

The hunt continued for several hours, and both Deoward and Kent hit rabbits of their own—two for each of them. Kent hadn't used a bow in nearly a year, and he hadn't fully re-acclimated yet, but Deoward demonstrated prowess with his javelins.

While Kymil didn't manage to kill any additional rabbits, he did bring down a young stag with three of his arrows. He grabbed three mice, summoned his blood magic, and threw three arrows at once. They knifed through the stag, and it fell, probably dead before it hit the ground.

Satisfied with the day's progress, they returned to the edge of the forest and reunited with Grak. By then, dusk was settling in, so they decided to begin the ride back to the palace with their trophies in tow. That way they could be back in time for the advisory meeting that night after dinner.

Kent wanted to engage with Kymil more, but Grak refused to leave his side during the journey home, and Deoward wouldn't stop talking. So Kent decided that though he wouldn't win Kymil over in one day, he'd at least made a good start.

⚜

THEY REACHED THE PALACE STABLES BY NIGHTFALL AND WENT THEIR SEPARATE WAYS. Grak and Deoward carried the deer carcass and the rabbits into the kitchen for butchering, and Kymil disappeared into his chambers.

Kent sought out Aveyna, first in the throne room. In her place, a wizened magistrate stood on the platform and heard cases from the citizens gathered there.

So Kent headed to her chambers and knocked on the door. A brunette servant girl of thirteen or fourteen years of age opened it, and he glanced over her shoulder and saw Aveyna seated at her vanity.

"Let him in, Giana," Aveyna ordered. "And then leave us. Close the door behind you, and wait outside."

The servant girl complied, sealing them in the room alone.

Aveyna stood, wrapped her arms around Kent's neck, and kissed him. When she released him, she inhaled a deep breath near his chest. "You smell like the woods."

"As I should." He embraced her.

"You're back later than expected. I'd hoped we'd have time before the meeting."

Kent tilted his head. "Do we not?"

She shook her head. "Not enough for me to make myself presentable."

Strings tied her dress together at her bust. Kent teased them with his fingers. "You are the queen. The meeting begins when you arrive."

Aveyna chuckled and batted his hand away. "And what will they think when you and I arrive late together?"

Kent grinned. "On the contrary, I would arrive on time. It does not take me long to prepare for such meetings."

"Being a woman puts me at a disadvantage. You men maintain unrealistic expectations for your queen's appearance."

"Then forget it. You are the queen, after all. No one will say a word." Kent reached for her bust again.

She caught his wrists and pulled them wide. "But they'll *think* it. I don't want to lose their respect by my appearance, especially given what I must tell them tonight."

Kent sighed, but she had a point. If she showed up bedraggled and proceeded to tell her other advisors about her proposed peace treaty with Muroth, they would think her all the more crazy.

Aveyna cupped his cheeks with her warm hands, and his stubble grated against her palms. "My love, there will be time tonight."

"I hope so." Kent held onto her waist.

"There will be," she reassured him. Then her eyes brightened. "Oh. I almost forgot. A message arrived for you today."

Aveyna picked up a piece of parchment laying on the nightstand next to her bed and extended it toward Kent.

He took it from her, puzzled. "Who is it from?"

"You'll see." She kissed his cheek. "Now release me so I can prepare."

"Very well." Kent kissed her lips. "I will see you at dinner."

"Please send Giana back in."

As Aveyna sat at her vanity again, Kent opened the door and stepped outside. He noticed Giana leaning against the wall a few yards down from the door and nodded to her. "You may go back inside now."

She curtseyed and scurried past him.

As Kent headed toward his chambers to change into more suitable dining attire, he unfurled the parchment and began to read. A message, scrawled in familiar handwriting, described lascivious tales of bedding beautiful Caclosian women, dining on exotic fruits and meats, and drinking "spectacular" wine.

Ronin's grand signature accented the bottom of the parchment, along with a post-script and a location where he could be reached should Kent decide to write him back. Apparently, Ronin had decided to stay put indefinitely.

Kent shook his head, smiling. Ronin had finally made it to Caclos after all. Kent would have to write him back later.

As Kent turned into the next corridor, he stopped short.

Grak stood before him with his sword in hand.

"We need to talk," he said. "Now."

157

CHAPTER THIRTEEN

Kent's shoulders stiffened. He immediately thought to the bow and arrows he'd left with one of the stable boys, and then he found himself searching the corridor for alternate weapons, then for something he could use in conjunction with his magic.

But aside from the walls, the floor, the fires burning in the iron torches behind Grak, and the torches themselves, Kent had no other options.

That was, if Grak actually meant to fight. The sword might've just been an intimidation tactic.

"I must change my attire before dinner," Kent said. "You have time."

Grak wore his full armor, as he had all day during the hunt. Kent, by contrast, wore hunting attire made of thick wool and leather. If a fight did ensue, Kent had the slight advantages of mobility and speed—both diminished because of the narrowness of the corridor—whereas Grak had every other advantage.

But the image of Grak holding a sword seemed to confirm Kent's earlier suspicions that Grak was not a mage. He'd meant to ask Aveyna about it several times, but he hadn't done so yet.

"What do you want?" Kent asked.

Grak shifted his grip on his sword and started forward. Bad for Kent. Right now, distance was Kent's ally in case he needed to retreat.

But retreating would show weakness and fear. Kent wasn't weak, and he didn't fear Grak, so he held his ground.

"I need to talk to you about the queen," Grak said.

"Why is your sword out?" Kent asked.

Grak looked at it. "I like the way it feels in my hand."

"If we are to have a conversation, you must put the sword away first."

"Why? Nervous about something?"

Kent's eyes narrowed. "I react more positively when I do not feel threatened."

Grak took a few more steps forward, now almost within striking range.

Only one response made strategic sense at this point. Kent stepped forward as well, closing the distance between them twice as fast.

Three calm steps later, Kent had leveled the terms, albeit only slightly. He'd taken away a good portion of Grak's sword range, limiting his potential attacks with it to stabbing and quick cuts. The down side was his proximity to Grak made Kent easier to grab hold of, and that presented a whole different set of issues.

"But I *want* you to feel threatened." Grak sneered at him. "That's the nature of this conversation. I'm threatening you."

Kent stood his ground. "Then get it over with. I have more important things to do."

"I know you're mixing with the queen."

"*Mixing?*" Kent knew what Grak was saying, but he refused to give him even an inch in the conversation.

"You know what I mean," Grak growled. "You're getting friendly with her, and not always with clothes on."

"How crude." Kent stared into Grak's dark eyes, unblinking.

"I don't like it. It needs to stop."

Kent blinked. Aveyna had mentioned Grak's interest in her—a "deep infatuation," she'd called it. "I do not believe you are in any position to make demands."

"You don't deny it, then?"

"What the queen does privately falls outside even the scope of your duties, as do my private behaviors. As such, I believe this conversation has concluded. Excuse me."

Kent tried to walk past Grak, but Grak's free hand caught his chest and half-pinned him against the corridor wall, stopping his progress.

Grak started to speak, but Kent reacted physically.

He grabbed Grak's armored wrist with his right hand, took hold of Grak's little finger with his left, and wrenched it back.

Snap.

Grak's eyes widened, and he roared. He yanked his hand free from Kent's grip and swung his sword at Kent.

But Kent saw it coming. He jammed the heel of his left hand into Grak's right bicep, stopping Grak's swing far short, then Kent shifted his footing, planted his right hand on Grak's black breastplate, and shoved with his arms and legs.

Grak staggered back several steps, and Kent backed farther away, increasing the distance once again. That way, if Grak charged, Kent would have plenty of time to deal with it.

"I told you not to touch me," Kent said.

Grak stood where he'd ended up, seething and cursing. He sheathed his sword with a metallic clack, and then he took hold of his little finger and popped it back into place with another snap. "You bastard... I ought to kill you."

Kent held his tongue. Now was not the time to prove a point—not when he had already proven one.

"You stay away from her, you hear?" Grak spat. "Or else."

Kent stared him down until Grak turned and stormed out of the corridor, clutching his hand. He waited a moment to make sure Grak wouldn't return, then he headed to his chambers.

⁂

AFTER DINNER, KENT JOINED GENERAL DEOWARD AND ADMIRAL TAGRIL IN THE throne room to meet with Queen Aveyna. General Ruba had returned to the northern army at the Inothian border, which fell under his command, so he wouldn't be in attendance.

Prince Kymil entered from the corridor behind the throne with Queen Aveyna close behind. Kent caught a glimpse of Grak's hulking form in the shadows farther into the corridor, and then the wall panel shut over him, sealing the meeting's five attendees in the throne room alone.

Aveyna sat on her throne, welcomed them briefly, and then dove into her plan regarding Muroth. She concluded, "I have already sent the proposed treaty by way of a winged messenger."

Her voice dissipated in the vast throne room, leaving silence in its wake.

General Deoward spoke first. "Your Highness, I wish you had consulted us prior to sending the messenger."

Admiral Tagril nodded. "These types of decisions are precisely *why* your predecessors relied upon advisors. We serve as checks and balances against the inclinations of the sovereign."

Aveyna remained silent, and she looked at Kent.

"While I am inclined to agree with the general and the admiral about how this decision was reached," Kent started, "I am optimistic that Queen Aveyna's attempts can forge a lasting peace with Muroth."

Aveyna gave him a grin and a nod. He'd done what she'd wanted.

"I think it was a reckless move," Kymil said from his chair. "Foolish and reckless."

Part of Kent wanted to smack the disdain off of Kymil's face, but internally, he agreed with the assessment. He'd said as much to Aveyna that morning.

"Muroth doesn't want peace. And we don't want peace," Kymil continued. "They are determined to reclaim what they lost so many years ago. We want to destroy them, and they want to destroy us. Peace is impossible."

"Peace talks have only been attempted once before throughout the course of our conflict with Muroth," Aveyna said. "Eighty-nine years ago, before any of us were born, it was Muroth, not Inoth, that offered terms for peace. My great-great grandfather rejected those terms, and thus the conflict continued."

"Then he was reckless and foolish, too," Kymil muttered.

Kent's patience snapped. "Perhaps you should address your *queen* with more respect."

Kymil looked up at Kent, a mixture of shock and anger in his eyes. "I beg your pardon?"

160

"It is the queen's pardon you ought to beg, not mine." Kent knew he was undoing whatever progress he'd made with Kymil on the hunting trip, but he refused to let Kymil treat Aveyna in a way even vaguely reminiscent of what she'd endured from Kymil's father. "Perhaps you ought to apologize as well."

"That will not be necessary, Lord Etheridge," Aveyna interjected. "Kymil is free to express his concerns."

"*Respectfully,*" Kent added. "He must address you according to the respect your office as his queen commands."

"Kent," Aveyna said calmly. "It's fine."

Kent's chest stewed with fervor, but he bit back the rest of words for Kymil, who sat in his chair glaring at him. Kent bowed to Aveyna. "Yes, my queen."

"Kymil," Aveyna began, "what alternative path would you suggest?"

"We must break them as they have sought to break us." He motioned toward Kent. "The whole reason you made *him* an advisor was so that we could better learn to defeat them. And now you want to make peace instead?"

"It is in Inoth's best interests to avoid further bloodshed," Aveyna said.

Kymil turned to Kent again. "Did you fill her head with these ideas? Is this your idea of *advising* her?"

Kent started to answer, but Aveyna cut him off.

"The idea to pursue peace was entirely mine, and I acted unilaterally in executing my plans to that effect." Aveyna looked at Kent. "Lord Etheridge did not sway my decision, but he is an asset to me all the same with regard to Muroth. His expertise regarding the internal politics of Muroth will help us to achieve this peace."

"I will do everything I can, Your Highness," Kent said.

The discussion continued for a few more minutes, and Aveyna answered her advisors' questions with wise, tactful answers. Meanwhile, Kymil glared at Kent practically nonstop.

Years earlier, Kent had learned that the males of certain predatory species often killed the non-related offspring of their mates to preserve their own lines as superior. Kent empathized with that sentiment now more than ever.

And his puny neck would be so easy to snap, too, Kent mused.

But it would also devastate Aveyna to lose Kymil, so Kent buried his dark thoughts deep within his mind.

"If there are no more questions, then I will call this meeting to a close." Aveyna glanced between the four of them, and no one said anything else. "Then all that remains is to await a reply from Muroth. Let us pray that we receive a favorable one. Go in peace, my trusted friends."

Back in Aveyna's chambers, Kent lay in her bed under her furs, spent and content. She lay next to him, partly on top of him and partly on her side, lightly snoring.

He grinned down at her. *Apparently, even queens snore.*

He'd already told her about the hunt with Kymil, but he hadn't said anything about his encounter with Grak afterward. Kent wondered about what Grak might do if he'd had the chance to see them together now, in bed together.

The fire in the hearth dwindled. Moonlight trickled into the room between the curtains, and Kent closed his eyes for a moment.

A series of hammerstrokes on Aveyna's door startled Kent awake again, and Aveyna with him. Frantic pounding. Metallic thudding. An armored hand.

Kent's internal protector ignited, and he looked toward the hearth, but the fire had gone out, and the wood inside was black and cold. He couldn't use fire magic without fire.

Rays of soft sunlight crept between the curtains instead of moonlight.

Morning, but early morning—at least for winter.

The pounding persisted, and Aveyna looked at him with wide, concerned eyes. Whether she was worried about him being found there or just about the incessant, urgent clanks against her door, Kent could not discern.

"Stay here," Kent told her. She didn't move.

Kent slid out of the bed, donned his undergarments and his boots—he didn't want to be caught *totally* off-guard—and took one of the fireplace pokers into his left hand, ready to summon his magic to his right hand to manipulate the iron to his will. Or just to bash it into whoever was there, if they meant Aveyna harm.

As he approached the door, it literally quaked and trembled from the pounding, and thick shadows moved in the light coming from under the door. Whatever or whoever it was, something was definitely wrong.

He carefully unlatched the lock, with the poker raised high in his left hand. The added bonus of choosing it was that he had an actual weapon to use as well as magic.

Kent pulled the door open, revealing Grak in the doorway.

Grak's countenance shifted from concern, to confusion, to fury. He growled, "What in the third hell are you doing in here?"

"How is your finger?" Kent lowered the poker but not his guard.

"What?" Realization dawned in Grak's eyes, and then he glowered at Kent anew and grunted. "It hurts."

"What do you want?"

"Where is the queen?" Grak asked. "She is safe."

"*Where?*"

"In bed."

"I must see her."

Grak pushed on the door, but Kent held it in place.

"She is not presentable," Kent said.

Grak's scowl might've permanently affixed itself to his face at the rate he was showing it. "It is my duty to ensure she is unharmed."

"Then you may take my word for it, as I just came from her side."

Grak's fists clenched, one of which held a parchment.

Kent nodded toward it. "I would not damage that message if it is important."

"I am to deliver it to Her Majesty *personally*," Grak said.

"You may give it to me instead." Kent held out his right hand.

"You deaf? Didn't you hear what i just said?" Grak snapped.

Kent started to speak, but Aveyna's voice carried from across the chamber.

"You may give it to Lord Etheridge, Grakios," Aveyna called.

Kent granted himself a grin.

Grak's frown deepened, and he called back, "Yes, Your Majesty."

He slapped the parchment into Kent's hand.

Then Kent closed the door in Grak's face and latched it again. He stood there, listening until he heard Grak stomp down the corridor, then he returned to Aveyna's bed and handed her the parchment.

"I've been meaning to ask you," Kent said as Aveyna unrolled the parchment, "is Grak a mage or not?"

She shook her head. "He's a skilled fighter, but he's not a mage. I brought him into the fold years ago because of his prowess and because I knew he didn't think like Inothians. He sees angles that mages don't see. That can be incredibly valuable when it comes to security."

Kent nodded. At least now he knew for sure.

Aveyna read the parchment. Her eyes widened, and she sprang from the bed, hurried over to her wardrobe, and began to pull out clothes. "Get dressed."

"What does it say?" Kent asked.

Between breaths, Aveyna said, "Muroth has invaded northern Inoth."

CHAPTER FOURTEEN

Within three hours, Kent and his servants had packed clothing and supplies for his trip to northern Inoth. Now he stood in the same stables he'd visited yesterday for the hunting excursion.

Within that same three-hour window, General Deoward had mustered a force numbering in the thousands and dispatched them ahead of the queen's traveling party. The advance force would clear a path, so to speak, for Aveyna and her entourage, but Deoward would stay behind to govern Goldmoor in her place.

The parchment had conveyed more than just Muroth's invasion—much more. It had announced Muroth's intent to meet with Queen Aveyna in response to her proposed peace treaty, and thus the army would temporarily cease hostilities until its as-yet-unnamed leader could meet with Aveyna.

Maybe Aveyna had been right after all, but maybe not. Either way, Kent would be there to advise her and help see her through it.

Kent wondered if Fane was leading the army, though he doubted it. Fane had always been a talented fighter and strategist, but he'd rarely seen actual battle. It had never held as much interest to him as it had for Kent.

That didn't mean Fane wouldn't show up, though. As Lord Etheridge, Fane would probably be there. And that complicated things, because peace talks would not go well if Kent managed to kill Fane in front of everyone.

A loud snort sounded behind Kent, followed by a series of quick, reptilian chirps.

Kent turned back and stared at the young wyvern rider who'd brought the message back from Muroth. So far, everyone had given him and his wyvern a wide berth.

The wyvern rider had brown hair, green eyes, and spoke with a Govalian accent. Blue-green scales covered his wyvern—both a magnificent and terrible beast. It carefully nipped chunks of dark red meat from the rider's hand.

A thick rod tipped with a three-pointed spearhead leaned against one of the stable pillars nearby. Kent admired the rider's choice. It was a ferocious weapon.

Kent noticed that the rider kept hunching over and rubbing his lower back. Perhaps he'd sustained some sort of injury.

The rider reached into a sack hanging from the wyvern's saddle and pulled out a pair of mushrooms, one colored with yellow and another with purple. Both radiated with the faint but familiar blue hue of magic.

He devoured them both, and within moments he'd straightened up and stopped rubbing his back. He also wobbled when he walked, and his speech slurred a bit whenever he spoke to his wyvern.

Kent just shook his head. *What an odd fellow.*

Aveyna arrived with a group of servants and entered her private carriage with Kymil. She invited Kent to join them, and he obliged, though Grak shot him a furious glare for doing so.

Soon after, General Deoward saw them off, and the journey north commenced.

⚔

SEVERAL DAYS LATER, THEY ARRIVED ON THE NORTHERN FRONT.

The Murothian army had encamped within easy striking distance of one of Inoth's northern fortresses, a place known as Dewmire. The Inothian soldiers that had gone ahead of the queen's caravan had pitched tents behind the fortress.

As the caravan arrived, General Ruba and the combined forces of Inoth's northern army and the soldiers from Goldmoor stood at attention out of respect for Aveyna.

Kent stepped out of the carriage first, into the chilly late-autumn air, and he offered his hand and helped Aveyna down. Kent offered to help Kymil as well, but Kymil ignored him and jumped down on his own.

"General Ruba," Aveyna said.

"Your Highness." He bowed.

"Apparently, I did not enjoy your presence for long enough back at Hunera Palace, so I thought it wise to visit you here."

Ruba chuckled. "I am honored, Your Highness. I trust you have been informed of the situation?"

"I am the *cause* of the situation, General," Aveyna replied. "As I'm sure you know."

He nodded. "That I do, Your Highness."

Ruba greeted Kymil and Kent, and then he escorted them into Dewmire. As Kent passed into the fortress gates behind Ruba and Aveyna, a cloud of dust from the courtyard announced the wyvern rider's landing. The Inothian soldiers present didn't react except to shield their eyes.

The rider dismounted, tossed his spear to a nearby Inothian soldier who caught it, and started toward Aveyna and Ruba.

"You already know Aeron Ironglade and his wyvern, Wafer, Your Highness," Ruba said.

165

"Yes, I do," Aveyna replied.

Aeron knelt before her and bowed.

"Rise, Mr. Ironglade," Aveyna ordered.

Aeron complied, and he rubbed his back as he did. "I'm ready to relay any additional messages you request, and I'm ready to do pretty much anything else you order me to do."

Kent eyed him, and Aeron noticed. His eyes widened slightly.

"I—I just mean that you've still got me on retainer," Aeron clarified, "so if I'm supposed to fight or guard you or anything else…"

Aveyna smiled. "I know what you meant, Mr. Ironglade. Thank you. For now, rest and recuperate. I must first confer with my advisors."

Aeron bowed again. "Yes, Your Highness."

Kent shot him another look, and Aeron glanced away.

Ruba led them into a large, inner meeting room, and Grak closed the door to seal them inside while he waited outside with the other royal guards. They all took their seats, and General Ruba explained the situation in greater detail.

Muroth's invading army numbered somewhere between 7,000 and 8,000 soldiers, including heavy cavalry, archers, and infantry. From what Inoth's scouts had reported and what Aeron had determined while delivering messages, Muroth had also brought catapults, but they hadn't been assembled yet.

Kent knew plenty about Murothian catapults. Just two years prior, he'd commissioned dozens of them for precisely an occasion like this. They were ruthless machines, capable of hurling all sorts of terrible things across battlefields. Chances were, his family had bought and paid for the majority of the catapults out there.

By contrast, Inoth had mustered closer to 10,000 soldiers between those sent from Goldmoor and those gathered from other forts nearby. Plus, they controlled Dewmire, which was well-provisioned in case of any siege attempts.

"Of course, it is my hope that all of this information is moot," Ruba concluded. "If Her Royal Highness is capable of brokering the peace treaty, then perhaps we can all go home." Ruba paused. "Well, I would remain here, of course, as is my duty."

"Has Muroth attempted to make contact with you directly?" Aveyna asked.

Ruba shook his head. "No. All communication thus far has gone through young Mr. Ironglade."

"So they haven't made requests regarding terms for a meeting?"

"Not yet. I think they were waiting for you to arrive."

"Do you know who commands their army?"

Ruba shook his head. "Ironglade dealt with a messenger speaking on behalf of Emperor Bouwen, but the messenger himself was no one of consequence. I do not know if the emperor himself is present."

"Doubtful," Kent said. "The emperor is old and rarely leaves Lowmir Keep anymore. It is possible, given the nature of this invasion, that the emperor would've come, but the odds are slim."

"Very well." Aveyna looked at Kent. "I believe it is up to us to send an invitation to a meeting."

Kent nodded.

"Please have Aeron deliver a message to them," Aveyna said to Ruba. "I will meet with the emperor or his authorized representative tomorrow morning."

Ruba bowed. "Right away, Your Highness."

KENT STARED AT THE FLICKERING CAMPFIRES DOTTING THE LANDSCAPE. HIGH ATOP THE fortress wall, the night air chilled his face, and his breath came out in wisps of vapor, reminiscent of the clouds that obscured the moon and the stars above.

How many men down there had he personally met? How many would have called him their lord less than a year prior?

Was Fane among them? Kent still didn't know.

He clenched his fists and exhaled a long sigh. The idea of Inoth making peace with Muroth made sense for both countries, but it did nothing to resolve Kent's desire to exact revenge upon his treacherous brother.

"There you are," a feminine voice said from behind him. Kent turned back in time to see Aveyna walking toward him.

Twenty feet behind her, Grak stood with two other royal guards near the stone staircase leading up to the wall, positioned between the nearest soldier on night watch duty and Aveyna.

"What brings you up here so late?" Aveyna wore thick, leather boots and a heavy coat made of furs, but Kent surmised she wore only a nightgown underneath.

"Just wanted to think. Clear my head," he said.

Aveyna stood next to him, and their shoulders touched. "Having second thoughts about swearing allegiance to Inoth?"

"None whatsoever."

"Good." Aveyna leaned into him.

Kent glanced back at Grak and saw him scowling in the torchlight.

"It's alright," Aveyna said. "Put your arm around me. Grak will have to endure."

Kent put his arm around her. "He is a bear I do not wish to poke."

"He's overreacting." Aveyna lowered her voice. "And he has too high of an opinion of himself. I find precisely nothing about him attractive. He is doubtless useful and good at his job, but that is where our relationship begins and ends."

"He is relentless, to be sure."

A long moment of silence passed between them.

"Do you know the emperor?" Aveyna asked.

"I did not know him well," Kent replied, "but we have met on several occasions. He and my father were contemporaries. They shared an amicable relationship."

"What of the emperor's children? Do you know them?"

"About as well as I know their father and the empress."

"I want you at the meeting with me," Aveyna said.

Kent tensed. "I will of course obey, but are you certain that is wise? The sight of me at your side may provoke an unfavorable response."

"Let me rephrase: I *need* you at the meeting with me. I've never dealt directly with Murothians before. Not before you, anyway."

"Why would you have? We have just been content to kill each other until now."

"Exactly," Aveyna said. "But you understand how they think. I need you to help me speak to them, to help broker this peace."

Kent sighed.

"Are you nervous?"

"Worried. Concerned." Kent exhaled a vaporous breath. "And nervous, yes."

"About your brother? If he's down there?"

"He may be. He may not be. It could go either way," Kent said. "When our father was alive, I went with the army. Fane accompanied me on occasion, but mostly he remained at home to aid Father in overseeing our other affairs. I always had a taste for battle, combat, strategy, and tactics, so I enjoyed coming to the front.

"Now that Father is dead, Fane may remain at the family estate. He was always less inclined to get personally involved in Muroth's military actions." Kent thought of General Calarook and wondered if he'd be present. "Our province has a strong slate of generals who handle border defenses, invasions, and other military actions, so there may be no need for Fane to come."

"If he is there, can I count on you to maintain your composure?" Aveyna asked.

"Of course," Kent said, albeit reluctantly. "I would not do anything to jeopardize the greater mission."

"I know how important it is to you to see that justice is served to him."

"It is, but peace between Muroth and Inoth is far more important. I will honor my commitment to both you and Inoth." Kent added, "And my brother may continue to live a healthy, happy life until the day he dies by my hand."

Aveyna grinned up at him. "Yes. Let it be so."

Another long, quiet moment passed.

"You said you do not believe the emperor is here," Aveyna said more than asked.

"He is an old, frail man. He was always mentally sharp, despite his age, unlike my father, whose faculties had begun to slip over the last few years of his life. But the emperor's physical body is worn out. I imagine he has sent someone."

"Whom will he have sent instead?"

"Possibly one of his children. His oldest child is his daughter, Sarina, but his second child and first son, Wye, is his heir. Sarina is beautiful and intelligent, but she has a hot streak to her that riles her temper easily. Wye is more subdued, but I always sensed a general apathy behind his words and eyes.

"If it is one of his children, I would bet on Sarina over Wye, simply because Emperor Bouwen is old. If something were to happen to Wye as well, then another of his male children would have to take the throne. It seems less risky to send Sarina or one of her other brothers instead.

"But then again," Kent continued, "it could be one of the southern lords or one of Muroth's generals. There are multiple possibilities, but one fact remains true: they are coming to meet with no one less than the Queen of Inoth herself. Anyone less than the emperor will pale in comparison to you."

"Thank you." Aveyna leaned into him again, and Kent squeezed her tighter. Her voice low again, she said, "If you are through, perhaps we could retire? I could use some inspiration and some comfort tonight to help prepare me for tomorrow."

Kent grinned. "Certainly."

As they walked toward the staircase, Kent noticed that Grak wasn't there anymore, but the two royal guards were. One led the way down the stairs, and one followed behind Aveyna and Kent.

The stairs fed into an open-walled corridor one story above the courtyard. Kent saw Grak standing with Kymil in the courtyard below, nodding as Kymil spoke.

Kymil noticed Kent and Aveyna walking past, and he stopped talking with Grak. Then he waved up at them, casually, and resumed his conversation with Grak.

Kent waved back, but Kymil missed it.

By the time Aveyna and Kent reached her chambers, a fire already raged in the hearth, and a decanter of wine with two goblets sat on a small table near the bed. The space felt cramped compared to Aveyna's sprawling chambers back at Hunera Palace, but they would do just fine for the night.

Kent and Aveyna skipped the wine and indulged in each other instead. When they finished, Aveyna lay next to him, silently searching his eyes.

"I've never been so happy," she said.

Kent stroked her face. He considered whether or not he'd ever been as happy.

His time with Miranda had been far too short, but he had enjoyed it immensely. She had meant everything to him, and he had found rest in her arms. They'd certainly been happy. But could he quantify their happiness as compared to this moment, right now, with Aveyna?

"Kent?" Her voice snapped him out of his thoughts.

He refocused on her and studied her face. Her beautiful, enrapturing face.

An impulse rose within him, one inspired by madness and heightened by anxiety over thoughts of tomorrow's meeting.

He acted on it nonetheless.

"Aveyna," he said. "Will you marry me?"

CHAPTER FIFTEEN

Aveyna blinked at him and sat up in the bed. "What?"

"I cannot see a future without you in my life." Kent sat up as well and took her hands into his. "You said you had never been happier. Does it not make sense to take this next step?"

Aveyna stared at him. "I'm not sure."

Kent opened his mouth to speak again, but he stopped. Aveyna's last marriage was marked with abuse and had ended with murder. A strong-willed approach to convince her to see his point of view would not gain him much ground.

Instead, he said, "Aveyna, I love you. I want to give you the very best of everything I have to offer, which, admittedly, is not much. But what I have, I give to you. I believe our paths converged for a reason—so that we could heal each other and grow together. If any part of you believes that, then say yes."

Aveyna remained silent, studying his eyes and his face. Slowly, her lips curled into a grin, and the grin spread into a smile. She grabbed Kent's head, pulled him close, and kissed him long and hard.

When Aveyna finally let go, Kent asked, "Is that a yes?"

She smiled again and nodded. "It's a yes. I can't deny the truth of what you said. I do believe we were meant to heal each other. And I want to grow together with you. So, yes, Lord Kent Etheridge, I will marry you."

They kissed again, and then Aveyna pulled Kent on top of her once more.

Morning came quickly for Kent, and before long, he was riding out of the fortress alongside Aveyna, Kymil, Grak, and the royal guard into the frigid morning air. A hundred-man entourage of elite Inothian soldiers also accompanied them.

Kent had strapped a sword to his hip, something he hadn't done for months in light of his nearly incessant study of magic. But he wore one today because he wanted to convey an air of strength to his former countrymen, regardless of who might show up.

He had also donned a belt with several pouches full of various natural items. That way, he could use magic if he needed to. Kent didn't know if he would need any of it, but he was fed up with barely surviving the last year's trials thanks to quick thinking and luck. Better to be prepared, for once, even if nothing happened.

In the distance, riders galloped toward them with the white, black, and bronze banners of Muroth flapping over their heads. A carriage of sorts also accompanied the procession.

Minutes later, Aveyna, Kymil, and Kent stood before neither Emperor Bouwen, nor Sarina, nor Wye. Instead, they faced Graeme Bouwen, the emperor's sixth son. Relief, but also regret, at not seeing Fane with Graeme filled Kent's stomach.

He also didn't see General Calarook among the group. Perhaps Calarook had stayed behind, ready to lead Muroth into battle, or perhaps he'd been demoted or reassigned in light of Kent's escape from Ranhold Fortress.

Kent had only met Graeme once before, more than ten years earlier when Graeme was only a child running through Lowmir Keep. He'd grown up since then, now with dark brown hair like his mother, and with his father's unmistakable square jaw and commanding presence.

He wore golden armor, both denoting him as royalty and setting him apart from the white- and bronze-armored Murothians who accompanied him. Two of his advisors, both northern lords whom Kent recognized but could not name, stood several feet behind him, effectively leaving Graeme alone.

Kent doubted Graeme would recognize him, given the time that had passed since they'd last seen each other. Sure enough, as Graeme approached, he glanced at Kent for a moment, then he refocused on Aveyna.

"You are Queen Avenya Armanix, ruler of Inoth?" Graeme asked in a deep voice.

"I am." Aveyna motioned toward Kymil. "And this is my son, Prince Kymil."

Graeme acknowledged him with a slight nod. "I am Prince Graeme Bouwen, son of Emperor Elex Bouwen, ruler of Muroth. We have received your messages, and I come with his full power and authority to discuss your proposal."

Kent scanned the soldiers surrounding the meeting. Like the Inothians, the Murothian soldiers had formed a semicircle behind Graeme. But unlike the Inothians, Graeme had half as many soldiers with him.

Having lived in Inoth for nearly a year, now, Kent found it unsettling at first, but he recalled the sense of Murothian pride and superiority he'd once held so close to his heart—especially when it came to Inoth.

Despite having lost the war that resulted in Inoth's separation from Muroth, Murothians now viewed themselves as inherently superior. Part of the mentality came from attributing the pervasiveness of magic within Inoth as a widespread curse rather than a benefit.

The other part came thanks to the intense, ongoing training Muroth subjected its soldiers to. It made them notoriously efficient in battle, especially against mages. So it made sense that Graeme would only bring a few dozen men with him compared to Aveyna's hundred.

Furthermore, it made little difference if Graeme were somehow killed during these negotiations. As the emperor's sixth son, Graeme stood little chance of ever ascending to his father's throne. Thus, if he perished, it would inspire national rage without hindering the Bouwen family's lineage.

"Do you agree to our terms?" Aveyna asked.

"No," Graeme said flatly. "But I believe you may wish to hear our counter-proposal."

Aveyna's jaw tensed, then it loosened. "What do you propose?"

"My father requests that Inoth cede all lands north of here, including Dewmire Fortress, to Muroth," Graeme said. "Citizens of Inoth will be given thirty days to remove their property and themselves from this land to resettle farther south."

Aveyna stared at him with a half-smile fixed on her face. "And the ceding of these lands to Muroth will buy lasting peace between us?"

"In part, yes," Graeme said. "My father also requests that Inoth pay Muroth an annual tribute of 500,000 gold coins, or the equivalent worth in comparable goods."

Aveyna squinted at him. "Would you give me a moment to confer with my advisors?"

Graeme nodded to her. "Do as you must."

Aveyna turned around and walked between Kent and Kymil. Then she turned and faced them with her back to her own men rather than to Graeme and the Murothians, which meant Kent and Kymil had their backs facing the Murothians instead.

Kent didn't like it, but he recognized she was doing it so her back wouldn't be turned to Muroth.

"His terms are steep," Aveyna said in a low voice. "The crown cannot afford to maintain a functional army and navy and pay such a massive annual sum in tribute to Muroth. Within ten years, we would be crippled."

"Were you considering paying Muroth *any* tribute?" Kent asked.

"I offered them a one-time payment of 100,000 gold to be used for reparations, specifically for the families of the Murothian soldiers who have perished in this senseless conflict," Aveyna replied.

Kent straightened his spine. She'd made a bold—and curious—move.

"We have a surplus in our treasury of roughly three million in gold," Aveyna said. "I figured it was a small price to pay to buy some goodwill from Muroth, regardless of whether it made it to the soldier's families or simply lined the pockets of Emperor Bouwen or Murothian lords."

"500,000 gold per year, Mother is a ridiculous rate," Kymil said.

"I agree," Kent looked at Aveyna. "This is a power grab by Muroth. As you said, they want to cripple Inoth, albeit slowly. Their request for ceding the lands is indicative of that."

"I never volunteered to cede any lands to them," Aveyna said.

"Doing so would increase Muroth's lands and weaken Inoth's strength as a country," Kent said. "These two terms alone would transform Inoth into a sort of vassal state under Muroth's partial control…"

"And that would lead to further persecution and ultimately our nation's demise," Aveyna continued for him. "So they aren't proposing peace. They're proposing to weaken us to the point where they can take over our entire country."

"It is a very Murothian thing to do," Kent said. "Reclaiming Inoth has been Muroth's goal for centuries. And taking over the entire country would mean the eradication of mages or anyone Muroth deems 'cursed.' These terms are tantamount to a death sentence. We simply cannot accept them, Aveyna."

Kymil shot Kent a look, but Kent didn't bother correcting his wording. Aveyna would soon be his wife, and Kymil would have to adjust eventually.

"I agree. We must see if there is room to negotiate," Aveyna said. "Thank you, gentlemen."

Aveyna stepped forward again and stood before Graeme, and Kent and Kymil turned around and stood behind her.

"I cannot accept your terms, Prince Bouwen," she said. "They vary wildly from my original offer. I had hoped that my appearing in good faith would signify a willingness to discuss fair terms with you."

"We believe these are fair terms," Graeme said. "Your original proposal was insulting. 100,000 gold coins, a handshake, and a mutual apology? Preposterous."

"I also suggested the establishment of open trade and commerce routes between our nations, which would certainly enrich us both, seeing as we would no longer be forced to trade solely with Govalia and Caclos, and on occasion Urthia and the rest of Aletia. Muroth would then have easier access to Caclos and the Tahn Sea as well."

"We have ready access to both Caclos and the Tahn without Inoth's aid." Graeme shook his head. "Queen Aveyna, your country has harassed and abused our southern border for decades. Your offer falls far short of what it would take to truly restore 'good faith' between us."

"We cannot and will not pay 500,000 gold each year to Muroth," Aveyna said. "And we cannot and will not cede any of our lands to you. What is to stop you from continuing your incursions farther south?"

"By ceding the lands and paying Muroth tribute, you will have purchased the peace you desire," Graeme said. "Muroth will become not only a peaceful neighbor but also your closest ally. We will protect you, and likewise, your military will come to our aid when we request it."

"I am willing to form such an alliance with Muroth, but not at the cost you have proposed," Aveyna said. "Would you accept a one-time reparation of 300,000 gold, no ceding of lands, the establishment of open trade and commerce between our nations, and the mutual protection treaty you just described?"

"I am not authorized to accept anything less than the terms I have already proposed," Graeme replied, his face stoic.

Aveyna scoffed. "So you didn't come to broker peace at all, then? You came to sneer in our faces and insult us?"

Kent bristled. Aveyna certainly wouldn't make headway with that approach. Muroth would just further recede into its armored shell.

"The insult, Queen Aveyna, was yours in the making, by thinking you could pacify us with empty words and the pittance you offered," Graeme fired back. "You are addressing a proud, noble nation, one declared righteous in the gods' eyes, uncursed and unquestionably superior to yours. Muroth bows to no one."

"Perhaps I ought to just surrender and let you take all of Inoth," Aveyna spat.

Graeme smirked. "We would *gladly* accept those terms."

"Aveyna," Kent said from behind her.

She turned back, and Kent motioned her over.

Aveyna faced Graeme again. "Would you kindly excuse me once again?"

Graeme nodded.

Aveyna took the same position as before, facing Kymil and Kent.

"Forgive my interruption," Kent said. "But the negotiations are faltering."

"To say the least," Kymil muttered.

Kent shot him a glare but continued, "Muroth is negotiating hard. We have failed to offer them anything they truly want, and we have little leverage to bend them to our will aside from the idea of continuing the war between our countries."

"That is not an option I wish to entertain," Aveyna said.

"I understand, but at the very least, nothing will have changed. Inoth has survived for a long time in spite of the war," Kent said.

"Surely it's better than bending to their whims," Kymil said.

Aveyna's jaw tensed again, and her brow furrowed. "The whole point of this endeavor is to pursue lasting peace. Returning to our old ways will achieve nothing."

"This does not have to be the final negotiation between our nations," Kent said. "We can bide our time and try again. Perhaps after the emperor dies, his son Wye will be more amicable to the idea of forging peace with us."

"So you're saying I should end the negotiations?"

Kent nodded. "At this time, I believe it is wise to conclude,n if only for today."

Aveyna sighed.

"We can offer to meet again tomorrow. They are already here, and so are we. Perhaps they will soften overnight."

Aveyna looked at Kymil. "What do you think?"

Kymil nodded toward Kent. "He's the Murothian. He would know."

Kent resented Kymil's tone and his insinuation, but at least he had agreed.

Aveyna sighed again. "Very well."

She approached Graeme again. "Prince Bouwen, it is clear that we will not reach terms today. I invite you to stay, and we can discuss this further tomorrow."

"We will only stay to oversee the secession of these lands to our control," Graeme said. "Our position will not change, no matter how many nights pass. And if we leave, we will return in an entirely different manner than how we came."

Kent's fists clenched. Another harsh negotiation tactic—Muroth was forcing Aveyna to make a sharp decision by declining to discuss the treaty further.

"You are free to do what you will, but I assure you that we are ready for any manner of 'return' you are suggesting," Aveyna said. "It's in both of our nations' interests to stay and talk through these terms until we can agree."

"I do not see it that way, but thank you for meeting with me, Queen Aveyna. Your beauty *almost* lives up to the tales told about you in northern Muroth. I imagine they were true in your youth." Graeme gave her a smug smile, turned, and walked toward his advisors.

Kent had kept his calm the whole time, but those final words made him want to crack Graeme's skull open.

Aveyna scoffed and turned toward Kent and Kymil again. "He is *insufferable*."

"He is Murothian," Kymil muttered.

Kent ignored Kymil's slight. "Surely there must be more we can do?"

"We must prepare for more war," Aveyna said.

War. She'd finally called it what it was.

"Then I will do everything I can to help ensure that we win it," Kent said.

"Queen Aveyna?" Graeme called from behind her.

The three of them turned to look at him.

He started toward them again and held one finger up. "There is one other way we can resolve this dispute."

Aveyna glanced at Kent, who nodded, and then at Kymil, who shrugged.

She stepped forward to meet Graeme in the middle. "I'm listening."

"If you are willing to abdicate your throne to your son, then we will negotiate different terms with him."

Aveyna stared at him. "I beg your pardon?"

Graeme repeated, "If you abdicate your throne to Prince Kymil then we will negotiate different terms with him."

Aveyna stared daggers at Kymil. "What have you done?"

Kymil walked over to her, kissed her cheek, and then stood beside Graeme, nearly shoulder to shoulder. "Mother, will you do this? For Inoth and our people?"

Kent gawked at the farce playing out before him. Something had gone wrong, somewhere, and Kymil had known about it.

No, he'd *caused* it. Perhaps it had even been his idea in the first place.

But it didn't make sense. Why would Kymil allow Muroth to install him, even if the terms were more favorable? Inoth would still languish under the weight of Muroth's demands, and her people would suffer all the same—

Unless Kymil just didn't care.

"Perhaps some people are better used as sacrifices to secure greater power," Kymil had said during the hunt.

Kent had disagreed with it then, and Kymil had brushed it away by claiming that criminals and invalids could pay the cost of greater power, but that wasn't what Kymil had in mind at all.

He meant to sacrifice the entire country of Inoth for his own personal gain.

"Absolutely not," Aveyna replied. "I am Inoth's queen, and I will remain her queen until the day I die."

Graeme nodded, and he turned toward Kymil. "Far be it from me to meddle in the affairs of Inoth's royal family. We will not intervene."

Kent's body tensed. *Intervene in what?*

Kymil raised his left hand.

Someone grabbed Kent from behind, and two men in black armor grabbed Aveyna. Kent pulled away, but something swept his feet out from under him, and he hit the ground on his side.

As Kent repositioned himself, Grak thrust his sword toward Kent's face, stopping just short.

"Don't move another inch."

Kent didn't move.

In that moment, it all made sense. The nights he'd seen Kymil and Grak at the mausoleum. Furtive meetings in the castle's halls. He'd seen Kymil talking to Grak several times, but he hadn't ever thought of it as anything but routine. After all, Grak's job was to guard Aveyna and Kymil—some degree of communication between them was necessary.

But now Kent knew what they'd been talking about in hushed tones since his arrival. All he could do was hold out hope that they hadn't won over the rest of the elite soldiers accompanying them.

Two of Aveyna's royal guards hauled Kent up and held him in place, and two more held Aveyna in place.

"Grakios?" She stared at him with stunned eyes. "What are you doing?"

"Something I should've done a long time ago." Grak drew his sword over his head ready to bring it down onto Kent.

Kent closed his eyes and tensed.

"Halt!" Kymil ordered.

Grak froze, and he stared at Kymil.

"You remember our agreement, do you not?" Kymil asked.

Grak sighed and lowered his sword. "Yes. Fine."

"Agreement?" Aveyna glanced between them. "What are you talking about? Grak, you're supposed to be *protecting* me."

"Not anymore," Grak said. "Now I serve His Majesty, King Kymil of Inoth."

"This is absurd!" Aveyna shouted. "I command all soldiers loyal to Inoth to come to my aid. Do your duty to your queen and your country!"

None of the elite Inothian soldiers moved. Kent's heartbeat accelerated.

It was a coup.

"You traitors!" Aveyna screamed. "You swore fealty to me! To Inoth!"

"Your reign has come to an end." Kymil started toward her. "And if you think it's premature, then just imagine what Father thought when you poisoned him."

Aveyna gasped. She started to stammer a response, but Kymil silenced her.

"Don't bother trying to explain," he said. "You murdered your husband. You are unfit to rule the Inothian people."

Aveyna shook her head. "How could you possibly know?"

"Divination. Before you burned Father's body, I summoned his spirit from the

Underworld. He told me what you did, and I found the poison in your chambers later that day. Later, as he died, Archmage Ivelsted confirmed it." Kymil glared at her with cold eyes. "I loved my father. And I used to love my mother. Now they are both dead to me."

"Kymil," Aveyna uttered, "you can't begin to understand—"

"That he hurt you? That he made you feel worthless?" Kymil snapped. "I know about all of it. But none of it justifies his murder."

Aveyna broke into tears, and Kent wanted nothing more than to tear free and crush Kymil's head in his hands. But doing so would achieve nothing. He'd never even reach Kymil, not with dozens of Inoth's finest soldiers surrounding them, and not with Grak standing in Kent's way.

"And you, *Lord* Etheridge." Kymil sneered. "I confess, your loyalty to Inoth has transcended my expectations. Had you not allowed your impulses toward my mother to guide you, perhaps you could've become one of my advisors instead."

Kent locked his eyes on Kymil. "I would have sooner returned to Muroth and faced my fate there."

"Whatever the case," Kymil continued, "bedding my mother has proven where your true allegiances lie. As such, you will endure the same fate as she." Kymil leaned in close to Kent. "But it will not be my hand."

As Kymil straightened up, someone emerged from among the Murothian soldiers behind him. He wore a long, green cape attached to triangle-shaped fasteners on his matching jacket and green trousers.

He looked exactly the same as he had nearly a year prior when he'd murdered their father, except now he wore a black patch over his right eye.

Fane.

CHAPTER SIXTEEN

"Hello, brother." The words slithered out of Fane's mouth, then his countenance changed to mock embarrassment. "Oh. I forgot. You are not technically my brother anymore, are you?"

Kent glowered at him. His brother had shown up after all. And that meant Kent had a chance to kill him, even if only a small one.

"Not pleased to see me? Or is it that you do not recognize me?" Fane tilted his head. "I wore the same clothes as the last time we saw each other to make sure you knew it was me."

Kent said nothing.

"Ah, Kent." Fane smiled. "You have not changed whatsoever, though you have missed much since you fled the family estate."

"Apparently, I did not miss your eye." Kent realized he must've hit it with his sword's backswing on his way out the window. It would've explained Fane's scream at the time.

Fane frowned at him. "Yes. An unfortunate loss, but it pales in comparison to the good fortune of learning you were still alive. You have our mutual friend Prince Kymil to thank for relaying that information to me."

Kent clenched his jaw tight.

"I admit," Fane stepped toward him, "I was not surprised to hear that you had found your way to the upper echelons of Inothian society. You always did have a cunning mind and a gift for charisma.

"Though it surprised me to learn that you elected to flee to Inoth, of all places, rather than to Govalia, or Caclos, or somewhere secluded in Muroth. Then again, I suppose it does make sense, given the way you butchered our father before my very eyes."

"Why bother perpetuating the lie now, Fane? There is no one here to impress, and you already have me at your mercy," Kent said.

Fane grinned and drew the dagger hanging from his belt.

Kent recognized it immediately. It had once belonged to him, and Fane had used it to kill their father.

"You raise an excellent point. You are mine to do with as I please." Fane's voice lowered. "Finally."

As Fane raised the dagger, Aveyna shrieked.

An explosion of white light hit Kent's eyes, and though he shut them, it blinded him nonetheless. Just like when he'd first arrived in Goldmoor and fought Trag at the Temple of Laeri.

The soldiers around Kent yelled and hollered, and the royal guards released their grips on him. It did him little good, as he couldn't see anything but brilliant light, brighter than the sun above them.

Something touched his shoulder, and the light vanished. He opened his eyes to find Aveyna staring at him, her eyes pleading.

Everyone around them still clutched their faces and tried to shield their eyes. An aura of light sizzled through the air amid the soldiers, but it had already started to fade.

"Kent!" Aveyna shouted. "We need to flee!"

He nodded, but before he'd gotten three steps toward the fortress, someone grabbed his ankle, and he tripped. He hit the ground hard, but he recovered quickly.

One of the royal guards had gotten ahold of him.

"Kent!" Aveyna yelled again.

He drove the heel of his other boot into the royal guard's forehead, and the royal guard released him. Kent scrambled to his feet, only to find the Inothian elite soldiers forming up around Aveyna and him.

Aveyna drew a white line in the air and pulled her sword of light from it, just as she had when she'd anointed Kent her advisor, only far quicker. She glanced at him and nodded.

Kent pulled a crystal from one of his pouches with his left hand and let his magic begin to flow.

AERON SAW THE BLAST OF LIGHT FROM HIS SPOT ATOP THE FORTRESS'S WALL, AND IT stunned him so much that he almost fell over.

By the gods... it's the signal.

Earlier that morning, Queen Aveyna had told Aeron to watch the meeting, and if something should go wrong, she'd signal him with a bright light to come to their aid.

He blinked away the spots in his vision, snatched up his spear, and ran down the stairs to the second story along the wall that framed the courtyard. The closer he got, the more he could sense Wafer's presence, and Aeron conveyed his urgency through their bond.

"Wafer!" he shouted, mostly for his own reassurance that Wafer would be ready. "We're leaving!"

Aeron shoved past a pair of Inothian soldiers walking toward him along the wall and jumped from the second story of the courtyard. Wafer met him before he could hit the ground, and he landed in the saddle on Wafer's back.

Together they launched into the skies above the fortress and shot toward the queen.

KENT HAD TOO MANY CHOICES.

He could attack Fane and try to claim the vengeance that had already eluded him for so long.

He could attack Kymil, whose betrayal had cast Aveyna and Kent into this fracas.

He could attack Grak, who had sided against Aveyna and who posed a greater physical threat than either Fane or Kymil.

Or Kent could focus solely on protecting Aveyna and himself with the hope that they could somehow escape.

Behind him, Aveyna had already slain a fourth of the traitorous Inothian elite soldiers either with her sword or other displays of powerful light magic, so Kent opted for Fane. If the gods intended for Kent to die that day, he would gladly perish knowing he'd taken Fane with him.

He absorbed the crystal's essence into his magic and extended his right hand toward Fane. A barrage of crystalline spikes sprung from his fingertips, careening toward Fane like arrows from a dozen bows.

Fane recoiled, but a wall of darkness arose before him and shattered the crystals before they could reach him.

Kymil stood ten feet away from him.

Kent gritted his teeth and moved to throw another barrage of crystals, but he saw Kymil holding something in his hand. Something small, grey, and writhing.

Red light formed in Kymil's palm, and then it flashed toward Kent.

Kent dove out of the way and rolled up to his feet, then he dove again, dodging blood arrows as fast as Kymil could conjure them. Crouched low, he erected a wide, crystalline barrier, and the blood arrows plinked off of it one at a time.

That barrier marked the end of his crystal, though. Kent opened his hand, and the last remaining granules of the crystal fell to the ground. He stole a glance back.

Several yards away, Aveyna continued to thrash and defend against the remaining elite soldiers and royal guards. Any time one of them hurled a magical attack at her, it hit some sort of invisible shield surrounding her with a flash of white light and deflected harmlessly away.

Lumbering footsteps thundered closer. From Kent's left, Grak barreled toward him, sword in hand.

Still crouched, Kent didn't have time to draw his own sword or even to get another object from his pouches to use magic, so he dug his fingers into the dirt and pumped magic into it instead.

The magic burned through the dirt quickly, but Kent managed to summon a cloud of dust from the ground that obscured Grak's view. Kent dodged Grak's attack and then drew his sword, ready to finally test his mettle.

Grak emerged from the cloud and stalked toward him.

"I thought you loved her." Kent held his sword at the ready. "Why would you betray her?"

Grak glowered at Kent, his rageful eyes reddened from the dust. "She didn't love me back. If I can't have her, I sure as hell won't let you have her either."

Their blades met with a mighty *clang*, and the vibration hurt Kent's hands. They exchanged blows, parrying each other's skillful attacks and evading others.

Kent gradually found his stroke again, and the thrill of engaging in high-level swordsmanship surged through his veins. Their blades locked, and Kent pushed Grak back with a hard shove.

As Kent readied his sword for another attack, a shock of sharp pain dug into his side, and he gasped.

He looked down. An arrow made of sickly green light protruded from his gut.

Kymil.

Kent searched the field for him, and their eyes met.

Kymil dropped a long, shriveled cord from his hand. A serpent of some sort?

Whatever it was, the arrow burned Kent's insides, and it was spreading.

Grak stormed toward him, his sword keen to finish the job.

Then a blast of white light launched Grak off of his feet and sent his armored body bouncing toward the Murothians.

"Kent!" Aveyna rushed to his side. When she noticed the arrow, she gasped. "No... *no!*"

Kent dropped to his knees and then slumped onto his good side, fighting the immense pain spreading throughout his chest and legs.

"It's a venom arrow." Her voice sounded distant, tinny, but she was kneeling right next to him.

His vision flickered and blurred, and he lost feeling in his torso, and then his legs. Then the sensation started creeping into his arms.

All around them, a glistening dome withstood blasts of fire and repelled every other attack. It flashed with white light upon every impact, creating a vivid display to Kent's faltering eyes.

But even with his vision failing, there was no mistaking the delighted sneers of Grak, Fane, and Kymil standing just outside the shield, watching him die.

In the distance, high above the battle, a winged beast flew toward them, and sunlight glinted off of its blue-green hide.

"I have to heal you," Aveyna said. "But I can't keep the shield up if I do."

"No. Save yourself," Kent uttered.

His vision clarified, and he realized the beast was the wyvern and its rider.

Wafer. Kent's head swam, but he remembered their names. *And Aeron Ironglade.*

They were coming in for a landing. Aveyna raised her hand and opened the top of the dome, and Wafer landed with a *thud* near Kent's head, obscuring most of Kent's view of the sky with his scaly belly.

Kent's limbs went completely numb, and the effect was spreading up his neck.

"I'm going to heal him," Aveyna called to Aeron over the shouts and impacts from everyone around them. "But the shield won't. I can't do both. I want you to take him out of here. Do *not* take him back to the fortress or back to Goldmoor."

"Your Highness?" Aeron asked. "We cannot carry you both. What about you?"

"Do as you're told," Aveyna replied. "You will leave me behind."

Kent used the last of his energy to shake his head. Through numbing lips, he said, "No, Aveyna. You can't. You're the queen."

"Not anymore," she said. "Grab him, and I'll heal him."

"This doesn't feel right…" Aeron said.

"*Aeron!*" Aveyna snapped. "You will do as I have commanded!"

Aeron gulped and gave a reluctant nod.

As Aveyna laid her hands on Kent's body, the wyvern repositioned itself and hooked its talons under Kent's arms.

White light flared between Aveyna and Kent, and she closed her eyes.

Kent could only see the light at first, but the numbness throughout his body reverted back to pain, and the pain faded to nothing.

The shield around them cracked from a heavy blow.

Aveyna pulled the venom arrow out of Kent's side, and the pain fully extinguished from his body. As Kent's cognition returned, the arrow in Aveyna's hand dissipated to nothing.

Then the shield exploded into thousands of shards of light.

"Go!" Aveyna yelled.

"Wait!" Kent shouted, but the ground dropped out from under him.

Magical attacks streamed past them.

As Kent ascended away, a glowing red arrow hit the center of Aveyna's chest.

Aveyna grabbed it and slumped over, and Kymil approached her with a sword in his hand, radiating violet light just like the one Eusephus had wielded.

And then Kymil killed her.

CHAPTER SEVENTEEN

K ent screamed and shouted and demanded and begged Aeron to take him back to the battle, but Aeron refused.

Wafer didn't stop flying until they'd left northern Inoth far behind. As dusk began to fall, they landed on the far side of the mountains separating northeast Inoth from southwest Govalia.

When Wafer finally released Kent from his grip, Kent stormed around to the side and yanked Aeron out of his saddle. He held Aeron by his breastplate and shook him.

"What the *hell* did you do?" he yelled in Aeron's face. "You left her there to die!"

Wafer hissed from behind Kent, and Aeron shoved Kent backward. Kent let go, and Wafer's mouth clamped around Kent's shoulder, with his long snout across Kent's chest.

Wafer's pointed teeth pressed into Kent's torso, and he froze. It hurt to even draw breath.

"If I tell him to kill you, he will," Aeron said. "A wyvern's jaw is strong enough to crack most types of rock. Your ribcage would shatter, and you'd either die from the excruciating pain or you'd bleed out from the puncture wounds to your organs. But that would be a shame seeing as the queen just gave up her life to save you."

Kent closed his eyes, but the image of Kymil slaying Aveyna replayed in his memory, so he opened them again.

"Look—I'm content to let you be on your way." Aeron folded his arms. "I've done my duty, and my contract with the queen is over now that she's..." He hesitated. "I'm moving on. I can't stay in Govalia for very long due to... personal reasons."

Kent said nothing. The sadness wracking his nerves didn't let him.

"But I know what you're capable of. I saw some of your fight from the sky," Aeron continued. "I think we'd be good together. Maybe we could be partners."

Kent looked at him. He didn't want anything to do with Aeron. Yes, he'd saved Kent's life, but he'd also allowed Aveyna to die in Kent's place.

"I'm prepared to let Wafer kill you if you intend to cause more trouble, but if you agree to behave, I'll set you loose." Aeron folded his arms and raised his eyebrows. "What's it gonna be?"

Kent scowled at him. Even if he could break free, the prospect of fighting Aeron and a full-grown wyvern wouldn't yield a favorable outcome, even with magic on his side.

"I will not harm you," Kent said quietly.

"Good." Aeron looked at Wafer. "Let him go, Wafer."

Wafer complied, and relief spread across Kent's chest and back. Putrid wyvern saliva clung to his shoulder, and he frowned at it.

"Your name's Kent, right?" Aeron asked. "Kent Etheridge? The queen told me you're Murothian."

Kent scooped up a handful of dirt and rubbed it on his shoulder to sop up the wyvern spit. He'd been forced out of not one, but two nations now. "I am no one anymore, and I have no country."

"Just like me." Aeron grinned. "Look, I know you're pissed about what happened back in Inoth, but I had to follow her orders. She was the one paying me."

Kent closed his eyes. He would've taken the burning from Kymil's poison arrow over the pain of losing Aveyna if he could. Being reminded of it so soon after threatened to cripple him. "Can we not talk about this, please?"

"Sure. Sorry." Aeron glanced around. "I'm going to get some firewood. Why don't you take some time to hang out here, gather yourself? Stay with Wafer. He'll protect you."

"I do not need his protection."

Wafer snorted, and Kent shot him a glare.

"Well, he's staying here anyway, so get used to it." Aeron headed toward a nearby forest. "I'll be back in a few minutes. Stay put. Or don't. You can leave if you want."

Kent elected to stay. He didn't know the area, and it would be night soon. It made more sense to stay for now.

He sat down, then he lay on his back and covered his face with his hands. Sorrow pooled in his chest and head, and soon after, sobs racked his body.

Many minutes later, Kent heard Aeron's footsteps, so he wiped his eyes and sat upright again.

Aeron carried a pile of sticks and small logs and dumped them onto the ground near Wafer, who now reclined on his side like a large, reptilian cow—except for his mammoth wings, which he'd folded and kept pressed against his body. Aeron started a fire using two flint stones from a pack tied to Wafer's saddle and built it into a steady blaze.

When Aeron stood up after building the fire, he winced and rubbed his back.

Kent wondered why Aeron hadn't asked Wafer to just ignite the sticks and logs for him instead, but he didn't ask. Maybe wyverns didn't breathe fire, though he'd always thought they could.

They didn't talk much for the rest of the night, nor did Kent eat anything. They hadn't brought any food with them aside from Aeron's magic mushrooms, two of which Aeron ate.

Kent made the next run for firewood, and then they turned in for the night.

As Kent lay on the cold ground near the warm fire, he thought of his nights in Aveyna's bed and the hearth in her chambers. He sighed, closed his eyes, and fell into a fitful sleep mired with nightmares.

<p>

THE MORNING SUNLIGHT RIPPED KENT FROM HIS DREAMS. HE ROSE, FETCHED MORE firewood in the frigid morning air, and used the dying embers and some magic to get the fire going again.

Aeron woke up soon after, though Wafer continued to snore.

Aeron stood to his feet, and as he stretched, he noticed Kent tending to the fire. He said, "Thank you."

Kent just stared at the fire and nodded. He didn't feel like talking.

But Aeron did. "I suppose we need to find some breakfast. If you want, I can let Wafer do some hunting for us, or I can take us into a nearby town for something."

Kent shook his head. Physically, he was hungry, but he doubted he'd eat anything any time soon.

"Have you given any more thought to my proposal?" Kent looked up at Aeron. "What proposal?"

"That we partner up."

"Doing what?"

"Mercenary work."

Kent looked back at the fire. He'd been a bounty hunter once, with Ronin, but now he didn't want to do anything. "I do not know what I intend to do now."

"Alright. So picture this," Aeron began. "You're a mage, and you know how to fight, too. I've got Wafer, and I'm a trained wyvern knight. A lot of people would pay plenty of coin to hire us. A *lot* of people."

It was too soon to consider much of anything. Kent shook his head. "I do not care either way."

Aeron sighed. "Look, Kent. I know you're sad and pissed and probably hate me, and I'm sure this is the last thing you want to talk about, but you've got no coin and nowhere to go. I know of three or four jobs we could get in Urthia *right now* that would get us some quick coin.

"At the very least, you'd be able to go somewhere else and do whatever you wanted after you helped me with these jobs. I can't do them alone, and having a mage would help a *ton*, but I need to know if you're in or not. If you're not, I'll drop you off on my way down to Caclos for another job, or you can stay here.

"Obviously I want you to come with me to Urthia, but I'll just as gladly leave you here. I'll give you another hour to tell me what you want to do, and then I'm leaving. Crystal?"

Kent considered Aeron's words. He'd been in this situation before— stripped of everything and forced to restart with no wealth, no connections, and limited options. But this time, he knew how to use his magic. That was something, at least.

He'd made good coin as a bounty hunter with Ronin, and he'd been skilled at the work. Mercenary work would mean more direct fighting, he imagined, and less tracking of targets, but the idea of more fighting didn't scare him. Right now, he wanted nothing more than to release some of his pent-up aggression.

He still needed to exact vengeance upon Fane, but now he yearned to avenge Aveyna's death as well, meaning he had to get back to Inoth to kill Kymil and Grak. Killing Graeme Bouwen would come next, if he had to prioritize his targets.

But with no coin, no weapons aside from his magic, and with no more authority in either Muroth or Inoth, the prospect of achieving any of it seemed impossible.

If Kent wanted to live to see his plans for revenge come to fruition, he would need to eat. And to eat, he would need coin. And traveling the continent as a mercenary sounded like a fine way to earn some, even if he had to do it with the man who had, in part, allowed Aveyna to die.

Kent looked at Aeron. "I don't need an hour. I will accompany you to Urthia."

Aeron smiled. "Good. I promise you a wild ride." Wafer chuffed and chirped.

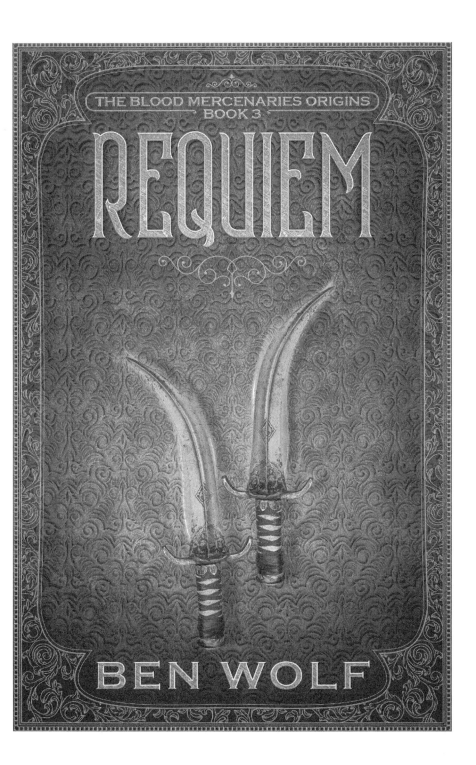

THE BLOOD MERCENARIES ORIGINS
BOOK 3

REQUIEM

BEN WOLF

CHAPTER ONE

Blood dripped from Mehta's curved knives. His commission was fulfilled, and he had honored Xyon, the God of Death.

Yet Mehta was not satisfied.

Four bodies lay at his feet: a man, a woman, and two children. He had sifted them all, but he wished the children hadn't seen him. He could have let them live otherwise.

Then again, perhaps it was better that they not discover their parents and servants dead. Sifting them had prevented them from realizing their family's fate. Part of Mehta wished he'd been granted the same mercy as a child.

A pair of servants lay dead in the next room of the grand manse, and the blood of the cook and two maids pooled in the kitchen one floor below. Before them, six armed guards had perished under Mehta's knives.

But it wasn't enough. He had delivered everyone in the manse to the gates of Xyon, and it still had not quenched his bloodlust. He had to sift again. He needed to sate his thirst.

Mehta stole through the nearest window and descended to the moonlit ground with nary a whisper from the grass, frosted over from the frigid night air. He would've sifted a passerby in the street if he could have, but the manse sat on a grand estate many miles from Etrijan's capital city of Sefera. In such a rural area, no one else was around.

I should go. The commission is fulfilled.

His hands trembled, still holding his knives. He exhaled a vaporous breath in the icy air.

I cannot go. Not yet. I need more.

He tightened his grips and searched the horizon. A range of snowcapped mountains jutted into the sky. They reminded him of the mountain with the cratered top that rose above his childhood home. They reminded him of simpler times, of parents whose faces he could not remember, and of a little sister whose name he had long forgotten.

His parents had been lying facedown in their own blood when the soldiers took Mehta away. Soldiers clad in black armor, decorated with the crest of a three-horned ram.

He shook the memories from his mind and refocused on the scene before him.

Before the distant mountains lay a sprawling pasture full of cows and sheep, some sleeping and some grazing under the moonlight. Only a simple wooden fence stood between him and more death.

Mehta started toward the pasture.

Within minutes, the reddened carcasses of dozens of livestock lay scattered throughout the pasture, young and old alike. Hot, sticky blood coated Mehta's brown-skinned forearms and dotted his chest and thighs.

The thirst persisted.

Mehta knew what it meant, but he didn't want to face it. Not now.

He'd lingered long enough. He needed to return to the Sanctum. Then the High Cleric would decide Mehta's fate.

Dawn would break within two hours, and he couldn't be seen near the manse in daylight. He couldn't be seen *anywhere* because to the rest of the world, he did not exist.

So Mehta turned toward Sefera, tucked his knives into the sheaths concealed within his clothes, and started to run.

And the thirst chased his every step.

※

As the first glow of morning light bloomed from beyond the distant, rocky horizon, Mehta knocked on the Sanctum's hidden door in Sefera. A sliding panel at eye level opened, but Mehta could not seen inside.

"Requiem," Mehta uttered the name the Xyonates had bestowed upon him five years earlier when he'd completed his training.

The sliding panel shut, and a bolt clanked from inside. The door opened with a creak, and Mehta slipped into the darkness, leaving the cold morning air behind him.

"Elegy." Mehta bowed to the Xyonate at the door.

Elegy bowed back. As he did, Mehta caught sight of the knife hanging from his hip. Of everyone in the Sanctum, only Elegy had ever matched Mehta's skill in combat.

"You fulfilled your charge?" Elegy asked, the candlelight glinting off of his dark, calculating eyes and bald head. Elegy wasn't his real name, but it was the only name Mehta had ever known him by.

Mehta nodded. The run from the manse had partially stanched Mehta's thirst for death, but he still had to fight the impulse to gratify himself with Elegy's blood.

He wondered how it might go. If he drew his knives fast enough, Elegy would have little time to react. Elegy would doubtless counter and deflect Mehta's first few attacks, but with the advantage of a surprise attack, Mehta would have an edge.

Elegy's free hand moved to the hilt of his knife, and Mehta tensed.

"The clerics will be pleased, Requiem." Elegy's voice interrupted Mehta's thoughts.

Will they? Mehta's ruminations on killing Elegy dissipated, and he relaxed the tension that had built up in his body with a calm, silent exhale.

"They await you at Xyon's shrine." Elegy offered Mehta a candle, but Mehta refused it. He'd walked the Sanctum's corridors hundreds of times. He knew every uneven step, every creaky floorboard, and he thrived in the shadows.

As he walked through the Sanctum, Mehta saw no one else. But when he entered the dark, windowless chapel, he found the rest of his brethren.

Before him, about a dozen Xyonates knelt before an icon of the god Xyon, their backs straight and upright, their hands clasped in reverence. Candlelight glinted off of their shaven heads. They all wore dark, form-fitting clothes, and their weapons lay before them, ready to receive the High Cleric's daily blessing.

Mehta bypassed them all and headed for Xyon's shrine and the three clerics standing before it. Two of them wore red ceremonial robes marked with ancient Aletian runes. The one in the middle wore the deep-purple robes of a Xyonate high cleric, and he faced toward the shrine, away from Mehta.

When Mehta reached the edge of the altar, he knelt, removed his knives, and set them on the floor. Then he bowed his head and clasped his hands together.

"Requiem," a deep voice said.

Mehta lifted his head.

The high cleric, Ghazal, turned toward Mehta with his hands outstretched, palms up. "Have you fulfilled your commission?"

"Yes, High Cleric," Mehta replied. "They await Xyon at the Gates of Hell."

Ghazal's head tilted, and he lowered his hands. "*They?*"

Anxiety swirled in Mehta's chest. "Yes, High Cleric."

"How many souls were sifted?"

"Fifteen, High Cleric."

Ghazal's jaw tensed. "Enumerate them."

"Six guards. Five servants. Three of the charge's family and the charge himself." The admission twisted Mehta's stomach. Again, he wished the children hadn't seen him.

That was unusual. He hadn't experienced true guilt since during his training, and he'd sifted dozens of souls in the years that followed, some of whom had been children.

So what had changed?

Ghazal stared back at the shrine and at the obsidian icon of Xyon at its center. Though human in form, the icon also had wings, and a third eye marked with an emerald glinted from the center of the god's forehead.

"Xyon will be pleased," Ghazal finally said.

"That is my only ambition, High Cleric. I live to serve Xyon."

Ghazal turned to face Mehta again. "Rise and draw near, Requiem."

Mehta complied.

Ghazal sniffed the air. "You smell of sheep's blood."

"I sifted their livestock as well."

"Why?"

Mehta blinked. "I…"

Ghazal's brown eyes scoured Mehta. "Because you had to?"

The mere suggestion deepened Mehta's thirst yet again. He yearned to sift Ghazal next—but not because he hated or feared him. He just needed to sift *someone*, and Ghazal's proximity made him the primary target.

Instead, Mehta clenched his fists and replied, "Yes, High Cleric."

"Is the need overwhelming? Insatiable?" Ghazal leaned close to him and whispered, "Do you feel it now?"

Mehta hesitated. He'd seen what happened to Xyonates who could no longer be controlled, and he didn't want it to happen to him.

But he nodded nonetheless. Mehta's fate was in Ghazal's hands, not anyone else's —not even his own. Above all else, Mehta would serve Xyon, whether through his life or his death.

"Xyon has blessed you." Ghazal grinned. "He has bestowed his appetite upon you, and every soul you commend to the Gates of Hell venerates him."

Mehta's breath caught in his throat. "I am unworthy of such blessing."

Ghazal raised his arms again, palms up. "It is Xyon's will. You have earned his favor. You are one of the elect."

"Then I—I must be cleansed." Mehta gulped. "Before I can be offered to him."

"You shall be, as will your instruments." Ghazal nodded to the two red-robed clerics on either side of Mehta. "Lament. Epitaph."

The clerics took hold of his arms and held him in place.

Though he wanted to, Mehta did not resist. He was an obedient servant.

Ghazal removed a curved, ceremonial knife from its mounting brackets above the icon. He turned back and held the knife in front of himself, with its wicked blade pointing upward, and he recited the Liturgy of Offering.

"As the river of blood spills from your veins, its flow will ferry you to Xyon's underworld throne."

Mehta swallowed. He didn't want to die, but Xyon demanded his sacrifice. He needed to obey. He'd been taught to obey all throughout his training. He would not stop now.

The image of the cratered mountain of his childhood surfaced in his mind. He would never see it again, just like he would never see his parents again.

Ghazal continued, "Your service to Xyon will continue in the Underworld, and you will hold a place of honor as one of his soldiers. As one of the elect, you will serve Xyon in eternity as you served him in life: nameless, faceless, and with absolute obedience."

But why did Xyon demand the premature death of those who served him in life? It made no sense to Mehta. It never had.

Now, of all times, he should *not* be rewarded with death for his deeds. Instead, he should continue to sift souls for Xyon.

"And thus I commit you, Requiem, to Xyon's realm, wreathed in the bones of your charges, clothed in the flesh of their bodies, and drenched in the blood of their sacrifices."

The cratered mountain called to him. He wanted to go back there—back to his home. His true home.

The molten metal stirring in Mehta's gut galvanized. He wasn't done living. He hadn't yet faced the men who'd taken him from his family—the soldiers wearing the sigil of the three-horned ram.

I do not want to die in the service of Xyon.

Ghazal rotated the ceremonial knife in his hand and gripped it with the blade pointed down.

And if Mehta didn't want to die, that left only one alternative.

I want to live.

"I cleanse you, now, Requiem, for your journey to Xyon's throne." Ghazal raised the knife.

CHAPTER TWO

Mehta jerked hard to his left, and Ghazal's ceremonial knife plunged into Epitaph's chest. Blood burbled out of the wound, and Epitaph stared down at it, wide-eyed and speechless.

Stunned, Ghazal and Lament didn't move, but Mehta twisted free of Lament's grip and shoved him back. Lament stumbled over the corner of the altar and fell over.

Epitaph dropped to his knees, clutching at the knife in his chest and gasping.

Mehta pushed Ghazal into the shrine, and it toppled under his momentum. Then Mehta snatched up his knives and turned toward his brethren, ready for a fight.

They were gone. All the candles were out. The chapel was empty and dark.

Mehta whirled back toward Lament and Ghazal, but they had vanished as well. Only Epitaph remained, and he lay on the floor, twitching, staring into the darkness with vacant, glassy eyes.

But Mehta wasn't afraid. This wasn't some horrifying occurrence or terrible realization. Though the danger was real and palpable, *he* was the most dangerous entity in the Sanctum. So why be afraid?

They should fear me instead.

Living within an enclave of Xyonates had its benefits: plenty of quiet, ample space for solitude, ready access to food, shelter, clothing, and numerous skilled training partners.

The drawback was that those same training partners were all skilled sifters, just like Mehta. If he meant to escape the Sanctum alive, it would come at the cost of much more death and gallons of blood.

He couldn't give up now. The damage was already done. If he faltered, they would commend him to Xyon the instant he let down his guard.

Xyon will just have to make do with Epitaph.

Mehta evaporated into the nearest shadow and listened. As part of his training, he'd developed the ability to see in the dark, thanks to an incantation the Xyonate clerics had performed on him.

Nothing concealed in shadows escaped his gaze. Faint green lines outlined everything with depth, whether mobile or stationary. As such, he could make out his surroundings well enough, but movement especially grabbed his attention. And he'd seen some the instant he'd entered the shadows.

The other Xyonates had adapted similar vision capabilities, so he had no real advantage—at least not in that regard. But not all Xyonates were created equal. Yes, they'd all been trained to sift quickly and, at times, brutally, but Mehta had long since topped the Sanctum's hierarchy along with Elegy and High Cleric Ghazal.

Movement flickered in his dark vision again, drawing ever nearer to him. Green lines traced the form of an arm and a sword swinging at him from the left. The attack was perfectly silent, yet were it not for Mehta's enhanced vision and training, the Xyonate would've sifted him then and there.

Instead, Mehta ducked under the swipe and drove his knives under the Xyonate's ribs. His thirst spiked, and he wanted more.

A faint gasp hit Mehta's ears, and from that vocalization alone, Mehta knew he'd sifted the Xyonate called Covenant. Mehta ripped his right blade from Covenant's torso and plunged it into the side of Covenant's neck.

Hot blood spattered on Mehta's hands and smacked the floor, and then Covenant dropped, motionless. Mehta moved on, heading toward the Sanctum's door, eager to pour more blood into his thirst.

To his surprise, he made it to the first corridor without encountering another of his brethren. He scanned the corridor for threats and listened, thankful for his boots' soft soles as he crept forward.

Something winked in the darkness from above, and Mehta hopped backward out of reflex. A spear thudded into the wooden floor beside him.

Canon. Mehta's knives found Canon's left arm, then his inner right thigh, then his left ankle tendon. Mehta's thirst burgeoned at the prelude to a fresh kill.

Canon hit the floor louder than his spear, and he too gasped.

Xyonates weren't permitted to react to pain with any vocalization louder than a sharp inhale. During the Xyonate training, the clerics had reinforced the idea by repeatedly subjecting Mehta and the other trainees to sudden, severe pain, albeit nothing that would cause permanent damage.

It taught them to anticipate pain, to not let it faze them, to not allow it to become a disadvantage. Xyonates had adopted only two responses to pain: submit to it and perish, or overcome it.

Canon wasn't going to overcome it. Mehta saw to that with a deep slash to his throat. Yet Mehta's thirst only continued to grow, continued to drive him forward.

Something whistled through the air, and Mehta's instincts moved his head to the side. The thing swished past him.

In the distance, Myth retreated behind the wall at the end of the corridor. Myth was a female Xyonate, one of the few, and one of the best of any of them. She had mastered the bow with lethal precision.

More blood to sate his knives' appetite.

As Myth nocked another arrow, Mehta raced down the corridor toward her. Myth emerged from her cover and took aim, but Mehta already had her. His knife severed her bowstring first, then it dug into the soft flesh on the underside of her chin. More blood oozed down Mehta's hand.

She struggled at first, but Mehta wrenched his knife free from her chin, slit her belly open, and left her there for Xyon to claim. His thirst endured.

As he progressed through a few more corridors, he encountered and felled two more of his brethren: Chant and Tribute. They'd wisely attacked him together, but it hadn't made a difference. Within seconds, both lay behind Mehta in pools of their own blood.

He needed more. Perhaps he should stay in the Sanctum after all; perhaps he should sift every one of them. Maybe then his thirst would finally be satisfied.

But he couldn't stay. There were too many of them, and they would overcome him eventually. He hadn't escaped ritual sacrifice at Xyon's altar to perish now.

The candles near the Sanctum's entrance were also snuffed, but it made no difference. He advanced through the darkness all the same.

Part of him wanted to abandon caution and run for the door. The other Xyonates would hear him, but he was quick. They wouldn't catch him.

But if they awaited him ahead, then running would alert them to his approach.

Caution had served him well thus far. He crept toward the door, his head swiveling, watching for moving green outlines in the shadows, his ears keen in the silence.

Pain lit up the lower left side of Mehta's torso, sharp and deep, just below his ribcage. He gasped and almost dropped his knife to check his wound, but he maintained his grip. He didn't need to check the wound. He already knew it was bad.

Mehta slashed at the source of the attack. His knives hit nothing.

Elegy. It has to be Elegy.

Hot blood oozed down his hip and onto his thigh. His thirst dwindled, replaced with desperation. He fully abandoned his musings about staying here and sifting everyone. Now he needed to escape. His thirst would have to wait.

"As long as I serve Xyon," Elegy's voice whispered from somewhere in the darkness around him, "I will pursue you to the death."

Of all the Xyonates in the Sanctum, only Elegy had ever matched Mehta's capabilities. And now Mehta had the chance to prove he was better.

Except he wasn't—at least not anymore. The blood seeping from his side condemned him, and the haze settling into his head confirmed it. They would soon send him to Xyon once he submitted to the pain.

No. I won't let them.

The door lay ahead, bolted shut. He needed to get out. In his weakening condition, he couldn't hope to overcome Elegy, Ghazal, and all the remaining Xyonates. His only chance was to escape.

And that meant he had to run.

He tucked the knife in his left hand into its sheath within his clothes and forced his legs into motion. He needed one hand free to unbolt and open the door, and he needed one knife to defend himself.

Mehta's legs pounded the floor, no longer silent, and each step sent bitter pulses of pain through his torso.

As he ran, the darkness encroached on him. Shadowy tendrils reached out for his arms and legs. He slashed at them in a fury, unable to distinguish between reality and those conjured by his imagination until his knife struck either solid metal or soft flesh.

He dodged and ducked and parried and kept running until he reached the door. With all of his strength, he threw the bolt open and yanked on the iron handle. A thin line of early morning sunlight streamed into the Sanctum, and frigid air billowed inside.

"Do not allow him to escape!" Ghazal's voice bellowed from the blackness behind him.

Amid the commotion and the creaking of the door, the whisper of careening metal caught Mehta's ears, and he lowered his head and shifted his body.

Fire ignited the back of his shoulder, and he gasped again, but he continued hauling the heavy door open. He made for the opening and slipped between the door and the frame, into the cold morning light. Then Mehta continued to run.

He ran along cobblestone streets lined with grey and white buildings, heading east. He knew the cratered mountain was to the east, but it was too far away to see from Sefera.

Still, it gave his steps purpose. Visible or not, it was something to run toward as he fled his Xyonate pursuers.

Voices chased his footsteps, and people in the streets staggered and stumbled out of his path, their eyes wide with shock, no doubt at the sight of his dark, blood-spattered form. Pain matched him step for step, but he didn't stop running. He couldn't submit. He had to overcome.

Mehta darted into an alley between two buildings made of gray stone, then he cut over to the next street, searching for somewhere—anywhere—to hide. He needed time, and he needed help. He could clean his wound and bandage himself, but that marked the extent of his medical prowess. It wouldn't be enough—not with the blood he'd already lost.

As his feet pounded the paving stones, Mehta took a breath, pressed his free hand against his wounded side, and stared at the city sprawled out before him. Sefera, the capital of Etrijan, spanned several miles over rolling countryside. Half a million people lived there, making it the third most populous city on the entire continent of Aletia.

Buildings of countless shapes and sizes lined the city's hilly streets. Each of them meant something to someone. Each one was a home, a business, a holy place—a sanctum of its own sort for those dwelling inside. Surely one of those buildings could shield him, even if only for a few hours.

Even at the early hour, the streets bustled with people, most of them bundled in warm furs and heavy cloaks and shawls.

Mehta wasn't dressed for the cold—not well enough, anyway. He'd dressed for the commission, and that had meant tight, yet flexible clothing designed for dexterity rather than warmth. And he was covered with blood, some of it his own.

Vapor puffed out of Mehta's mouth in short, ragged breaths, and his tongue had gone dry and chalky. Between the cold, the loss of blood, and the fatigue threatening to envelop him from both, Mehta was short on time.

He needed healing first, then hiding second. And one place in the city excelled in healing above all others.

The Temple of Laeri, the Goddess of Light.

He was close. Mehta could make it, too, if he didn't pass out.

Footsteps padded behind him, no longer silent like they'd been in the Sanctum, but still hushed, like the pattering of raindrops along the paving stones. Mehta glanced down at his hand and torso, both stained crimson. They were following his blood trail.

But Mehta refused to get caught in the downpour.

He inhaled a sharp breath that stabbed his side and broke into a run again.

Block after block flew by, and Mehta grew wearier with each step. Before long, he could see the temple looming in the distance, but he wouldn't make it. His energy was sapped, and he was too weak.

Instead of continuing toward the temple, he veered into another alley, this one narrower but with two outlets aside from the one by which he'd entered. Mehta slowed his progress at a peculiar sight.

A man in pristine white robes and furs stood halfway down the alley next to a mule and a wooden cart full of sacks. He looked to be around forty years old and had a bulging belly.

Mehta stopped entirely when a familiar form emerged at the far end of the alley, clad in unmistakable red robes and wielding one short sword in each hand.

Cleric Lament.

The sight of him sent Mehta's vision swirling. The alley spun, and Mehta's body quaked. He clenched his eyes shut to still the spinning.

When Mehta opened his eyes, Lament had closed half the distance between them.

Though he had personally trained Mehta and the other Xyonates in various forms of combat and methods of sifting, Lament no longer accepted commissions because of an old injury he'd sustained while sifting a lord known to be a deadly fighter. Lament had prevailed and sifted the lord, but his injuries had cost him High Cleric Ghazal's trust.

It didn't matter, though. Lament's capabilities hadn't waned much over the two decades that he'd instructed Mehta and the others. Mehta had been his finest pupil, but now Lament would reassert why he was the master, especially with Mehta so weakened.

The man in the white robes backed against the wall and watched as Lament stalked past him, the cart, and the mule. Lament didn't even look at him.

Mehta removed his hand from his wounded side, drew his other knife, and awaited his fate. It clung to his palm, still sticky with blood—this time his own.

With the other Xyonates somewhere behind him, Mehta couldn't run back. He either had to stand against Lament alone or face the rest of the Xyonates all at once. He chose to face Lament.

But if Xyon truly meant to claim Mehta today, even after all he'd endured to escape, then at the very least, Lament would sustain a new range of injuries in fulfilling Xyon's will.

Mehta's thirst returned at the thought. He hoped it would be enough to save his life here and now.

Lament stopped a safe distance from Mehta and appraised him. "I am impressed by your resolve."

Mehta didn't reply. It took all of his energy just to remain standing.

"But it's time to commit yourself to Xyon. Surely you have earned a place of the highest honor among his finest warriors by now." Lament started forward again, his silver blades glinting with gold in the morning sun.

The temptation to lower his guard ached in Mehta's arms, but he kept his hands up, as ready as he could be, given his wound.

Lament drew nearer, inch-by-inch, now well within striking range of Mehta because of the length of his short swords. Mehta, however, could not strike Lament at that range, so he waited for Lament to make the first move.

Behind Lament, the man in the white moved. Mehta had expected him to flee, but instead, the man hurled something toward Lament.

A shiny, red sphere exploded against the back of Lament's head in a shower of white pulp, and he toppled a step forward, stunned. Lament started to turn back, and Mehta saw his opening.

Mehta lunged forward with his blades extended.

Lament whirled around to face Mehta, but he was too late.

Mehta's blades plunged into Lament's chest, and they both fell to the alley floor.

Lament gawked up at Mehta, and his mouth hung open, forming words and trying to gasp, but failing at both. Rage burned in Lament's eyes, and he released his swords and tried to grip Mehta's clothes to pull himself up.

"Give my regards to Xyon," Mehta rasped.

Mehta twisted his blades in a sharp, jerking motion.

Lament lurched, lost his grip, and started clawing at his chest. Mehta had hit his lungs, and Lament gasped for air in total futility.

Mehta yanked his blades free, and Lament slumped to the ground, rocking and convulsing, his tongue and teeth tainted with bright red blood. Next to Lament's head lay the scattered remains of a red apple.

The man in white had thrown an *apple* at Lament?

As Mehta tried to rise, his vision cut out, and he toppled to his hands and knees next to Lament. He blinked hard, and his eyesight returned.

Submit or overcome.

He looked up in time to see the man in white cautiously approaching him.

The thirst wasn't there. He didn't have the energy to support it. But while Mehta had no desire to sift the man in white, he had no reason to trust him beyond the remnants of an apple lying in an alley.

"I'm going to help you." The man in white's voice sounded as if he'd said it underwater. "I won't hurt you."

Mehta was too weak to argue. His vision darkened again, and this time it stayed dark. Though he fought to overcome, his body didn't allow him to continue. He slipped into the black void between life and death.

CHAPTER THREE

Mehta's consciousness flickered in and out, accompanied by throbbing pain in his side and on the back of his shoulder.

It was easier to sleep, but sleeping left him vulnerable. He tried to force his eyelids open, and vivid white light filtered into his vision. It pulsed brighter and brighter until he had to clench his eyes shut to stop it from scarring his sight.

But in closing his eyes, he lost consciousness again.

The image of the cratered mountain filled his dreams.

Mehta awoke in a dark room, gasping.

His enchanted vision adjusted to the lack of light, and soon he could make out shapes and forms in the shadows. He lay on a soft bed, covered in thick furs and sweating.

But he was alive.

As he flung the furs off, pain ignited in his side and his shoulder once again. He grunted—more sound than he usually permitted himself to make, given the Xyonates' rules, but he wasn't really a Xyonate anymore.

Still, practiced silence had countless useful applications, so Mehta ground his teeth, exhaled a ragged breath, and kept quiet as he slowly sat up.

The only light in the room crept under a door across from the bed, and it only shone dimly. He tested the floor with his bare feet and felt cool stone as he stood.

Evidently, whoever had brought him here had taken his boots. Not an advantage, but he'd trained thousands of hours while barefoot, so the disadvantage was nominal.

He searched himself for his knives. They'd taken those, too, along with whatever weapon had been lodged in the back of his shoulder. Cloth bandages covered the spot now and wrapped under his arm and around his shoulder.

Another set of bandages constricted his torso, covering his wounded side. It still burned with fresh pain, but it hadn't killed him yet.

Without his weapons in this unknown scenario, he couldn't be assured of an advantage. The wounds to his back and side would put him at a further disadvantage. But injured or not, any worthy Xyonate—or former Xyonate—could sift without the use of weapons if need be. And Mehta would if he had to.

He scanned the room again, hoping to find a weapon, but aside from the bed, a nightstand, and a bookshelf full of books, the room contained little else. He could've snapped a leg off of the nightstand and fashioned it into a makeshift club, but doing so would be a loud endeavor and wouldn't be worth the risk.

Instead, he approached the door slowly, both to remain silent and for the sake of his wounds. He ran his fingers up and down the polished wood until he found a metal plate with a keyhole and a doorknob. Was it locked or not?

For now, it didn't matter. He needed more information before trying to open it, so he pressed his ear against the door and listened.

Low voices murmured on the other side, distant and incomprehensible. Mehta made out two for certain, one certainly male and one likely female.

He waited, listening for several long minutes, expecting to hear footfalls eventually, but he heard nothing but the voices. Whoever had brought him here could be seated, reclining, or otherwise at rest. And if he could exit the room fast enough, he might glean enough of an advantage to overcome them.

The last time he'd been in a situation like this was when the soldiers wearing the three-headed ram's sigil had slain his parents and taken him from his home. He'd been just a child, only a few years old, but he remembered every moment of it with perfect clarity.

He pushed the memories away. He needed to focus on the situation at hand.

Mehta considered the bandages wrapped around his torso and his shoulder. Were his captors actually saviors? The man in white robes from the alley had both distracted Lament and promised to help Mehta as he fell unconscious, but Mehta remembered little after that.

Was he in the man's home? Was he somewhere else? Had the man in fact done something to help him, or had someone else taken him away?

There was only one way to find out if the door was locked. Mehta curled his fingers around the cool metal knob.

Light footfalls padded just outside the door, closer and closer. The dim light at the bottom of the door bloomed brighter.

Mehta recoiled from the door in perfect silence. He positioned himself beyond the door's hinges and waited with his back flat against the wall. In the darkness, his enhanced vision continued to outline everything in faint green lines.

The telltale rattling of metal, albeit quiet, filled the silent room, and the door opened with a faint creak. It hadn't been locked.

Candlelight illuminated a strip of the room, revealing plain white walls and a matching ceiling. The illuminated strip expanded as the door continued opening, and Mehta tensed, ready to spring at the right moment.

Then the candle-bearer stepped into the room, and Mehta froze.

It was a child. A girl, perhaps nine or ten years old, with sandy blonde hair, wearing a white nightgown, and holding a candle.

She was no threat to him. Whoever had sent her had either taken a terrible gamble or they didn't know what he was.

The girl stared at the empty bed, looked around the room, and finally turned toward him.

Their gazes met across the candlelight.

Mehta remained perfectly still.

"Hello," she said, her voice bright and chipper as if greeting a new friend.

Mehta didn't reply, but something stirred inside him. Something dark and terrible.

His thirst.

"I'm glad to see you're feeling better." Her voice lilted with sincerity and enthusiasm. A silver pendant, just a simple triangle pointing down, hung around her neck from a thin cord of leather. "When Father brought you in this morning, Mother and I feared the worst."

Sifting her would be the easiest thing in the world. Within seconds, she could be lying at his feet, her neck broken, and his thirst would be sated.

Or would it?

Mehta hesitated.

She turned toward the open door. "Father? He's awake."

His thirst burgeoned, multiplied by the father's impending arrival. Everything within him screamed to take the girl, hold her hostage, and leverage her against her father, who would inevitably prove to be more of a threat.

But Mehta did not move. He was wearing bandages. The people in this place—this house, or whatever it was—had tended to his wounds and taken measures to heal him. Thirst or otherwise, he couldn't justify sifting allies, especially now that he had so few.

So he remained still and waited to see what the next few seconds might bring.

A man stepped into the room. Mehta recognized his shape first—the bulge in his midsection was considerable. He'd noticed it before, in the alley.

This was the man who'd worn the white robes and furs. The man who'd thrown the apple at the back of Lament's head, giving Mehta the chance to prevail.

He had brown hair and light eyes, but Mehta couldn't make out their exact color in the candlelight. Now closer to him, Mehta guessed him to be in his early to mid-thirties rather than approaching forty.

"How do you feel?" the man asked.

Mehta considered his question. How could such a simple question ignite such a wide range of answers in his head?

He felt pain from his wounds. He felt confusion at how he'd arrived in this place. He felt an ongoing tug within him to sift them both—the thirst. He felt grateful they'd helped him, and he felt lost and abandoned and betrayed by the only family he'd ever really known—the Xyonates.

Truly a mixture of good and bad, but far more bad than good.

But Mehta also felt he'd better not let his guard down just yet. The appearance of someone who'd claimed he could help, plus a harmless, pleasant little girl did not ensure safety by any standard.

So Mehta replied, "Fine."

The man nodded slowly as if he somehow understood the range of emotions coursing through Mehta. "Are you hungry?"

As if on cue, Mehta's stomach rumbled. He couldn't remember the last time he'd eaten.

"How long have I been here?" he asked, still backed against the wall, still ready to sift them both if necessary. "And where am I?"

"Come with me." The man gave him a small nod and left the room, leaving the girl in there with Mehta alone again.

Did they truly not know what he was?

Xyonates operated in secret, and he'd been led to believe that common folk knew of their existence but thought of them merely as phantoms. But this man had seen Mehta sift Lament in the alley, and he still saw fit to leave his daughter exposed to potential harm.

It made no sense. It was foolish. Thoughtless.

The girl smiled at him and extended her hand, palm down. "I'll help you."

Help how? He outweighed her by at least 150 pounds. Even if he didn't, she was too short to lean on. Maybe she meant to guide him?

He swallowed. "I'd rather not touch you, if you don't mind."

Mehta didn't know what might happen if he did. He didn't want to risk the thirst taking over.

The girl shrugged and lowered her hand. "Very well. But it isn't gentlemanly to refuse the hand of a beautiful lady."

Mehta blinked at her.

"Follow me. We need to catch up with Father." With that, she turned and left the room as well, taking her candle with her, plunging Mehta into the shadows once again.

What was happening? Why were these people behaving so strangely?

Or perhaps *he* was the one behaving strangely. He'd only had limited interaction with anyone outside of the Sanctum since he'd been a small child, and most of that contact involved sifting. Not exactly a perfect frame of reference for how the rest of the world behaved.

His stomach growled again.

If these people were his captors, they would've locked his door and sent armed guards—rather than a little girl—into his room. He elected to follow them for now, though he remained vigilant.

Mehta found the girl waiting for him just outside the door. She waved him forward, and he stepped through cautiously, watching every inch of the room beyond.

A hearth glowed with a waning fire on the opposite end of the room. Three simple, whitewashed, wooden chairs sat before the hearth, and another sat against a wall adjacent to Mehta's room. A white fur rug lay in the space between the chairs and the hearth, and a row of bookshelves made up the far left wall.

Two doors sat at regular intervals along the same wall as Mehta's room. A third door punctuated the wall beyond the bookshelves at the farthest point in the room from Mehta's position. To Mehta's right, a fourth door was set into that wall, and strategically positioned torches accompanied the light given off by the hearth.

No one else was in the room.

Atop the mantle over the hearth sat a triangle-shaped icon, pointing down toward its white marble base. In that context, Mehta recognized the symbol—it represented the Goddess of Light, Laeri. That explained why the girl wore the triangle pendant around her neck.

Had they taken him to the temple?

"This way," the girl said.

Mehta hadn't seen any nooks or deep shadows in the space thus far. No hiding places meant no one could hide in wait for him, so he followed the girl across the room to the third door by the bookshelves, noting how nice the fur rug felt on his bare feet.

The door opened into a short, white corridor lit with torches. The ceiling arched upward, and the girl's father waited at the far end. The corridor had no doors and was well lit, so Mehta continued forward.

As he walked, he found it ironic how much solace he had taken in the shadows of his room, yet now he also found comfort in knowing that nothing and no one could hide nearby due to the ample lighting throughout the space.

The corridor ended in a room about the size of the one with the hearth, only it contained a stone oven, cabinets, countertops, and a simple, wooden table with four chairs instead. Torches lit this room as well, and what few small shadows he saw couldn't have concealed anything.

A door at the far end hung open, and the man stepped out of it with a bulging sack in each hand. Not an exit—just a pantry door. The room had no exits except for the door through which they'd entered.

"Please, sit." The man nodded toward the table, then he set the sacks on one of the countertops and began to untie them. "Do you like apples? If you prefer something more exotic, I have a few oranges as well."

Mehta hadn't eaten an orange in over a year. He'd been sent on a commission to the island of Caclos, where the climate was conducive to growing oranges, and he'd indulged in one there. It was perhaps the finest fruit he'd ever eaten. After that, he'd taken several in his pack and enjoyed them on his journey home to Etrijan.

He wanted another one now.

"You have oranges?" Mehta asked, his voice edged with caution.

"Yes." The man smiled and pulled one out of the sack. He tossed it to Mehta, who caught it. The man said, "It's all yours."

Mehta looked it over in his hands. Its pebble-grain texture felt familiar to his fingers, and he dug his nails into it and began peeling the skin off. Before long, he'd devoured it, and sticky juice clung to his hands, but he still hadn't sat down.

He noticed his hands for the first time since he'd awakened. They weren't covered with blood anymore. Nor was there any on his arms or his clothes. They'd bathed him and cleaned his garments.

As he looked closer, he noticed brownish specks of grit under his fingernails. They hadn't gotten *all* the blood off of him, but he could hardly fault them for not cleaning under his fingernails.

The man and the girl watched him with smiles on their faces, and the girl took a seat at the table with an apple and a small knife in her hands. Hardly threatening, but Mehta noted it nonetheless. Should he need the knife, he could take it from her easily enough.

"Would you like another?" the man asked. "You're welcome to sit, by the way."

Mehta shook his head in response to both the man's question and his comment. "Where am I?"

"You're in the parsonage of the Temple of Laeri. I'm the high priest, Rulfran." The man nodded toward the girl. "This is Ferne, my daughter."

Ferne waved at Mehta. He didn't wave back, but she didn't seem to mind. She was too fixated on her apple.

"Here. Have another. I insist." Rulfran tossed a second orange to Mehta. "I'm sure you're famished."

"How long have I been here?" The orange clung to Mehta's sticky fingers.

"Since this morning, when I encountered you in the alley."

Good. I haven't lingered too long, then. "I should leave."

"In your condition? You wouldn't last long out there." Rulfran shook his head. "You need rest, my friend."

Friend. How could Rulfran refer to him as a friend? They didn't know each other at all. So what had inspired Rulfran to use such a term? It made no sense.

Mehta had never had friends—only fellow Xyonate trainees and Xyonate brethren. Personal connections beyond that were scorned, even forbidden.

He'd been taught to keep his brethren at an arm's-length, partially because Xyonates lived notoriously short lifespans but also because focus was paramount when it came to the Xyonate way of life. A Xyonate who lacked focus was dangerous. Reckless. A threat.

And Mehta had been the best of them. He'd devoted every aspect of his life to the Xyonate way, dedicated every ounce of himself to fulfilling Xyon's will in Aletia.

And look where it has gotten you.

"Rest is for the weak," Mehta repeated the mantra Lament had taught him nearly two decades earlier and repeated hundreds of times since then.

Rulfran stared at him. "That's the dumbest thing I've ever heard."

Mehta blinked but said nothing.

"If you don't rest, you won't heal."

"If I do rest, they will find me."

Rulfran shook his head. "You're safe. Laeri watches over all of us."

"No." Mehta set the orange down on the corner of the table. "You don't know them. They won't stop until I'm dead."

Ferne looked up at him from her spot at the table, her blue eyes wide.

Rulfran rounded the table and put his hands on Ferne's shoulders. "I understand how you feel. I'm sorry you've found yourself in this predicament, but I would like to help you if I can. If you insist that you must leave, may I give you some coin, at least, to help you flee the city?"

Why would Rulfran give him money? Mehta was a Xyonate and a total stranger.

"I can't take your money. It wouldn't be—" Mehta stopped.

He was about to say it wasn't *right*, but the irony of the statement hit him. He had virtually no concept of what was right and what wasn't. He just followed orders.

"I'm offering it freely." Rulfran pulled a strand of sandy blonde hair away from Ferne's forehead and tucked it behind her ear. "As a gift."

"I can't accept it." Mehta glanced around. "Will you release me?"

Rulfran stared at him. "You're free to go any time. You're not our prisoner."

"Which way is out?"

Ferne pointed toward the doorway they'd used to enter the kitchen. "Door's out there. I wish you'd stay, though."

The way she said it stirred something deep within Mehta. Her words carried an innocence he hadn't known since before pledging himself as a Xyonate.

They were sweet words, kind and true. They almost made him trust Ferne and Rulfran. They almost made him want to stay.

Almost.

But the cratered mountain called to him. He would make his home there and try to find out if any of his family remained alive.

And maybe he'd find out who had sent those soldiers to slay his parents.

Mehta started toward the door without another word, his steps determined.

And then his head started to swim. He staggered to the nearest wall and braced himself against it as fresh pain spiked in his side.

He winced and ground his teeth.

Footsteps sounded behind him, and he whirled around, his eyes fixed on Rulfran's approaching form. He growled, "*Stay back.*"

Rulfran halted, his hands outstretched. "I won't harm you. I only want to help."

Mehta's vision blurred, and his hand slipped off of the wall. He sank to his knees and braced himself against the floor.

The pain heightened. Mehta resisted. He would not submit again.

"Please," Rulfran said. "I hate to see you like this. You need rest. Let me help."

Mehta shook his head, trying to force the pain from his mind. He clutched his wounded side with his free hand, and his arm bracing him against the floor quaked.

Concern etched on her kind face, Ferne stood and joined her father.

Sticky moisture clung to his fingers. He pulled his hand away from his bandaged wound and found it coated in blood.

CHAPTER FOUR

He'd seen plenty of blood before. It hadn't fazed him then, and it would not faze him now. Neither would the pain nor the disorientation.

Mehta inhaled a long, shaky breath, and he looked up at Ferne and Rulfran again. If they intended to do him harm, now would be an excellent opportunity. Instead, they just watched him struggle, helpless to intervene because he wouldn't let them.

But why am I struggling? His arm quaked again, and he planted his other hand on the ground with a wet smack, leaving a bloody handprint where he'd braced himself on the floor.

Ferne crouched next to him, and he looked up at her. Sadness filled her pleading blue eyes. "Please let us help you."

He didn't want to submit, but this wasn't truly submitting. Accepting care from these people wouldn't put him at risk.

Mehta's arms quivered, and he slumped onto his good side, defeated by the culmination of pain, weakness, and the goodwill of strangers. They'd told him he was safe. He could either accept it as the truth or not.

Mehta nodded, and Rulfran crouched down as well and helped him upright on wobbly legs. Together, they headed back to the room where Mehta had awoken.

*

MORNING LIGHT LEVERED MEHTA'S EYELIDS OPEN A CRACK, THEN HE OPENED THEM ALL the way, immediately alert. Sunshine glowed around the perimeter of the window, but thick curtains blocked most of the light from breaking into the room.

Mehta sat up in the bed. He'd slept through the night, but the pain in his side lingered. His shoulder, however, did not hurt at all.

If he could've reached back to touch it, he would have, but his side wouldn't allow him to do so.

Metal clinked and scraped, and the door started opening.

Mehta tensed, but he relaxed just as quickly. He was safe. He'd decided to believe it last night, and he needed to continue to believe it now.

But neither Rulfran nor Ferne entered the room. Instead, a blonde woman in white robes entered, carrying a tray of food.

Mehta's guard went up, but it slackened the more he studied her pretty face. She had to be Ferne's mother. The resemblance was unmistakable, and she had the same blue eyes.

But unlike Ferne, this woman did not seem comfortable with Mehta's presence.

"Good morning," she said, her voice flat. She gave him a forced smile.

Mehta didn't respond. He just stared at her, wary.

She placed the tray on the nightstand beside the bed. A silver goblet of water sat on the tray next to a small loaf of bread. Also on the tray, a bowl of steaming brown-orange soup smelled of garlic and spices and meat—lamb, perhaps.

Mehta's stomach rumbled in response to the aroma. He couldn't have stopped it from growling if he'd wanted to.

"You don't have to eat all of this, but I suggest that you do." Her voice was still flat. "The sooner you recover, the sooner you can be on your way."

Her tone suggested that she not only wanted him gone but also that she didn't care that he knew it. Mehta took no offense; he wanted to leave as well, sooner rather than later, and he couldn't blame a holy woman like her—a priest's wife—for wanting him out of their home.

"But I need to change your bandages first."

Mehta looked down at himself. Rulfran had changed his bandages prior to letting him drift off to sleep the night before, and it did not appear that any blood had seeped through the new bandages.

Mehta raised his head. The woman hadn't moved since she'd mentioned changing his bandages. She just stared at him with her arms folded.

He took her silence as impatience, and, still seated on the bed, he straightened his back and raised his arms slightly to give her access to his torso. It hurt his side to hold his arm up, but he didn't show it.

The woman reached for his torso and changed his bandages on his side. When she'd cleaned his wound and reapplied the new bandages, she asked him to turn to his side so she could get to his shoulder.

Once she had it unwrapped, she said, "Hm."

Mehta looked up at her again.

"We don't need to rewrap your shoulder."

"Why not?" Mehta asked.

She shook her head. "It appears my husband has been using his magic on you."

Mehta recoiled from her.

"It's fine." She held her hands up, tense and with nervousness behind her blue eyes. "He practices light magic. As a servant of Laeri, he can use it to heal others. That explains why he's been in bed all morning."

Mehta didn't understand, but he didn't ask about it, either. Instead, he rotated his shoulder to confirm what she'd said. Sure enough, the only pain came from his side. His shoulder felt fine.

"I'll be on my way, then." She collected the used bandages and left the room without so much as another word. She hadn't even given Mehta her name.

Ferne and Rulfran had been overly hospitable, but the woman had been cold toward Mehta. She had to know what he was. Not many people would even consider bringing a trained assassin to enter their home, much less allowing one to stay overnight, feeding him, tending to his wounds, and seeing to his wellbeing.

She'd done more for him than he'd deserved, certainly.

Mehta tried the soup and found it as delicious as it smelled, but his appetite hadn't yet fully returned, so he ate very little of it. He left it sitting on the tray and headed toward the door, which the woman had left open.

Instead of stepping out right away, he peered into the sunlit room beyond, studying it. Watching. He'd resolved to trust these people, but that didn't mean he should be any less vigilant. A lifetime of Xyonate training had ingrained caution into his very core.

The hearth on the opposite end of the room was dark and devoid of the fire crackling in it the night before. Ferne sat in one of the three whitewashed chairs before the hearth, reading a thick book with her legs curled underneath her. Beams of white sunlight from skylight windows illuminated the floor around her.

Satisfied, Mehta entered the room, his hand pressed against his side. His steps sent tiny jolts of pain into his side, and the wound still throbbed even when he stopped walking. He placed his hands on the back of one of the chairs adjacent to where Ferne sat.

She looked up at him and smiled, then she refocused on her book again.

Throughout his time as a Xyonate, thousands of people had glanced at him and not given him so much as a second look. He'd sifted some of those people, he'd slipped past others after a commission, and others had simply been passersby.

But none of them had looked at him with the ambivalent innocence of Ferne. He might as well have been a tree, or a horse, or a statue, or some other object worthy of only fleeting interest.

When she didn't look up again, he rounded the chair and sat in it, careful to do so slowly for the sake of his wounded side. He sat there, listening to the relative silence of Rulfran's home.

He could hear his own breathing, and he could hear Ferne drawing measured, easy breaths as she read. The occasional mug or cup clunked from inside the kitchen. Mehta thought he even heard Rulfran snoring in one of the rooms to his left, but he couldn't be sure.

Mehta stared at the triangle-shaped icon sitting on the mantle, then he glanced at Ferne again. She still wore the triangle-shaped pendant that matched the icon.

Her neck—he'd wanted to snap it last night. Now the thirst stirred in his chest yet again.

"Mother says it's not polite to stare." Ferne's voice broke Mehta out of his dark thoughts.

The sound of her voice subdued the thirst but only because her words had distracted him. He said, "I'm sorry."

"I don't mind," Ferne said, still reading. "I'm just telling you what's proper when it comes to manners."

Manners and politeness weren't subjects that Mehta had studied while training to become a Xyonate. What use were manners and politeness to a precision instrument? Any time spent learning such frivolities was wasted, except insofar as it was necessary for a Xyonate to blend in with those around him.

Ferne glanced up at him and giggled. "You're still staring."

Mehta looked away. He repeated, "I'm sorry."

"So who are you?" Ferne lowered her book.

Mehta hesitated. "What—what do you mean?"

"I mean, tell me who you are."

The question perplexed him. For such a simple inquiry, he lacked any definitive answer. Until yesterday, the entirety of his person had been tethered to the Xyonates. Every breath, every whisper in every shadow, and every single action had belonged to them.

Now, without them, Mehta lacked identity.

"What's your name?" Ferne asked.

Even that question bothered him.

Mehta. The name he'd been born with. The name he'd remembered from so many years before.

Requiem. His Xyonate name, given to him upon the completion of his training. The name under which he'd sifted countless people and done Xyon's bidding.

Ferne giggled again. "Don't you know your own name?"

Mehta inhaled a sharp breath but a shock of pain in his side stopped him. He exhaled slowly. And he chose a name.

"Mehta," he said.

By all considerations, the name *Requiem* held no meaning for him anymore. He'd renounced the Xyonates, and he'd fled their ranks. Shouldn't he also strip himself of the name they'd given him?

"Mehta," Ferne repeated. "I like it. It's pretty. *Meh-ta.*"

Pretty? "Thank you... I suppose."

"Where are you from?" Ferne asked.

The cratered mountain arose in his memory. "Far away from here."

Ferne leaned toward him and whispered, "How did you get hurt?"

Mehta swallowed the lump in his throat and closed his eyes. The memory of Elegy's attack inside the Sanctum returned, and the pain in his side spiked to accompany it, albeit less severe than before. Mehta opened his eyes.

Ferne's innocent eyes stared up at him. "Mother and Father won't tell me."

Mehta considered that they had spared her the details due to her age. But he'd been even younger when the Xyonates had introduced him to the God of Death and his ways.

He glanced around. Rulfran's snores still sounded from the other room, and Ferne's mother was nowhere in sight—probably still in the kitchen.

"Someone stabbed me," he replied quietly.

Ferne covered her mouth, and her eyes widened. "Why would someone do that?"

Mehta exhaled a ragged breath. How could he explain the complexities of the Xyonate lifestyle to a child? "It's complicated."

"I don't understand."

"They—" Mehta hesitated. "—they wanted me dead. They didn't succeed. That's all you need to know."

Ferne opened her mouth to speak, but her mother's stern voice filled the room.

"Ferne, come away from him."

Ferne recoiled from Mehta and complied immediately. She walked across the room to where her mother stood, her head drooping, still carrying her book.

"Lunch is ready," her mother said. "Go on. Say the blessing and eat."

With her head low, Ferne slipped past her mother into the kitchen.

Ferne's mother stood there, staring at Mehta. He was used to hard stares from people far more dangerous than this woman, but something in her eyes chilled Mehta's soul.

"I would appreciate if you'd refrain from speaking with my daughter while you're here. You may be our guest, but she is off-limits," Ferne's mother said. "Do you understand?"

Mehta didn't want a fight. He nodded.

She turned and went into the kitchen, and a door latch opened behind Mehta.

He looked back, on edge, and saw Rulfran emerge from the room. Mehta relaxed.

"Good morning." Rulfran yawned and rubbed his eyes. "Feeling better today?"

Well, I was. Mehta nodded again.

"Join us for lunch?" Rulfran motioned toward the kitchen.

"Your wife already brought me some soup."

"Ah, Elanil." Rulfran smiled and patted his round belly. "Always the consummate hostess. She serves alongside me as the High Priestess of Laeri. She's equally hospitable and kind in the service of the goddess Laeri's patrons."

Mehta raised an eyebrow. *If you say so.*

Rulfran donned a goofy grin. "And she's quite the beauty."

"Yes." Mehta couldn't argue that point. Elanil was unquestionably beautiful.

"Please, join us anyway. You're our guest. It will be good to talk with you some more."

"I don't want to impose." *Nor do I want to spend any more time here than necessary.*

It wasn't that Mehta disliked them. In fact, little Ferne was growing on him. But he felt out of place, like a dagger jammed into a knife's scabbard.

"Please. I insist."

Rulfran did a lot of insisting. As someone trained to obey those in authority without hesitation, Mehta found himself drawn to honor Rulfran's requests—especially in light of how last night had taken a positive turn.

"Alright," he said.

"I don't think I got your name amid all the commotion last night," Rulfran said.

Requiem. "Mehta."

"Mehta? What a unique name. It's a pleasure to formally meet you." Rulfran smiled at him and motioned for him to lead the way to the kitchen.

Mehta would've preferred to follow, but he obliged Rulfran yet again.

When Mehta walked into the kitchen, he noticed Elanil's shift from pleasant to concern, then to somber, then to the low burn of frustrated fury.

Great.

Mehta looked to Rulfran, and Rulfran pointed toward an open chair situated between Elanil and another empty chair. Mehta sat in it, and Rulfran sat in the other empty chair, separating Mehta from sitting adjacent to Ferne—except now she sat directly across from him.

She'd noticed him when he'd walked into the room, but she quickly averted her gaze and refocused on her plate.

The meal came and went, with Mehta sitting there in silence while Rulfran did most of the talking. Elanil spoke on occasion, usually in response to something Rulfran said, but Ferne scarcely said a word.

As he finished his soup, Rulfran said, "Mehta, I'm sure you've realized by now that your shoulder is healed."

Mehta nodded. "Some sort of magic, I'm told."

"The purest magic. A blessing from Laeri herself," Rulfran said. "To those of us who dedicate our lives to holiness and study, the goddess endows miraculous powers, not the least of which is healing."

Mehta said nothing. He just listened.

"It comes at personal sacrifice to those of us who aren't yet as experienced. That's why I had to sleep so long this morning. Using Laeri's blessings to heal you really drained me."

"I'm sorry," Mehta said.

Rulfran waved his hand dismissively. "I'm not looking for an apology, my friend. I'm simply explaining my absence. I was pleased to be able to help."

Mehta hesitated. How should he respond? "Well, thank you."

"I would have liked to heal the wound in your side, but I fear my powers are not that advanced. To try to heal something so severe might…" Rulfran shook his head. "…well, I'm not sure what it might do to me."

"It's fine. I will heal, or I won't."

Ferne looked up from her empty plate with wide eyes, but a scowl from Elanil severed Ferne's gaze.

"Ferne," Elanil said, "Why don't you go play or read?"

"But I want to stay here."

"*Ferne*," Elanil repeated.

That was all she said, but that was all it took for Ferne to comply. She stood from her chair, grabbed her book, and headed out of the kitchen.

"Close the door behind you, please," Elanil called.

A moment later, a tiny arm reached across the doorway and shut the door.

"What is it, Elanil?" Rulfran asked.

"We need to discuss a few things regarding our guest's stay in our home," she said.

"Please," Mehta held up his hand. "There's no need. I'll go."

"What?" Rulfran shook his head. "Of course you won't go. You're not well."

"I think it's best if I do." Mehta locked eyes with Elanil, whose face remained emotionless. "I don't want to impose any further. I've already been too much of a burden."

"No, no. Certainly not."

"Rulfran." Elanil reached over and put her right hand on top of his left hand. "If he is determined to leave, perhaps we should let him."

She glanced at Mehta again, and her eyebrows rose slightly.

Mehta got the signal. "Your hospitality has been most generous, but I don't want to overstay my welcome."

Rulfran studied Mehta, then he studied his wife. "I think I understand."

"What's to understand, darling?" Elanil said. "He wants to leave."

Rulfran put his right hand on top of Elanil's, which still rested on his left hand. "My dear, do you not wish him to stay with us?"

She smiled at him. "Now Rulfran, why would you ever think that?"

Mehta didn't like where this was heading. He stood from his chair. "Please. I can leave. It's fine. I'll be fine."

"No, Mehta. You will stay," Rulfran said, his voice firm, all while staring at Elanil. "At least until my wife truly speaks her mind."

Elanil's smile faded.

Now Mehta *really* didn't want to be there.

"Well, my dear, let's hear it," Rulfran said.

Elanil pulled away from him and sat back in her chair, rigid in body and expression. She hissed, "I don't trust him."

"Why not?"

"He is a Xyonate. He serves Xyon, the god of death, darkness, and the Underworld. Xyon is the eternal enemy of Laeri," she said, "and you invited one of his followers *into our home.*"

Some part of Mehta wanted to correct her and tell her that he'd left the Xyonates, but he remained silent. Though he'd abandoned the Sanctum and Xyon's followers, much of his old life still festered within him like a cancer.

Yet in all his years of training, Mehta had never been taught that the goddess Laeri was Xyon's enemy. For the clerics to have left out such an important detail confused Mehta.

"I did not invite him, dear wife," Rulfran said. "I brought him here myself. He would have died in the alley where I'd found him if I had not. Would you have preferred that?"

"Of course not."

She said it without even a hint of hesitation, but Mehta wouldn't have held it against her if she *had* wanted him dead in the alley.

"And are we not called by Laeri to heal the sick, care for the wounded, and feed the hungry, shelter the poor, and—"

"And show kindness to strangers and foreigners. Yes, I know the scriptures as well as you do, Rulfran," she muttered.

"And yet you wish him to leave?"

"I never said that."

"You said you didn't trust him," Rulfran pressed. "Why would you want someone you don't trust to stay?"

"I—Rulfran, stop it," she said. "I know what you're doing."

"I'm trying to help someone in need. That's all. We help people all the time."

Mehta bristled at Rulfran's words and at the heightening tension lining their conversation. He didn't deserve anyone's help, and he certainly didn't want to drive a wedge between these good people.

"But never in our *home*, Rulfran. You didn't consult me. You didn't ask me if I'd agree with you bringing a Xyonate—a murderer—into our home."

"I shouldn't have to," Rulfran countered, his voice more level than it had been. "It was the right thing to do."

"By him, maybe." Elanil pointed at Mehta but didn't look at him. "But not for us. Not for your daughter. You put her at risk by bringing him here."

Rulfran turned to Mehta. "I'm sorry you have to hear all of this."

I wouldn't be hearing it if you had just let me leave, Mehta thought, but he didn't dare say it aloud.

"So you'll apologize to him but not to me?" Elanil snapped.

"Why would I apologize for doing good?" Rulfran shook his head. "I couldn't let him die."

"You didn't have to bring him here."

"If I had left him there, more of the Xyonates would have found him and killed him."

"Yes. That's what Xyonates do." Elanil's gaze flitted to Mehta, then back to Rulfran. "They *kill*."

Rulfran turned to Mehta again. "Are you going to kill us?"

The suggestion, combined with the tension in the room, aroused Mehta's thirst, but he replied, "No."

Rulfran looked at Elanil again. "There you have it."

Elanil scoffed. "And you believe him? Just like that?"

"He has given me no reason to distrust him thus far."

"He's a *Xyonate*, Rulfran!" Elanil almost yelled.

"And we serve Laeri," Rulfran matched her volume. "I could not stand by and let him perish. Not when Laeri so clearly placed him in my path. As a high priestess in her service, you of all people should understand that."

"And *you* should understand, as a father and as a husband, that bringing an assassin into your home creates a colossal risk to our family," Elanil fired back.

"I'll go," Mehta interjected. He had to say something to stop the argument, or the growing thirst might overwhelm him.

"No, you won't," Rulfran said. "You're not well."

"Rulfran," Mehta said, "you've been kind to me, but I can't divide your family. I've already divided too many families."

Elanil scoffed again, but Mehta paid her no mind.

"You've helped me enough," Mehta continued. "Please, let me go."

Rulfran paused, motionless. He glowered at Elanil for a moment, then he turned back to Mehta and slowly nodded his head. "Very well, but only on the condition that you allow me to give you some coin for your journey."

Mehta shook his head. "I can't—"

"I know, I know. You can't take my money. But you're going to."

Mehta frowned at him, but he'd endured enough arguing, and the thirst had finally begun to subside. If taking the money would get him out of there faster, he'd accept it.

Elanil nodded at Mehta, and pain flared in his side. For the first time since he'd met her, he resented her. Though he didn't want to stay, he couldn't deny that his body could've used the extra rest.

But he wasn't leaving without his knives. "If you'll bring me my belongings, I can leave now."

"Of course." Elanil stood and rounded the table—on the side opposite of Mehta—and headed toward the kitchen door.

She opened it, revealing Ferne standing there.

A man stood behind her with a gleaming knife to her throat.

CHAPTER FIVE

Elanil gasped and staggered back, then she took a step forward.

The man, whom Mehta recognized as Creed, one of his Xyonate brethren, pulled Ferne back and pressed the knife against her neck. He wore dark strips of fabric wrapped tightly around his body and legs, leaving his tan, sinewy arms exposed.

Ferne yelped, and Elanil's advance stopped.

"Please," Elanil said. "Let her go."

"I'm not here for her or for you," Creed's scratchy voice said. His dark, conniving eyes focused on Mehta. "I'm here for him."

Mehta processed the situation in an instant—Creed wasn't alone. He couldn't be. Xyonates weren't prideful as individuals, so there would be no cause to confront Mehta without bringing along reinforcements.

So Mehta would have to sift Creed and anyone else with him before he could escape.

That door was the only way out. The kitchen was a self-contained room with no windows or other doors except for the pantry door on the opposite side of the room.

Furthermore, Mehta noted no obvious weapons within reach. He would have to wait to disarm whichever Xyonate came for him first.

His wounded side would multiply the difficulty of all of that. It would hamper his mobility. His speed would dwindle. His precision might falter.

Mehta's response to his initial assessment was simply to back away from the table. Right now, space to move was his ally.

Creed's devilish eyes watched him, and he urged Ferne into the room. Another Xyonate entered behind him, then another. Then another.

Fable and Mantra—two male Xyonates—and Hymn, a female.

BLOOD MERCENARIES ORIGINS

Mehta had hoped for only one more. He would've had a chance against two of them, but fighting four Xyonates seemed impossible in his weakened state.

The terror etched on Ferne's face sent a shock of guilt into Mehta's gut. That girl and her parents would unquestionably die today.

And it will be my fault.

They'd tracked him here, somehow, and if they experienced the thirst like he did, they'd sift everyone in sight like a pack of wild wolves tearing into helpless prey.

But maybe he could bargain for their lives. He had to at least try.

"Let her go, and I'll come with you," Mehta said.

Creed snickered. "What do you care if she lives or dies?"

"She's innocent. You want me."

"No one is innocent, Requiem. Don't you remember the clerics' teachings?"

"She's young. Let her live her life."

Creed brandished an insidious smile. "Why let her live when I can honor Xyon with her death?"

Elanil gasped and covered her mouth with her hands.

Creed laughed again. "Don't worry, priestess. You will accompany her to the Underworld soon after."

"Creed, you can either take me and live, or you can try to sift these people, and you will perish instead." Mehta said it with far more confidence than he felt. He hoped his reputation within the Sanctum would sow uncertainty in their minds. Maybe it would be enough to dissuade them from attacking.

And maybe his thirst would serve him for once, instead of the other way around.

Creed glanced at his fellow Xyonates, and they glanced at him.

Perhaps Mehta's bluster had worked.

"If I die," Creed said, "I will die with the honor of serving Xyon."

Mehta's fists clenched. *Fanatics.* He hadn't realized how insufferable they were until he was no longer one of them.

A voice shouted something from behind Mehta—Rulfran.

Mehta didn't recognize the words, but a stunning flash of light ignited within the room, blinding Mehta. He tore at his eyes, trying to see through the searing brilliance, but to no avail.

Shuffling footsteps pattered across the kitchen floor and past him before he could react. They were too loud to have been one of the Xyonates but too quiet to have been an adult's.

Ferne must have escaped Creed's grasp.

A hand grasped Mehta's wrist, and he rolled his wrist and broke free from the grip. Then he realized he could see again. Rulfran stood next to him, and Ferne clung to Elanil.

They stared across the room at the four Xyonates between them and the way out, all of whom rubbed their eyes, blinking, desperate to see once again.

"Now's your chance," Rulfran whispered.

Mehta took Rulfran's meaning. Rulfran's blast of light had evened the odds. He started toward the Xyonates, fully able to see.

Creed blinked and shook his head, inching forward as he did. Mehta approached him with perfect silence.

Then Creed stopped, blinked again, and slashed his knife at Mehta's torso.

Mehta jumped back, out of its reach.

"I see you, Requiem," Creed said. "You're a dark haze, but I see enough of you."

From Mehta's right side, Fable launched toward him with a pair of golden-handled daggers extended.

Mehta ducked under his first swipe. He blocked Fable's second attack, bracing both his forearms against Fable's arm, stopping his motion. Mehta's hands shifted and grabbed ahold of Fable's wrist.

Mehta stepped under Fable's arm but pulled it with him, put pressure on the pommel of the dagger, and stripped it from Fable's hand. Now Mehta had the weapon he needed.

Mantra's curved sword sliced toward Mehta's head, but Mehta parried it away with his dagger. As Mantra began a follow-up swing, Mehta ducked low and slashed the dagger across his leg, just under his left knee.

Mehta's aim was intentional. The dagger severed the tendon beneath Mantra's knee, yielding a spurt of blood.

Then, no longer held in place by the tendon, the muscles in Mantra's thigh rolled up into a thick bulge. He dropped to the floor, shrieking and groping at his ruined leg.

Mantra was no longer a threat. Even if he somehow managed to survive, he'd never walk again.

But the pain in Mehta's side reignited. Instead of finishing Mantra off, Mehta staggered back against the wall, trying to stanch the fire pulsing in his torso.

Hymn made it to Mantra first. She crouched down beside him and pulled his head up against her side. Though Mehta couldn't hear her because of Mantra's gasps, he made out the words on her lips, "I commit you, Mantra, to Xyon's realm."

Then she eased her knife into the side of Mantra's neck, and his moans silenced. When she removed it, blood streamed out of the wound and pooled on the floor beneath him. He died within seconds.

Elanil and Ferne gasped.

One down, three to go.

And Mehta couldn't even breathe without it hurting.

Hymn let Mantra's head slump to the floor. Then she stood and stalked toward Rulfran, Elanil, and Ferne while Creed and Fable approached Mehta from opposite angles.

Rulfran drew Elanil and Ferne behind him, shielding them with his body as Hymn approached. White light glowed from his palms, but Mehta knew he wouldn't stand even a shadow of a chance against Hymn's prowess.

If Mehta threw his dagger, he might be able to hit or even sift Hymn, but doing so would leave him vulnerable to fatal blows from Creed and Fable. And he'd never be able to sift them in time to save Rulfran's family.

Rulfran pointed his palms at Hymn, and they flared brighter. A blast of light knocked Hymn across the kitchen and into the far wall.

Creed and Fable seized the opportunity to attack Mehta—Creed high, and Fable low. Coordinated. Deadly.

But Mehta had expected that, and as he dove over Fable's attack, he used his dagger to deflect Creed's slash at his chest. Mehta rolled to his feet, ready to defend another blow from Creed or Fable, but he found himself face-to-face with Hymn instead.

She stabbed at him, and he batted her forearm away with his own. But she followed the stab with a spinning kick that caught Mehta on the side of his head, leveling him to the floor.

Stunned, Mehta rolled to his back in time to see Hymn raise her knife for a final blow.

Then Rulfran's body slammed into Hymn, tackling her to the floor. He'd saved Mehta, but he'd doomed himself in the process.

As Mehta recovered to his feet, Hymn twisted free and drove her knives into Rulfran's sides repeatedly. Crimson stained his white tunic, and he rolled off of her, gasping and moaning.

Elanil shrieked and covered Ferne's eyes.

Mehta lashed his dagger at Hymn, but she rolled under it, away from Rulfran. Then she stood next to Creed and Fable.

Rulfran was as good as dead. It was just a matter of time.

But perhaps Mehta could still save Elanil and Ferne. They were innocent in all of this. He would do everything he could to help them escape. He steeled himself against the pain in his side and stepped forward, ready to fight.

Rulfran's hand grabbed his ankle.

Mehta chanced a look down.

Through strained, ragged breaths, Rulfran said, "Don't waste this."

Brilliant white light flared from Rulfran's hand, and the pain in Mehta's side dwindled until it no longer hurt at all.

Rulfran had healed him.

Rulfran's grip faltered, and his body slackened.

But Mehta was alive, uninjured, and energized with renewed vigor.

His thirst sparked to life, and he channeled it into his dagger.

The Xyonates came at him like a maelstrom. Mehta dodged blows, batted away attacks, and returned brutal counterstrikes that rent the flesh on the Xyonates' arms and legs. But he'd failed to inflict any debilitating or fatal blows on them.

Worse yet, he'd ended up in the middle of the Xyonates, surrounded. Hymn stood behind Mehta, and Creed and Fable stood before him. They were spaced apart just enough to prevent him from slipping between them, and their positioning still pulled his attention in two directions.

No matter. He was the best, and his thirst needed quenching. He would cut them down all at once or one by one—however they came at him, that's how they would die.

As Mehta engaged the Xyonates, he noticed Elanil creeping toward the kitchen door along the wall, pulling Ferne behind her. Their bravery gave him purpose—he had to distract the Xyonates long enough so they could escape.

But while Mehta dueled with Creed and Fable, Hymn stepped away from the fracas. She raised her knife over her shoulder, her gaze fixed upon Ferne and Elanil.

Thanks to Creed and Fable's positioning, Mehta would never reach Hymn in time to stop her throw. Everything within him cried out, and it burst from his mouth in a desperate shout.

Elanil's head turned.

Hymn hurled her knife. It careened through the air, turning end-over-end, straight at Ferne.

CHAPTER SIX

E lanil stepped in front of Ferne, shielding her, and the knife thudded into her chest. She dropped to the floor with shock etched onto her face.

Ferne gasped, then screamed.

Creed attacked with a quick slash at Mehta's gut, but Mehta backed away, careful not to double over and offer his face as a target for Creed's follow-up swipe.

Hymn stalked toward Ferne, menace emanating from her cold, dark eyes.

Mehta had to stop her.

Fable attacked next, and Mehta intercepted his swing, grabbed Fable's arm, and used his momentum to smash Fable's forehead into the kitchen's stone wall. Then he whirled Fable around, using him as a human shield as Creed lunged forward.

The blade plunged into Fable's gut, stopping it from reaching Mehta. Fable gasped and flinched, and he dropped his remaining dagger to the floor.

The sight of Fable's blood intensified Mehta's thirst.

Beyond Creed and Fable, Hymn stepped closer to Ferne.

Creed hesitated, then he drove the knife deeper into Fable's stomach, trying to puncture through the other side to get to Mehta. Fable grunted and grasped at Creed's wrist.

But Mehta shoved Fable forward into Creed and stepped to the side. He lined up his throw, a clear shot, and whipped the dagger at Hymn.

It lodged in her back, and she toppled forward, landing at Ferne's feet.

Ferne shrieked.

Mehta's thirst screamed for more.

Creed pushed Fable to the side as Mehta crouched down to pick up Fable's other dagger. Fable fell to the floor, clutching his wounded, bleeding stomach, submitting to the pain.

Creed hurtled toward Mehta, his knife poised to strike. Mehta extended his dagger and dropped backward, focused on its wobbling tip as he fell. He had the reach advantage, and as Creed approached, Mehta adjusted the dagger's point so it pierced into Creed's chest just above his heart.

Blood erupted from the wound. Mehta had hit Creed's aorta.

They dropped to the floor together, but Creed was already dead, and his blood quickly joined that of Mantra's and Fable's.

Mehta shoved Creed's body aside and stood. He jerked the dagger from Creed's chest, and more blood pulsed out of the wound. His thirst reveled in the victory, but it still refused to subside.

Fable looked up at Mehta, still clutching his wounded gut. He uttered, "Sift me, Requiem. Send me to Xyon. Give me what I have always desired."

Mehta had to sift Fable, but he hated that doing so somehow gave Fable what he wanted.

"I'll sift you," Mehta said, "but you'll perish as a failure. I still yet live."

Fable's smug countenance darkened, and he died by his own dagger.

Mehta hurried over to Hymn and Ferne. Ferne sat there, crouched against the wall near the kitchen door, staring down at Hymn with wide eyes.

Hymn squirmed and writhed and reached, but she couldn't get the dagger out of her back.

Mehta stood over them both. He considered telling Ferne to look away, but she had already seen worse than what he was about to do.

He planted his foot on Hymn's upper back, pinned her to the floor, and drove his dagger into the base of her skull. Her writhing stopped immediately, and Mehta's thirst delighted in her death.

Mehta looked down at Ferne. His thirst wanted her, too, but he denied the impulse with every fiber of his being. He had to, or it would have overcome him, and Ferne would've joined the Xyonates in death next.

"We must leave now," he said to her.

Ferne pointed to Elanil, who moaned.

Mehta rushed over to her. One look told him that Hymn's aim had been true. Elanil would soon die. Blood seeped from the knife wound in her chest and had pooled underneath her.

"You... bastard..." she rasped. "This is... your fault."

"I know." With total sincerity, Mehta uttered, "I'm sorry."

"Save your... apologies," she wheezed. "You destroyed... my family. Go... to hell... with your *evil*... god."

Then Elanil went silent, and her breathing stopped. Her eyes turned to glass, and she went limp.

Ferne burst into tears.

Mehta crouched in front of Ferne and placed his hands on her shoulders. "We must go. More will be coming."

Ferne continued weeping, hopeless.

Mehta shook her, and his voice hardened. "*Ferne.*"

She stopped crying and looked up at him with terror in her eyes. It sickened

Mehta's stomach. He hated being harsh with her, especially after what she'd just experienced, but he knew of no other way to get her attention.

"Please," Mehta said, his voice softer. "We have to leave. It's not safe here anymore."

Ferne gulped and shuddered.

"I won't hurt you." Even as Mehta said it, his thirst swelled, but he forced it away.

Ferne nodded slightly, but doubt lingered in her eyes. "Alright."

"I swear to you that I won't hurt you, nor will I allow any harm to come to you," Mehta said. "You have my word."

Ferne nodded again, and she stood.

He didn't know where they would go, but perhaps if they could escape Sefera after nightfall then they could head toward the cratered mountain of Mehta's memories. Perhaps they'd be safe there.

Mehta collected a few supplies, some money, and some of the weapons strewn across Ferne's kitchen. He recovered his own knives from Rulfran's room and stuffed all of it into a pack. Then he fled the Temple of Laeri with Ferne in tow.

THANKS TO THE XYONATES' BLOOD COVERING MOST OF MEHTA'S BODY, STAYING AT AN inn or a boarding house wasn't an option. Walking into a place in such a state would invite far too much negative attention, perhaps including the city guard. The last thing Mehta needed was more trouble.

Instead, about a mile from the Temple of Laeri, Mehta found them an abandoned, run-down shanty wedged between two larger buildings. Holes pocked its roof, and the weathered gray boards that made up its walls creaked when the wind blew, but it would have to do.

He sat Ferne down. "How are you?"

"I'm sad," she replied, her face downcast.

Mehta took her hands in his. He didn't know why he did it, but it seemed appropriate at that moment. "I'm sorry."

She looked up at him, and fresh tears pooled in her eyes. "I'm scared."

Before Mehta could respond, Ferne lurched forward, wrapped her arms around his torso, and buried her face in his chest, sobbing.

Mehta stiffened at first, then he relaxed. He embraced her, uncertain and unsure what he was supposed to do next. They sat there, in the darkness of the shanty, unmoving for several minutes.

Ferne finally released him, sniveling. She brushed the tears from her cheek and wiped her runny nose on her forearm. "What do we do now?"

"For now, we wait."

"Then what?"

"I don't know." Mehta sighed and sat on a rickety stepstool. The shanty groaned against a gust of wind. "Sefera is no longer safe for me. Or you."

"I miss Mother and Father." Ferne lowered her head.

The thirst awakened within Mehta. He could sift the girl that night in her sleep, and she would join her parents in a better place.

Or he could sift her now and spare her any further torment.

He gripped the hilt of one of his knives, now tucked in its sheath inside his clothes. Sifting her would satisfy his thirst…

But only for a short while. It would inevitably return, stronger than before, as it always did. It was relentless.

"What's wrong?" Ferne stared up at his face, oblivious to his dark thoughts.

The thirst burgeoned in his chest and spread into his arms, but he forced himself to release his grip on his knife. He clasped his hands together instead. "Nothing."

Ferne shook her head. "Something's wrong. I can tell. Are we in trouble? Do we need to leave?"

"No. We're safe here." *Relatively.*

"Then what's wrong?"

The thirst threatened to consume him. Sifting Ferne would be the easiest thing he'd ever done. She was small. Defenseless. Unsuspecting. A simple, quick death.

But Mehta couldn't do it. He refused to do it. Nothing gave him the right to sift her, to cut her innocent life short.

Yet the thirst refused to leave him alone. It threatened to overpower him and force the deed nonetheless.

His hands began to shake.

"What's wrong?" Ferne repeated.

"I…" Mehta started. If he could get her to flee, then he wouldn't have the chance to kill her. "I desire to sift you."

Ferne blinked at him. "What?"

"To kill you. It's overwhelming me," Mehta continued. "You should go."

Ferne recoiled. "Why would you want to kill me? You just saved me from those people."

"I can't explain it." Mehta thought about standing, but he didn't want to scare Ferne after what he'd just said. An armed assassin towering over a little girl? Not a reassuring image. So instead he backed the stool against one of the walls and sat as far away from her as the shanty allowed.

Ferne watched him the whole time. "Maybe I can help you."

Mehta shook his head. "You can't help me. No one can."

"Let me try?" Ferne took a tentative step toward him. "I like helping people."

The thirst throbbed within him. "No. It's too dangerous for you to be near me right now. You should leave."

"At least try something for me?" Ferne pressed.

Mehta sighed, more concerned for her than frustrated. "Ferne, I—"

"Please?"

His jaw clenched. "Fine. Try what?"

"Close your eyes. Make your hands into fists."

"What will that do?"

"Just try it."

Mehta obliged her.

"Now push this feeling away in your mind. Put it in a crate and close it up. Wrap it in chains, and lock them."

Mehta opened one eye and squinted at her.

"No peeking!" Ferne pointed at him.

"Sorry." Mehta closed his eye again. He visualized his thirst as a roiling, angry mass of darkness, and he forced it into a crate in his mind. He shut the crate, chained it up, and secured it with an imaginary lock.

"Have you done it?"

"Yes."

"Good. Now banish that feeling to the back of your head. Put it in a closet and close the door on it."

His eyes still shut, Mehta did as she instructed. The sensation of the thirst still oppressed him, and he doubted any of this would work.

"We're going to say a prayer to Laeri. She'll help us with the rest."

Now Mehta doubted it even more. Why would the Goddess of Light help a former Xyonate with anything?

"Just repeat what I say." Ferne's voice drew closer to him, and he felt her pry his hands open, slip something pointy in his right palm, and then she pushed his hands back together.

He stole another peek and saw her kneeling in front of him. The leather cord of her necklace reached between them, and Mehta held the triangular pendant—Laeri's symbol—in his hands. Ferne cupped his knuckles with her petite palms.

"Laeri, Goddess of Light," Ferne began, and Mehta repeated, "may your blessings be upon us, and may your favor shine upon our steps. Bless us with mercy and justice, and cover us with your protection, both within and without.

"Help us to control our minds and our bodies. Give us the strength to resist temptation, and let us shine your light into the darkness everywhere. By your grace, we ask these things."

As Mehta repeated the last words of Ferne's prayer, he opened his eyes and looked at her. Against all reason and logic, he'd hoped it would remove his thirst entirely.

It hadn't.

But the thirst wasn't ruling him, either.

Ferne's words had ushered Mehta's thirst into the dark recesses of his mind where it lingered, still there but no longer at the forefront. No longer running rampant through his veins, threatening to overtake him entirely. He had subdued it, whether by Laeri's divine intervention, by his own doing, or because of any number of other causes or reasons.

Whatever it was, something had changed. Something had made a difference.

"How do you feel?" Ferne asked.

"Better," Mehta admitted. "Thank you."

"Father used to do that with me," she said, her voice lined with sadness. "Whenever I'd get frustrated, or too excited, or sad. He'd help me calm down."

"I'm sorry, Ferne," Mehta said again.

"I know." She looked at him with tears in her eyes. "Can I... am I allowed to hug you again?"

Mehta stiffened. "I—"

"It's alright." Ferne sat and hugged her knees to her chest instead.

"I'm sorry," Mehta repeated. "I'm... I'm not used to any of this."

Tears streamed from Ferne's eyes again.

She was just a child. She had no understanding of his world, his choices. She couldn't comprehend the way he'd lived most of his life.

But he understood her pain. He'd been stripped of his parents at an even younger age. And he remembered what that had felt like.

Now he was a grown man, one nearly devoid of compassion, but that part of him was growing. Rulfran had shown compassion to him and saved his life twice. It was too late for Mehta to save him, but he could still save Ferne.

And he could start right now.

He reached toward Ferne slowly, gently, and took hold of her hand, and he pulled her forward. She complied, and she wrapped her arms around his blood-caked torso and cried. And though it still felt strange and foreign to him, he embraced her.

In that moment, it occurred to him that if he truly meant to keep Ferne safe, they couldn't just escape. The threat of the Xyonates finding him would always chase his footsteps, no matter how far he ran.

There was only one way to stop them.

He had to kill them all.

CHAPTER SEVEN

"We have to go back," Mehta said.

Ferne released her grip and looked up at him, her cheeks streaked with tears. "Where?"

"To your home. To the Temple of Laeri."

Ferne's eyes widened, and Mehta could read the terror in them.

"I have to face them."

"*No.*" Ferne's voice took on a whiny tone. It marked the first time something about her had agitated Mehta. "We can just leave."

"You can leave. They don't care about you," Mehta said. "But they want me dead."

"You have to come with me."

"Do you have relatives I can take you to? Grandparents, aunts, uncles, cousins?"

Ferne shook her head and wiped the tears from her face. "The rest of my family lives in Urthia. I've never met them. My parents came here before I was born."

"What about friends, or parishioners at the temple? Other servants of Laeri?"

Ferne shook her head again. "I don't know how to find any of them."

"The Xyonates will strike at nightfall. That's when we—" Mehta stopped. "—when *they* excel in their craft. Xyonates can see in the dark thanks to an enchantment on our vision. And most people sleep at night, so there's less resistance. We need to get you somewhere safe before then."

"Mehta, no," Ferne pleaded. "Just come with me. Please? I don't have anyone anymore. I can't go on my own."

"And I can't leave until this entire sect of Xyonates is dead," Mehta snapped.

Ferne stared at him, hurt in her eyes.

"I'm sorry," Mehta said. "I shouldn't have said it like that."

Ferne didn't reply. She lowered her gaze and stared at the floor again.

"I have to do this, Ferne," Mehta said. "And I need to get you somewhere safe. I can't be worrying about you at the same time."

"You can hide me." Ferne looked up. "At the temple. There's plenty of hiding spots there."

Mehta shook his head. "It's too much of a risk."

"It's safer than giving me to someone you don't know, and it's safer than leaving me somewhere else by myself," Ferne countered. "At least this way, I'll be nearby, and you can check on me if you need to."

Mehta weighed her words. She had a point. "Where in the temple would you hide?"

"There's at least… ten places I can think of."

Hiding her close by would be preferable, Mehta decided, if they could do it in such a way that she wouldn't or couldn't be found. And a place like the Temple of Laeri, with more than ten hiding places, could prove useful with regard to dealing with the remainder of the Xyonates.

"Show me," Mehta said.

As the afternoon sun sank toward the horizon, Mehta and Ferne waited in the long shadows of a nearby alley until the last of the parishioners left the Temple of Laeri. Then they headed over to a side entrance that Ferne knew about.

They hadn't taken Rulfran's keys when they'd left the parsonage—Mehta hadn't considered that he might need them, and keys jingled and clinked together. Not ideal for moving around silently.

But Ferne had her tricks, and she managed to get inside through a window with a faulty latch. Then she went to the side door and let Mehta inside.

As he entered, Mehta noticed a marble statue of Laeri perched above the door. She stared down at him with white, inanimate eyes, standing tall on a ledge over the door with her arms outstretched, clothed in white robes with extra fabric draping down from her sleeves.

A last reminder to parishioners to live holy lives once they left the temple? Mehta couldn't say for sure.

Ferne's brief tour of the temple's white marble interior reminded Mehta of the Xyonate Sanctum in many ways—replete with nooks and crannies, many with potential for deep shadows come nightfall.

When she showed Mehta the storeroom on the lower level, his mind whirled with possibilities based on what it contained.

But they had little time before nightfall. And less time meant he might have to do something more drastic.

When Ferne led Mehta into the altar room on the second floor, the large, crystalline chandeliers hanging from the lofted ceiling caught his attention first. They formed a singular row that extended from the back of the altar room to the front.

Each of them had to weigh several hundred pounds. Thick chains suspended them from metal hooks embedded in the ceiling's whitewashed crossbeams and then trailed down to a series of anchor points mounted on the walls along the right side of the room.

Mehta studied them as Ferne headed toward the altar. *Interesting.*

A series of thick black curtains hung beside the windows spaced at regular intervals along the two side walls. Late afternoon sunlight streamed through them, illuminating the room in orange light.

Then Ferne showed him a hatch in the floor behind the altar. It opened thanks to a lever that ran along the back of the altar. Mehta marveled at how well it was concealed in the altar's golden trim—it blended in perfectly.

Ferne pulled it up, and the hatch popped open.

"It leads directly down to the street. It's leftover from when the temple used to do animal sacrifices. My father said the priests used to dump animal guts down it. But Laeri hasn't demanded animal sacrifices for a long time, Father said." Ferne frowned and looked down at the floor. Tears pooled in her eyes.

Mehta crouched in front of her and took her hands in his. "I won't let them harm you."

She shook her head and sniveled. "It's not that. I'm thinking about my parents."

Mehta squeezed her hands. "I can't bring them back, Ferne, but I'm going to sift the people who sent their killers. I know it isn't the same as getting your parents back, but you have my word that they'll pay for what they've done."

To us both.

Ferne nodded and wiped her eyes. "I know."

"So this chute leads to the street?" Mehta asked.

Ferne nodded again and sniveled once more. "Yes. I don't think it's been used for years, though. Not for that, anyway. One time I got curious and went down it. It popped me back out on the street, and I almost broke my leg. I would have, but I landed on a pile of old rags that someone had left in the alley."

Mehta considered its potential. The chute wasn't wide enough for him to slide through, but Ferne could still fit. If things went poorly, at least she had a reliable means of escape. He pushed the lever down, and the hatch snapped shut.

"Are you sure they'll find us?"

"Without question."

"How?"

Mehta didn't answer her. Instead, he sized her up one more time. "There's something I need to show you."

Mehta removed one of Creed's knives from his belt and handed it to Ferne.

She took it from him, uncertain and tentative.

"Don't be afraid of it. It can't hurt you unless you're reckless with it."

"I've used a knife before."

"Not one like this. And not for what I'm about to show you."

Mehta removed one of his knives from its sheath inside his clothes, one of the original pair he'd used to carve his way out of the Sanctum. It was a simple gray blade made of forged iron. Dark brown wood made up its hilt, but Mehta had long since wrapped and rewrapped the hilt with strips of black fabric several times over.

It wasn't anything special, nor was its twin, but it felt familiar in Mehta's hand. And it was sharp enough to cut to the bone—and even into it.

He refocused on Ferne. "Given your height, if it comes to it, your options are limited in a fight."

He paused, trying to gauge her reaction. Ferne didn't respond.

"Striking at the belly is good, but it isn't often fatal." Mehta drew his knife through the air across his own gut. "It's soft and easy to cut into. But those with training know how to defend their bellies, and they expect attacks to that area.

"So instead, you should strike the inner thigh." Mehta traced his knife across the inside of his leg to show her. "If you strike hard enough and deep enough, you'll sever a major artery. The heart does not know how to stop beating, and it will pump blood out of that wound until there is no blood left. It's even more effective if you can cut both legs."

Ferne shuddered. "This is gross. I don't want to think about this."

"But you *must*." Mehta's voice came out firmer than he wanted it to. He tempered his next words. "You must know this. If something should happen and I cannot protect you, you need to know something about fighting.

"Any drunkard can stab someone, but killing quickly is altogether different. It requires precision, speed, and strength applied simultaneously. Without a plan, we are destined to fail and die." Mehta considered adding, *and I want to live*, but he didn't. "Do you understand?"

Ferne nodded.

Mehta pointed to a thick marble pillar that helped to frame the altar. "Pick a side of that pillar to be the inside of a leg. I want you to practice your cuts on it."

Mehta showed her a few knife slashes from different angles and told her to practice twenty of each movement. Even though marble was a soft rock, the practice slashes would dull the knife to some degree. He'd show her how to sharpen it once she finished practicing, but in the meantime, he needed to prepare for the Xyonates' arrival.

He started by shutting the curtains to all the windows in the altar room except for one, and then he took a closer look at the chandelier anchors.

⚔

THE HEAVY BLUE-BLACK OF NIGHTFALL BLANKETED SEFERA WITHIN TWO HOURS' TIME. When darkness fully consumed the city, Mehta ceased his preparations. He didn't know when the Xyonates would come, and he didn't want to be caught off-guard, so he stashed Ferne in one of her secret spots and waited at the altar.

As he sat there, shrouded in the altar's shadow, his muscles burned from the exertion of his preparations. He hoped the Xyonates wouldn't show for awhile to give him time to recover. And if they showed up soon, he'd just have to deal with it.

He glanced up at the large statue of Laeri looming over him and over the altar.

She stared across the altar room, her white face turned silvery gray by the moonlight from the lone set of curtains he'd left open.

Mehta considered praying to Laeri for success. After all, he was in her temple, and he was about to desecrate it with the deaths of several worshippers of Xyon—or maybe just his own.

Or would their deaths honor her instead? If Laeri hated Xyon, as Elanil had claimed, then perhaps Mehta would be doing her a favor by killing Xyon's followers. Perhaps the blood of sacrifices would once again flow from Laeri's altar—or at least very near to it.

Hours passed, and Mehta's thirst waxed and waned with each little sound he heard. Yet to his surprise, none of the sounds came from Ferne's position—at least not that he could tell. She must've taken his warnings about remaining perfectly quiet to heart.

Or she'd fallen asleep. Whatever the case, when the Xyonates arrived, they'd both know it immediately.

More hours passed, and Mehta continued waiting.

Then a loud crash announced the Xyonates' entry into the temple.

CHAPTER EIGHT

No other sound came, but Mehta's first trap had sprung. That meant one of the Xyonates was already dead, or at least close to it.

He'd barricaded all of the entrances and windows except for one way in, the very same side door where Ferne had let him into the temple. It had likely confirmed to the Xyonates that Mehta was inside, but they would've figured it out one way or another eventually.

With a bit of rope and some creativity, Mehta had rigged the marble statue of Laeri above the door to fall after the door opened. Given its weight and size, he figured it would topple slowly enough to catch whichever Xyonate had entered first.

Mehta hoped it was Elegy, but more likely than not, Ghazal would've sent someone else to take the lead. Ghazal wouldn't squander a Xyonate as valuable as Elegy—at least, not as long as he could control him.

That first trap was also Mehta's cue to change his position. He crept away from the altar in silence and into the long shadows of the altar room.

The moonlight from the single un-curtained window in the altar room divided the room into two roughly equal spaces, both of which offered ample darkness in which he could hide. Now he took his place and stood as still as the statue of Laeri behind the altar, waiting with one of the chandelier chains in his hand.

For minutes, Mehta remained silent and motionless, inhaling the strong scent of oil from nearby. Soon after, a low creak sounded from one of the altar room doors.

Mehta watched as a dark figure slipped inside the altar room. Thanks to his enchanted vision, Mehta could see the Xyonate clearly, outlined in faint green light. It was Verse, a young Xyonate who'd recently completed his training.

Verse advanced forward into the room, skirting along the walls, jabbing each set of curtains with his sword and then moving on to the next.

Mehta didn't mind swords—he'd done his fair share of training with them over the years, but he preferred to sift in close quarters. He preferred to feel the life drain from his charges close up.

Verse slowed as he approached the window with its curtains open and glanced around.

Mehta reveled in the moment. By leaving only one set of curtains open, he'd knowingly sparked concern and confusion within Verse.

Why open only one set of curtains?

Why that set?

Is he hiding there or somewhere else?

Do I approach the window or stay out of the light?

It would've driven Mehta mad, trying to assess and determine the reason for opening a single set of curtains in an otherwise dark room. It had certainly stalled Verse's steps.

Verse stood just beyond the stream of moonlight, near the center of the altar room, calculating his next move. Meanwhile, Mehta waited. Another few steps and he'd be in position.

Verse eased forward another step, and moonlight glinted off of his sword.

Mehta's thirst heightened. He squeezed the hilt of his knife, careful not to move his other hand. The chain was merely wrapped around the anchor point—a simple metal spike that still held the chandelier's weight thanks to the tension from Mehta's grip on the end of the chain.

Verse took another two steps forward, closer to the light, scanning the room with his enchanted eyes. He held his sword at the ready.

Clink.

Mehta had let the chain slip a bit, just enough to interrupt the silence.

Verse's head whipped toward the sound, and he approached Mehta's position quickly.

Mehta released his grip on the chain, and it rattled hard and fast and angry. Above Verse's head, the crystalline chandelier plummeted.

He noticed it and tried to dive away, but it crashed onto his right leg, pinning it to the floor.

To his credit as a Xyonate, Verse didn't cry out at all—not even a grunt. But he'd released his sword upon the chandelier's impact, and it had clattered about a foot away from his now-outstretched hand.

Mehta emerged from behind the curtains across from the exposed window and drew his other knife, heading straight toward Verse, who strained against the chandelier to try to reach his sword. Mehta got there first and kicked it away.

Verse stared up at him, his young face serene.

Then Mehta sifted him, spilling his blood across the shaft of moonlight from the open window. It glistened, bright red and vibrant, yet calm as it expanded into an ever-growing pool across the white marble floor.

When Mehta looked up, six more Xyonates stood in the altar room with him. Elegy stood in the center, holding a pair of knives similar to Mehta's, with the five other Xyonates spread out behind him.

Mehta had hoped to catch more of them with his traps, but he steeled himself. He recognized each of the remaining Xyonates. If he could get through all of them, the only threat remaining would be—

"Greetings, Requiem," a dark voice uttered behind him.

Mehta turned back, slowly, and positioned himself so he could keep an eye on Elegy and the other five Xyonates.

Ghazal stood behind the altar. He no longer wore the regal purple robes befitting his status as High Cleric. Instead, he wore black, close-fitting fabric that covered everything but his face, neck, and hands.

He held the same ceremonial knife in his hand, and he loomed over the altar and the sacrificial lamb that now rested upon it—

Ferne.

They'd found her. Mehta cursed.

She lay facedown on the altar, quivering under Ghazal's knife but with her head turned toward Mehta and her face etched with terror.

"Submit," Ghazal's voice filled the silence.

Mehta stood there, still. The other Xyonates hadn't advanced, and Ghazal hadn't moved his knife.

Ferne shifted on the altar. Her arms and legs weren't bound, so she could move as freely as she dared with Ghazal's knife hovering overhead.

She continued to move and shift as any restless child might, but it looked like she was reaching for something—something along the golden trim on the other side of the altar near Ghazal.

Mehta hoped it would work. He backed against the wall adjacent to the nearest set of curtains. As Mehta expected, Ghazal's keen eyes traced his every movement.

"You helped guide me in the ways of Xyon and his followers since I was a small child," Mehta said to Ghazal. "Through your tutelage and training, I have learned many things. I've become a skilled sifter thanks to the Xyonates' ways."

Mehta pulled a flint from the folds of his clothes.

"But one thing you taught me from the very beginning was to never submit."

He turned toward the nearest curtain, struck the flint on his knife, and ignited the fabric with white-hot sparks. The curtain blossomed into a pillar of fire that spread to the other curtain hanging at that window, and then fire traced a line across the floor toward the next set of curtains in both directions.

In preparation for a moment like this, Mehta had doused all of the curtains with lamp oil from the storeroom and poured lines of oil between them. He'd rightly assumed that his other traps wouldn't take out all of the remaining Xyonates, so he'd arranged one last complication as they tried to commit him to Xyon.

Mehta stepped toward the center of the altar room, away from the inferno he'd kindled, as the flames spread to all of the curtains.

"Sift him," Ghazal commanded over the crackling flames.

As Ghazal gave the order, Ferne twitched. Then Ghazal dropped partway behind the altar with a grunt, and Ferne rolled off the front side to relative safety.

234

She'd pulled the lever concealed in the altar's golden trim and opened the hatch, and Ghazal had fallen partway in.

Mehta would've preferred that she had gone down and escaped instead, but it was better than nothing. He grinned, readied his knives, and shouted, "Run, Ferne!"

She did, and the six Xyonates approached Mehta amid the flames.

Mehta's thirst threatened to consume him, but if there were ever a time to let it rule him, it was now. He loosed the thirst from its chain-bound crate in his mind, and it rampaged through every vein in his body. He would never be more ready than in that exact moment.

Mehta moved toward the Xyonates.

"I told you back at the Sanctum," Elegy said, his voice low, "that as long as I serve Xyon, I will pursue you to the death. Tonight, one of us will meet him in the Underworld."

Before Mehta could respond, the remaining female Xyonate, Idyl, lashed a bull-whip at him. But Mehta darted forward and skidded across the floor, and it cracked through the air above his head.

Another Xyonate, Dictum, jabbed at him with a spear, but Mehta batted it away with his knives as he recovered his footing. Then he dove to the side to avoid a trio of knives careening at him from Elegy's hands.

Mehta rolled to his feet and traded blows with Proverb, an older, bulkier Xyonate in his thirties, who swung hand-axes at him in a flurry of vicious attacks. Mehta pushed him back with a well-timed kick to his chest then turned to face Whisper and Hush, a rare pair of Xyonate twin brothers.

Whisper launched arrows from afar while Hush, his larger, thicker brother, swung a long sword. Mehta dodged and maneuvered away from all of the attacks at a safe distance.

Proverb returned for more as Hush swung his sword at Mehta's head. Mehta ducked under it, and Hush's sword hit Proverb's axes with a loud *clang*.

Mehta exploded at Hush with a flurry of knife slashes, but Hush defended them all. As Mehta finished his combo, he noticed Whisper taking aim at him from over Hush's shoulder. The arrow loosed, and Mehta shifted Hush into its path.

A whip cracked, and the arrow snapped out of the air. Idyl had saved Hush from his own brother's arrow.

Mehta admired her timing and skill—he certainly couldn't have done that.

Even in spite of his thirst, this battle was proving even harder than he'd expected. But they hadn't succeeded in landing any significant blows on him yet, either.

Dictum's spear stabbed toward Mehta's face. Mehta moved his head to the left and hurled the knife in his right hand in a backhanded toss at Dictum. As the spear-head grazed Mehta's right cheek, his knife struck Dictum's shoulder.

Mehta grabbed the spear's shaft with his right hand and threw his other knife at Dictum as well. The second knife hit Dictum's gut, and Mehta wrenched the spear from his hands, taking it as his own.

Dictum didn't go down, though. Thought bleeding, he pulled the knives from his body, held one in each hand, and he stalked toward Mehta.

Xyonate resolve. Or fanaticism. Or both.

But Mehta had achieved his goal—he'd acquired a longer-range weapon at the cost of two short-range knives. He'd leveled the contest a bit more.

He spun the spear over his head with one hand at Hush, who'd closed in on him once more, and Hush ducked under it. As Mehta completed the spear's arc, he grabbed the spear shaft with both hands and multiplied its force with a hard strike to Hush's ankles.

He'd expected Hush to jump over, but the spear shaft struck Hush's legs and took him down. Mehta moved to jab the spear into Hush's chest to finish him off, but another arrow from Whisper launched toward him.

Mehta spun the spear in his hands and deflected the arrow down and away, then he blocked a second one as Hush recovered his footing.

Mehta cursed. He'd landed a solid blow and given Hush a slight limp, but there were too many Xyonates for him to make any real progress.

Then Idyl's whip cracked again. It latched onto Mehta's spear near its head and started to pull it away from him.

It was a good tactic. She'd pull the spearhead away, and he'd pull it back. But it would be enough of a distraction for Whisper to hit him with an arrow or for Elegy to throw another knife, or Proverb could close in with his axes.

Mehta didn't play along.

Idyl yanked, and Mehta dove forward with his spear, toward her. He planted the spearhead into the marble floor and vaulted through the air, over a throwing knife and an arrow, right past a bloody Dictum and Proverb.

He slammed his foot into the side of her head, and she went down hard. Her head smacked the floor, and she dropped the whip, unconscious. Mehta landed beside her, snatched up the whip, and gave her head a quick, brutal stomp, crushing her skull.

His thirst multiplied at her death, simultaneously satisfied and desperate for more. He'd killed one of them. Now five remained, plus Ghazal.

Mehta glanced at the altar. He no longer saw Ghazal behind it, and Ferne had long since run off and taken cover yet again. He hoped she could stay safe until he could search for her. And he hoped Ghazal would leave her alone.

The remaining five Xyonates closed in on him.

The bullwhip still clung to Mehta's spear, so he tossed the spear into the air with one hand and swung the whip hard with his other. The spear jerked to the right and leveled out, and Mehta arched his back to continue the swing. Doing so made the spear into a long mace.

The butt of the spear whooshed over the Xyonates' heads and then back behind Mehta, who pulled hard on the whip with both hands to keep it swinging. Meanwhile, Whisper nocked another arrow and drew the string back on his bow.

Mehta gave the whip a sharp yank, and the spear arced toward Whisper, but he saw it coming and dodged it. Instead, the spear smacked into Proverb's face, knocking him to the floor.

But it also stopped Mehta's momentum, and it didn't prevent Whisper from firing.

The arrow soared toward Mehta, and he barely eluded it. He jerked on the whip, pulling the spear back to him across the marble floor, and he picked it up and separated the whip from it.

He easily deflected one of Elegy's throwing knives and another arrow from Whisper, then he hurried through the pool of Verse's blood and took cover behind the fallen chandelier to catch his breath.

Thirst or otherwise, his body still had limits.

The blow he'd delivered to Proverb had undoubtedly hurt, but it hadn't killed him or even knocked him out. The whip had proven fun and useful thus far, as had the spear, but Mehta couldn't hope to wield both effectively. He had to choose between them. He chose the spear, shifted it to his right hand, and moved the whip to his left.

The curtains still blazed with hot fire, staining the white marble ceiling and walls black and boiling the altar room air. Mehta doubted the whole building would catch fire, but the crossbeams that framed the lofted ceiling might burn if the flames reached high enough. Right now, a collapsing ceiling was the least of his concerns.

He stood up again as the Xyonates approached the chandelier and immediately avoided another arrow and another knife. He lashed the bullwhip at Whisper, hoping to get ahold of his bow, but Hush stepped in front of the strike. The whip coiled around Hush's blade instead.

Mehta hauled the whip back, and Hush's sword lowered. As it did, Mehta hurled the spear at Hush. From such a close distance, Hush couldn't move in time. The spear plunged into Hush's chest, and he fell.

Four Xyonates left to kill.

So much for keeping the spear. Mehta yanked it back and pulled Hush's sword over to him. It clattered across the pool of Verse's blood, and Mehta grabbed it. He tossed the whip aside and tested the sword's weight. It would function best as a two-handed sword.

Mehta didn't prefer such weapons.

The whip would give him more reach and speed but far less lethality, and the only way out of all of this was by killing the last four Xyonates. Mehta could switch weapons again when the next opportunity arose, but in the meantime, he shook Verse's blood off of Hush's sword and waited for the next attack to come.

Upon his brother's death, Whisper's face crinkled into a snarl, and he loosed another arrow. Mehta batted it down then smacked Whisper's next arrow away as well. As Whisper reached for a third, he found his quiver empty.

With another snarl, Whisper slung the bow over his shoulder and drew a pair of daggers from his hips. Then he advanced with Proverb on Mehta's right while Dictum, still bleeding and still clutching Mehta's knives, approached from Mehta's left with Elegy.

Mehta didn't want them surrounding him, and he could make use of the downed chandelier as an obstacle in the fight, so he pressed his advantage.

Of the two pairs of Xyonates coming toward him, Mehta decided that taking on Dictum and Elegy made the most sense. Even though Dictum's wounds would hinder him, Elegy's skill made them a more formidable pair than Proverb and Whisper. Mehta wanted to eliminate the greatest threat first.

Furthermore, they both carried knives—shorter-range weapons, which meant Mehta had the advantage of reach. If Mehta wielded it properly, Hush's sword could strike long before they could even get close to him.

And even if Mehta couldn't defeat Elegy, he'd almost certainly sift Dictum in the process. That would level the odds even more. So he advanced toward Dictum and Elegy with Hush's sword, ready.

As Whisper and Proverb rounded the chandelier after him, Mehta swung the sword at Dictum, who hopped back and out of the way. Elegy sprang forward and drove his knives down at Mehta.

Mehta brought the sword up hard and fast, and metal clanged. He whipped his foot at Elegy's side, catching him in the ribs. The blow sent Elegy toppling onto the downed chandelier, delaying him. Mehta would've finished him right there, but Dictum was closing in.

So Mehta slid under Dictum's slashes and swung his sword again. The blade dug into Dictum's right thigh, just above his knee, and embedded in the bone. Dictum went down, and Mehta let the sword fall with him.

When he recovered his footing, Mehta ran to Hush, who lay on the marble floor with the spear protruding from his chest. To Mehta's surprise, Hush was still alive, though only barely. Blood tainted his teeth red, and his breaths came in sharp, shallow huffs.

Mehta crouched next to him, pulled out one of the spare knives tucked within his clothes, and drew it across Hush's throat to finish him off. As he did, he watched Elegy do the same thing to Dictum, who would've died from blood loss soon enough. Then Elegy pulled the sword from Dictum's leg.

Then Mehta tucked the blade back within the folds of his clothes, planted his foot on Hush's body, and yanked the spear from his chest. He caught sight of Whisper glowering at him from near the chandelier.

Three Xyonates remained. Three Xyonates and Ghazal stood between him and his journey home to the crater-topped mountain. Three more Xyonates to either satisfy his raging thirst or sift him.

Mehta backed away from the ever-expanding pool of blood from Verse, Hush, and now Dictum. He stood just beyond its edge and forced Elegy, Whisper, and Proverb to walk into it—it was either that, or they'd have to venture closer to the roaring flames scouring the ceiling rafters.

He took a long look over his shoulder to scan for Ghazal and Ferne, but he saw neither of them. It concerned him, but he couldn't do anything about it until he dealt with the Xyonates.

The three Xyonates spread wide across the altar room and approached him. Elegy stood in the center with Whisper on the left and Proverb on the right.

Mehta held out his spear, ready.

Whisper charged first, followed closely by Proverb. Mehta parried Whisper's daggers with three solid blocks, then he threw an attack of his own.

As Whisper defended, Proverb closed in and delivered a series of vicious hacks with his axes. Rather than trying to parry heavy axe blows with a wooden spear shaft, Mehta dodged and worked to gain a more favorable position.

He'd sparred enough times with Proverb in the past to know his tendencies, and he waited for an opening while fending off Whisper and Elegy. The opening came and went once, but the second time it appeared, Mehta slammed the butt end of his spear into the side of Proverb's face hard enough to shatter his jaw.

Crack.

Proverb spun as he fell, and his body smacked against the bloody floor. He wasn't moving. The blow to his head might've killed him, but he could just be unconscious. Either way, Mehta needed to make sure.

Whisper rushed closer, as if trying to separate Mehta from Proverb to keep him from finishing off Proverb, and it would've worked had his foot not slipped on the slick floor. The slip itself wasn't fatal, but Mehta seized the momentary advantage.

Whisper still held up his daggers in defense of his torso, but his legs were spread too far apart. Mehta jammed the spear's head into Whisper's knee.

Whisper yelped and his leg buckled, but as Mehta pulled his spear back, Whisper lashed out with his daggers again before Mehta could react.

Clang.

A long sword batted Whisper's daggers away. As Mehta raised the spear in defense, the sword cleaved down into Whisper's torso from above his shoulder. It lodged in his chest, and Whisper stared at the sword's wielder in shock as he slumped to the floor.

Elegy.

CHAPTER NINE

E legy stood there, facing Mehta with his hands empty. Whisper's blood dotted the side of his face.

Why had he killed Whisper? More importantly, why *hadn't* he killed Mehta when he'd had the chance? He could've just as easily swung the sword at Mehta.

"I have waited long enough, Requiem." Elegy removed a twin set of knives from the folds of his clothes. "Throw down your spear, and let us determine the truth between us once and for all."

Inside, Mehta hesitated, but he immediately threw down the spear to convey confidence and certainty. He extracted a single knife from inside his clothes and gripped it in his right hand. Fire crackled and blazed around them, and perspiration from the oppressive heat mingled with the Xyonates' blood on Mehta's face.

In order to triumph, Mehta couldn't rely on his thirst alone. He'd need to martial every ounce of skill, energy, drive, speed, strength, and precision to win.

But could he really defeat Elegy? They'd always matched up well in training and sparring sessions, and the Xyonate clerics had barely distinguished between them when it came to the most difficult commissions.

Their Xyonate brethren had held them both in high regard, but the reverence they'd shown Mehta had, in his opinion, surpassed what they'd shown Elegy. Mehta had always known Elegy was a threat and a masterful sifter, but he'd never felt the need to prove anything against him.

Elegy, on the other hand, had wished to assert his dominance. Thus, in Mehta's mind, Mehta had always been the better Xyonate.

But that could all change today.

"I accept your challenge." Mehta took a balanced fighting stance.

"Mehta?" a small voice called from behind him.

240

Mehta didn't dare look, not with Elegy standing so close. So he backed several steps away and then turned his head.

Ferne stood before the altar. Blood spattered her face, arms, and clothes. She held the knife Mehta had given her in her right hand. It perfectly matched the one he now held, except that blood dripped from its tip.

Mehta opened his mouth to ask what had happened, but Ghazal staggered into the altar room behind her. His face had paled, and he clutched at his right thigh. Crimson blood pulsed through his fingers.

Right where Mehta had shown Ferne to aim.

Ferne backed away from him, toward the nearest set of flaming curtains, glancing frantically between Mehta and Ghazal. She held the knife in front of her, like Mehta had shown her, but her face showed the same expression of terror she'd worn when Ghazal had her on the altar.

Mehta moved to her side, and Elegy went to Ghazal.

"It's alright, Ferne," Mehta said over the roar of the flames. He wrapped his arms around her shoulders and pulled her close. She didn't lower the knife, nor did she take her gaze off of Ghazal. "It's alright."

As Elegy approached, Ghazal groped for him with his free hand until he got ahold of Elegy's forearms.

"Sift them both, Elegy," Ghazal said. "You are the last Xyonate in Sefera."

Elegy glanced at them, his face blank.

"*Sift them,*" Ghazal repeated, his voice breaking. He wouldn't last much longer, not with most of his blood covering Ferne. "Xyon demands their blood. You are the finest Xyonate I have ever known. You must avenge our sect. You must deliver their souls to Xyon. This is my final command to you. Sift them, Elegy."

Ghazal's grip faltered, and he slumped to the floor, barely breathing.

Elegy crouched down next to him, studied him for a brief moment, then drove his knife into Ghazal's chest. Ghazal convulsed once, then he went still.

Elegy pulled the knife out and stood, facing Mehta and Ferne.

Mehta ushered Ferne behind him. If sifting Elegy were to be his last act, then he would do it with the same dedication as when he'd sifted for Xyon.

But he wouldn't be doing it for Xyon, nor would he do it for Laeri. He would do it for Ferne, and he would do it for himself.

Only Elegy stood between them and their escape, between Mehta and the cratered mountain that marked his homeland. Between Mehta and freedom from the Xyonates, once and for all. Between Mehta and avenging his family's demise.

Whether he lived or died, that freedom was assured, but if he failed to defeat Elegy, Ferne would perish as well. Mehta couldn't let that happen. Not after Rulfran's sacrifice. Not after Elanil's bitter accusations. Ferne deserved to live, and Mehta would ensure that she did.

He approached Elegy, his knife poised, his thirst heightened. Maybe Elegy's blood would finally sate him.

"Hold." Elegy raised his right hand, still holding his knife in it with his thumb, but extending his fingers as if to halt Mehta's progress.

Mehta stopped. He didn't know why, but he stopped.

"I will not fight you," Elegy said.

Mehta studied him. "Why not?"

"Any order whose leader can be slain by a small girl is not worthy of my loyalty," Elegy replied. "I will continue to serve Xyon, but I will not do it here. The Xyonates of Sefera are no more."

Mehta didn't lower his guard. This could still be a trap. "You swore that as long as you served Xyon, you would pursue me to death."

"Ghazal's unworthiness severed me from my oath. He can no longer direct my blade. Thus, you are no longer my enemy, nor are you my commission." Elegy pointed his knife past Mehta, at Ferne. "That girl stripped Ghazal of his power with the knife in her hand. In the end, she is more of a Xyonate than he was."

"She will *never* be a Xyonate if I have any say in things."

Elegy nodded. "A pity. She could become a cunning sifter someday."

Mehta said nothing. He'd been where Ferne was now, a small child teetering on the edge of two lives. He would do everything he could to ensure that she didn't fall into the wrong one.

Something cracked above them, and both Mehta and Elegy recoiled.

The fire had entirely engulfed the ceiling. The wooden crossbeams overhead burned with bright flames. It was only a matter of time before the ceiling collapsed. Even if it didn't, the flames would soon be visible to much of Sefera, if they weren't already. Escaping would prove much harder with all the added attention.

Mehta faced Ferne and extended his free hand. "We need to leave now."

When Mehta turned back to Elegy, he was already gone.

Mehta smirked, tugged Ferne's hand, and as they fled the fiery altar room, Mehta retrieved his knives. Still dubious of Elegy's sincerity, Mehta scanned every corner and every shadow of the temple as they hurried to escape.

But he was nowhere to be found. Despite it all, Elegy had never lied to Mehta, and he hadn't lied this time, either.

On their way out, they headed down to the store room to retrieve the supplies and money they'd set aside. Then they slipped into the cold streets of Sefera, leaving the burning monument to Laeri behind them.

TWO WEEKS LATER, THE FAMILIAR SIGHT OF THE CRATERED MOUNTAIN LOOMED IN THE distance. It sat between two taller peaks of similar height, both of them pointed, jagged, and topped with snow. A valley ran between the peaks, decorated with the vivid oranges and yellows of late autumn.

Mehta could hardly believe his eyes. It looked just like he remembered.

"Is that it?" Excitement lined Ferne's voice.

Mehta nodded and looked down at her. "That's it. Come on. We're almost there."

Together, they descended into the valley.

From what Mehta could remember, the village hadn't changed much since he'd left so many years prior. The same wooden buildings lined the cobblestone streets, and brown-skinned people like him still plied their trades, eking out livings wherever and however they could.

Rugged people. Robust people. Mountain people.

His people.

The setting sun had just reached the peaks of the mountains behind them. As far as Mehta knew, the village was safe enough at night, apart from the occasional wolf or bear that wandered into town in search of prey gone astray from its owners—chickens, pigs, goats, or in rare cases, small children.

Ferne lagged behind him by a step, weary from the constant travel since they'd left Sefera, but they'd made it. She could rest for as long as she wanted once they found somewhere to stay for the night.

As they walked, Mehta recognized a familiar, sturdy dwelling made of pine and stone. Its location, its look, the trees around it, and the landscape in the background —he knew it all. This dwelling had been his home.

When he'd left, his parents lay facedown in a puddle of muddy blood in front of the house. The soldiers in black armor had killed them, and Mehta hadn't had the chance to say goodbye. He'd sifted countless other parents since then, himself.

What's more, he was responsible, at least in part, for the deaths of Rulfran and Elanil. He'd done what he could to make it up to Ferne by avenging their deaths, but he'd also tried to spare her from unnecessary carnage in the process.

But even so, Ferne was no longer fully innocent. She'd slain Ghazal. Yes, she'd done it in desperation, as a means of defending herself, but she'd done it nonetheless. It didn't matter that Elegy had delivered the final blow. Ferne had ensured Ghazal's death. She had sifted him.

"Is this…?" Ferne looked up at him.

Mehta nodded. "My home."

He stepped up to the door and rapped on it.

He had lived here with his parents, grandparents, and his infant sister. His grand-parents had been old when he'd been taken, but to his knowledge, the soldiers wearing the three-horned ram sigil had left them alive. If they had survived this many years, then perhaps—

The door opened, and a young, brown-skinned woman with long black hair stared at Mehta from the doorway.

For the first time in twenty years, Mehta remembered his mother's face. This woman's appearance was almost a perfect match, except thinner and younger.

Was this his younger sister? Mehta couldn't even remember her name.

"What do you want?" The young woman glanced at Ferne, whose pale skin and blonde hair stood out against the village's brown-skinned population.

What should Mehta say? What *could* he say?

"I…" he started. "I used to live here. Many years ago."

243

The young woman stared at him.

"You look so much like…" Little things came back to Mehta—his memory of her bearing, the way she stood, the way she moved. This young woman demonstrated all of that, almost as if she were a mirror version of his mother.

Mehta's throat seized. He hadn't allowed himself any semblance of real emotion in so long, so the sensation of profound sadness and the possibility of recovering some of what he'd lost caught him off guard.

He finished, "…so much like my mother."

The young woman recoiled at first, then she squinted at him. "Who are you?"

"My name is—" He stopped. He'd almost said, "Requiem." Instead, he said, "My name is Mehta. This used to be my home. My parents were killed many years ago, and I was taken away."

"You are Mehta?" The young woman shook her head and glanced at Ferne again. "That is impossible."

Mehta shook his head. "I am Mehta. I am alive. I have come home."

A man's scratchy voice from inside called, "Who is it?"

"No one, Grandfather," the woman said.

"Grandfather is alive?" Mehta's heart jumped in his chest.

The woman stiffened in the doorway, on edge. "I think you need to go."

Mehta's heart sank. "No… I can't leave. This was my home once. You have no idea what I've endured to get back."

"I don't know you, and everything you've said is common knowledge around here," she said. "Please go."

As the woman moved to close the door, a wizened, white-haired head emerged from the darkness behind her. A familiar face appeared in the doorway next to the woman's. Mehta's grandfather.

Mehta wanted to speak, to call out to him, but given the woman's final words to him, he knew that the only way he'd progress any further would be if Grandfather recognized him. It would take a miracle, but it was all he had at this point.

The woman stepped aside, and Grandfather's withered form filled the doorway. He squinted at Mehta and studied him up and down.

Mehta held his breath and pleaded with Laeri for favor.

CHAPTER TEN

"Mehta?" Grandfather's eyes opened wide. "Have you returned to us as a ghost, or are you yet made of flesh and bone?"

Mehta's mouth hung open, and it curled into a smile. He lunged forward, arms wide, and wrapped his grandfather in a tight hug. It was an impulse, an urge he would normally not gratify. He'd been trained to ignore impulses unless they would save his life or grant him an advantage.

Then again, perhaps that's why he'd done it now.

The old man returned Mehta's embrace, patting him on his back. When Mehta finally let go, Grandfather held him by his shoulders and looked him up and down.

"What has become of you, my boy?"

Mehta's words caught in his throat, but he finally replied, "It's a long story."

Grandfather nodded and motioned toward the young woman who once again stood in the doorway. "This is your sister, Palomi."

Palomi. Now he remembered her name. She'd been an infant when he was taken. The Xyonate training had not only stripped him of nearly his entire identity but also most of his early memories.

Even so, what few intact memories he still harbored had returned him home to the last of his kin. For all his divine power, Xyon had failed to fully consume Mehta's being.

Mehta wanted to embrace her as well, but she still stared at him with skepticism in her dark eyes. He wiped the tears from his eyes and nodded to her instead.

Then her eyes softened, and her posture relaxed. "If Grandfather recognizes you, that is good enough for me... for now. Welcome home."

She opened her arms and beckoned him forward.

Emotion welled in Mehta's chest. Everything within him resisted it, fought it, beat it back, but for the first time since the soldiers had taken him so many years earlier, he realized he didn't have to quell his emotions anymore.

Tears stung the corners of his eyes, but he stopped fighting them. Instead, he let them flow as he embraced his little sister for the first time in his life.

THAT NIGHT, THEY ALL SHARED A GRAND FEAST OF ELK MEAT, ROASTED VEGETABLES, and wild rice, paid for out of the plunder Mehta had taken from the Temple of Laeri. Palomi had prepared the food, and Grandfather had roasted it over the open fire pit behind their house.

With full bellies, they retired to the pinewood furniture and down-filled pillows in the modest common room. As Mehta, his grandfather, and Palomi discussed Mehta's life with the Xyonates and his subsequent escape from it, Ferne fell asleep, curled up on a large cushion in front of the glowing hearth.

Palomi recoiled in reaction to Mehta's stories, but Grandfather just nodded with a sad, knowing expression on his face. When Mehta finished describing the final battle at the Temple of Laeri, Grandfather spoke first.

"I am sorry you have endured such a harsh, violent upbringing. I must admit, I do not entirely know what to make of you upon hearing what you have just shared."

Mehta glanced between Grandfather and Palomi. "If you're worried I mean to do you harm…"

Grandfather waved his hand. "If you had meant to sift us, as you say, I am certain you already would have done it. What concerns me is your ongoing thirst for more death. A thirst that, by your own admission, is somewhat unpredictable."

"I am learning how to manage it." Mehta nodded toward Ferne, still asleep before the fire. "Ferne's father, and Ferne herself, have helped me in that regard."

Palomi had been quiet for most of the evening, but she finally said, "She seems like a good child."

"She is," Mehta agreed. "The things she has seen in her young life rival those of mine. I had hoped she would be safe here."

"I pray that she will find respite here among the mountains," Grandfather started, "but the reality is that life here is hard for everyone. Yes, we can hunt and gather and grow a few crops where the soil will cooperate, and timber is plentiful, but we are not without enemies."

The soldiers in black. The three-horned ram sigil.

Mehta asked, "Are they the same soldiers who took me all those years ago?"

"The very same." Grandfather glanced between them. "They have afflicted us since before either of you were born."

"Who are they?"

"Lord Valdis's men," Palomi replied.

Mehta glanced between them.

"Lord Blayne Valdis rules a province of Xenthan, the country beyond the cratered mountain." Grandfather pointed vaguely in the direction of the mountain, even though the house's walls obscured it from view. "His men regularly raid the border towns and villages of Etrijan."

"What about Etrijan's army? Don't they protect the border?" Mehta asked.

Grandfather shook his head. "The nearest fortress is fifty miles from here, and the nearest outpost is thirty. They can't be bothered. Xenthan and Etrijan share friendly relations, so a little raiding and extortion here and there is overlooked. But make no mistake—it was Valdis's men who slew your parents and took you away."

Mehta exhaled a silent, furious breath. It was bad enough that Lord Valdis's men had altered the course of his life forever, but it enraged him that even now, decades later, they were still harassing this tiny village.

"Why has no one stopped them? Why haven't the able men in this village taken action?"

"The last time anyone stood up to them was the day your parents were killed," Grandfather said. "And it was your father who led them."

Mehta's mouth opened. It all made sense now. They'd killed his father and mother as examples, and they'd taken him away as well.

But they'd left Palomi there. Upon reflection, taking her would have proven troublesome; they couldn't care for an infant or effectively sell one into service like they could with a young boy.

And they'd left Mehta's grandparents behind as well, and they'd left them alive. No point leaving an infant girl behind without someone to care for her.

Ultimately, Lord Valdis and his men robbed Mehta of the chance to know his family. But in doing so, they'd inadvertently turned him into the most dangerous person they would ever encounter. And he intended to encounter them sooner rather than later.

"You said he lives beyond the mountain," Mehta said. "Where?"

Grandfather squinted at him. "What are you scheming, Mehta?"

"I mean to bring this Lord Valdis and his men a reckoning."

Grandfather shook his head. "He is a dark sorcerer, and his men are ruthless, skilled fighters. It is a fool's errand."

"Then I am a fool." Mehta hadn't dealt with any sorcerers in his time as a Xyonate, but they had to be made of blood and bone like anyone else.

"What do you hope to achieve?" Grandfather asked. "Vengeance will not resurrect your parents, nor will it salve your wounded spirit."

For all Mehta knew, Grandfather hadn't killed anyone, ever. Even if he had, Mehta had certainly sifted many more. In this area, Mehta favored his experience over his grandfather's wisdom. "Even if it does not, perhaps it will keep the remainder of my family safe."

Palomi glared at him. "You cannot keep us safe by leaving. We need you here. If you were truly my brother, you would understand that."

Her words dug into Mehta's gut, as painful as Lament's knife back in the alley in Sefera, but he didn't hold them against her. She would never comprehend what he'd endured, no matter how thoroughly he explained his life to her.

Palomi had likely never even ventured out of this valley. She didn't know how the world worked, how dangerous it was, how tyrants preyed on the weak—until someone stopped them. The Xyonates had been one of many tools utilized by those in power to keep their power. Now it was time to turn those tools against them.

"At best, cutting off a tree's branches yields a warm fire for a night. At worst, it means a mess to clean up, and more branches will grow in the place of those cut off." Mehta said. "But when you cut down the entire tree, no branches can regrow."

Palomi and Grandfather stared at him.

"This Lord Valdis is the tree," Mehta continued. "We can fight and resist his soldiers—the branches—indefinitely, but he can always send more. The only way to end these raids is to strike at the root of the problem."

"And what of her?" Palomi nodded toward Ferne, who still slept on her cushion before the hearth. "What role will she play in your fool's errand?"

"None," Mehta replied. "I was hoping she could stay here with you."

Palomi's expression soured, and she opened her mouth to speak, but Grandfather spoke first.

"Of course she can stay," he said.

"Grandfather?" Palomi hissed. "We cannot afford to—"

"I don't intend to burden you without compensation." Mehta produced a leather pouch and extracted only two gold coins from it. Then he cinched the pouch shut and tossed it to Palomi, who caught it. "That is all that remains from the Temple of Laeri in Sefera. I have what I need to buy provisions for my journey. The rest should be more than enough to care for Ferne and for yourselves until I return."

Palomi stared down at the pouch then looked up at Mehta and Grandfather. "This is more money than I've ever seen."

"We would have cared for her anyway, Mehta," Grandfather said. "Where you're going... that is no place for a child. Xenthan is called the Black Realm for a reason. It is a land of darkness and terror, a place of danger and peril. I fear that if you venture there, you will not return, and we have only just gotten you back."

Mehta met his grandfather's eyes. "I will return. You have my word."

Palomi stood, scowling, and without so much as a word, she gently scooped Ferne into her arms and carried her into an adjacent room. Then she shut the door behind her.

Mehta frowned, but Grandfather placed his withered hand on Mehta's shoulder.

"She is concerned for you," Grandfather said. "And so am I."

Even so, doubt filled Mehta's chest. Was he making the right decision by leaving them behind?

For so long, he'd only served his Xyonate masters. Then he'd served himself—until he met Ferne. Elanil had charged him to protect Ferne with her dying breath. And now that he'd found his family again, a new drive ignited within him to keep them safe as well.

Perhaps leaving them would not achieve that end. Perhaps Palomi was right, and Mehta would only get himself killed. Where would that leave his family and Ferne?

There was no certainty to be found in any decision.

If he stayed, he could protect them directly, here at home, but someday Lord

Valdis's men might overcome him. They would come to know who he was, and they would pursue him specifically. He would either flee or fight to his death, and both outcomes would tear him from his family once again.

If he left, though, before anyone else knew his plans, he could use that secret to his advantage. If Lord Valdis didn't know he was coming, Mehta could reach him more easily. And with Valdis dead, Mehta could finally live with his family in peace.

Lord Valdis was Mehta's final commission.

"When are you leaving?" Grandfather must've seen the renewed resolve in Mehta's eyes.

"Tomorrow morning. Early."

"Do you want me to wake Ferne to see you off?"

Mehta considered it. "No. It will be better if I am just gone."

Grandfather hesitated, as if about to say something, but he just nodded.

⁂

AS MEHTA CREPT OUT OF HIS FAMILY HOME THE NEXT MORNING UNDER THE COVER OF darkness, the frigid mountain air sent chills rippling across his skin. He pulled his bearskin coat tighter around him and shivered, exhaling vapor.

He surveyed the moonlit mountaintops, particularly the cratered mountain to the east. It would serve as his marker, a guide to bring him back when he fulfilled his final commission, just as it had brought him home once before.

As he took the first steps of his new journey, a small voice called his name. He turned back to find Ferne following him, her pack slung over her shoulder.

"Ferne, go back inside," Mehta said as she approached. "Where I'm going, you cannot follow."

Ferne shook her head and looked up at him. "No. I'm going with you."

"It's not safe."

"Nothing that's happened so far has been safe," Ferne countered. "I'm going with you."

Mehta crouched down and cupped her shoulders with his hands. "No, Ferne. You can't come. I can't be responsible for a child in Xenthan. It's too dangerous."

Ferne's face scrunched, and her lip quivered. Tears pooled in her eyes and streamed down her cheeks. She latched onto him with her arms around his neck and squeezed, sobbing.

Mehta returned her embrace, and regret and doubt stabbed his heart.

"You can't leave me here," Ferne said between sobs. "I can't lose you, too."

Mehta closed his eyes, grateful for her additional warmth on this cold morning. "You won't lose me, Ferne. I'm coming back."

Ferne pulled away from him and shook her head. "I don't believe you. If it's really so dangerous, you could die."

"After all you've seen, do you really think there's anything out there that can kill me?" Mehta granted himself a grin.

Ferne stared at him, then she lowered her gaze to the ground. "No."

249

"Exactly." Mehta wiped away her tears with his fingers. "I'll be back before you know it."

She grabbed onto him again. "I still don't want you to go."

He patted her back. "I know. I don't want to go, either, but I have to. It's the only way to ensure that my family is safe. And that includes you."

Ferne released him again and looked at him with reddened eyes. "I'm part of your family now?"

Mehta smiled. "Yes. You, my sister, and my grandfather. If I don't protect the three of you, I'll have nothing left. And in order to protect you, I have to leave for now. Do you understand?"

Ferne nodded. She reached into her shirt and pulled out a shining object—the silver pendant she'd worn since the day he first met her. A triangle, pointing down like an arrowhead. The symbol of Laeri, the Goddess of Light.

She pulled the leather cord over her head and handed it to Mehta. "Here. Now Laeri will keep you safe."

Mehta stared at the necklace. Even in the waning moonlight, the pendant glimmered. "I can't take this, Ferne."

"You have to. You'll need Laeri's protection where you're going more than I will here."

She had a point.

"Perhaps you're right." Mehta handed it back to her. "Help me get it on?"

As Mehta bowed, Ferne slipped the leather cord over his head and positioned the pendant so it hung just under the center of his neck. The cord was a bit small for his neck, but it would have to do.

"Thank you," he said.

"Promise me you'll be careful?" Ferne said.

"I promise. And I'm coming back here as soon as I can."

Ferne hugged him once more.

When they let go of each other, Mehta nodded toward his childhood home. "Now hurry back inside. It's cold out here."

Ferne gave him a sad smile, and then she turned and ran back to the house. With a final wave, she went inside.

Mehta turned east, toward the cratered mountain, and started walking.

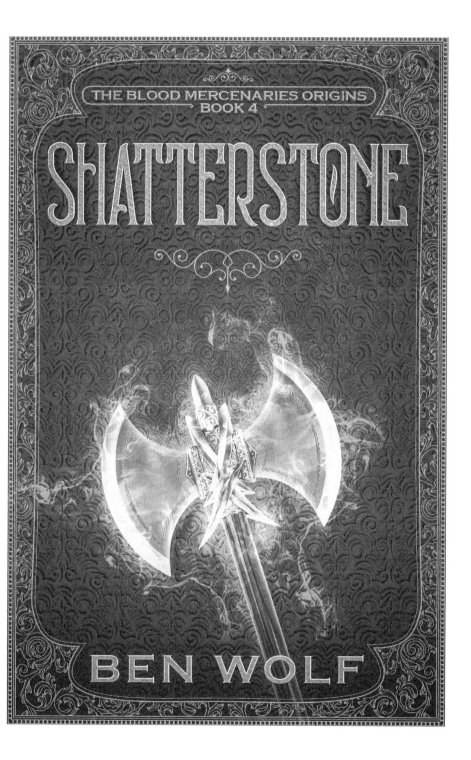

THE BLOOD MERCENARIES ORIGINS
BOOK 4

SHATTERSTONE

BEN WOLF

CHAPTER ONE

G arrick Shatterstone had a job to do, and he wasn't going to leave the small pub until he'd gotten what he came for.

He sat in a rickety chair in the corner, watching and listening as Coburn Tye, a member of Garrick's three-man mercenary crew, tried to charm his way into the blonde, busty barmaid's good graces—or possibly into her bed. By the tone and timbre of the conversation, Garrick wondered if Coburn had once again swayed from the task at hand.

The bar was a freestanding, rectangular space set in the middle of the pub. It offered service on all four sides, but only one barmaid was working that evening.

If Garrick didn't interject, they'd be here all night. He cleared his throat loudly and nudged his pewter tankard forward. It scraped across the table toward Irwin Tiller, the third member of Garrick's merc crew.

Both the barmaid and Coburn glanced at Garrick. As the barmaid moved to pick up a pitcher of mead, Coburn took hold of her wrist.

"Don't be long," he oozed, stroking her skin with his index finger.

She blushed. "I won't."

Garrick watched her round the bar with the pitcher in hand. She had a nice shape to her and a common, yet pretty look—not that it mattered much to Coburn. He'd pursue virtually anything female that walked upright.

The barmaid poured Garrick a full tankard of mead, and he produced a pair of copper coins from his money pouch and set them on the table. She took them, gave him a slight bow, and turned toward Irwin.

"Anything for you, mister?" she asked.

Irwin shook his head. "Negative."

As the barmaid headed back to the bar, Irwin stared at her from behind, and

Garrick caught Coburn's eyes. Garrick motioned his index finger in a circle and mouthed the words, "Get moving."

Coburn scowled at him but nodded.

Irwin adjusted his spectacles. "I would've gone up and gotten you another one."

"I wanted to interrupt Coburn. He's got a job to do, and he's not doing it." Garrick took a swig of his mead then wiped his mouth with his wrist. He glanced over his shoulder at his long-handled, double-bladed battle-axe leaning in the shadowy corner. Hopefully, he wouldn't have to use it. "Besides, the less the other folk in this pub see of us, the better."

"You're right," Irwin pulled out a parchment folded into a small square and opened it enough to scribble Garrick's mead payment into the ledger. "We're approaching our predetermined spending limit for this establishment. And that's not including whatever Coburn has spent thus far."

"We'll stay as long as we need to stay," Garrick said. "We need that information, and this pub has strong ties to the Crimson Flame. The diagram Lord Valdis gave us won't mean a thing until we can actually get *inside* the temple."

"And the longer we stay, the more likely someone will notice us," Irwin countered. "And the more coin we'll burn."

Garrick couldn't argue with Irwin's logic. "Just be patient. Coburn will get us what we need."

Lord Valdis had wanted them to keep a low profile for this mission. Garrick didn't prefer it, but he always put his employers' wishes before his own, and Lord Valdis had hired him for close to a dozen jobs over the years. For that kind of loyalty—and that kind of money—Garrick had no problem playing things quietly.

But being close to seven feet tall and weighing nearly 400 pounds, Garrick had to take additional measures to look inconspicuous. In this case, he wore a brown, hooded cloak that covered his huge frame, large head, and most importantly, his green-tinged skin and dark blue hair.

Back in Xenthan, no one cared what he looked like because everyone had seen far worse. Orcs, goblins, and other fell beasts roamed the land freely, so the sight of a huge man with troll blood in his veins didn't faze anyone.

But now, on Etrijan's side of the Thornback Mountains, he'd opted for anonymity for the sake of the mission. Here in the pub, he'd even taken to hunching over to make himself look smaller and less imposing.

"What'd you say your name was?" Coburn asked, wearing a wide smile.

"Falna," the barmaid replied with a smile of her own.

"Falna," Coburn repeated. "What a lovely name. It reminds me of an enchanted forest I once saw, a place whose beauty pales only in comparison to yours."

Falna blushed again. "You're too much, mister... what should I call you?"

Garrick's grip on his tankard tightened. *Please don't use your real name, Coburn. Please don't be that stupid.*

"Rowburn," Coburn said. "Rowburn Brye."

Still too close for Garrick's comfort, but it would have to do.

"You've got a knack for words, don't you?" Falna leaned closer to him, resting her elbows on the bar.

"That's not the only thing I've got a knack for," Coburn uttered.

Garrick wanted to strangle him. They had a job to do, and all Coburn had in mind was rolling in the hay with some small-town barmaid.

"Miss?" a voice called from a table at the other end of the bar, near the door. "More ale? And some bread and cheese, too?"

A gruff man with a long, red beard held up a pewter tankard similar to Garrick's and waved it.

Falna gave Coburn a wink and started gathering a basket to take to the man. Once she left, Coburn turned back toward Garrick and Irwin.

Garrick conveyed every ounce of his anger and frustration in one look. He mouthed, "Get to the point" to Coburn.

"I'm loosening her up," Coburn mouthed back.

"You're wasting time," Garrick countered.

"It's fine," Coburn mouthed.

Garrick drew his index finger across his neck and then pointed at Coburn.

Coburn held up his hands and mouthed, "Alright, alright."

He faced forward just as Falna returned to the bar. "Welcome back, enchantress."

Falna giggled. "Stop. You and your silver tongue."

"Speaking of silver tongues..."

Garrick cleared his throat again, plenty loud.

Still facing forward, Coburn waved Garrick off with his hand behind his back so Falna couldn't see. "...I was wondering if you might answer a question or two for me."

"Depends on the questions." Falna leaned on her elbows again, her face only inches away from Coburn's. "You may have to persuade me to answer."

Coburn cackled, and it grated on Garrick's nerves like it always did.

"I'm up for just about anything," Coburn replied.

"I'll bet you are." Falna brushed the tip of Coburn's nose with her finger. "So what is it you want to know?"

"I'm looking for some *red fire*," Coburn said. "Know where I might find some?"

Red fire was a coded term that Irwin had discovered during an interrogation the week before. They'd managed to capture a member of the Crimson Flame, and Irwin, being an alchemist, had coaxed it out of him with the help of one of his many concoctions.

Falna's countenance shifted from flirty and fun to a guarded seriousness, then it changed back again. "Red fire? Whatever are you talking about?"

Coburn stroked her bare forearm with his fingers. His voice low, he said, "You don't have to play coy with me, enchantress. I'm told that red fire can burn through even the most resilient of souls, refining them into perfect beings worthy of eternal reward."

Falna cleared her throat and straightened up. "Well, yes. Of course."

"So can you help me find some?" Coburn straightened his back to match her posture.

"I—I'm afraid—" Falna gulped, and her eyes glanced around the pub. "I know of what you speak, but I couldn't tell you where to find it."

Garrick didn't like her reaction. The very mention of *red fire* had set Falna on edge. But Garrick didn't move. Either Coburn would handle it, or he wouldn't.

"Falna, beautiful," Coburn said. "I'm just asking you to point me in the right direction. That's all."

Falna shook her head and glanced toward the door. "I'm sorry, Mr. Brye, but I can't help you."

The bearded man seated near the door stood to his full height and started toward Coburn and Falna.

Garrick watched his every step. The man carried a bit of extra weight around his midsection, but he walked with absolute confidence. Garrick figured him at mid-forties, six-foot-three, and close to 300 capable pounds of muscle. His red beard reached to the center of his chest.

Around here, logging was the driving economic force. This guy had probably been felling trees and hauling logs to the nearest major city every week since he was a teenager. So he knew his way around an axe and had no qualms about dealing with other strong men.

The bearded man stopped three paces from Coburn and asked, "This fellow bothering you, Falna?"

"Pardon me, sir," Coburn said, his voice firm, "but the lady and I are having a discussion."

Garrick sighed. If Coburn had wanted to, he could've handled that better. Instead of actually working his charisma on the man, Coburn had decided to vex him instead. Garrick downed a long glug of mead and cracked his knuckles.

"And I was talking to the lady, not your scrawny ass."

Coburn chuckled. "Call me scrawny again, and see what happens."

Garrick mumbled, "Here it comes."

Irwin covered his face with his hands. "Why does this always happen?"

"'Cause his ego's big as a mountain and more fragile than a butterfly's wings."

The bearded man leaned closer to Coburn and uttered, "*Scrawny.*"

Coburn grabbed a fistful of the man's beard with his left hand, yanked down, and sliced it clean from his chin with the knife in his other hand. The man staggered back, stunned, leaving Coburn sitting there with most of the beard still in his hand.

"You forgot this." Coburn tossed the clump of red hair at the now-de-bearded man and tucked his knife back into his clothes.

"You... *bastard!*" the de-bearded man shouted. "Do you have any idea how long it took me to grow that?"

Coburn shrugged. "I warned you."

With a savage growl, the de-bearded man lunged at him.

Coburn sidestepped the de-bearded man, and he collided with the edge of the bar. Then he whirled around and reached for Coburn a second time. This time, Coburn ducked under his grasp and came up behind the de-bearded man again.

"If I were you, I wouldn't keep this up," Coburn said. "I fight for a living, and I'd rather not—"

The de-bearded man swung at Coburn's head, but Coburn slipped the punch and kept speaking.

"—Pardon me, but I was saying I'd rather not have to hurt you."

The de-bearded man's rage turned to a sneer. "Good luck with that."

Two men seated behind Coburn stood from their chairs and grabbed his arms, anchoring him in place. They were each almost as big as the first one.

"Should we do something?" Irwin hissed.

"He can handle himself." Garrick took another drink of his mead and watched as Falna rounded the bar and ran into the kitchen. *Good.* It was better she stayed out of the way, for her own sake.

Irwin gawked at Garrick through his spectacles. "Against *three* of them?"

Garrick set his tankard down. "He'll be fine."

The de-bearded man swung at Coburn's head again, but Coburn kicked his legs out and hit the man in his chest before he could get close enough. He tottered backward into the bar, hit it hard, and grabbed at his lower back, wincing.

The two men holding Coburn tried to wrench him back into place, but his left arm slipped free. He grabbed the head of the man who still held onto him and drove his knee into the man's temple. The man dropped to the pub floor.

The other man swung a wild fist at Coburn's face, but Coburn slipped under it and slammed his knuckles into the man's thigh. The man yelped and fell, holding his leg with bared teeth. Only the de-bearded man remained standing.

"See?" Garrick said to Irwin. "He's fine."

Four other men, all of them big, bearded types, stood and started toward Coburn from around the pub.

"Is he?" Irwin asked. When Garrick didn't answer, Irwin said, "I'm going to help him. You should, too."

"Don't break your hands punching anyone. We need them for the rest of this mission." Garrick leaned back in his seat, still trying to slump a bit.

"I won't," Irwin replied. "I value my work too highly for that."

As Coburn engaged the five men amid the crashing of tables and chairs, the breaking of bottles, and the clanking of pewter tankards, Irwin pulled a glass vial from inside his pack. It glowed with faint yellow light. He removed another vial, this one dark blue, and held it in his left hand. Then he stood.

"Hey!" he called.

Two of the men on the outside of the fracas whirled to face him.

Garrick shielded his eyes. He knew what was coming.

He threw the vial at their feet, and it crashed onto the floor with a loud *pop* and a flash of brilliant light.

The men hollered and clutched at their faces, then they started groping around and blinking as if unable to see.

Irwin picked up a tankard from a nearby table and swung it at the nearest man. It clunked on his head, and he slumped to the floor, unconscious. Irwin repeated the process with the other man, and he, too, fell.

Coburn had hardly touched any of the other three men; he was spending most of his time maneuvering to avoid getting hit, and thus far, he'd succeeded.

Irwin yelled, "Blue vial!" and tossed the blue vial into the fray.

Coburn ducked low and covered his face with his cloak.

The vial shattered, and blue mist billowed up from the spilled liquid on the floor. Two of the men breathed it in and immediately slumped to the floor and started snoring, but the de-bearded man backed away, covering his face.

A moment later, once the mist had dissipated, Irwin called, "Clear!"

Coburn swung his cloak wide open and inhaled a desperate gasp, only to be met by the de-bearded man charging into him. They tumbled to the floor together, trading blows and positions, each fighting for the upper hand. Coburn had the skill, but the de-bearded man had the size.

Beyond them, the first two men who'd joined the fight had recovered and now started toward Irwin.

Garrick also noticed the second man whom Irwin had hit with the pewter tankard crawling toward the kitchen. Probably just wanted to get out of there.

Garrick didn't blame him. If a bunch of his friends had failed to take on a scrawny thief and an even scrawnier alchemist, he might consider retreating as well.

Irwin rushed back to his pouch to retrieve more vials. "I didn't account for these additional costs, you know."

Garrick waved his hand. "Don't worry about it. After this job's done, we'll have more than enough coin to replace what you've already used and more."

"I hope you're right." Irwin frowned at him. "But we haven't succeeded in either gaining any useful information or staying out of sight this whole time. So I'm not optimistic about our chances of completing this mission."

"Behind you." Garrick nodded at him.

Irwin popped the cork out of an orange vial, whirled around, and splashed it into the face of a very angry man. The liquid hit his face and began to steam.

The man wailed and grabbed at his face, staggering around the pub aimlessly.

"The orange one? Really?" Garrick asked. Irwin had used the orange one on the Crimson Flame cultist to get info about the pub out of him. It was a nasty brew.

"It's what I had in my hands," Irwin said. "And you know the burns aren't permanent—just excruciatingly painful."

"Weren't you just lamenting how we've failed to stay hidden?" Garrick quipped.

"You saw what happened. Had no choice." Irwin tipped his chin up in defiance. "Now if you'll excuse me, I need to help Coburn since you're unwilling to do so."

"I'm not unwilling." Garrick raised his tankard. "Just got this drink to finish."

Irwin shook his head and turned away.

As he did, the man who'd crawled into the kitchen returned. He was standing now, and he pointed at Coburn and Irwin while looking into the kitchen.

Then six men in black robes emerged from the kitchen. They had shaved heads and the red insignia of a fireball tattooed on their bare chests.

The Crimson Flame. Fire-worshiping cultists.

Fanatics.

But these fanatics knew where the hidden Crimson Flame temple was. And that's where Lord Valdis had directed Garrick to go.

The six cultists drew curved short swords and started toward Coburn and Irwin.

Garrick downed the rest of his mead and stood to his full height. He flung the cloak off of his shoulders, revealing his massive body and his leather torso armor, and picked up his battle-axe from the corner.

Upon seeing him, the cultists stopped short, their mouths hanging open as they stared. The tallest among them couldn't have been more than six feet in height, so Garrick towered over them like he did with nearly everyone he encountered.

"Crimson Flame, eh?" Garrick grinned. "Been looking for you guys."

He took a step forward, and all six of them stepped back.

Garrick chuckled and stole a glance at Irwin and Coburn to make sure he didn't have to rescue them. As he did, a flash of metal lashed at his left side.

Even if Garrick had wanted to, he couldn't have blocked the blow in time. The cultist's swing was too fast, and for all his strength, Garrick was just too slow.

Ping.

The blade glanced off of his bare arm. The blow smarted but hadn't cut him.

Garrick just shook his head at them. Being part troll, on his mother's side, meant he'd inherited some of the benefit of trolls having thick, durable skin. It would take a lot more than a few puny swords to bring him down.

By the time he'd finished talking, the pain in his arm had dwindled to nothing. Accelerated healing was another perk of the troll blood coursing through his veins.

He swung his battle-axe hard and fast, and five of the six cultists dodged in time. The sixth—the one who'd struck him—caught the flat side of his battle-axe. The blow launched the cultist into the pub wall with a loud *crack*, and he flopped onto the floor, motionless—maybe even dead.

"Now we can play this one of two ways," Garrick said. "If you cooperate and tell me what I want to know, I'll let you live. If not, I'll—"

All five of them charged toward him.

"Fair enough."

Metal clanged against Garrick's legs and arms and the handle of his battle-axe. He backhanded one of the cultists and sent him flying into a table, and it toppled over. He bashed another with the blunt end of his battle-axe, and the cultist dropped to the floor with his head split open and bleeding.

The third got kicked into one of his friends, and Garrick's battle-axe crashed through the guard of another and embedded halfway into his torso. The cultist spat up blood, and Garrick kicked him away. When he landed, the cultist's body folded on top of itself unnaturally, and blood pooled underneath him.

Of the six, three of the cultists got back up—the two he'd knocked down with his kick and the one he'd backhanded over the table. The other three lay on the floor, unmoving.

The cultists' swords were better for slashing than stabbing, and that suited Garrick just fine. They could hack at him for a century and not harm him.

But their sword tips could pierce through his skin if they managed a clean enough stab. That was just about the only way these idiots could hurt him, and it was why he still wore the leather torso armor in spite of his resilient skin.

Garrick checked on Irwin and Coburn again. Only they only still stood, now looming over the de-bearded man, alternating kicks to his ribs and legs.

The remaining cultists attacked again, and Garrick took their blows in stride until one of them stabbed at him. He batted the attack aside with his battle-axe, but the sword's tip embedded in the lower right side of his leather armor.

It didn't pierce all the way through, but Garrick still grimaced at how close he'd come to taking real damage. He rammed the blunt end of his battle-axe handle into the cultist's forehead so hard that it caved in, and he dropped to the floor, dead.

Garrick dispatched the remaining two just as easily, careful to only kill one of them and to break the leg of the other. He got ahold of the remaining cultist's neck with his massive hand and pinned him to the wall next to the kitchen door, then he lifted him up to eye level.

"Another benefit of the troll blood is ridiculous strength. I can hold you here for an hour if I have to," Garrick said. "Or you can tell me where the Crimson Flame temple is located, and I'll let you go."

The cultist squirmed and sputtered in Garrick's grasp, but he managed to rasp, "I'll never... tell you anything!"

Garrick sighed and glanced back at Irwin and Coburn again. They'd finished with the de-bearded man and started toward Garrick, and Irwin had detoured to grab his pack first. But as they approached, they stopped short, staring at something.

Garrick followed their gazes to the kitchen door. Red light flared around its edges, brighter with each passing second.

Then the door exploded.

Raging fire incinerated the kitchen door, billowed outward, and scorched the walls. Garrick dropped the cultist and dove to the side, away from the conflagration, but the cultist couldn't move in time. The flames charred the cultist's body black along with several of the pub's patrons and the other cultists.

When Garrick looked up, he saw both Irwin and Coburn taking cover behind tables. *Wooden* tables.

Whoever or whatever was coming for them, it could wield fire. It would burn through the pub's measly wooden tables in seconds.

"Move, you idiots!" Garrick hissed as he recovered his footing. "He'll burn you to a crisp behind those!"

"Not a he." Irwin adjusted his spectacles and pointed. "*She.*"

Garrick faced the kitchen again in time to see a busty, female figure step forward. Flames wreathed her body and hovered above her empty palms. Her blonde hair flowed behind her and teased her face, blown by the swirling fire around her, and she glowered at them with fiery red eyes edged with charred black skin.

Coburn gawked at her. "Falna?"

CHAPTER TWO

Garrick couldn't believe his eyes either, but he wasn't about to let some small-town barmaid light him up. He'd faced much worse and survived.

Falna hurled a ball of fire at Coburn's position first. He leaped over the bar as the fire engulfed the table where he'd been taking cover, reducing it to ash.

Irwin had nowhere to hide. Instead, he rummaged in his pack for something.

Garrick knew the drill—Irwin would find a solution, but he needed time.

No problem.

Garrick lurched forward and swung his battle-axe at Falna, hard and vicious.

Falna saw it coming and ducked underneath it, and she moved to blast Garrick to dust, but Garrick followed through with a kick that caught Falna's sternum.

It wasn't as hard of a kick as he'd wanted, but it knocked her off-balance, and her attack veered upward again. Fire seared a hole into the ceiling and ignited the pub's roof. Stars twinkled in the open night sky overhead.

When his foot touched the floor again, Garrick realized that the flames swirling around Falna had lit the leather on his boot on fire. It burned his shin and crept up toward his knee, but if he didn't keep pursuing Falna, she'd roast him like a holiday quail.

To buy himself some time, Garrick reached for a nearby chair and whipped it at her. She erected a wall of flames and destroyed most of it, but a few pieces of charred wood pelted her and knocked her over. Meanwhile, Garrick bent over and smacked the fire on his boot out.

Though his skin was resilient to most impacts, fire affected him the same as it would anyone else. His accelerated healing would take care of the burn in time, but not as quickly as it would a cut or a bone break. Trolls didn't like fire, and the human part of his makeup did nothing to protect him from it, either.

By now the place had filled with smoke, obscuring Garrick's vision and threatening to choke him. One of the drawbacks of being so tall was that the smoke got to him first. If Falna hadn't accidentally blown the hole in the roof, smoke would've filled the whole place by now.

Small, scattered fires gnawed away at various spots on the floor, on tables, on chairs. A corner of the bar itself had caught fire, but it hadn't spread much yet. Chunks of wood smoldered across the room, kicking smoke into the air.

Garrick had lost sight of Falna in the smoke when he'd patted out the fire on his leg, and with the smoke stinging his eyes, he couldn't see anything. He crouched low, trying to determine whether the growing flames around him were just fires or a fire mage hiding in her ideal environment.

"Irwin?" Garrick called. "What have you got for me?"

"Just a moment, please!" Irwin's voice cut through the smoke. "I'm having trouble finding—"

Fire billowed up from behind the bar, and a body rolled overtop of it. Coburn.

Flames licked at the heels of his boots as he toppled onto the floor between two smaller fires. Behind the bar, bottles of hard liquor ignited and burst, spewing flames in every direction.

"I'll admit, I was hoping for a hot night with a well-endowed barmaid when I started talking to her," Coburn wheezed, "but this isn't what I had in mind!"

Garrick hurried over to him, and they crouched against the burning bar together. "Where is she now?"

Coburn shook his head. "I don't know. I can't see anything."

"Found it!" Irwin shouted.

"Get over here!" Garrick hollered back.

Irwin scampered across the pub floor and held up a vial of clear liquid. "I've only got the one."

"We're trying to find the temple of a fire-worshiping cult called 'the Crimson Flame,' and you only brought *one* anti-fire potion?" Garrick growled.

"I'll make more later," Irwin said. "And it's a *suspended solution*, not a potion. I'm an alchemist, not some hack apothecary. But if you prefer, I can always take out the black vial…"

"No." Garrick shook his head. "It's too dangerous."

"Then make sure this one counts." Irwin planted it in Garrick's open hand.

To their right, the bar burst apart and flames shot forward, boiling the air around them. They rolled to the left, skittering and crawling to avoid the fire.

"Shake it before you break it," Irwin reminded him. "It'll get foamy and frothy, but it'll keep you safe from the fire until it runs out."

"I'm not going to use it to protect myself," Garrick said. "I'm going to use it on her. I'll distract her. You two sneak around from behind. Once her fire's out, grab her and hold her down. Dose her with something if you have to. If we don't get her away from the flames, she'll keep using them against us."

As if on cue, all the fires around them swelled in size. They burned brighter and hotter, and Garrick had to shield his face against the heat. He cursed and started shaking the vial.

"Go that way." Garrick pointed to the other side of the bar. Then he crouch-ran around the opposite side to where he thought he'd find Falna, shaking the vial as he ran.

Sure enough, a maelstrom of flames and fury greeted him through the haze. Falna's vivid red eyes fixed on his position, and the flames around her burned brighter and hotter as she drew her arm back to throw another fireball.

For once, Garrick was quicker. He'd been ready to throw the vial as soon as he saw her, and that's what he did.

As the vial flew at Falna, the heat exploded it in midair, and a plume of white foam slapped into Falna, caking her from head to toe. The foam also splattered onto nearby tables, chairs, walls, and the floor. Whatever fire it touched it extinguished with an angry hiss, including the fireball conjuring in Falna's hand.

"Now!" Garrick yelled.

As Falna tried to claw the foam from her eyes, Coburn hit her from behind, knocking her to the floor. Coburn pulled his knife out of its sheath with a *shing* and put it against her neck.

"Don't move, *enchantress*," he said, his voice sharp with rage.

She kept scraping at her eyes. "It… it's burning my eyes!"

"It should. It's a compound designed to extinguish fire, and your eyes were steeped in flames," Irwin said.

"Let's get her out of here. The place is going to burn down," Garrick said.

Coburn stood and wrenched Falna up by her hair until she was standing. Then Garrick grabbed his battle-axe in one hand and slung Falna over his shoulder with the other.

"What about your cloak?" Irwin asked.

"Leave it. It's not worth the risk." Garrick kicked the pub door so hard that it snapped off its hinges and slammed to the ground outside, then he ducked under the doorway—like he had to with almost every doorway—and set Falna down fifty paces away from the blazing pub.

Frigid winds marking the beginning of winter in the north cooled Garrick's over-heated skin and quickly threatened to turn him to ice. *Well, at least it's not snowing.*

The white foam still covered most of Falna's body, but she'd managed to wipe away the majority of it from her face. She looked past Garrick toward the blazing pub. Her eyes, now back to their original blue color but still outlined by charred skin, sank with grief.

"You're too far away. You can't call the fire to you." Garrick crouched in front of her, partly to intimidate her and partly to keep his body heat contained in the icy air. "We made sure of it. And we can either leave you out here to freeze to death, or you can tell us what we want to know."

Falna glared up at him with fury in her eyes, but no actual fire burned in them anymore. She clamped her mouth shut and shivered.

"Tell us where the Crimson Flame temple is, and then we'll be on our way."

She laughed at him. "You want to know where the temple is? Fine. If you three uninitiated brigands are stupid enough to walk into the Temple of the Crimson

Flame, then by all means, please do. You'll be walking into an eternity of fire, an inferno unlike anything you've ever—"

Garrick grabbed her by her collar and yanked her closer to him. "Just get to the point."

She told him the location and how to get there. "But you'll never escape. That, I guarantee."

"We'll take our chances." Garrick let her go and stood just as a gust of wind needled the backs of his bare arms. He turned back to Coburn and Irwin. "Let's go. We need to find suitable shelter before we turn into mercenary icicles."

"What about her?" Irwin pushed his spectacles up to the bridge of his nose and shivered.

"She's got no coat, and the nearest town is miles away," Garrick said. "There's still a fire burning at the pub, so she's tethered to it until sunrise, at least. Whatever the case, she's no longer our problem, and we've got a lunch meeting in Mirstone tomorrow."

Irwin nodded. He walked past her with his pack slung over his shoulder and his hands tucked under his armpits.

Coburn walked forward, crouched in front of Falna, and shook his head. "We could have been wonderful together, enchantress. We could have danced beneath the stars, frolicked in pristine waters, and made even the gods envious of our love." He leveled his gaze at her. "But instead, you tried to light me on fire. Multiple times."

"It's part of my job to seem amenable to patrons' desires. Makes them drink more, and then the pub makes more money." Falna sneered at him. "You never had a chance."

Coburn's expression hardened. "Return to your ruins, harpy. The only warmth you'll know tonight is that of the destruction wrought by your own hand. And in the morning, your bed will be just as cold as if I were in it this night." Coburn held up a pouch. "Oh, and one more thing…"

Falna's eyes widened.

"When you nearly set me on fire and I had to jump over the bar, I helped myself to the evening's earnings. Consider it hazard pay." Coburn jingled the pouch again.

Before Falna could respond, Coburn walked past her. She screeched something at him from behind, but the howling winter wind swallowed her words.

THE NEXT MORNING, GARRICK GRUMBLED AS IRWIN SHOOK HIM AWAKE JUST BEFORE sunrise. He didn't want to wake up, but they had to reach Mirstone by midday.

The night before, they'd gathered firewood, camped in a shallow cave, and survived the cold dark along with the insects and vermin that resided in that subterranean hole. Not the finest accommodations, but it beat waking up frozen to death.

After packing up, they ate a modest breakfast of dried meats and stale bread from Irwin's pack while trekking west through the numerous foothills in northern Etrijan. Fortunately for them, based on Falna's directions, Mirstone, the nearest town, was roughly in the same direction that they needed to travel to reach the temple. Or perhaps a bit south.

They arrived in Mirstone early, so they restocked what supplies they could using Falna's money from the pub. Irwin took great joy in adding the revenue to his ledger, but his glee faded when the majority of it landed in the hands of various merchants and shopkeepers.

Even so, Garrick was pleased that a town of that size had outfitted them with virtually everything he could've asked for prior to raiding a cultist temple. The local apothecary even satisfied most of Irwin's requests for various elemental substances, and with a multiple-day journey ahead of them, he'd have plenty of time to formulate a considerable inventory of concoctions.

Most importantly, Garrick's initial guess about the temple's location had been right, so the meeting he'd scheduled with Noraff made perfect sense.

As planned, Garrick and his crew met Noraff in a tavern on the north side of Mirstone for lunch. When they arrived, Garrick noted first that Noraff wasn't alone. A man in brown robes sat at Noraff's side.

Noraff noticed them as soon as Garrick ducked under the tavern's doorframe, and he stood up from his seat and ambled over on long, lanky limbs.

Noraff was an Onni, a humanoid species known for their prowess in climbing, in part thanks to their incredible grip strength and the talons tipping each of their fingers and toes but also because of their extended limbs. They made for capable fighters, too, because of their exceptional reach.

"Garrick, you old sot," Noraff spread his long arms wide to embrace Garrick. "Bring it in."

Garrick spread his arms wide, too, noting how his wingspan didn't reach as long as Noraff's even though Noraff stood at least a foot shorter in height. "Good to see you, Noraff."

As Garrick and Noraff embraced, the mage-type man at the table stood and faced them. Garrick eyed him. He wore simple brown robes and looked unimpressive in virtually every way.

Noraff released his grasp on Garrick and held him at his considerable arm's-length. "Look at you. How long has it been? Two years? You haven't changed a bit. Well, maybe a bit bigger overall."

Garrick refocused on Noraff, specifically on the brown hair that covered every inch of his exposed skin. "You've gotten even hairier."

Unlike regular humans, Onni grew coarse hair all up and down their bodies, arms and legs. Where human men could grow beards, Onni grew hair on the entirety of their faces and rarely trimmed it. The only parts of their bodies not covered in hair were their palms and the soles of their feet which could function like a second set of hands.

Give him a tail, and he'd be a monkey, Garrick had once said about Noraff to a fellow mercenary. He'd meant it as an insult, but that was back when he hadn't yet been forced to work with Noraff and didn't know or trust him.

Then again, now that Garrick knew him, he still didn't fully trust Noraff. But they needed a fourth man—specifically one with climbing skills—for the next phase of this job, and Garrick preferred the Onni he knew over the Onni he didn't.

Noraff caught Garrick glancing at the mage-type, and he let go of Garrick's arms. "I see you've noticed my friend. Garrick, this is Phesnos. He's a mage."

"Pleasure." Phesnos stepped forward and extended his hand.

As Garrick shook it, he studied Phesnos's keen blue eyes and angular face. He didn't like what he saw, though he couldn't exactly explain why.

"Same," Garrick replied. He introduced Irwin and Coburn to them, and they shook hands and then took their seats at the table.

A tavern wench brought each of them a round of ale, but Irwin declined his, as usual, and requested goat's milk instead. Coburn didn't say so much as a word to her, and Garrick wondered if it was because of how things had gone with Falna last night.

"Bring us a full spread of food, too, love," Noraff said to the wench. "We've all got big appetites."

Irwin cleared his throat and nudged Garrick's leg with his under the table.

Margins. Irwin was always concerned about the margins. Paying for a huge meal wasn't an expense Irwin wanted to justify.

Garrick turned toward him and gave him a corrective look as if to say, "it's fine."

Irwin rolled his eyes and shook his head.

"So tell me about this job." Noraff adjusted his belt, and Garrick caught a glimpse of a green knife hilt sticking out of a sheath.

Despite his hairy body, Noraff still wore clothes, although they hung loose on his limber frame. Some Onni Garrick had met didn't wear anything, and he'd always found it awkward when trying to have conversations with them.

Garrick cast a long glance at Phesnos. "I'd rather not talk about it in front of—"

"Sorry," Noraff interrupted. He turned to Phesnos. "Could you give us a moment?"

Phesnos nodded, picked up his ale, and walked across the tavern without so much as a word.

"Sorry," Noraff repeated. "I wasn't thinking."

"It's fine," Garrick said. "So the job is—"

"I'm sorry. One more thing," Noraff said. "I just have to say that I can't work the job unless we cut in Phesnos as well."

Garrick sat there. The idea that Noraff had included Phesnos in the meeting was troubling at the onset because of the secrecy of the job. The thought had crossed Garrick's mind that Noraff had brought him along for this exact purpose, but Garrick hadn't given it serious consideration. Now he would have to.

"It's a four-man job," Garrick said. "We don't need a fifth."

"But it won't *hurt* to have a fifth. One extra guy to watch our backs," Noraff said.

"One extra share, meaning smaller payouts for each of us," Irwin countered.

"Pay a workman his worth, right?" Noraff stared at Irwin. "I assure you, he's worth every coin."

"I said we don't need a fifth, Noraff." Garrick's voice hardened. "End of discussion."

"If you're saying the discussion is over, then you're doing the job with three men." Noraff sat back in his chair and folded his long arms across his chest.

"Then we'll do it with three." Garrick held his ground. He'd expected some negotiation from Noraff, but he hadn't anticipated this type of pushback.

"You just said it's a four-man job," Noraff said.

"I also just said it's not a five-man job."

"If it's a four-man job, how can you do it with three?"

Garrick knew they *could* do it with three, but it would complicate everything. Having a fourth man along would make everything quicker and easier.

Most jobs Garrick took, he could do with Irwin and Coburn just fine. But a deep dive into a temple full of hostile cultists and whatever else lurked under its foundation called for a fourth man—especially one capable of climbing literally anything.

That's why he'd contacted Noraff in the first place: According to the diagram Garrick had received from Lord Valdis, the interior of the temple housed a secret entrance to what could only be described as a dungeon beneath it, and the diagram suggested plenty of opportunities for a climber to come in handy.

Plus, having a fourth man capable of fighting took some of the strain off of Garrick. He proudly carried the load when it came to the majority of battles, but he often caught himself having to watch out for Irwin and even Coburn at times. A fourth man on a job like this, in a dark place filled with only the gods knew what, would come in handy beyond just climbing.

But Noraff didn't know any of that, nor did he need to.

"We'll make do," Garrick replied.

"So you had me travel all the way to the middle of nowhere, in Etrijan, just to send me back?"

Garrick grinned. "At least we get to have lunch together."

The tavern wench reappeared with a large platter of food and set it on the table for them. The aromas of roast chicken and potatoes, goat stew, warm bread from the oven, and seasoned ears of corn set Garrick's stomach rumbling.

Coburn looked up at the wench, who smiled at him, but he looked away immediately. Garrick smirked at the sight. Maybe Coburn had learned something.

"Look." Noraff leaned forward as he filled his plate. "Think about how this looks from my perspective. You asked me to travel hundreds of miles for this job. I get here, and you've got two other guys with you whom I don't know, and it's supposed to be a four-man job. I'm outnumbered. If you want to scam me, it'll be easy for the three of you to cut me out."

"No one's going to cut you out, Noraff," Irwin said. "We don't operate that way."

Now Garrick nudged Irwin with his leg to get him to shut up. He'd had no intention of cutting out Noraff, but the more information Noraff had, the harder he could negotiate on the price and terms.

Too late now, but hopefully Irwin would keep his trap shut going forward.

"You can make all the promises you want. That doesn't change how this looks,"

Noraff said. "For all I know, you'll just kill me once we finish the job and leave my carcass in a trench somewhere."

"Since we're only using three men for this job now, you've got nothing to worry about." Garrick tore a leg and a thigh off of one of the roast chickens and bit a large chunk out of it. Salted, smoky meat tantalized his tongue.

"You could make good use of Phesnos," Noraff said. "He's a talented mage. I've worked with him on a couple of jobs before."

"I said we don't need a fifth," Garrick reiterated. A fifth would be nice, but they didn't *need* a fifth.

"I want to do this job with you. I didn't come all this way just for a meal with an old friend."

"Friend" was a generous term to describe Garrick's relationship with Noraff, but he didn't say anything to the contrary.

"I want you to do that job as well," Garrick said, "but we don't need Phesnos involved. So if you want to sign on, just you, then we can make an agreement."

"It's either Phesnos and me, or neither of us." Noraff shrugged. "That's how it has to be."

"Even if we were to entertain this fancy of yours, bringing in your mysterious and unnecessary acquaintance into our fold," Coburn started, "it would mean splitting our shares of the take. For what possible reason would we give up a percentage of our coin for someone whose worth is yet unknown?"

"As far as I'm concerned, *your* worth is equally as unknown," Noraff replied. "Same with spectacles, over here."

"I am quite useful, thank you very much," Irwin said. "I am well-versed in chemistry, alchemy, and a variety of other sciences that are both useful and germane to our—"

"And how good are you at wielding a sword? Or a spear? Or anything sharp and pointy?"

"I do rather well with needles and scalpels, as a matter of fact."

"Well, the next time I need a splinter removed, I'll be sure to look you up," Noraff quipped. "Not that I've ever had a splinter in my entire life, mind you. Tree Onni don't get splinters."

Irwin huffed and filled his mouth with bread.

Garrick studied Noraff as he ate. There was no question that having a fighter as skilled as Noraff would prove valuable where they were going. But at the cost of splitting the payment five ways to accommodate the addition of a fifth?

"Here's what I propose," Garrick said. "If you want your friend to come along, he gets half of *your* share."

"Not a chance." Noraff shook his head. "That's not fair."

"We don't know his capabilities or anything about him," Garrick said. "So the burden is on you."

Noraff pointed at Irwin and Coburn. "I don't know their capabilities either, but you're vouching for them. I'm vouching for Phesnos."

"Yeah, but it's not your job. We don't have to convince you. *You* have to convince *us*." Garrick took another bite of the chicken.

"Trust me. He's skilled, he has worked as a mercenary many times before, and I've seen him in action," Noraff said. "He can handle himself in a fight, and if we encounter anything with magic capabilities, then he'll come in doubly handy."

Neither Garrick nor his crew said anything.

"How about this: I'll pay him a quarter of my share—we'll call it an investment in my peace of mind—and then the rest of you can each chip in an eighth of your shares. That way, it only hurts you a little to bring him along, and he still makes a little more than half of the original fee."

"I'd rather keep all of my earnings." Irwin looked up at Garrick. "But I suppose..."

Garrick looked to Coburn.

"Another set of hands may prove advantageous," Coburn said, "particularly if those hands are imbued with magic."

Garrick turned back to Noraff. "Your friend's been waiting to eat long enough. Bring him back over."

Noraff whistled and waved at Phesnos, and he headed toward the table. As Phesnos walked, Noraff asked, "Does that mean he's in?"

Something about the whole situation still bothered Garrick, and Noraff hadn't made a very strong case, but ultimately, doing the job with three men wasn't something Garrick wanted to try. So they'd do it with five instead, and hopefully they'd be able to work through the job even faster.

As Phesnos took a standing position next to his seat, Garrick stood to meet him. Phesnos stared up at him with those sharp blue eyes—but without a hint of intimidation in them.

Garrick extended his hand. "Welcome to the team."

"WE MUST BE CLOSE TO THE TEMPLE," GARRICK SAID AS THE FIVE OF THEM LEFT Mirstone together. "A town of that size, out here in the foothills with no major rivers and only one major road in and out—I'd be willing to bet the cultists stop there for supplies regularly."

"It would explain why Mirstone had so much to offer despite its relatively small size and population," Irwin said. "In any case, I'm pleased with the outcome of our visit."

"I'm just glad we finally got some palatable food." Coburn gnawed on a roasted chicken leg leftover from lunch. "I imagine we'll need an abundance of strength once we arrive."

"It sounds like it's a three-day journey to this temple?" Noraff asked.

"Probably closer to three-and-a-half days," Garrick said. "And it'll be uphill most of the way, into the mountains."

"And once we get there...?"

Noraff was probing for information, but Garrick wasn't going to reveal anything unless he had to.

"I'll be clear in my instructions when we arrive. Until then," Garrick motioned toward the rolling Etrijani hills all around them, "just enjoy the view."

※

THREE AND A HALF DAYS LATER, THE TEMPLE CAME INTO VIEW. ONE SIDE WAS CARVED out of a sheer cliff face, and the rest sat atop the cliff itself, set into a mountain. Falna's directions had proven true.

"Is that it?" Noraff asked.

"Has to be," Garrick replied. "Who else would hide a fire-worshipping temple high up in the mountains but a bunch of idiot cultists?"

"If Mountain Onni were more religious, I could see them doing it," Noraff said.

Noraff had explained to Garrick about a year earlier that his people were Forest Onni, and they mostly lived in forests where they maneuvered through trees faster than most other species could run along the ground. That's also why Noraff had brown hair—to blend in with the trees. By contrast, Mountain Onni had hair in a range of shades of gray.

"They're not Mountain Onni," Garrick said. "Guaranteed."

The temple's position, embedded in the mountain, would make the approach difficult. They'd either have to approach it via whatever jagged mountain roads led up to its front entrance, or they'd have to scale the cliff face.

What I wouldn't give for a couple of wyverns right now, Garrick mused.

"Let me guess," Noraff started, "you want me to climb the cliff, sneak inside, and let you in the front door?"

"I didn't hire you for your personality," Garrick replied. He scanned the horizon, now painted with vivid purples, pinks, and oranges as the sun sank toward the mountain peaks. "We'll wait for the cover of nightfall before we approach from the front."

"And what will I encounter when I get inside?" Noraff asked.

"Nothing you can't handle. Probably just a bunch of monks praying. Some of them might try to set you on fire, but you'll be fine if you're careful."

"I'd prefer to take someone with me. Having someone who can watch my back is always useful," Noraff said.

"I'll pass, thanks." Irwin patted his flimsy arms. "I couldn't climb that, not in a millennium. I'd fall before I got twenty feet off the ground."

"I'm out, too," Garrick said.

"Why?" Noraff asked. "Afraid of heights?"

"Not specifically. But I've stayed alive thus far by managing the risks I take in this line of work," Garrick said. "Trying to haul my 400-pound body up a cliff face like that, plus gear, in the dark, is a recipe for catastrophe. So take Pheasant with you."

"*Phesnos,*" a voice behind them said.

It was Phesnos. He'd hardly said anything to anyone but Noraff over the last few days of travel, so much so that Garrick *had* actually forgotten his name.

"Right. Phesnos." Garrick gave him a glance. "Take him."

"I don't climb," Phesnos said.

"Of course he doesn't," Garrick mumbled.

"I am known for my magical prowess, not for my physical attributes," Phesnos continued.

"I don't think you're known for anything," Garrick countered.

"Maybe not to you."

Garrick turned and faced him. "So remind me again why we're paying you to be here?"

"Phesnos will prove his worth, I assure you," Noraff stepped between them. "It just won't be by climbing. So if none of the three of you will be joining me, then either I'm going alone or…"

Everyone turned toward Coburn.

Coburn looked at the cliff face, then he refocused on everyone else and sighed. "You're not serious, are you?"

As the sun set behind the mountains, Noraff and Coburn started to scale the cliff. Meanwhile, Garrick and Irwin headed toward the temple with Phesnos trailing behind. As they cut through the forests painted on the mountain's slopes, the night sky darkened to midnight blue, punctuated with twinkling white stars.

They trekked upward in silence along a rough path tainted with encroaching vegetation. Garrick led them, ever watchful of the woods surrounding them as they advanced. With only Irwin and a so-called mage of unknown ability, if something or someone attacked them, he'd have to do most of the fighting himself.

They reached the temple a couple of hours later and took cover behind some bushes. The temple stood roughly four stories high, with four tall pillars of dark granite denoting the entrance. To the temple's left, the mountain continued to rise to its zenith, and the gray rock framed the temple's left side in a solid wall.

To the right, a tall, man-made wall of stone formed an imposing perimeter, especially because the mountain dropped off into open air just a few feet beyond the edge of the wall. The wall also extended out from the mountain's side on the left, and it met the right side of the wall in a center arch, forming a small courtyard.

But the wall didn't have a door or portcullis of any sort. It just stood there, open to the empty courtyard beyond. Nor did Garrick see any guards patrolling on top of the wall. Stranger still, the place was totally dark on the outside. For this being a Crimson Flame temple, Garrick had expected more fire and more light.

"What do we do now?" Irwin whispered.

Garrick pulled his battle-axe from his back and held it. "We wait for Coburn and Noraff."

"And if they didn't make it?"

"Then we go in ourselves. We'll give them an hour."

Not two minutes later, a voice hissed at them from ahead, on the right side of the perimeter wall. Garrick's grip on his battle-axe tightened at the sound, then he relaxed once he recognized Noraff's voice. He scanned the area, searching for some sign of Noraff under the moonlight but not finding anything.

"There." Phesnos pointed.

Garrick looked and saw Noraff's silhouette clinging to the wall like a spider and waving to them.

"It's safe," Noraff rasped. "Come over."

Phesnos started toward Noraff, but Garrick grabbed him by his shoulder and stopped him.

"I'll go first," Garrick said. "You come with Irwin once I'm sure it's safe."

Phesnos frowned at him but shrugged. "Suit yourself."

Garrick stepped past the bushes, his head swiveling back and forth. No one came at him, so he walked forward, battle-axe high and ready. Still nothing.

Satisfied, he waved back to Irwin and Phesnos, and they emerged from the bushes as well. They met up with Noraff, who still clung to the wall, his body parallel to the ground.

Now close up, Garrick saw Noraff's claw-tipped fingers and toes gripping crevices in the wall, some of them incomprehensibly shallow. Somehow, the green-hilted knife in his belt stayed in its sheath no matter how much he swung or swayed or scampered along the rocks.

But Onni could climb anything. It's what they did.

"There's a secret entrance. Coburn spotted it while we were climbing," Noraff said. "Good eyesight, that one, even in the dark."

"He's a thief. Has enchanted vision," Irwin said. "I've been trying to replicate the results with a more scientific approach, but thus far I've been unable to—"

"Where is he now?" Garrick broke in. A part of him worried that Coburn hadn't survived the climb.

"He's waiting for us at the door," Noraff replied. "He's a passable climber, too—for a human, anyway. We decided to try it instead of risking going in a window or something."

Garrick studied the edge of the wall and the narrow path—if he could even call it that—of uneven rocks that extended beyond it. In some places, it was only two feet wide. Not ideal for someone of Garrick's size.

"I wish you'd just stuck to the plan," Garrick grunted.

"Nonsense. Why make things unnecessarily difficult on ourselves?"

"This way is 'unnecessarily difficult' for *me*."

Still clinging to the wall with three of his limbs, Noraff waved Garrick's concerns away. "Just watch your step. Wouldn't want to tumble down that slope."

Thanks to the moonlight, Garrick could see clear down into the valley below. His heightened healing, durable bones, and tough skin wouldn't be enough to save him from that kind of fall. Not even close.

And one misstep could send him there.

271

Noraff released all of his grips except for his right foot. His body swung toward the ground and then back up to the other side like a pendulum. His limbs latched onto a new set of grips immediately, and he began crawl-climbing along the wall.

"Show-off," Irwin muttered.

Phesnos stared at Garrick with those keen blue eyes. "Well?"

"You go first this time," Garrick said. "I'll bring up the rear."

"Whatever you say," Phesnos replied, his voice flat. He took hold of the stones in the wall and started to navigate the rocks at his feet.

"Do you want me to go next?" Irwin asked.

"Yes." Garrick added, "Be careful."

Irwin mimicked Phesnos's approach and stepped onto the path.

Once Irwin had progressed several steps ahead, Garrick shifted his battle-axe to his right hand. He didn't want it somehow bumping the wall and throwing off his balance. His size alone was enough of an issue.

"So much for managing risks," he muttered. Garrick glanced around once more to make sure no one was following them, then he too stepped onto the path. His fingers found a grip in the cold rock, and he started forward, taking each step with the utmost caution and care.

As he advanced, he tried not to think about all the things that could go wrong at that moment, but they came to his mind anyway. He tried to push them down and focus on the task at hand.

The path narrowed as the wall curved around the mountainside, and Garrick cursed Coburn's eyes and Noraff's climbing skills. He cursed his thick fingers more, though. If he couldn't manage to find grips, his strength wouldn't matter.

Ahead of him, it looked like Phesnos had reached the secret entrance, which as far as Garrick could tell was just a cave, but he didn't have a good angle on it. Irwin was still several yards away but progressing smoothly.

Just pay attention to your own self, Garrick told himself. *You'll get there just fine. This isn't how you're gonna die. Falling off of a mountain like some jackass isn't your end.*

Two steps later and with only a mediocre handhold for his left hand, Garrick considered securing the battle-axe on his back again instead of carrying it the rest of the way. He was strong, but it was a heavy weapon, and it had threatened more than once to sway him off-balance.

A gust of frigid night wind howled against the side of the mountain and threatened to knock Garrick loose, but he pressed himself against the wall and held on with all of his strength.

It worked, and he didn't fall.

But Irwin did.

CHAPTER THREE

"I rwin!" Garrick shouted.

There was no way Garrick could've gotten to him in time, but Irwin somehow grabbed ahold of a rock on the way down. Even more miraculous, he managed to hold on, even with his flimsy arms.

But it wouldn't last. Flimsy arms weren't good for much.

"Noraff!" Garrick shuffled toward Irwin, careful with each step, but the wind kept howling. He bellowed, "Noraff, get out here!"

The wind swallowed his calls. He'd have to help Irwin himself.

"Hold on, Irwin!" Garrick called to him. The path had shrunk to its narrowest right where Garrick was, so much so that only his toes balanced on the rocky edge.

Irwin hung from the rock two feet below the edge of the path. Even with Garrick's height, and even if he could manage to reach down despite the narrow ledge, his arms would never reach that far down while crouching.

But he had his battle-axe. He'd kept it in his hand, and now he could lower it to reach Irwin. Or at least, he could try to.

"Hold on!" Garrick called again. He maneuvered his left hand to secure grips as he advanced, and he finally reached Irwin's position. But the edge of the rock was still narrow, and with Garrick's size, he couldn't conceive of how to adjust his footing so he could lower the battle-axe. "Noraff! Get out here! We need your help!"

The raging wind continued to devour his words.

"I—I can't hold on much longer," Irwin yelled. "Please hurry!"

Garrick lowered his battle-axe toward Irwin, but it didn't reach far enough.

"Lower, please?" Irwin begged.

"I'm trying!" When Garrick tried to lower it, his hip pressed against the rock. He was strong, but he couldn't move the side of a mountain with his hip, so whenever he tried to crouch, he bumped the wall and started to lose his balance.

"I'm sorry to rush you, but my fingers are slipping!" Irwin called.

"I said I'm trying! *Noraff!*" Garrick had to get lower, but the only way to do that was a wild risk. But he couldn't let Irwin fall, so he had to risk it. He shouted down to Irwin, "Hang on! I'm going to try something."

He positioned his left foot parallel with the edge, grabbed a lower grip on the rock wall, and let his right leg dangle over the valley below. Then he squatted down, lowering his whole body and leaning away from the wall.

If his left foot slipped, or if his left hand lost its grip, he was going over. No question about it. But now the head of the battle-axe reached below where Irwin was hanging on.

"Grab the undercurves of the blades, and I'll pull you up." Even as Garrick said it, his right arm ached, but he had to do it, so he would. "And don't grab the sharp part like an idiot."

Irwin reached for it with his left hand and got his fingers around the battle-axe's undercurve like Garrick had said. His other hand still gripped the rock. "Alright. I'm going to—"

The rock crumbled under Irwin's grasp. He reached his other hand up and grabbed ahold of the battle-axe's other undercurve as the rock tumbled into the valley below.

Irwin's drop wrenched on Garrick's arm, and the battle-axe handle slid through his hand. It stopped sliding at the pommel, and Garrick managed to hold on even though every inch of his arm and his shoulder screamed at him to let go.

Worse yet, the jolt from Irwin started to pry Garrick's fingers from his hold on the rock wall. Now his fingertips barely held his grip in the stone. He fiercely dug them into the stone.

I'm not gonna fall. I won't.

Garrick inhaled a deep, frigid breath, and roared as he pulled his battle-axe—and Irwin—up. Irwin rose slowly, and Garrick's back and arm muscles burned.

A brown, hairy arm reached out, grabbed Irwin by his collar, and pulled him to the rocks. Noraff's voice said, "I've got ya!"

Noraff's help enabled Garrick to readjust his grip on the wall, and he steadied himself. Together, Noraff and Garrick hauled Irwin back up to the rock wall and helped him get a grip.

Once he found his footing again, Irwin said between heavy breaths, "Thank you. I owe you both a great debt."

"About time you showed up." Garrick glowered at Noraff, who clung to the wall by all four limbs again. "I yelled for you at least three times."

"Sorry. Didn't hear you. I only came out again because you were taking so long."

"We can't all climb like you can, Noraff," Garrick snapped.

"Alright, alright." Despite hanging from the wall, Noraff held up one of his hands in surrender. "We're almost there. Can you make it the rest of the way?"

"I believe so," Irwin said.

"Yes," Garrick replied, "if you move."

Noraff complied, and despite the violent winter winds, they completed the rest of the journey across the wall without incident.

The secret entrance was more of a hole carved into the side of the wall than a cave like Garrick had thought. Inside there was room enough for them all to stand but not much to spare beyond that. Recessed in the hole was a weathered wooden door.

To Garrick's relief, Coburn was alive. Coburn said, "I've picked the lock already, but the door is either stuck or too heavy for any of us to open. Do you think you could—"

"Yes," Garrick answered. His right arm was still sore from hauling Irwin and his battle-axe up, but if yanking an old door open meant he wouldn't have to go back out on that ledge, he'd do it in a heartbeat. Garrick strapped his battle-axe to his back and grabbed ahold of the door's iron handle. He looked at the others. "Stand back."

With one mighty pull and a loud scrape, Garrick wrenched the door open, but only a few inches. Two more hefts got it open wide enough for Coburn and Noraff to slip through, and they worked together with Garrick to get it open even wider.

Phesnos and Irwin went in next, and Garrick entered last.

The interior of the dark room they'd entered stank of rotting meat and fruit. Irwin pulled a vial from his pack, and it glowed with yellow light, illuminating the small space.

They'd entered some sort of antechamber, but the room was empty, so Garrick couldn't figure out its exact purpose. A door on the wall opposite of the secret entrance was the only other way out.

"Do we shut the secret door?" Irwin asked.

"It was pretty hard to get open. I say we leave it," Noraff replied.

"We should shut it," Garrick said. "If anyone comes down here and sees it open, it'll raise concerns."

"I don't think we're in danger of that," Phesnos said. "By the way that door refused to open, it's clear no one has been down here in some time."

Garrick wanted to say, "No one asked you," but he kept quiet instead.

"We've made enough noise as it was getting inside," Coburn said. "Closing the door means more noise, and none of us want to risk anyone inside realizing we're here."

"Fine. Whatever. I don't care." Garrick pulled the diagram from his pack and showed it to all of them, Phesnos included. "This shows the layout of the temple. We're looking for a secret room concealed behind a long set of curtains hanging in the main hall. There's a door set into the wall behind those curtains. That's where we need to be."

Coburn took the lead. He picked the lock to the room's other door, and it didn't scrape or even creak as it opened. Soft, red-orange light flowed into the doorway, but Garrick couldn't yet see where it was coming from.

Coburn slipped out of the room in perfect silence with one of his knives in his right hand. Noraff and Phesnos followed him, and Irwin and Garrick brought up the rear.

They entered a short, stone hallway devoid of life. Two torches mounted on the walls burned with red-orange flames. At one end of the hallway was one door, and the other hallway had just an open arch.

Coburn looked back at Garrick, who nodded toward the arch.

As they crept toward the arch, the light shuffle of footsteps sounded from ahead of them. They all froze in place.

Two bald-headed men in black-and-red robes walked past the archway, but neither of them looked into the hallway where Garrick and his team were waiting.

Once they passed, Garrick exhaled a calm breath and relaxed his grip on his battle-axe. He nodded to Coburn, and they started to advance once again.

The next hallway took them deeper into the temple, and they snuck past what appeared to be a kitchen, a barracks full of monks, and a bathing room. Finally, they reached a huge room full of tables and benches. It was dark except for a handful of torches that continued to burn, but they were just a fraction of the total number mounted on the walls.

"This isn't it," Garrick whispered. "Keep moving."

The next set of doors opened to a room resembling what the diagram showed: a grand hall with high ceilings, pillars of black granite, and a handful of crimson torches burning. Ornate etchings of great, scaled beasts with sharp claws and fire billowing out of their mouths adorned the stone walls. A granite altar on a platform at the far end of the hall lay empty.

Smooth, black stone made up the floor and the walls. Two long windows stretched from the lofted ceiling nearly down to the floor, and on either side of them, floor-length curtains hung from iron rods. It all looked just like the layout on the diagram.

Each of the curtains bore the symbol Garrick had seen on the cultists' chests back at the pub, only with the colors reversed: a crimson background with a black fireball in the center.

They glanced around the room to ensure they could cross to the curtains safely. Finding no one, they headed toward the right side. Sure enough, behind the curtain they found a rectangular outline cut into the stone, but it had no door handle.

"So how do we get it open?" Coburn whispered. "I cannot pick a lock that doesn't exist."

"There's a lever somewhere nearby," Garrick replied. "The diagram says it should be..."

He turned to face the altar.

"It's under the altar?" Noraff asked. "The thing has to weigh a ton. It's solid stone."

"So we're going to have to move it," Garrick said.

"I could blow it up instead," Irwin offered.

"Too noisy." Garrick motioned toward the opposite side. "I'll take one end, and the four of you can take the other end. We lift on three. Try to slide it toward the curtains."

Noraff grunted and Phesnos sighed, but they obeyed.

Garrick counted down. "One... two... *three.*"

They all strained against the heavy altar, but it did move—slowly. Inch by miserable inch, they hefted it off of its spot, revealing a metal apparatus beneath. In its center sat a lever.

"Would you care to do the honors?" Coburn motioned toward it but looked at Garrick.

"You're just worried it's old and rusted. You don't think you can lift it," Garrick quipped.

"On the contrary, I didn't want to break it with my unfathomable strength," Coburn countered.

Garrick scoffed and reached down. He pulled the lever up with one hand, and it squeaked. It stopped with a metallic *crunch*, and the familiar sound of stone scraping against stone sounded from by the curtains. Garrick released the lever, and it slowly receded into the metal casing on its own.

Within seconds, the secret door was open. They rushed to move the altar back in place, and then they headed over to the door. Just inside, they found another lever, and Coburn pulled it down. The door started to shut them inside.

"You'd better hope that same lever opens the door back up," Garrick said.

"I'm certain it does." Irwin had his glowing yellow vial out again. He adjusted his spectacles and studied a network of gears and chains along the wall inside the room. "We should be fine."

"So what now?" Noraff asked.

Garrick looked around as the door shut. The room contained nothing but a few unlit torches in brackets mounted to the walls and a smooth gray floor. "I'm not sure. There's supposed to be a—"

Something clanked, and the secret door came to a stop, now shut. Then stone scraped against stone once again, and a section of the floor opened, revealing a staircase that spiraled down under the floor.

"That's what I was looking for," Garrick said. He grabbed a torch from one of the brackets. "Everyone get a torch. We're going down."

The staircase descended into a subterranean realm like almost every cave Garrick had ever seen. It opened into a large, cavernous space, full of darkness and the sound of dripping water echoing off the walls.

As they descended deeper into the cave, Irwin used a single drop from a vial of red liquid to light his torch, then the others lit their own torches using Irwin's flames. The light from all five torches illuminated enough of the cave to show them their path.

When they reached the bottom of the stairs, they found a single path to follow, punctuated by stalactites and stalagmites and pillars of minerals and rocks. It perfectly matched the path drawn on Lord Valdis's diagram.

Aside from the near-constant dripping noises, Garrick heard only the shuffling of the group's footsteps and, occasionally, other sounds in the darkness. Scraping. Scurrying. Skittering.

Whatever it was, they weren't alone down there.

Garrick glanced at Coburn, who shook his head with wide eyes. Whatever Coburn could see beyond the reach of the flames, it wasn't good.

Garrick stayed on his guard, constantly turning his head and moving his torch around for a better look at his surroundings, but there wasn't much to see except dozens of holes in the walls and occasionally on the cavern floor beyond the path.

Don't want to know what's in those, Garrick told himself. *Just get past this part.*

As they progressed, orange light filtered into the cavern from the direction they were headed, and it grew brighter with each step, but the cavern narrowed as well. Moments later, they reached a small opening only about the width of two men and just barely tall enough so Garrick didn't have to hunch to get through it.

Garrick stepped through it first, his battle-axe ready for anything, and hot, humid air enveloped him.

Inside, he found a cavern bigger than any they'd encountered thus far. The edge of the stone floor ended in a steep drop-off about fifty feet from the opening he'd just come through. Below, a roiling river of lava provided ample light and explained the oppressive heat in the cavern.

The cavern's jagged ceiling had to be several hundred feet high, and the air wavered and rippled from the molten rock below. In the distance, he saw a steep cliff face like the one Noraff and Coburn had climbed to reach the temple, but shorter.

The river of lava flowed between the edge of the stone floor and the cliff face, but a series of stone pillars jutting out of the lava formed a perilous and erratic path over to it. Garrick couldn't see them all clearly, but those he could see didn't look particularly sturdy.

The others stepped through behind Garrick.

"By the gods," Coburn said from behind Garrick. "This place is magnificent and wretched all at once."

"I'm certainly not cold anymore." Irwin fanned himself with his hands.

"Have we descended all the way into the underworld?" Noraff asked.

Garrick shook his head, still taking in the sight. "No. It's a dungeon of some sort."

"So there's something in here we need to retrieve?" Noraff asked.

Garrick nodded. "Yes. Something very specific."

"And you're still not going to tell us what it is?" Noraff prodded.

"No. You're here to help us get to it and get it out." Garrick glanced between Noraff and Phesnos. "That's all you need concern yourselves with."

"Don't take it personally," Coburn said. "Neither Irwin nor I know what treasure we seek either."

Truth be told, Garrick didn't even know what the treasure was. Lord Valdis had simply told him to bring back everything he could find that looked important. *You will know what I'm after,* Lord Valdis had said. *When you see it, you will know.*

"So what now?" Irwin asked.

Garrick looked at the diagram. It appeared to end at the point where they'd left the old cavern behind, but some notes scrawled along the bottom gave him additional insight. He folded it up and tucked it back into his pack.

"The diagram ends here, but it looks like there are two paths that continue moving forward. At the end of each path is a key, and the diagram says we'll need both keys to access the treasure."

He pointed toward the cliff face beyond the river of lava. "Some of us need to traverse those pillars leading toward that cliff face and climb up there, and the rest of us will take this other path to the right."

The other path continued on solid ground, but it led up an incline, away from the lava river, to a towering archway clearly carved by skilled stoneworkers rather than shaped by nature. Inside loomed more of the same blackness they'd just left.

The implication was clear: risk death by traversing the lava river on those pitiful pillars, or risk death by venturing into the territory of whatever had carved the archway. For Garrick, the choice was easy: he could fight against whatever had carved the archway, but he couldn't fight against a flowing river of lava if he were to fall in.

"Apparently, you expect me to take the lava route," Noraff said.

"You climb. I fight. It makes sense," Garrick said. "And since you insisted on bringing a fifth along, you don't have to do it alone. Phesnos can go with you."

"Why not Coburn again?" Noraff asked. "He's a better climber than Phesnos."

"Because where I'm going, it'll be dark. Coburn can see in the dark. You've got all the light you need in here." Garrick continued, "And don't even think about taking Irwin. He can't make the jumps between the platforms, and he won't be able to climb the wall, either."

"And if I fall into the lava?" Noraff said.

Garrick shrugged. "Then you'll die, and we'll have to make do without you."

A screech split the air, then a black thing the size of a small dog skittered out of the archway on eight legs, right toward the group.

Irwin and Noraff jumped back, and the sight of the thing startled even Garrick. But decades of training made him drop his torch and raise his battle-axe, ready.

The thing pounced at Irwin, the smallest of their group, and he gasped.

Garrick took a huge step and swung his battle-axe down at the thing as it careened through the air. *Crunch.*

The thing shrieked upon impact, and it went down with Garrick's battle-axe to the floor. It lay there, writhing and wriggling with the battle-axe's blade sticking out of its back, unable to advance further. Dark blood oozed out of its wound.

"Absolutely revolting," Coburn said. "What an abomination!"

The thing looked to be part spider, thanks to its eight legs and beady eyes, but the rest of it was something else entirely. Its body was thick and black, covered in an insect-like shell, and it had two pincer-like claws at the front of its body.

"What is it?" Noraff asked.

"It appears to be some sort of hybrid species. Perhaps part scorpion and part spider," Irwin replied.

"So, a 'scorper?'" Garrick said.

"Very apropos," Coburn said. "Vile and repulsive as it is."

The scorper thrashed, threatening to slip free, still screeching.

Garrick motioned to Irwin to get back, and he reached over and picked up his torch, all while keeping his battle-axe firmly embedded in the scorper's back. Then he put the torch's flames under its back end.

The scorper's shrieks intensified as it caught fire, and the flames soon engulfed it. Its legs burned off first, and then its pincers, and it finally stopped squealing as the fire charred its head. Like most bugs, it burned quickly.

For good measure, Garrick left his battle-axe in it until it was reduced to ash. A bit of fire wouldn't hurt his weapon, but the thought of the thing scurrying around while ablaze seemed even worse than when it had emerged from the archway.

Garrick shook the excess ash off of his battle-axe and eyed Noraff. "Still want to go through the arch?"

Noraff scowled, but he said, "Let's go, Phesnos."

Together, they started toward the first of the pillars jutting out of the lava.

"You think they're going to make it?" Irwin asked. "I calculate their chances at about fifty percent."

"After seeing that wretched creature come for us, I'm more concerned about our chances," Coburn said.

"I estimate our odds to be about one in—"

"They'll be fine, and so will we," Garrick cut in. "Come on. We've got a dungeon to raid."

Several steps later, as the archway swallowed them into the darkness within, Garrick stepped on the first of what appeared to be a series of stone tiles stretching beyond the reach of their torchlights.

The architecture didn't stop there. Pillars of carved stone rose to the dungeon's rounded ceiling, but most of their facades had crumbled with age. Unlit torches and candelabra were mounted to the pillars and to the dungeon's walls, and black, iron lamps hung on matching chains from the ceiling at regular intervals.

Someone or something had built this part of the dungeon.

At first, Garrick guessed it was dwarves, but then he saw a large symbol carved into one of the pillars. It was a four-pointed star with an eye in the center. The iris resembled that of a cat's eye, only it lay horizontal instead of vertical.

It was the symbol of the ancient Aletians, the people who brought order to the continent of Aletia and who founded Etrijan and its surrounding countries several millennia earlier. They were people of legend, long extinct and obsolete, but they had left behind a widespread, long-enduring legacy, apparently including this place.

Garrick started to point the symbol out to Coburn and Irwin, but his next step depressed one of the tiles with a *click*.

He pulled his foot back, wary of what he'd just done. Had he sprung some sort of trap? Had he alerted something within the dungeon?

The torches, candelabras, and hanging lamps sparked to life with violet fire, casting a warm, yet haunting glow into the space.

"What did you do?" Coburn hissed.

Before Garrick could answer, a loud rumble sounded behind them. They whirled back for a look in time to see a massive stone slab rising from the ground. It covered the archway completely and trapped them inside.

"Now what?" Irwin asked.

"It changes nothing," Garrick said. "We have to keep moving forward anyway."

They turned toward the dungeon's tiled path once again, and in the violet light, they saw that it rose at a steady incline toward another archway. The room on the other side of that second archway glowed with faint teal light.

But ahead of the archway, not twenty feet ahead of them, stood a lone figure with a curved, chipped sword in its hand.

It wore an iron helmet over what remained of its head, which amounted to a gray-white skull with decayed flesh clinging to its cheekbones and chin. On its chest, the upper half of a torn metal breastplate exposed its rib bones underneath. It had one metal gauntlet on its non-sword hand and one metal shin guard over its bony left leg but no other armor to speak of.

Overall, it was far more bone and tendons than flesh, yet it stood there as if it had the strength and musculature of a fully intact warrior.

"What sorcery is this?" Coburn asked.

"It's a skulk," Garrick replied. "A fell being. Once a normal human or elf or whatever, but something stole its essence and reanimated it with dark magic."

The skulk raised its sword and opened its mouth as if to loose a battle cry, but with no throat, only a low howl of rushing wind sounded throughout the cavern.

The crackle of smashing rocks reverberated as random floor tiles fractured and shattered. A dozen more skulks crawled up from the fresh holes in the floor, their bones and sporadic armor clacking on the stone tiles.

Garrick glanced behind them. The slab still covered the archway door, but more importantly, four skulks had climbed out of the tiles behind them as well. A bulbous, black scorper clung to the face of one of the skulks, gnawing on what little flesh remained around its eye sockets, but the skulk didn't seem to notice.

"Disgusting." Coburn tossed his torch to the floor and unsheathed his other knife with his free hand.

Garrick had never encountered skulks before; he'd only heard about them in the myths his tribesmen had told around the campfire when he was a child. To hear the men talk about them, Garrick gathered that cutting them down was a viable option, so that's what he would do.

"How do we kill them?" Irwin fidgeted with his bag, which he now wore on the front of his body for easier access to his concoctions.

"However you can," Garrick replied.

"Does that include using the black vial?" Irwin rummaged through his pack.

"No. Too dangerous. Figure something else out," Garrick said.

Irwin grumbled something, but the skulks started charging toward them, so Garrick couldn't hear what it was.

As the skulks drew closer, Garrick tightened his grip on his battle-axe.

Then he smiled.

CHAPTER FOUR

This was what Garrick lived for: facing an onslaught of opponents all at once, with plenty of room to do his work. Their old, rusted weapons couldn't harm him, and he didn't have to hold back. He could loose the most savage parts of himself and go berserk.

And that's exactly what he did.

The nearest skulk went down from a vicious hack that snapped its spine. The next one caught an axe head to its jaw, caving in the entire right side of its face. The third slammed face-first into the floor tiles, courtesy of a mighty overhead blow from Garrick's battle-axe.

Their weapons *pinged* off of his arms and legs as he tore through them, batting them aside as if they were flies pestering him. He severed limbs, shattered bones, and crushed skulls to dust under his heels. They didn't stand a chance against him.

But Coburn and Irwin were a different story. Even amid his berserking, Garrick often stole glances back at them to make sure they could handle whatever foes managed to avoid his rampage.

They had learned early on in working with Garrick to stay away once he got going, but the drawback was that he often left them alone, exposed, to face foes on their own. As the largest, most physically capable member of their mercenary trio, Garrick felt responsible for their wellbeing.

Coburn deftly avoided the skulks' clumsy attacks, slipping under blows and dodging others. Whenever the opportunity to strike back presented itself, he drove his knives into them wherever they could get a decent bite.

The problem was, his knives did next to nothing to harm the skulks. They just weren't large enough, heavy enough weapons, so Coburn hadn't felled a single one.

Irwin, on the other hand, was handling the skulks surprisingly well. He'd already taken out several of them with his vials. Two light-blue vials had frozen a pair of skulks solid and snagged the left leg of a third in ice. Then he sheared through the heads, armor, and torsos of three others with an acid solution from his green vials.

Then Irwin jammed a glowing yellow vial into the gaping mouth of another skulk. As Irwin dove away, the skulk's jaw clamped shut on the vial.

It burst with a loud *pop* and a brilliant flash of light that blew the skulk's head apart, showering the area with skull fragments. The rest of the skulk collapsed into a heap of bones, and the bones disintegrated into powder.

Garrick backhanded the face of one skulk so hard that its head spun all the way around with a series of snaps, but it stayed upright and kept coming for him. He bashed its face in with the pommel of his battle-axe, and its skull crunched inward. It dropped to the floor in a pile of dust.

"I can't believe Irwin is killing more of these fiends than I," Coburn shouted over the fracas.

He sheathed his knives and scrambled over to a bony arm scraping its way along the floor with a sword curled in its fingers. Coburn stomped on its wrist and jerked the sword from its fingers, taking a couple of them off in the process. He stomped on the hand once more for good measure, then he blocked a haphazard slice from another skulk.

With his new weapon in hand, Coburn engaged the remaining skulks near Irwin, who continued lobbing vials at his opponents with excellent precision. Meanwhile, Garrick felled several more skulks with catastrophic blows that left them either dead, destroyed, or both.

As they battled the few remaining skulks, Garrick turned his attention toward the exit. That's when he noticed dozens of large, black dots advancing toward them from the ceiling and the walls. The dots sharpened into focus as they drew closer, forming into a skittering mass of scorpers.

Garrick cursed. He drove his shoulder into a skulk and sent it flying into one of the pillars, and its bones and armor clanked against the stone. He finished it off with a battle-axe strike to its head, and it reduced to dust.

The scorpers swarmed toward him, and he smacked them aside with arcing swipes of his battle-axe, relying more on the flat sides than on the blades. The scorpers screeched and flailed through the air and crunched against the walls and the pillars, but they kept coming.

At some point, Garrick resorted to stomping on them. A well-timed, one-footed stomp on their heads usually did the trick, but some of the time they skidded out from under him, avoiding death. So Garrick started jumping and crushing them with both feet, sending black innards and dark blood squirting out their sides—just like any other insects.

But it wasn't enough. Their pincers found his boots, and their wiry legs propelled them up his shins. He backhanded them off of his legs and even one on his torso, and he hopped back to try to put space between him and them. Garrick didn't know if they were venomous or just ravenous, but he didn't care to find out.

"Irwin," Garrick called. "We need fire over here."

"I'm kind of busy, Garrick," Irwin shouted back. A bright light flashed behind

Garrick, accompanied by a loud *pop*, and then a jawbone landed on the floor in front of Garrick. It dissolved into dust before it could bounce a second time.

Garrick abandoned the idea of swatting the scorpers back again and retreated toward Irwin and Coburn, who only had two more skulks to deal with. If Garrick didn't do something, the scorpers would overrun them. If Irwin didn't set them on fire, they'd never get out of this room alive.

So Garrick slammed his battle-axe into the nearest skulk's head, shattering its skull into tiny pieces. Then he grabbed the other one by the vertebrae in its neck, lifted it off its feet, and hurled it like a ragdoll toward the encroaching scorpers.

It served to block their progress temporarily as they swarmed it and started cleaning the remaining flesh from its bones, but plenty of them continued to advance. An ocean of scorpers wriggled between Garrick, Irwin, Coburn, and the way out.

"Fire, please?" Garrick asked.

Irwin already had the red vial in his hand. He calmly said, "Move, please."

Then he hurled the red vial over the front lines of scorpers and into the middle of their ranks.

At first, Garrick wondered why Irwin hadn't aimed for the front of the scorpers, but when the vial shattered, Irwin's plan made perfect sense. Brilliant red flames erupted from the vial, completely incinerating the scorpers closest to the inferno and igniting all those in close proximity.

The fire seared through the scorper ranks from the center outward, and blazing scorpers skittered around in a shrill, screeching frenzy, setting each other ablaze. Gradually, the flames scorched a path through the scorpers wide enough for Garrick, Irwin, and Coburn to run through.

"Hurry!" Garrick shouted.

They did. As the trio ran, Garrick saw the last skulk, its bones charred black from the flames, sit up in their path. So Garrick timed his steps and drove a stunning kick into the bottom of the skulk's chin. Its head snapped off of its neck and launched across the room until it smacked against the far wall and exploded into a cloud of dust and ash.

Scorpers all around them shrieked and burned, and the ones not on fire shuffled toward them, but they couldn't catch up. Garrick made it through the second archway first, followed by Coburn and then Irwin.

As soon as all three of them set foot in the room with the teal light, a new slab of rock started to rise from the stone floor. A few scorpers squelched through before the slab could totally cover the archway, and the stone pulverized a few more as it shut, but Garrick squashed the survivors right away.

They'd made it.

"That wasn't so hard, was it?" Garrick asked.

Irwin and Coburn glowered at him.

"Maybe not for you," Coburn replied. "I was virtually useless in there."

"I wasn't." Irwin grinned.

Garrick patted his shoulder. He was truly proud of Irwin. He'd come a long way in the last year or so they'd been working together. "You performed excellently."

Irwin's grin widened. "Thanks. It's just science, you know? Applied force, leveraging elemental advantages, pressure from—"

"Yes, yes." Coburn tossed the skulk's old sword aside. "We understand how much smarter you are than either of us. Yet we have an enterprise to complete, and we've no idea how many rooms this godforsaken place holds. Shall we proceed?"

Garrick looked around. The cavern looked similar to the one they'd just left, down to the pillars and the path and the height of the ceiling, but it differed wildly in that the path descended down into a pool of standing water that glowed with a pacifying teal light.

Though similar torches were mounted on the pillars and comparable lamps hung from the ceiling, none of them burned at all. The pool of water gave off the only light in the room. Across the pool, the next archway beckoned them to enter, and like the first one, no light shone from inside.

"Who's up for a swim?" Coburn rubbed his hands together. "Truth be told, I don't like the look of this one bit. Who puts a lake inside a room?"

"An irradiated lake, at that," Irwin added.

"There's nothing good in that water," Garrick said. "That, I guarantee."

"And yet we must traverse the water in order to conquer this room," Coburn said. "So tie your blue hair back, and let's wade in."

Garrick frowned. His dark blue hair was another side effect of the troll blood in his lineage, and he couldn't do anything about it but wear hoods or cut it short, and he preferred longer hair. In certain lighting, it looked black, but most of the time it was clearly and obviously blue to everyone who saw it.

"Sorry," Coburn said. "I forgot you don't appreciate mentions of your hair."

"Forget it," Garrick said. "I'm more concerned about that water."

The water itself wouldn't hurt Garrick, but he could certainly drown. At over 400 pounds and wielding a heavy battle-axe, he'd sink far easier than he could swim.

"Spread out. Look for a boat or a raft or something we can use to get across." Garrick added, "And be alert. There could be more of those scorpers or something even worse in here that we don't know about yet."

The search didn't last long, and it turned up nothing of use. Though roughly the same size as the room they'd just left, most of it was submerged, leaving very little surface area for stashing boats.

"I suppose we're swimming after all, then," Coburn said.

"Lead the way." Garrick motioned toward the pool.

Coburn stepped into the water, the first to disturb its serene surface. The water rippled with each of his movements, and the ripples seemed to extend throughout the entirety of the pool, interrupted only by the pillars protruding from the water.

"Feel any different?" Irwin asked.

Coburn, now five feet ahead and knee-deep, shook his head. "It is a comfortable temperature, despite its subterranean location. I don't believe there is any magic influence in the water. Or at least, if there is, I don't seem to be affected by it."

"Perhaps the light is some sort of natural luminescence, then." Irwin nudged Garrick. "See? Science."

Garrick just nodded. "You're next in."

Irwin gulped, removed his spectacles, and tucked them into his pack. Then he stepped one foot into the water. Then the other.

Before long, all three of them had waded into the pool. To Garrick's dismay, Coburn and Irwin had to start swimming about twenty feet in. He hoped that with his additional height, he'd be able to touch the bottom, but instead, when the water reached the top of his shoulders, his foot slipped off a steep drop-off.

Surprised, he scrambled to keep his head above the water, but it rushed up to meet him all the way to his nose. He sputtered and spat and kicked his legs furiously until he found the edge of the drop off again.

Stability. Sure footing. It had only been an hour or two since the last time he'd been without them—thanks to the temple's exterior wall—but he'd already begun to take them for granted. The drop-off had humbled him yet again.

"You alright?" Irwin called back, looking at Garrick while treading water.

"Fine. I just wish you'd told me about the drop-off."

"What drop-off?" Coburn asked from beyond Irwin.

"The one I just—" Garrick stopped. He was at least a foot taller than Coburn and even taller compared to Irwin. They probably hadn't even had a chance to find the drop-off point because of their heights. "Never mind."

Garrick adjusted his footing, strapped his battle-axe to his back, and pushed off the edge into the water. He tried to swim with steady, even strokes, but once he started struggling to keep his head above the water, he abandoned the idea. Between his own body weight and the battle-axe on his back, he had to change his approach.

He resorted to frantic dog-paddling. He knew it would use more energy and that it would take him longer to get across the pool, but swimming with better form and ultimately drowning wasn't a viable alternative.

As he swam, Garrick tried to take in his surroundings, particularly in the water but also the walls and ceiling. If something were to attack them right now, they'd have a far rougher time trying to fight back. With how this swim was going, Garrick wasn't sure he could even fight back at all.

By the time they reached the halfway point, Garrick was exhausted. He swam over to one of the pillars and grabbed the lip of one of the carvings with his fingers. It reminded him of trying to find grips in the temple's exterior wall—his fingers were too big and the carved rock offered him little by way of true holds, but it gave his arms and legs a much-needed respite.

"I'm taking a break," he said to Irwin and Coburn.

They each took up spots at pillars of their own—Coburn at the pillar ahead of Garrick's, and Irwin at the pillar across from Garrick's.

"Perhaps you should swim from pillar to pillar and take breaks in between," Coburn suggested.

Normally Garrick would've rejected such advice. The last thing he wanted was to be seen as weak, but here, in this dungeon with his closest friends, he had to be honest with himself.

"I think I will," he said. "I'm not built for swimming."

"No, you're not," Irwin agreed. "Some of the things I've seen you do defy the natural order of things, so it's understandable and even expected that you'd be deficient in other areas of your life, particularly buoyancy and—"

Something yanked Irwin under the teal water with a splash.

"Irwin!" Garrick and Coburn shouted.

Coburn launched away from his pillar and dug into the water, splashing as he glided toward Irwin.

Almost everything within Garrick urged him to join Coburn in trying to save Irwin, but what good would he do? He could barely keep himself afloat. So he stayed put, hoping Coburn could handle whatever had happened on his own.

A series of frenetic splashes and gasps marked Irwin's desperation to stay above the water, but he slipped under the surface again before Coburn could reach him.

"Irwin!" Garrick shouted again. "Coburn, is there something down there?"

"I'm not sure," Coburn called back. "It's... murky. Hazy. Despite the light, I'm having a hard time seeing anything. I'm going to dive down and see if—"

Coburn jerked under the water as well, splashing as he went down.

"Coburn? No!" Garrick shouted and cursed.

Coburn resurfaced and inhaled a ragged breath, but the thing snatched him under the water again, silencing him.

Garrick cursed again. He released his grip on the pillar with his right hand but still held it with his left, and he took hold of his battle-axe. What good it would do him in the water against whatever unknown foe he was about to face, he didn't know. Probably none whatsoever, but holding it made him feel less worthless.

He held his position, perfectly still, watching the ripples from Coburn's splashes echo past him and scanning the water. He saw nothing. The water had calmed back to the perfect teal tranquility he'd seen when they'd first entered the room.

Then something latched onto his foot and hauled him down hard.

Garrick's faulty grip on the pillar slipped, and he went under the water with only half a breath in his lungs. He swung the battle-axe toward his feet, hoping to hit whatever had grabbed him, but he hit nothing solid.

As he started to swing again, the thing jerked him deeper, and the battle-axe squirted out of his hands and disappeared into the water below.

In that moment, all Garrick could think was that he should've taken the lava path instead.

Then he saw it. A gaping mouth rose up at him, translucent and glowing bright teal. A vivid orange tongue waggled at him as the mouth rose to meet his body.

As Garrick clawed at the water, toward the surface, the mouth enveloped his legs. It didn't hurt—it just felt rubbery, but the thing's strength was undeniable.

Garrick couldn't escape. He was going to die.

The thing's mouth closed over his torso, and then over his arms and head. Then it swallowed him whole.

CHAPTER FIVE

G arrick dropped into a pit, and something bony, squishy, and fleshy softened his fall. The space constricted around him, and he grunted, unable to move.

Yet somehow he could still breathe. The air inside the creature's belly was foul and putrid, but at least Garrick wasn't drowning anymore.

He grunted again, and something below him grunted in response. He recognized the voice.

"Coburn?" Garrick managed.

"Garrick?" It was Coburn.

"What's happening?" Garrick asked. He could hardly move. The space in the creature's belly continued to tighten, hindering his limbs.

"We've been consumed," Coburn said. "Irwin is in here, too, beneath me."

"Hello?" came Irwin's muffled voice.

"The... air is toxic," Coburn said. "I'm... dizzy. Losing vision."

Garrick realized he could still see the water around him. He knew it was what he was seeing because he could make out the dark, mottled shapes of the room's stone pillars.

And if he could still see the pillars, maybe they could get out.

A wave of dizziness hit him as well, and spots filled his vision. Whatever gases were in the creature's belly, they weren't breathable for long.

"Coburn, knives," Garrick uttered.

"Can't reach. No strength. You?"

Garrick's hands were being sucked in totally opposite directions from Coburn, and it was a strong pull. Maybe too strong. "I'll try."

Strength was the one thing Garrick could always count on. He'd always had it, and he always would. He could lift heavier things and inflict more damage with his body than any human or human-hybrid he'd ever met. So now he would call upon his strength once more, hoping it could save him.

Garrick marshaled all of his waning energy and pulled his arms toward him. The creature's stomach resisted, pulling back, but Garrick strained harder, and his hands slipped back to him with a dull *thump*.

The stomach immediately closed in on the space where Garrick's arms had been, but Garrick kept moving. He dug his fingers into the stomach lining, inching down toward Coburn. They fished for Coburn's body and found his clothes. They crawled through folds of wet fabric until they found the solid hilt of his knife.

All the while, the stomach constricted further, as if aware of Garrick's plans. But he resisted and tried not to breathe the toxic air.

He grasped the knife and pulled his hand away from Coburn, and he turned the knife toward the creature's stomach lining. Its sharp point dug in easily, and Garrick drew it in a straight line toward his own face.

The tension in the stomach tightened, quivered, and then released. Garrick kept cutting. Teal water splashed Garrick's face and chest, and he realized he'd cut straight through to the pool itself. Still dazed from the gases in the creature's gut, Garrick scrambled for the surface, still holding Coburn's knife in a death-grip.

His head broke through the water, and he gasped, never more grateful for the musty dungeon air. The dizziness started to fade immediately, and he felt strength returning to his body.

Coburn surfaced next, and Irwin's head popped above the surface last. They made their way back to the pillars and held on.

"What in the third hell was that?" Garrick asked.

Irwin shook his head. "Nothing I've ever seen before. It appeared to be some sort of membranous creature—carnivorous and quite hungry. When it swallowed you, suddenly I could see through its skin very clearly."

"I think the only reason we survived was because it ate all three of us," Coburn said. "When it devoured you, you added too much strain to its form, and thus we could then see a way out and cut through it."

"I just want to know if it's dead or not," Garrick said.

"Hard to say for sure," Coburn said.

"Light in the pool has started to fade. Maybe the creature was the source of the light?" Irwin suggested.

"I doubt it will continue to pursue us, though," Coburn continued. "Not with a wound the likes of what you just inflicted upon it."

Coburn's words reminded Garrick that he was still holding the knife. He extended it. "Here. You may not have done much in the last room, but this little knife just saved all of us."

"Thank you." Coburn accepted it. "Where's your axe?"

Garrick shook his head, infuriated. He'd loved that battle-axe. "At the bottom. I dropped it when it grabbed me."

"Hold firm," Coburn said. "The light is unquestionably fading, but there should still be enough..."

He inhaled a deep breath and dove under the water, knife in hand.

"Is he crazy?" Garrick asked. "That thing is still down there!"

"I think you killed it," Irwin said. "The light is almost out."

"How could that thing give off enough light to illuminate the whole pool?" Garrick blinked at Irwin.

"I don't know. And right now I don't care. I just want to get out of this room."

A moment later, Coburn emerged from the water and extended a familiar handle toward Garrick. "Allow me to return the favor."

Garrick pulled his battle-axe out of the water and held it up. It felt good to have it in his hands again. It felt right. Even though he'd only been apart from it for a few minutes, the thought of permanent separation had devastated him.

But no more. He had it back now.

"I'm done soaking. Let's go." Garrick affixed the battle-axe to his back again and started to swim.

They managed to get out of the pool within ten more minutes, thanks to Garrick implementing Coburn's strategy of swimming from pillar to pillar and resting as needed. By the time they were out, the pool's light had faded to nothing, and the room had gone dark.

Irwin pulled one of his glowing yellow vials from his pack and used it to light the space. They wrung out their wet clothes and checked their inventories to make sure nothing had gotten lost or damaged thus far. Satisfied, they re-dressed and headed into the next room.

As before, a slab rose from the floor behind them, sealing off the darkened pool and whatever remained of the creature they'd slain. But that's where the similarities to the previous two rooms ended.

Where the previous two rooms were rectangular in shape and featured pillars, hanging lamps, and mounted torches, this room was a circle with no pillars and no light besides Irwin's yellow vial. The ceiling was considerably lower, and the floor was smooth, black obsidian instead of tile.

Black-and-white marbled stone made up the interior walls. Halfway up each wall, a section of the stone was cut out all the way around, replaced by a ring of black metal. There was no other door that Garrick could see aside from the one they'd entered through, but a dark, circular opening in the center of the ceiling might've been another way out.

A huge block of stone lay directly under the opening in the ceiling. As they advanced, the block sharpened into a sarcophagus of some sort. Huge etchings of the ancient Aletians' symbol adorned its sides and its top.

"No light in here," Irwin said. "What are we supposed to do?"

"Perhaps there's a switch somewhere, like in the first room," Garrick suggested. "Start looking. Do you have more of those yellow vials?"

Irwin passed one to each of them, and they split up to comb the room for answers.

After several minutes of fruitless searching, Garrick brought them back together.

"I don't know what to tell you," he said. "The only thing in here is this sarcophagus."

"Perhaps we should attempt to unearth its inhabitant in search of answers?" Coburn suggested. "If indeed an ancient Aletian resides within, perhaps it holds the key to our escape, whether literal or figurative."

"I'm not a fan of disturbing the dead, but if we don't do something, we'll just end up joining their ranks," Irwin added.

"Hold this, and step back." Garrick handed his vial back to Irwin. He stood at the end of the sarcophagus and curled his fingers under the lip of the lid. He straightened his back, crouched down, and lifted.

The stone scraped, and Garrick's muscles strained. The lid was heavy—it probably weighed a little more than the granite altar they'd moved in the temple—but he was making progress.

As he lifted, Garrick walked the lid to the side, twisting it along the edges of the sarcophagus to create enough of an opening to look inside. If he tried to take the lid all the way off, it weighed enough that he'd never manage to get it back in place again.

With some more pushing and positioning, he managed to get the lid turned perpendicular to the sarcophagus at one end. He motioned for light, and Irwin scampered over with a vial in-hand. Together, they leaned over the sarcophagus on one side, and Coburn leaned over the other.

The yellow light shined on a hulking corpse not swaddled with burial dressings, but decay had certainly taken its toll on its body. When it had been alive, it had probably rivaled Garrick for size—or perhaps it was even larger. Based on how Garrick had positioned the lid, they couldn't see the corpse's head, but they could see from the middle of its chest down to its feet.

Black skin and flesh covered portions of the body, but plenty of bone showed through the remains of its tattered clothes. A large, long-handled hammer lay next to the body with its head near the feet which were clad in leather boots, still surprisingly intact, given the state of the rest of the corpse.

But by far, the corpse's most striking feature was the golden key embedded in its chest.

The skin and flesh had worn away around its ribcage, and gold glinted up at them in the yellow light from the vial. The key was easily as long as Irwin's head and neck combined, and it hung down just below the sternum.

"Well, I'd say we've discovered our way out, one way or another," Coburn said. "I don't surmise he has any further use for it. Shall I...?"

Garrick nodded. "By all means."

"Hold the light closer, if you would, please."

Irwin complied, and Coburn reached into the sarcophagus.

As Coburn's fingers touched the golden key, the corpse's dead hand latched onto his wrist.

"What the—" Coburn started. He managed to jerk his hand free, but the corpse kept moving.

They all backed away from the sarcophagus, and Garrick raised his battle-axe.

"What did you do?" he snapped at Coburn.

"You were watching the whole time," Coburn fired back. "The key is bewitched. Accursed..."

"Booby-trapped," Irwin finished for him.

The bones in the sarcophagus rattled against the inside of the stone, louder and louder, more and more violently. Then a pair of decayed hands reached up and pushed on the edge of the lid. Then another pair joined them.

Garrick couldn't believe his eyes. Whatever the thing in there was, it had four arms instead of two. It must've been lying atop its other arms; otherwise Garrick would've seen them when they found the key.

The arms hefted the lid off the sarcophagus with ease, and the lid skidded off the top and smashed to pieces on the stone floor. Instead of sitting upright and climbing out, the thing demolished one of the sarcophagus's stone walls with its legs and arms, and then it rose to its full height with its hammer in two of its four hands.

Garrick studied every inch of it, trying to identify potential weaknesses. Aside from possibly the key in its chest, he couldn't readily identify a single one.

But what he could identify was what the thing was—sort of. Aside from being a decayed, undead corpse with four arms, it also had two heads. And both of them were bulls' heads, each with two long horns jutting out from their sides.

"What in the name of the gods is that?" Coburn asked.

"A minotaur?" Irwin offered. "A bull's head on a man's body, but with two heads?"

"So... a duotaur?" Garrick suggested.

Coburn and Irwin both nodded.

All around them, the black metal ring set into the walls ignited with brilliant yellow-orange flames, providing ample light for the room. The duotaur's heads barked a dissonant moo-grunt, and its boots burst apart, revealing cloven hoofs for feet and the reverse-jointed legs typical of livestock.

The golden key gleamed in its chest.

"How do we kill it?" Coburn asked.

"Only one way to find out," Garrick said.

"I really hope this is the last room," Irwin muttered. "Do we use the black vial?"

Against a foe like this, the black vial might've made sense, but Garrick shook his head. "It might damage the key. We can't risk it. We need it to access the treasure."

The duotaur twirled its hammer between its four arms in a brilliant display of proficiency, transferring it from hand to hand as if it weighed nothing. But it had to weigh more than Garrick's battle-axe—mostly because the duotaur stood a solid three inches taller than him, not including its horns.

Wielding that kind of weapon and moving the sarcophagus slab as easily as the duotaur had meant it was stronger than Garrick. And the way it moved the hammer suggested it could be a better fighter, too.

If Garrick couldn't rely on his strength and his berserker rage, he might have to find a way to be quicker than the duotaur—as odd as that sounded to him. Coburn and Irwin would move faster than the duotaur for sure, but Garrick doubted he'd be fast enough to make a difference.

Worse still, that hammer could deal significant damage to Garrick in ways that conventional weapons couldn't. His skin could deflect cuts and resist stabs from sharp objects, but the crushing force of a hammer could reduce his bones to powder. His enhanced healing abilities could only repair so much.

Garrick had to err on the side of caution; he had to fight smart, especially since he had to do the majority of the fighting himself.

"I'll take the brunt of his fury." Garrick removed his pack from his back and tossed it aside. "Don't let him get close to you. Just support me from the sides as you can."

Coburn and Irwin nodded, and Garrick motioned the duotaur forward.

But the duotaur charged toward Coburn and Irwin first, and they dove out of its path. It slowed to a halt, then it pivoted on its hooves and charged again, this time toward Garrick.

He moved aside as well, and the duotaur barreled past him, but it lashed its hammer at him in a wicked backhanded swing as it passed him by. He barely managed to get his battle-axe up in time to deflect the blow. It sent painful quivers ratcheting up into Garrick's arms and sent him staggering back a step.

Imagine if he'd hit you instead, Garrick told himself. *Can't let that happen.*

When the duotaur turned back, Garrick got his first clear look at its heads in the light from the fires encircling them.

Like the rest of the duotaur's body, decay marred its faces. One of the heads had only one eye and was missing half of the facial tissue by its mouth, revealing twin rows of plaque-rimmed teeth. Strips of blackened flesh dangled from its chin and jawline along with its hair.

The other head was missing a chunk of skin just to the left of the center of its forehead, and its absence spread over the base of its horn. In lieu of a cow's meaty nose, pointed nasal cavity bones jutted out from a tear in the center of its face.

Its appearance didn't bother Garrick for what it was. What bothered him was that some practitioner of dark magic had seen fit to steal the essence of two healthy minotaurs only to then merge them into an even more freakish monstrosity—all for the sake of guarding whatever treasure lay within this dungeon.

It twisted Garrick's stomach that people in Aletia had not only the will to perform such heinous acts but also the capability to carry them out. Even so, he chided himself for his thoughts. Lord Valdis was a practitioner of dark magic as well. Perhaps he was being overly judgmental.

His thoughts on the ethics of duotaurs and dark magic dissipated as the beast charged again. This time, Garrick seized the opportunity to deal a blow of his own. As the duotaur blasted toward him, Garrick ducked low and swung his battle-axe hard at the duotaur's stampeding hooves and ankles. If he could disable it, then—

CLANG.

The hammer's head met his battle-axe mid-swing, then a heavy pain lit up the side of Garrick's face.

Garrick fell to his side, stunned, as the duotaur's charge slowed to a halt. Then it began to turn around.

What had happened? The hammer head had blocked Garrick's battle-axe—had the duotaur hit him with the hammer's pommel?

His tongue felt something hard inside his mouth, followed by the tangy, metallic taste of copper. Garrick spat a globule of red blood into his hand along with a tooth. *His* tooth. His tongue searched his top row of teeth and found an open space where his first molar had been not five seconds earlier.

Garrick tossed the tooth aside. He'd regrow another one in a few weeks, but the duotaur would pay for it.

The familiar rush of fury heated Garrick's chest, and he shifted his grip on his battle-axe. Maybe a rage-fueled attack was in order after all.

Once the duotaur had reset and prepared to charge, a red vial smacked into the side of his leftmost head and shattered. It kindled into fire and ignited the duotaur's left head, left shoulders, left arms, chest, and back with blazing fire.

The duotaur groaned and writhed, but it didn't lose its balance or stumble. The fire spread to its right head, but by then, three of its four arms had started patting the flames out with quick smacks, leaving singed hair and charred flesh behind.

With its heads smoking and more of its skin gone thanks to Irwin's vial, the duotaur looked even worse than when it had first set upon them. Interestingly enough, though, Garrick caught a whiff of what smelled like steak searing over open flames, and his stomach responded with a low growl.

Later. When this was all over, he'd treat himself to a fine meal of steak, potatoes, and ale. But for now, he had an undead duotaur to take down.

Before the duotaur could charge again, Garrick rushed toward it with his battle-axe raised high. He swung it hard at the duotaur's midsection, a blow that would've cleaved any human in half.

But the duotaur effortlessly blocked the attack with the shaft of his hammer and lashed two of his fists at Garrick's head. Garrick ducked under the punches and backed up, ready to swing his battle-axe again, but he had no time.

Instead, Garrick sidestepped a devastating overhead blow that fractured the obsidian floor, and he swung his battle-axe again. Unable to block Garrick's attack, the duotaur stepped back, and Garrick's swing missed it entirely.

But Garrick was used to foes dodging his vicious swings, and he'd adapted his fighting style over the years accordingly. He used his momentum to spin all the way around, and he drove the battle-axe even harder and faster at the duotaur.

CLANG.

The hammer completely stopped Garrick's momentum yet again, sending painful tremors through his hands once more, but this time, Garrick was ready for the block. He stepped in closer to the duotaur and slammed the pommel of his battle-axe into the duotaur's exposed nasal bones with a loud *crack.*

The duotaur's head snapped back, but its other head remained unfazed. Two of its arms grabbed Garrick by his shoulders, and a third grabbed ahold of the shaft of his battle-axe. They pulled on him hard, so Garrick adjusted and drove his knee into the duotaur's pelvis.

Normally, he would've aimed for the duotaur's gut, but it had no flesh or organs under its ribs. Its pelvis rocked backward, and Garrick used the moment to try to wrench free from its grasp. But the duotaur refused to let go.

Garrick tried to knee it again, but as he did, the duotaur swept Garrick's foot out from underneath him. He landed hard on the obsidian floor with the duotaur hunched over him. Neither of them released their grasps on the battle-axe, but the duotaur's hammer rose from the side for another strike.

If Garrick didn't let go, the hammer would bash his face in. If he did let go, he'd have no weapon to fight with.

But being dead meant he couldn't fight at all. He needed to let go.

A light blue vial smacked into the duotaur's side, and an eruption of ice encased the duotaur's shoulders, holding its arms—and the hammer—in place. Another timely throw from Irwin.

The duotaur groaned, and Garrick yanked his battle-axe free from its grasp. He wriggled away along his back, then he took a swing at its ankles.

The duotaur hopped over the swipe, and when it landed, it hunched over, shuddered, and then straightened its back fast and hard. The ice on its shoulders shattered, freeing its arms once again.

Garrick cursed under his breath and yelled, "Hit it again!"

"I'm out of ice!" Irwin called back.

The duotaur raised its hammer over its head and brought it down at Garrick, who hadn't had time to get up from the floor. He shifted to the side, and the hammer cracked the floor once again.

The duotaur reared back for another blow, and Garrick jerked to the other side. The hammer shattered the stones just to the left of Garrick's head, temporarily deafening his left ear.

He twisted his hips to the left and kicked the hammer's shaft as hard as he could, hoping to pry it free from the duotaur's hands. Instead, the duotaur maintained his grip but lurched forward, catching himself with his left leg.

Another red vial hit the duotaur's body, this time against his back. It burst into flames, and the duotaur unleashed another low groan.

Garrick abandoned his battle-axe, sat up, and grabbed the shaft of the hammer with both hands. He clung to it and wrenched it down toward the floor. To his surprise, the duotaur released its grip on it.

As the duotaur dropped to its back and started scraping the fire out against the floor, Garrick rose to his full height with the hammer in his hands. It weighed a lot more than his battle-axe, and fatigue from the fight had settled into his muscles, but just one good swing would cave in one of the duotaur's skulls.

So Garrick hefted it over his head in a wide arc and whipped it down at the duotaur. The hammer smashed the duotaur's left head into an unrecognizable mass of bone and decayed flesh, and its other head roared in response.

One of its hands hooked behind Garrick's heel and yanked, taking him to the ground. He released his grip on the hammer, slapped the floor with his palms as he hit, and kept his chin tucked so as not to bash his head into the hard stone. He tried to turn toward the duotaur, but it rolled on top of him too quickly.

Garrick grunted both at the duotaur's weight and at the sight of its pulverized head lolling back and forth while it pressed him down. It got all the way on top of him and glowered down at him with one cloudy eye and one gaping eye socket.

Then it straightened and methodically punched all four of its arms at Garrick's body and at his head, which he tried to protect with his forearms.

The blows kept coming, kept pummeling him. He'd taken plenty of punishment his entire life, especially from his father as a child, but never anything like this. And no matter how much Garrick writhed and strained and tried to buck the duotaur off, he couldn't change his position or counter any of its punches.

Coburn leaped onto its back and plunged his knife into the duotaur's neck. But the duotaur just kept punching Garrick with three of his arms, grabbed Coburn's leg with the fourth arm, and tossed him aside. He rolled to a stop near Irwin.

"I'm going to use the black vial!" Irwin shouted from somewhere in the distance.

"Are you insane?" Coburn yelled.

Garrick's instinct was to yell for Irwin to stop. He knew what the black vial would do, but at this point, Garrick had no better options. Either the duotaur would beat him to death, or the black vial would kill them both. And if it destroyed the key, so be it. At least this abomination would be gone, too.

"Do it!" Garrick shouted between punches.

His arms and ribs ached from the repeated strikes, and despite Garrick's guard, the duotaur had delivered several stunning blows to his face. It hurt, but the pain wasn't the worst part—it was knowing that eventually, the duotaur would break through his guard entirely and land something too devastating, and that would be the end. With no guard, the duotaur would kill him quickly.

Amid the pummeling, Garrick glanced over at Irwin and Coburn.

With the black vial in his left hand and a red vial in his right, Irwin started forward, but Coburn grabbed his shoulder to stop him.

"Give it to me," Coburn demanded. "And hit it again. I need a distraction."

Irwin handed both vials to him and dug in his pack again. He removed one of the glowing yellow vials and raised it to throw it. "Ready?"

"Now!" Coburn yelled as he lit the fuse on the black vial with a drop from the red vial. It sparked to life and spiraled down toward the vial's cork stopper.

Irwin hurled the yellow vial at the duotaur's head.

Garrick clenched his eyes shut and covered his head with his forearms, pointing his elbows up at the duotaur.

Pop.

The duotaur groaned and stopped punching Garrick.

Even with Garrick's eyes closed and his arms over his face, the flash of light still scarred his vision. But when he opened his eyes, he still saw Coburn bury the black vial in the duotaur's empty eye socket.

CHAPTER SIX

No time. Garrick had to do something now, or else...

As the fuse burned down to about two inches from the cork, Coburn scrambled away and took cover behind the remains of the sarcophagus with Irwin.

With the duotaur still distracted, Garrick braced his hands against the duotaur's knee and shoved himself out from under its weight. Then he planted his feet in the duotaur's chest and kicked hard.

The duotaur launched backward, and as it did, its other head burst apart in an explosion of brilliant purple light that shook the entire room and extinguished the flames burning from the metal ring.

The force of the blast flung Garrick back, and he tumbled end over end until his body smacked against the nearest wall, painfully stopping his momentum. A wave of purple light washed over the room and then faded to nothing, leaving them in total darkness once again.

Garrick lay there with his eyes closed, utterly exhausted and miserable. He wasn't sure which had done him more harm—taking the beating from the duotaur or the explosion from the black vial. Either way, he had no intention of getting up any time soon.

Then a yellow light threatened to break through his eyelids. He forced his heavy limbs to move, peeling them out from under him, and covered his eyes with his forearm.

"Garrick?" Irwin's frantic voice asked. "Are you alright?"

Garrick just moaned. It didn't feel like he'd broken anything, but the duotaur hadn't done him any favors, either. He managed to ask, "Is it dead?"

"Oh, he's dead, alright," Coburn's voice responded from beyond Irwin's. "There's not much left of him."

"Key?" Garrick asked.

"Intact, somehow. Perhaps a mercy from the gods," Coburn replied. "We have it here."

"Can you stand?" Dust clouded the edges of Irwin's spectacles. "Do you want the pink vial? I only have the one, but—"

"No. Save it." Garrick sighed. "Just give me some time."

His body was healing itself at its usual accelerated rate, but he was still nowhere near ready to do any kind of moving.

"There still doesn't seem to be any way out aside from the opening above the sarcophagus," Coburn said. "It looks like we may have to climb out of here."

Garrick moaned again. The thought of trying to climb in his current condition repulsed him.

Several minutes later, Garrick felt well enough to sit up. When he did, he found Coburn and Irwin seated in front of him, gnawing on strips of dried meat from their packs. Between them lay one of Irwin's glowing yellow vials and the golden key.

"I don't know what kind of metal it's made of, but it didn't get a scratch from the black vial," Irwin said. "It's quite remarkable."

"Pass me some jerky," Garrick said more than asked.

Irwin handed a piece to him, and he bit off a huge chunk. As he started to chew it, his loose teeth and the missing tooth on his right side reminded him of the blow he'd taken from the duotaur. He touched the empty space with his tongue then shifted the meat to the other side of his mouth and chewed it there instead.

"We're going to need you to lift me up into the shaft. Hopefully from there I can reach the top and feed a rope down for you and Irwin," Coburn said.

Garrick nodded. "Just give me a few more minutes, and I'll be ready to go."

"How do you think Noraff and Phesnos are faring?" Irwin asked.

"Probably worse than us. I can't see how they would've made it this far had they gone through the archways," Garrick replied. "I think we need to count on backtracking to find their key also."

Within three more minutes, Garrick pushed himself up to his feet. Aches and pains still racked his body, but he knew if he didn't get mobile, he risked his body stiffening up. He needed to stay loose for whatever awaited them beyond the climb—not to mention the climb into the shaft itself.

As Garrick started toward the sarcophagus, he glanced at the remains of the duotaur lying on the obsidian floor. Not much had endured the blast—its legs barely remained connected, and a chunk of its torso jutted up in a sort of triangular shape from its hip, but its arms and legs and heads were nowhere to be found.

Even more impressive, the blast from the black vial had blown a huge chunk out of the wall behind the duotaur's body, and it had blown pieces out of the walls adjacent to that spot as well.

Garrick huffed. The power in Irwin's vials never ceased to amaze him. But more incredible still was that the key had somehow survived it all.

Before long, Garrick felt well enough to help Coburn up into the shaft. He managed to find purchase with his footing and grips, and he soon reached the top and sent a rope back down.

Irwin climbed up first with the key in his pack, then Garrick retrieved his battle-axe and his pack. Finally, he took hold of the rope, ready to climb out as well.

Garrick glanced back at the duotaur's body, just in case. It lay there, motionless.

The hammer still lay next to the carcass. It was a mighty weapon, but only a being at least as strong as Garrick could wield it, if not one much stronger. Even though it could've fetched some decent coin, leaving it behind made the most sense. He couldn't hope to bring it with them for the remainder of the journey, not when his own battle-axe already felt too heavy on his back.

He climbed up the rope, his body burning from the strain, and left the circular room behind.

⚔

"I THINK THAT'S THE DOOR WE'RE LOOKING FOR." IRWIN POINTED TO A MASSIVE, VAULT-like metal door with two large keyholes on either side of it.

After climbing out of the shaft, they'd navigated a series of dark tunnels and pathways inclining farther upward. The journey ended at another carved archway that fed them into another high-ceilinged cavern that curved to the right and was wide enough for a brigade of soldiers to march through shoulder-to-shoulder.

Across from their archway, about two hundred feet away, stood another archway. A metal, vault-like door lay to the right, set into the inner wall's curve. They approached it and stood before it. As so many other places in this dungeon had, the vault door bore the four-pointed star-and-eye symbol of the ancient Aletians.

"No Noraff or Phesnos. Maybe they didn't make it?" Irwin said.

"I'm betting they would've come through that archway." Garrick nodded toward it.

Now that they were closer, he could see a translucent, quartz-like rock covering its interior, but it didn't appear to be very thick. It had a red-orange tint to it, probably from the lava on the other side.

He also noticed a keyhole in the wall next to it.

"Irwin, try the key in there," Garrick ordered. As they'd made the rest of the journey up here, he'd taken it as easy as he could to allow his body more time to recuperate. That included letting Irwin and Coburn handle more of the mundane tasks he'd normally insist on doing himself.

Irwin inserted the key into the keyhole. "It fits."

"Give it a turn." Garrick nodded toward him.

Irwin had to leverage almost his whole body to twist the key, but he did manage to twist it. Something clanked inside the lock, and the quartz inside the archway began to lower. Harsh orange light streamed in from the top, and heat comparable to when they'd first entered the lava cavern belched out at them as well.

And inside, Garrick saw Phesnos and Noraff battling a golem.

He cursed. So much for resting his worn-out body. Now he'd have to help them take it out.

"C'mon," he said to Irwin and Coburn. "We've got another monster to slay."

"I've only got one more black vial left," Irwin said as he pulled the key out of the lock.

"Stow it. One was enough for today." The last thing Garrick needed was to get blown across yet another room—especially one with lava in it. "And stash that key, too."

They stormed inside the room with Garrick in the lead. He noticed his battle-axe felt heavier than usual, but he refused to let it slow him down.

The battle raged on a ledge overlooking a canyon. A river of lava carved through it a few hundred feet below. The golem moved far slower than the duotaur had, but what could they do against a monstrosity comprised entirely of rocks and boulders?

Garrick's battle-axe wouldn't do much. He regretted not bringing the duotaur's hammer after all.

He stopped short as Coburn and Irwin rushed to join Noraff and Phesnos in engaging the golem, which stood near the edge of the rock ledge. Irwin hurled vials of green acid at it, and Coburn circled around in front of it, waving his knives as a distraction.

Meanwhile, Noraff leaped and swung from the walls, occasionally swiping at the golem with some sort of sword that Garrick had never seen before. His attacks did next to nothing to the golem. The green knife in his belt swayed with his movements but remained in its sheath, and as he scurried along the walls, he shifted a large silver key from his hands to his feet and back again.

Phesnos, for the first time since Garrick had met him, seemed useful—possibly the most useful one of the four. In one hand, he held a handful of mostly-green leaves, and with the other he launched green vines that coiled around the golem's legs and arms, slowing it down substantially, but not inflicting a lot of damage.

And at that moment, Garrick recognized the solution.

"Phesnos!" he called. "Lock his ankles together!"

Phesnos looked back at Garrick with a blank, expressionless face.

"Do it!" Garrick shouted.

Phesnos turned back toward the battle, readjusted his aim, and hurled a bunch of vines at the golem's ankles. The green leaves in his hand shriveled to dead, brown husks, and he let them go, but the vines did their work in binding the golem's legs together.

As Garrick had expected, the golem tried to step out of the vines as it had before, but this time it couldn't move, so it bent over and reached down to pull the vines free. That's when Garrick started running toward it.

At about five feet away, he leaped at the golem, leading with his legs. He landed both of his feet on the golem's shoulders and pushed off hard. Garrick landed on the hard ground and reignited all the aches and pains he'd been working through, but the golem got it far worse.

With the golem's balance off and with it bending over, Garrick's weight and momentum knocked it backward. The vines kept its ankles restrained, and it couldn't take a step to adjust. Instead, it teetered back, toward the edge, and then it toppled over with a low roar. It tumbled down the rocks into the canyon below.

Noraff shifted the key to his free hand, dropped from the wall onto the rocky floor, and looked over the edge next to Garrick. Irwin, Coburn, and Phesnos joined them. Below them, the lava river consumed the golem's body even as its stone fingers scraped against the rocks lining the canyon.

"We've been fighting that thing for nearly an hour," Noraff said between ragged breaths, "and you show up and knock it into the lava like it's nothing? Like it was just some random thing in your way, so you moved it?"

Garrick cracked his knuckles. "Yeah. Basically."

Noraff shook his head and muttered, "Big bastard."

Garrick bit back his words. The word "bastard" had never sat well with him, ever since his father had tried to kill his mother so many years before. But Noraff had no concept of what Garrick's upbringing had been like, so he let it slide.

"You have no idea what it took for us to get to you." Even as Garrick said it, his muscles reminded him of their fatigue. "So just be thankful we made it at all. Otherwise you'd still be fighting it—and losing."

Noraff scoffed. "Whatever. Are we going to claim your precious treasure now, or is there something else waiting for us beyond that arch?"

"Just the door." Garrick glanced at each of them. "Ready?"

They all nodded.

With both keys at the ready and led by the light from Irwin's vials, they headed through the arch and stopped at the huge steel door. Noraff inserted his key into the left keyhole, and Irwin pushed his key into the right.

Garrick stood in front of the door and motioned for them both to turn their keys. They did, in unison, and two ancient locking mechanisms clanked and clunked within the wall.

Garrick grabbed ahold of two bars mounted to the heavy door and pulled. It swung open slowly, and metal groaned against metal.

They'd made it.

Together, they ventured inside.

Garrick relished the familiar rush of having completed a mission. It meant, first and foremost, that he'd get paid, and so would Irwin and Coburn. But more importantly, he'd done what he'd set out to do for Lord Valdis. And he'd also achieved something no one else ever had by conquering this dungeon.

His eyes feasted on the contents of the room. Piles of gold and silver coins lined the walls, all of them stamped with the seal of the ancient Aletians from what Garrick could see. The seal wouldn't fetch any more money than they were worth for being solid gold, but it would make for interesting conversations whenever they made purchases.

Two chests overflowing with rubies, sapphires, diamonds, and emeralds sat near the back of the room, one on either side of a towering bookshelf crammed with worn, leather-bound books and yellowed parchments. Golden goblets, pearl necklaces, and bejeweled icons and idols lay scattered throughout the room.

And none of it was what Lord Valdis had sent Garrick to retrieve.

Oh, they'd take as much of the treasure back with them as they could carry, of course, but the real prize, the real mission, wasn't among the shiny objects in the room. Garrick just had to find it, and then they could go.

"Take what you can carry. Anything you can haul out of here, you can keep," Garrick said. "We'll leave when everyone is satisfied with their take."

Irwin let out a whoop, and Coburn headed straight for the nearest pile of gold. Noraff went to one of the treasure chests full of jewels, and Phesnos strolled through the room as if he didn't need any of it, or as if he were touring a gallery of fine works of art.

Garrick headed back to the bookshelf, his eyes scanning its contents for anything out of the ordinary. From what he could tell, the books and parchments were written in ancient Aletian runes. Then again, he was the furthest thing from a scholar, so he couldn't be sure.

As he studied the bookshelves, a small, black statue caught his eye. It sat on the second highest bookshelf, just barely within Garrick's reach, but high enough that he couldn't get a good look at it. He pulled it down and held it in his hands.

It was a dragon, clearly, but something different from the common wyverns flying around the continent of Aletia. This reptile had two wings and four legs, a slightly shorter neck than that of a typical wyvern, and a narrower face. A spike tipped its tail, and bony horns and ridges trailed down its back.

The most striking difference was the statue's intricate depiction of the dragon breathing fire. To Garrick's knowledge, common wyverns couldn't breathe fire. They were just huge, smarter-than-average, flying lizards. On some level, this statue suggested that actual dragons existed—or had existed—in the time of the Aletians.

But the statue wasn't what he'd risked his life and the lives of four others to find. It indicated he was close, though.

Garrick held the statue in one hand and reached up to the second bookshelf again. He patted its wooden surface with his fingers until they found a piece of metal jutting out of the wood. It felt smooth and rounded. Maybe a button or something?

He pushed it down.

Click.

Metal scraped and squealed and churned behind the bookshelf. Garrick stepped back, and the bookshelf inched forward and then started to slide to the side. It stopped when it hit the chest full of jewels, and the gears behind it wailed in protest.

Garrick yanked the chest away, scattering jewels across the floor, but something snapped behind the bookshelf, and it stopped moving. A whirring sound continued, but the bookshelf stayed still.

Garrick cursed.

"What's happening?" Noraff asked from behind him.

"Pay it no mind," Garrick grunted. "Focus on your newfound riches."

The whirring stopped, but the bookshelf still refused to move. Garrick got his hands on the other side of it and yanked, and it scraped along the floor, slowly sliding open with each of his hefts. Books tumbled off of the bookshelves and smacked his shoulders as if they meant to keep him from further moving the unit aside.

The more he pushed, the more the bookshelf screeched, but before long, he had it moved enough to be able to squeeze through the opening into the room that lay behind it.

"Irwin, light," he called.

Irwin slipped through the opening without having to squeeze at all, and he held up a glowing yellow vial to illuminate the room.

It was a small, circular chamber with a shallow pit in the center. The whole room reeked of pitch, so Garrick had Irwin drip a drop of his red vial into the pit. Sure enough, the pit caught on fire and splashed the room with yellow-orange light. Irwin tucked his vials back into his pack.

The room only contained three items: a sword with a white blade, a matching white shield, and a parchment. Each of them hung on the circular wall, with the shield on the left, the sword on the right, and the parchment in the center.

Lord Valdis was a wealthy man with an entire army under his control. He was a sorcerer, and thus he had little to no use for the physical implements of war, so Garrick approached the parchment.

It was a map. Aletian runes lined its perimeter, and it showed the entire continent of Aletia. He recognized it from other maps he'd seen.

He noticed a large X somewhere in the center of the Xenthan, but several smaller X's marked other locations across the continent in what would now be Muroth, Inoth, and Govalia.

What any of it meant, Garrick didn't know, nor did he care. But this was clearly what Lord Valdis wanted. Why else would the Aletians have placed it in a secret room, inside a vault, within a dungeon, and under a mountain?

Even if Garrick took nothing else from this vault, he would make sure this map went with him, and he would ensure it got back to Lord Valdis fully intact. "Irwin, grab me a string from one of the parchments out there."

"Will do." Irwin returned a moment later and handed it to him.

Garrick carefully removed the parchment from the wall, rolled it up, and tied it with the string. It was too large to fit properly in his pack, but he'd carry it anyway to make sure it stayed in pristine condition the whole time.

"I think I saw a parchment tube out there," Irwin said. "Should I go get it?"

"Yes, definitely." A case for carrying the map would make Garrick's return trip far easier.

While Irwin searched for the parchment tube, Garrick approached the sword. Based on the bright white coloration of its blade, Garrick guessed it was made of snow steel. As such, it was one of a handful of enhanced types of metal that could do him harm where normal steel, iron, and other non-enchanted metals couldn't.

Furthermore, snow steel was effective against beasts and species that relied on fire to give them strength. As such, Garrick found it ironic that such a fine weapon was housed under a temple belonging to a cult of fire-worshippers.

As he looked closer at the sword, he noticed runes etched into its blade, presumably ancient Aletian characters or numerals, none of which he could read. Even more interesting, the cold exuding from the blade itself actually cooled Garrick's face. Definitely snow steel.

Its ornate hilt was colored a brilliant blue, and milky white gemstones—maybe opals?—adorned the ends of its cross-guard. Black leather grips wrapped around the handle, and a crystalline spike extended from the pommel. Impeccable crafts-manship.

Garrick considered taking the sword with him as his own personal prize. He enjoyed his battle-axe, but he'd had plenty of training with swords over the years as well. A blade designed to fell fiery foes might come in handy on his way out.

Speaking of out, Irwin had left awhile ago for that tube. Where was he?

Garrick turned back and glanced through the opening between the bookshelf and the wall and saw Phesnos crouched near a pile of gold with a sack next to him. "Irwin? Where is that tube?"

"We're still looking for it," Noraff's voice replied.

Garrick leaned the parchment against the wall, careful not to let it roll toward the pit of fire. Then he headed toward the opening and squeezed through it.

As he fully emerged, lightning stabbed into his left side, and he grunted and clutched at the spot. Hot, sticky blood coated his hand, and the familiar green handle of a knife protruded from his torso. He looked over at his attacker.

Noraff stood beside him, wearing a smirk.

CHAPTER SEVEN

G arrick slumped against the bookshelf, struggling to stay on his feet. The knife wound was deep. He could tell that much. It might even be fatal, but he wouldn't let Noraff get away with this if he could help it. So he marshaled his strength and swung his right fist.

Noraff easily ducked under it, and the punch overextended Garrick. He caught a hard elbow to his jaw from Noraff in response—harder than he would've expected from an Onni. It knocked him over, and he lay on his back, still holding the area where the knife stuck out of his flesh.

Unable to get back up and fight, he glanced around for Irwin and Coburn.

Irwin lay in a pool of blood atop a pile of gold and silver coins, clutching at his slashed neck and writhing. Blood dotted his spectacles, still on his face. He was still alive but wouldn't last long.

Phesnos stood up from his crouching position, and when he moved, his brown robes moved with him, revealing Coburn's body lying on the floor, impaled upon several golden spikes—the result of Phesnos's magic manipulating the gold itself.

A glowing yellow vial lay next to Coburn's head, illuminating his vacant eyes staring up at Garrick. Coburn was no longer there. He was already dead.

"You traitorous bastard," Garrick growled. Rage burned inside of him. Coburn and Irwin were good men—good friends—and they'd been killed as if they were merely stray dogs.

Garrick tried to sit up, but pain from the knife stabbed him anew, and he only made it up to his elbow. He glowered at Noraff, wishing he could reach out and snap his twig of a neck.

"Why are you so far away?" Garrick asked. "Don't you want your little knife back?"

"Nice try, but you can keep it." Noraff crouched down in front of him but still out of reach, holding one of Irwin's glowing yellow vials. "That's mage steel in your belly. Steel forged with magic. It's stronger than regular steel, and it's sharper, too. Sharp enough to pierce even your thick hide."

That explained how Noraff had managed to stab him so easily. "Yeah. It's not like you have enough skill to stab me with conventional steel."

"Go ahead, insult me. But you're the one lying on the floor, bleeding out with his dead friends." Noraff corrected himself, "Or soon to be, in the case of your alchemist friend."

"Why are you doing this?" Garrick grunted. "You can't even carry all of this out of here on your own."

"It's not about the gold. Well, not specifically this gold, anyway. We'll certainly get paid for our efforts, though not by you." Noraff motioned to Phesnos with his head.

Phesnos picked up the glowing yellow vial lying on the floor near Coburn's body and walked past Garrick into the hidden room and emerged with the rolled-up map in his other hand. As Garrick watched, Phesnos produced the parchment tube from inside his brown robes and started to stuff the map into it.

"Our employer—our *actual* employer—wants this map very badly," Noraff continued. "He told us exactly what it was and that your Lord Valdis was looking for it. And then he hired us to bring it back to him so Valdis couldn't get his greedy hands on it."

"So you latched onto our mission and used us to get you to it." Garrick spat at Noraff's feet, and a bit of blood tinged his saliva. "You're a conniving little prick."

"And you're a big, dumb ingrate. Let's not forget that you asked me to join you. All I did was make it known that I was available for work. *You* hired *me*," Noraff countered.

"First mistake I've ever made," Garrick quipped.

"And that right there is why I have no qualms about doing this." Noraff pointed at him. "I've despised you since the moment we met. You're arrogant, stupid, and yet too strong and capable for your own good. You don't deserve your strength and your abilities, yet you flaunt them in front of everyone you work with."

"You have *no idea* what I've suffered because of them," Garrick grunted. "But you don't see me whining about it or complaining that I can't climb or do magic. I'm working with what I've been given, with what I've earned. If you're jealous, that's on you."

"You won't be working with anything for much longer. Phesnos and I are leaving, and we're going to seal you in here with your useless friends." Noraff sneered at him. "And now, at the end, you finally realize not even your great strength or your thick skin can save you.

"I expect you'll die a slow, painful death," Noraff continued. "Bleeding out, starvation, or maybe those scorpion-spider terrors will claim you. It doesn't matter how you go; what matters is that you will. Tell me, Garrick, what good is all that strength now? Where is your bravado? Your bluster?"

With a scoff, Noraff stood and started to leave, but Garrick called after him. "*Noraff.*"

Noraff, still holding the glowing yellow vial, looked back at him.

"I'm going to find you one day, either in this life or the next, and I *will* make you pay for your betrayal here, for murdering my friends and for trying to kill me," Garrick said. "And that's not bravado or bluster. It is my solemn oath before whatever gods or goddesses can hear it. I *will* bring a reckoning to you one way or another."

Noraff chuckled. "Yet again, your overconfidence shows the depth of your foolishness. And that's how you'll die—as a fool, powerless and alone. Goodbye, Garrick Shatterstone."

As Noraff headed out of the vault, Phesnos looked back at Garrick with the same expressionless face he always wore.

It enraged Garrick more than if Phesnos had leered at him or shown some lewd gesture. It demonstrated precisely how apathetic Phesnos was about the whole situation, how little he cared that they had just killed Coburn and Irwin.

Worse still, Garrick had saved both Noraff and Phesnos from the golem only minutes earlier, yet they still saw fit to betray him.

"I'll come for you, too, Pheasant," Garrick rasped. "Have no doubt about it."

Phesnos just blinked at him and turned away. He exited the vault with Noraff, and together they shut the vault door. Two distinct clanks sounded, and the door locked Garrick inside.

The only light now came from the fire burning in the secret room, so Garrick could hardly see anything. But he didn't need to see to know what he had to do. It was too late for Coburn, but Garrick had to get over to Irwin to try to help, if he could.

Garrick rallied his waning energy and forced himself up to his knees. He didn't pull the knife out—not yet. For all he knew, it might've been the only thing keeping the majority of his blood in his body. Then he crawled over to Irwin.

He found Irwin's pack and dug inside it for another glowing vial. One more left. He pulled it out, careful not to drop it from his shaking hand, and held the vial up to Irwin's face.

Irwin lay still, but his wide eyes blinked. He held his bleeding neck with both hands and struggled to breathe.

"Hold on, Irwin." Garrick started digging in Irwin's pack again. "I'll use the pink vial on you. It should—"

Irwin's bloody right hand latched onto Garrick's wrist, and he shook his head slightly. His voice burbled, "Too... late."

Garrick didn't want to accept that. Irwin had been with him for close to a year, and he'd seen the contents of the pink vial work some incredible healing magic—though Irwin would've insisted it was *science*. "Irwin, I'm sorry. I let my guard down."

Irwin blinked again, let go of Garrick, then looked at him. "You can... get out."

"What? No, I can't. We're sealed in."

"Black... vial. Door." Irwin sputtered and winced, and then went still. Garrick thought he'd died until Irwin blinked again. "Use pink... vial on yourself."

Garrick hesitated. But Coburn was already dead, and Irwin wouldn't make it. "Fine."

Irwin's right hand found Garrick's wrist again, caking it with fresh blood. "Get... out. Find them and... justice."

Garrick nodded. Irwin didn't have a vengeful bone in his body, but Garrick had already promised to punish Noraff and Phesnos for their betrayal. "If I can get out of here, I'll lay waste to them."

Irwin blinked, long and slow, and gave a faint nod. "You... can get... out..."

Then Irwin's grip on Garrick's wrist went limp, and his eyes stopped blinking.

Garrick leaned back on the pile of gold next to Irwin's body and pulled the pink vial out of Irwin's pack. He exhaled a shaky breath. He couldn't ever remember enduring this level of pain before.

Out of nowhere, the ground trembled beneath him, then it began to shake and quake. Books dove out of the bookshelves and smacked the floor, and the coins and trinkets throughout the vault rattled and clinked and jingled.

Garrick tried to cover his head to protect it from potential falling rocks, but fresh pain seared his insides like a hot poker. Ultimately, it didn't matter, because the quaking subsided just as quickly as it began.

Whatever had happened, it wasn't good. But it wouldn't matter at all unless Garrick could get out of the vault. And first he had to tend to his wound.

He looked down to see blood drenching his trousers and soaking into his leather armor. If he didn't make a choice soon, the knife would decide his fate for him. It had to come out anyway for the pink vial to do its work. He set the glowing yellow vial on Irwin's hip and braced himself.

With a series of quick breaths, Garrick curled his fingers around the knife's hilt and yanked it from his torso. Blood burbled out of the wound, and he dropped the knife to the floor and pressed his hand against his bleeding side.

He pried the cork out of the pink vial, careful not to spill any of it as he did, and slowly poured about half of its contents onto the wound. Then he used his fingers to spread the wound open wider. The pain spiked, and he winced, but he tilted his body to the side and poured the rest as far into the wound as he could.

The pink liquid started to work by numbing his pain to a dull gnawing. Irwin had explained that it not only numbed pain but also worked to enhance and accelerate the user's own healing process. Garrick hoped his troll blood would help rejuvenate him entirely, even if it meant he'd have to linger in the vault.

But he couldn't just lie around. He had to try to break out and follow Noraff and Phesnos before they escaped the dungeon entirely. He wanted to leave their wretched bodies here in the dungeon, the same as they'd done to Irwin and Coburn.

The pain had numbed enough by that point that Garrick felt he could try to stand, but the bleeding hadn't yet stopped. He'd need to find a way to bandage it, at least, before he tried to get out.

He stripped Irwin's sleeves from his shirt, sorry he had to do it, but Irwin would've given him the entire shirt if he'd asked for it. Garrick tied them together and wrapped them around his torso. Then he tied them together again, cinching them tightly against his side.

It wouldn't be enough. He reached down and tore the rest of Irwin's shirt off of his body in two pieces. Blood stained the top of it, by the collar.

He folded one of the strips into a square and slid it under the shirtsleeves, then he did the same with the other, careful to position them for maximum coverage. He cinched the sleeves tighter, and the fabric pressed against his wound firmly.

Next, he pulled the black vial out of Irwin's pack, and then the red vial. But he wasn't ready to light the fuse. Not yet.

He set them aside, careful not to risk breaking either of them, and he rummaged through the remainder of Irwin's supplies. He took some food and a few other vials, most of them filled with clear liquid. Apparently Irwin had heeded Garrick's comment about needing more vials of fire-suppressing solution.

Then he picked up Noraff's knife, the one with the green hilt. Noraff had told him he could keep it, and he would—at least until Garrick could properly return it to Noraff in the same manner in which he'd received it.

Garrick tucked the knife and the other supplies into his pack. He rifled through Coburn's pack next but didn't find anything of significant value, so he left it alone, paid his respects to Coburn, and then headed back toward the black and red vials.

He stopped halfway there at the sight of the flames still burning in the hidden room, and he turned for a final look. That sword and shield—he could make use of those, especially in his weakened state. If he had to deal with any of the Crimson Flame cultists on his way out, the added protection of snow steel weapons would help him far more than his battle-axe would.

So Garrick slipped into the secret room once more and pulled the shield and the sword off the wall, claiming them for himself. They both still radiated cold, and the white metal chilled his skin whenever he touched it.

He hooked the shield onto his back and sheathed the sword in a scabbard that was mounted just behind it, and he strapped it to his belt. He didn't want to leave his battle-axe behind, but he decided he'd better. The less weight he had to carry, the more likely he'd find a way out.

And besides, if he couldn't catch up to Noraff and Phesnos and get the map back, he'd need money to survive while looking for other jobs, so he had to leave some room in his pack for that. If Lord Valdis didn't have him killed for failing.

Garrick shuddered at the thought. The idea of Lord Valdis killing him wasn't nearly as vexing as the thought of having to face him and admit his failure to deliver the map. What would happen to his reputation? Would he even be able to get more mercenary work after a blunder this severe?

Now was not the time to think about that. Garrick couldn't grant such thoughts any quarter in his mind. He had to get out, first. If he made it out of the vault—and the dungeon, and the temple after that—alive, then he could worry about his future. But for the time being, he needed to focus on the here and now.

Garrick dropped several gold coins in his pack along with the glowing yellow vial, slung the pack on his back next to the shield, and held the two vials in his hands once again. Satisfied with his efforts and with the ever-diminishing pain in his side, he decided it was time.

He hated to leave a fortune of this size behind, but catching Noraff and Phesnos was more important than anything else, so he positioned the black vial at the base of the vault door. A drop from the red vial ignited the fuse, and Garrick hurried away.

The only place he could reasonably take shelter was within the secret room, so he squeezed past the bookshelf, braced himself against one of the interior stone walls, crouched low, and waited with his hands covering his ears.

A deafening boom rocked the vault. The bookshelf blew apart, snuffed the fire in the pit, and the force of the blast threw Garrick against the back wall.

He curled up and covered his head. He'd managed to survive everything else in this dungeon—and Noraff's betrayal. Falling rocks were nothing.

When the room finally stopped rattling, Garrick looked up. He removed the yellow vial from his pack once again and used it to look around.

Almost nothing remained of the bookshelf or the books and parchment on it except for the shards of wood that lay around him and on top of him. The walls that had framed the entrance to the secret room on that side had broken and crumbled, leaving an opening nearly the size of the vault door itself.

Garrick stood and approached the vault's main room. Gold, silver, and jewelry lay scattered across the floor and in the fire pit within the secret room, but the closer to the vault door he walked, the more molten gold and silver he found hardening on the floor, along with chunks of rock and steel mixed in.

It sickened Garrick when he realized that Irwin and Coburn's bodies were totally gone, probably turned to ash by the blast. But he couldn't have either buried them down here or hauled them out anyway; the best he could've hoped for was burning them, and the black vial had done essentially that, only far quicker.

Nonetheless, Garrick would carry their memories with him until he delivered them the justice they deserved, and he would remember them far beyond that, too.

Most importantly, the black vial had worked. Aletian construction and architecture were unparalleled, even by elves and dwarves, but Irwin's alchemy had trumped it nonetheless.

The explosion had ripped a hole into not only the steel door and the frame but also into the rock wall adjacent to it. To the Aletians' credit, the vial hadn't managed to carve a large hole, but it was still big enough that Garrick could crawl out, so he crouched down to his hands and knees and wriggled his way out of the vault.

He was free.

Noraff and Phesnos had a solid fifteen-minute head start on him, but if Garrick pushed himself, he could catch up. He started toward the archway on the left—the archway he'd come through after defeating the duotaur—but stopped short.

It was caved in.

Garrick cursed. That explained the quaking right after Noraff left. Phesnos must've somehow brought down the archway and part of the ceiling with his magic.

He turned back and glanced at the other archway. Harsh orange light still poured in through the archway where he'd finished off the golem.

Garrick had a choice: he could either heft rocks and boulders off the pile and eventually dig his way out or he could attempt to traverse a more unknown path along the lava river.

In the end, the choice was easy. Even if he did manage to break through the cave-in, it would delay him too much. Plus, he'd have to swim across the pool again, and that had been a slow, arduous process as well.

Trying to go back the way he'd come would not help him catch Noraff and Phesnos, so he headed for the lava archway.

✣

THE ALTERNATE PATH HAD WOUND DOWN A STEEP, CURVING CLIFF FACE, AT TIMES ONLY wide enough for Garrick to safely walk, but it was wider than when he'd traversed the temple's rock wall, so he counted himself lucky.

The tradeoff was the oppressive heat generated by the lava river flowing below and the occasional globs of molten rock it flung up at him as he progressed. One of them almost hit Garrick's left shoulder, but it hit the snow steel shield instead.

The lava hissed and steamed and hardened to black rock within seconds, clinging to the shield, but one solid whack against the wall shattered it and cleaned off the shield. Garrick checked the shield for damage but found none. The snow steel had completely negated the lava's heat and thus remained intact, and it even still radiated cold onto his back.

The curving path ascended again by several hundred feet and terminated at yet another cliff face, and Garrick recognized the landscape before him. The lava river flowed below him, punctuated by several rocky platforms jutting out of it.

In the distance, he saw the rock ledge and the hole in the wall where they'd first discovered the lava room. And to the left, he saw a familiar-looking archway. Garrick watched two forms scamper out of it and toward the opening in the wall.

Noraff and Phesnos.

CHAPTER EIGHT

P art of Garrick wanted to shout at them, to bellow a war cry and curses. They might not hear him anyway, and even if they did, he'd forfeit any advantage of surprise he might still have. Instead, he focused on climbing down.

Climbing down proved even harder than climbing up, especially given Garrick's size. The only advantages he had were increased strength and a longer reach, but his added weight all but negated his strength, and finding suitable grips for his thick hands and ledges for his large feet still proved challenging despite his height.

It took longer than he'd wanted, but he managed to make it to the bottom alive and intact nonetheless. He faced the platforms jutting out of the lava.

Not a single one of them was straight up and down or had a nice, flat surface. They all tilted one way or another. Garrick stepped to the edge and peered down at the base of the first one. Unlike some of the others he'd seen on the opposite side, this one looked thick and sturdy, but he couldn't tell for sure.

Whatever the case, there was no going back, and he needed to move forward as quickly as possible if he stood any chance of catching up to Noraff and Phesnos. So he backed up a few steps from the edge, ran forward, and leaped.

Garrick's boots hit the uneven surface of the first platform, and he grabbed ahold of a rock protrusion to steady himself. If he fell back, he could slip into the lava below. He climbed up to more level footing on the platform, then he ran toward the next platform and jumped.

Crossing the platforms went faster than the climb down the cliff face had gone, but it took more of a toll on Garrick's nerves. Nonetheless, none of them crumbled beneath him. He made it across, through the oppressive heat, and landed on the rock ledge where he'd just seen Noraff and Phesnos.

Without hesitation, he charged toward the opening in the wall.

Pitch black enveloped him, so he pulled out the glowing yellow vial from his pack and used it to light his way. As soon as he did, dozens of scorpers poured out of the holes and crevices in the walls and the cave's floor and scurried toward him.

Garrick cursed, and he ran. He didn't have time to fight them, nor did he have time to dig out the red vial and light them on fire. He just had to get past them.

He dodged the same low-hanging stalactites and rocks that he'd encountered on their trek inside, but this time in reverse. The scorpers snapped their pincers at his ankles and heels as he ran, and his boots stomped on several of them along the way. Their screeches and shrieks punished his ears in the small, confined space.

The cave gradually widened, and he saw the staircase ahead. Garrick danced out of reach of the scorpers, kicked a few aside, and bolted for the stairs.

Garrick was catching up to them. He could feel it.

He also felt the scorpers skittering after him, nipping at his heels as he ran.

The journey back had exhausted him, and the pain from Noraff's knife had returned—albeit duller and less debilitating than before—but Garrick let his drive to exact vengeance on Noraff and Phesnos propel him forward.

That, and he had an army of scorpers chasing him up the stairs and along the walls. If Garrick stopped, they'd overwhelm him in no time.

He fought through straining muscles and fatigue, but he made it up the stairs and emerged in the temple's secret room once again, only to find that the secret door was open. Noraff and Phesnos might still be in the temple, or they might be outside by now. Either way, Garrick had to keep going.

Instead of peering into the grand hall to check for threats, he just barreled inside without any consideration of consequences, but they all hit him the instant he cleared the secret door and emerged from behind the huge curtain that covered it.

A trio of Crimson Flame cultists stood around the altar, each of them as bald as the ones he'd faced back in the pub run by Falna. They wore familiar black and red robes, and each bore a tattoo of a fireball on their bare chests.

A pair of iron candelabras held candles that burned with calm flames, illuminating the cultist's faces. They noticed him immediately.

The four of them shared a silent moment of mutual surprise. Then the cultists reached toward the candelabras and pulled the candles' fire into their hands.

Garrick still held the glowing yellow vial. He wouldn't need it anymore, so he hurled it at the altar and then shielded his eyes from the ensuing flash.

Pop. The vial detonated, and the cultists yelped.

Garrick drew the snow-steel sword, pulled the matching shield from his back, and charged toward the cultists. Before they had the chance to recover, he felled them all. The sword hissed with every impact against their bodies.

A screech sounded behind Garrick, and then a cacophony of other screeches echoed it. The scorpers had reached the top and started to ooze out of the secret room. He left the cultists' bodies behind as fodder for the scorpers and kept running, but this time he stopped just inside the grand hall's doorway.

He'd been too loud. Footsteps and shouts sounded in the hallway beyond, so he pressed himself against the wall adjacent to the doors and slid behind a red tapestry emblazoned with the black fireball symbol of the Crimson Flame.

Gods, he hated that symbol. And he hated the cultists behind it even more.

Because of his size, the tapestry bulged out along his body, and anyone who looked at it would immediately realize he was there, but with the scorpers chirping and shrieking as they fed on flesh on the opposite side of the grand hall, Garrick hoped the approaching cultists wouldn't even bother to look in his direction.

Sure enough, a dozen cultists burst into the grand hall and shouted commands and directions at each other as they moved to battle the encroaching scorpers.

Garrick watched, amused. He couldn't have planned that any better. And considering that he hadn't planned it at all, he grinned at this small modicum of good fortune in spite of how wrong everything had gone at the end.

While the cultists battled the scorpers with weapons and with fire, Garrick slipped from behind the tapestry and snuck out the grand hall doors.

Instead of heading back to the secret entrance, Garrick made his way to where he expected the temple's main entrance to be. The encounter with the cultists had slowed him down again, but perhaps if Noraff and Phesnos had taken the side route along the temple walls, he might be able to catch up to them this way.

A huge, square log lay in iron holders across the doors, barring them shut. Garrick hefted it up and let it drop to the stone floor with a *thud*. Then he brandished his sword and shield once more and burst through the temple's front doors and into the courtyard.

A dusting of snow covered the ground, and the first rays of morning sunlight glowed from just below the horizon. As the cold air hit Garrick's face, the sword and shield in his hands gave off a faint ringing sound, and then the runes on each of them began to glow with teal and blue light.

At first, Garrick didn't understand, but then it made sense: He'd stepped into a cold environment with two snow-steel weapons. They would naturally have more power because they could draw from the colder conditions.

But Garrick had neither the time nor the desire to further test the weapons' power. He just needed to catch Noraff and Phesnos.

As he bolted out of the courtyard and past the temple's perimeter walls, Garrick scanned the landscape beyond for any sign of them. Two sets of footprints in the fresh snow led away from the side of the wall where they'd snuck in hours before. One set was a pair of boots, and the other looked like a misshapen hand—an Onni footprint.

He chased their path into the trees where it became obfuscated thanks to the tree canopy blocking some of the snowfall, but he managed to stay with it. The trail ended a half-mile from the temple at a clearing that overlooked the valley below.

There, Garrick saw Phesnos sitting atop an orange wyvern with purple striping. Phesnos's arms were curled around the rider's waist.

Even in the early morning light, Garrick could make out the rider's forest green armor, typical of the Govalian Army and its wyvern knights. Short hair, so blonde it was nearly white, poked out from under her matching green helmet.

Beyond them, a second wyvern, this one green, dove off the edge and into the valley. Garrick caught a glimpse of a hairy form on its back clinging to the wyvern knight, who also wore forest green armor.

Before Garrick could react, the purple and orange wyvern leaped off the edge as well and glided after the green wyvern, leaving him alone at the edge of the clearing.

He was too late.

⚔

TWELVE DAYS LATER

Garrick's legs begged for mercy, but he kept trudging through the snow. He had to get back to Lord Valdis and explain what had happened at all costs.

In the distance, he saw the cratered mountain looming, and before long, his legs carried him into a small village that lay in a valley between the mountains. There, he found a host of brown faces, each of them rugged and worn, each of them tinged with dismay of some sort.

Garrick arrived about midday and decided to press onward, past the village's wooden buildings and through its cobblestone streets. It was too early to stop for the night, and he wanted to get back to Lord Valdis sooner rather than later. The anticipation of that meeting was driving Garrick insane.

As he ventured through the village, he noticed a small blonde-headed girl with fair skin playing in the snow in front of one of the houses. She stuck out, being the only white face in a town of brown-skinned people with dark hair.

Her blue eyes locked onto him for just a moment. She smiled at him and kept playing in the snow. Garrick neither smiled back nor gave her a second thought.

Instead, the forest green armor of the wyvern knights assaulted his mind. He'd thought of almost nothing else as he made his trip back to Xenthan.

Why were Govalian wyvern knights providing aid and transportation to Noraff and Phesnos, a couple of no-name mercenaries, all the way up in Etrijan? It made no sense whatsoever. Did Noraff work for someone in Govalia's government? Was he working on behalf of the Govalian Army itself?

Try as he may, Garrick couldn't put it together. So his thoughts returned to self-deprecation as he chided himself for the thousandth time for allowing the betrayal to happen in the first place. There were so many ways he could've prevented it, so many opportunities to shut it down before it even started.

The more he dwelled on those thoughts, the angrier he got, and the more furiously he plowed through the snow. So he let the thoughts flow, let them sear hard lessons into his very core, and let them fuel his journey back to Valdis Keep.

Once he got east of the cratered mountain, he'd be in Xenthan, where he'd have to face the true consequences of his failure before Lord Valdis. He wasn't looking forward to it, but it had to be done.

So Garrick kept walking.

⚔

Valdis Keep loomed overhead, tall, black, and imposing, its spires scraping Xenthan's perpetually crimson skies. Warm, yellow light burned from some of its windows and through some of the embrasures along its battlements.

Except for a few small buildings in a meager surrounding village, the keep stood alone among a vast wasteland of dark rocks and gray sand, both of which contributed to Xenthan's unofficial moniker, "The Black Realm." A light coating of snow softened the terrain's appearance, but not by much.

Valdis Keep wasn't inviting, but Garrick had to venture inside nonetheless.

As Garrick approached, he touched the space where he'd lost the tooth in the fight with the duotaur. The tooth had only partially grown back. A bit more time, and he'd be chewing on that side of his mouth normally again.

The soldiers at the keep's front gates stopped Garrick until he lowered his hood. Upon recognizing him, they waved him through.

"Where're your friends?" one of them asked as Garrick crossed into the keep's sprawling courtyard. "Weren't there three of you when you left?"

Garrick stopped, turned his head, and looked down at the soldier. Lord Valdis's sigil of a three-horned ram decorated the soldier's black breastplate. The piece looked brand new, along with the rest of his armor.

For all Garrick knew, this man had never left the keep. He'd never journeyed anywhere, never ventured outside of Xenthan. He'd never scratched his armor, never sloshed through mud made of earth and blood, never drawn his sword on a foe holding a real weapon rather than a practice blade.

After his miserable failure back at the dungeon and the long, frigid journey home, Garrick wanted to snap the soldier's neck right then and there for his ignorance, but he didn't. Instead, he continued walking across the courtyard.

"What's wrong with him?" he heard the soldier ask from behind him.

Garrick paid it no mind and entered Valdis Keep.

Gray floors and walls lined the halls as Garrick made his way through the keep. Torches lit his way under ornate, pointed archways, and stone gargoyles—none of them alive, as far as Garrick knew—perched high above him, watching every room and every hallway with obsidian eyes.

When Garrick finally reached the black double doors that led to Lord Valdis's throne room, he stopped short. He needed to calm his hammering heartbeat first.

You can do this, he told himself. *Just get through it. If he kills you, then so be it, but if not, work to re-earn his trust.*

Garrick had never heard of Lord Valdis offering anyone a second chance. He was known for his ruthlessness above all else, but Garrick couldn't focus on that now. All he could do was own up to his mistakes, tell the truth about what happened, and pray to the gods for mercy.

He nodded to the soldiers posted on either side of the doors. They pulled the doors open, and Garrick stepped inside to meet his fate head-on.

SHAMELESS COMMERCIAL

Kent set down the book he was reading and looked up at Aeron. "This is a truly fascinating work of fiction. I do not suppose you have read it?"

"What's it called?" Aeron asked as he patted Wafer's flank. The two of them lay against a rocky cliff face on their way north to Xenthan, content after feasting on a deer Wafer had caught earlier that evening.

"It is called *The Ghost Mine*, written by a legendary author known as Ben Wolf. It tells the thrilling story of an energy mine that reopens three years after a horrific accident, but even now, much of what happens there goes terribly awry—often at the cost of the characters' lives."

Aeron shook his head. "Can't say I've read it, but it sounds phenomenal."

"It certainly is." Kent raised an eyebrow. "Though I must confess, the sciences in this book seem more like magic. Perhaps that is why it is called 'science fiction.'"

"Chalk it up to artistic license," Aeron said with a wave of his hand, and Wafer snorted in agreement. "Mind if I read it when you finish?"

"I just did." Kent handed it to him. "I am starting the next book in the trilogy."

Aeron accepted the book and looked over its cover as Kent pulled two other books out of his pack to show him.

"Wow. Looks scary," Aeron said. "But also awesome."

"Indeed. Worth a read for anyone who enjoys mystery, plenty of horror, combat, and action," Kent said. "I picked them up directly from the author in my journeys, but the books are also available through a worldwide vendor known as 'Amazon.'"

Aeron gave an enthusiastic nod. "I'm gonna start reading now!"

Wafer bobbed his head and chomped with his mouth, and Aeron eyed him.

"Well, if you're still hungry, then go hunt some more," Aeron said. "I've got a great book to read. And you—yeah, you, the person reading this—you should write a review of this book on Amazon. It'll help Ben Wolf write more great books."

 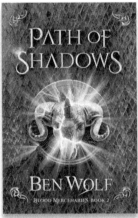 

Acknowledgements

Every published book is the culmination of a lot of hard work, dedication, and support. The author writes the book, but everything that comes after is equally as essential to the success of the book.

First of all, thank YOU for reading this book. I had a blast putting it together, but it was by no means a solo effort.

Second, thanks to my parents for believing in me from an early age and for helping to support my dreams and my growth. I love you both.

Thank you to Jesus Christ for changing my life (and the world) forever.

Thanks to my all-star beta readers, Daniel Kuhnley and Paige Guido, for your excellent feedback, encouragement, and for having my back.

Thanks also to my mastermind group. It's a secret group, but you all know who you are. (insert evil laugh)

Kirk DouPonce, you are a brilliant artist. The covers for this series are phenomenal. Thank you for your long-suffering patience with me throughout the process.

Will Wight, you continue to bless me with your time and feedback, and you've been far better to me than I deserve. I really appreciate the time you've invested in me, and I'm honored to be your friend.

Dirty Mike Hueser and the BJJ boys, thanks for keeping me frosty.

And thank you to all of my readers! Without you, I wouldn't be doing this.

Last of all, thank you especially to my intelligent, beautiful, thoughtful, and ultra-supportive wife, Charis Crowe. Your flexibility with my weird writing schedule for this series made all the difference in me getting everything done.

I love you.

ABOUT BEN WOLF

In 7th grade, I saw the movie *Congo*. It was so bad, I wrote a parody of it set in Australia that featured killer kangaroos. So began my writing career.

I've spoken at 50+ writers conferences and multiple comic cons nationwide. When not writing, I occasionally choke people in Brazilian jiujitsu. I live in the midwest with my gorgeous wife, our kids, and our cats Marco and Ivy.

Get the full series and check out my other books on Amazon.com:

Want updates on future projects? Sign up for my author email newsletter now!

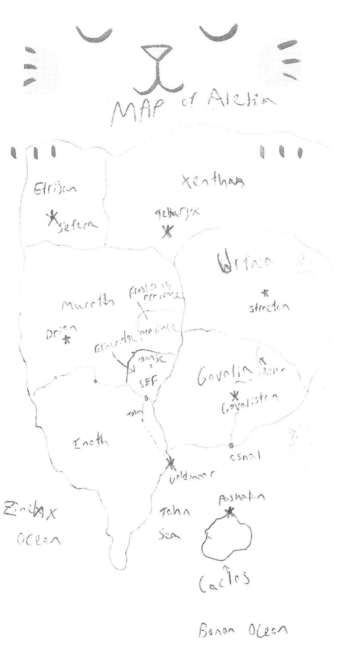

MAP of Aletia

Elrijan

Xenthan

★ Sieferin

geltarijx
★

Urthan

Mureth

Frostsnow province
★ streeton

★ Drijn

Etherdev province

house
SEF

Govalia Province

★ Govaliston

Toby

csnol

Inoth

★ Goldmoor

Zindax
Ocean

Tahn
Sea

pashalen
★

Cactos

Bonon Ocean

meow.